A

The Foundations of our Faith

SALZWASSER
VERLAG

Anonymous

The Foundations of our Faith

Reprint of the original, first published in 1863.

1st Edition 2022 | ISBN: 978-3-37500-212-1

Verlag (Publisher): Salzwasser Verlag GmbH, Zeilweg 44, 60439 Frankfurt, Deutschland
Vertretungsberechtigt (Authorized to represent): E. Roepke, Zeilweg 44, 60439 Frankfurt, Deutschland
Druck (Print): Books on Demand GmbH, In de Tarpen 42, 22848 Norderstedt, Deutschland

THE FOUNDATIONS OF OUR FAITH.

THE FOUNDATIONS OF OUR FAITH

TEN PAPERS READ BEFORE
A MIXED AUDIENCE OF MEN.

BY

PROFESSORS AUBERLEN, GESS
AND OTHERS

LONDON
STRAHAN AND CO. 32 LUDGATE HILL.
1863.

CONTENTS.

INTRODUCTORY.

As I have been chosen to deliver the first of the proposed series of Theological Lectures, it devolves upon me to explain the nature and aim of our undertaking. We have arranged to deliver a course of ten fortnightly lectures on the great foundations of our faith, the subjects discussed to follow the order in which they are presented in the Apostles' Creed, so that there should be a systematic and progressive connexion between them, while, at the same time, each lecturer endeavours to treat his particular theme in such a manner as to give it all possible completeness.

This undertaking has been suggested more especially by the experiences of the last year. These have tended to convince us that neither the public statement from the pulpit of Christian truths to mixed congregations, nor the religious instruction given to our young people, adequately meets the requirements of the day. There are undeniably many youths and many grown men in whom the trials and vicissitudes of life have awakened a desire more and more clearly to understand the faith they hold, in order to give a satisfactory account of it to all objectors. There are others, again, who no longer stand firm themselves in the religious beliefs of their childhood; doubts suggested from without have shaken their position; objections have sprung up within their own secret consciousness; they are perplexed with questions for which they can find no answer, which even the best course of religious instruction has failed to grapple with; they cannot escape from the spirit of the times; they shrink from exposing themselves to the ridicule of the many who treat a belief in the Bible as an obsolete prejudice; the increasingly bold tone of historical criticism fills their minds with a pleasant sense of freedom; the ever-widening sphere of modern science results in discoveries they hold to be irreconcilable with the truth of Scripture, so that, although they still retain a certain reverence for the spirit of the Bible, they can find no solution for the contradictions it seems to present.

We cannot, indeed, suppose that there are not some whose speculative difficulties are strengthened by a darker motive, to whom doubt, nay, even rejection of Christianity is welcome; because it is an irksome discipline, a disturbing influence to conscience, a weighty obligation to holiness of life, a barrier to sinful pleasure, that they are casting away as a foolish prejudice. For such men as these, the great essential is to renounce the evil and turn to the good; let them resolve to break with sin, and they will find new light break in upon their understandings.

But, at the same time, all doubters do not belong to this class. I can well believe that there are many who, so far from wilfully encouraging their doubts as a sanction to misconduct, can conscientiously assert that, since these very doubts have arisen, they are far more in earnest, both as regards morality and even piety, than they were in the days when they held a traditional faith lifelessly though implicitly. It is not ours to judge those who occupy this critical position; later, the Spirit of God may discover to them that their motives are more mixed than they now suppose, and at the present time many a one amongst their number feels uncertain, restless, and unhappy in his heart's core.

It is such as these whom we fain would serve. But it is desirable that, at the outset, we should mutually guard against delusive hopes. You must not come with the expectation or the desire to hear something startling, unexpected, novel, free from all human imperfection or error; what you do find, however, of error or imperfection you must lay to our charge, not to that of God's Truth. And we, again, when we have set forth the most important truths in the best way we can, must not imagine that we can take your convictions as it were by storm. In all that relates to mind, most especially in all that relates to God, we can never attain to mathematical certainty, to such evidence as forces immediate belief from every reasonable mind. The maturing of religious faith must necessarily be progressive.

What lies within our power is only this: to attest our own inward experience of the truth of God's Word; to adduce proofs of it; to give a rational explanation of it, and then to invite all to examine it theoretically and experimentally for themselves. And surely it is well worth testing the comparative value, for life and death, time and eternity, of a self-made religion, more especially if this consist rather in knowing what we do *not*, than what we *do* believe, and be founded less on our own experience than on hearsay. For incontrovertibly the very essence of religion must be positive, not negative; must be, not a mere consciousness of what we do *not* hold, but a simple and confident answer to these three questions: What do you believe? What are you sure of? What conception have you of God?

I.

WHAT IS FAITH?

AS we have to pass under review the principal verities of Christian faith, it is evident that we should first of all attain a right comprehension of what is meant by Faith. Accordingly, the question that I have now to discuss is the nature of faith, with special reference to the declaration, "He who believeth not shall be damned:"—A declaration this which has offended many, ourselves amongst the number: "He who believeth not shall be damned"! What harsh and horrible words are these! And this is a declaration of the God of love! Nay, this can be nothing else than a gloomy, tyrannical fanaticism. This is a doctrine which, could it find acceptance now-a-days, would pledge us to irreconcilable hatred towards the unbelieving, while "amongst the genuine children of the present century, it is considered barbarism to be prejudiced against any one on account of his religious opinions, much more to persecute him."

And yet this is Bible language; this is an expression of our Lord himself! Or can it be that this is a mistake altogether; and will some tell us that this intolerably hard sentence has no need to burden our spirits, since it belongs to that portion of the Gospel of St. Mark which is not authentic, and cannot, therefore, be proved to be the language of Christ?

It is indeed true that this sixteenth chapter ends with the eighth verse in one of the oldest and most valuable of our long-known manuscript versions; as also in that version lately discovered by Tischendorf in one of the Sinaitic monasteries; and that, according to indisputable contemporary testimony, the last twelve verses were also wanting in several manuscripts no longer extant. This is a problem which cannot be very certainly solved, but yet we incline to believe that the oldest manuscripts must in some way have got mutilated, for it appears quite improbable that the Gospel could originally have ended with the eighth verse, in which it is said of the women,—" Neither said they anything to any man; for they were afraid." It is evident that this is *not* a conclusion; we therefore infer that the right conclusion was in many cases lost.

I will not lay any particular stress just now upon the fact of such a critic as Lachmann accepting our reading of the New Testament, and giving these twelve verses in his edition; more important evidence of their authenticity exists in the harmony of our text with other indisputably genuine passages of Scripture. " He that believeth on the Son hath everlasting life," saith the Baptist; " He that believeth not shall not see life, but the wrath of God abideth on him" (John iii. 36). And the apostle Paul, in like manner, speaks of the wrath of God coming upon the children of disobedience or unbelief (Eph. v. 6); and, in 1 Cor. i. 18, after saying, " The preaching of the cross is to them that perish foolishness; but unto us who are saved it is the power of God," he gives, in the 21st verse, the conditions of the salvation: " It pleased God through the foolishness of preaching to save them that believe;" whence we must infer, that those who perish are those who do not believe. Thus we see that there is no escape from the position: it is a constantly recurring truth in Scripture, which finds its most concise expression in the words of our text, " He who believeth not shall be damned."

But still there are, it may be, some among us to whom this Bible statement is perfectly intolerable. Let such once grant that there is a life after death, and that this life is not the same in all cases, but an alternative of blessedness or misery; and then grant this for the moment—without binding yourself down to the conclusion—that what qualifies a man for misery or blessedness, is in point of fact his belief or his unbelief;

then, I ask you, which would be the more cruel, the more loveless conduct, to warn us in time, or to give us no warning at all? If a man were walking in darkness where the very next step might plunge him into the abyss, and one stood by him who knew his danger, say which were the greater cruelty, to startle him by screams, and drag him back were it even by the hair of his head, or to let him quietly wander on? You will all allow, that *granted* that blessedness or misery hinge on faith and unbelief, it is love, not unlovingness, that warns, and that the sin against love would be the withholding of the warning. But this very inference will but strengthen your opposition to the doctrine, to which we have for the moment assumed your agreement, the doctrine that links our eternal destiny to our belief. The Scripture indeed lays it down; you, however, reject it, and declare it intolerable. But may not your opposition arise from your conception of faith differing from the scriptural conception of it? Let us look into the matter, and consent patiently to follow me during a somewhat dry investigation.

What do we understand in our everyday life by faith? "I believe that such or such a thing has happened," we are in the habit of saying, meaning thereby, "I do not know it for a certainty, but I have sufficient ground for receiving it as a fact." It would be better, indeed, if I could say, "I know it; I know it positively; I have seen it; or I have some other equally indisputable source of certainty." Here, you perceive, there is a contrast drawn between believing and knowing; the word *believing* is used as the equivalent of uncertain or partial knowledge; is, therefore, something not much higher than an imperfectly founded opinion; and accordingly we have just heard that no one should be looked down upon for his religious opinions. But it is only writers of the present day who speak of these religious opinions; the Scriptures never do so. Such belief or opinion as this is in no way whatever to be identified with what the Bible calls faith.

In order to search deeper into the matter, we must now ask ourselves, How do we generally attain to any cognition whatever, whether it be a knowledge of external things, or a conviction as to some given truth? If we reflect upon it a little, we soon perceive that we must distinguish between the objects of our cognition as belonging to essentially different classes.

There are cognitions internal in the human mind itself, as for instance, and above all, the mathematical. Here, from the most simple, fundamental ideas of number and space, the laws of all reckoning and all measurement are step by step evolved, and any one who possesses good faculties can follow the process. This mathematical science is the most exact of all, nay, the only completely exact; but at the same time it gives us no living substance, no reality, nothing but distinct, precise, yet empty and abstract forms; and it would be a mere perversion to suppose that all other sciences could or ought to proceed upon mathematical principles, and that nothing was to be received as truth but what was capable of mathematical proof. The greatest mathematicians, who were at the same time decided Christians, Pascal, Euler, Newton, knew better.

If now we turn to the cognition of living realities, we find that these latter must reveal themselves, and we must receive their revelation; that is, we must have an organ which is capable of apprehending the evidence they give of their reality, and we must place trust in this apprehensive or verifying faculty, in order to build our conclusions thereon, and understand by thinking the fact verified. In this sense we may truly affirm that all our cognitions imply belief, and that without some sort of belief we could not establish any one of them. Goethe once called himself a believer in the five senses, and thereby expressed a truth which has a wider and higher range than he was perhaps aware of.

For, in point of fact, is it not a belief, a reliance, that you place in your senses? A light-giving body evidences its existence by its light. Your eye is the organ appropriated to the reception of that evidence. Accordingly, you perceive the light, and you believe the testimony of your eye-sight. You even believe it, though you know experimentally that there are such things as optical delusions. When a stick dipped into water appears to be broken, you are convinced by other sources of information, probably by touch, that it is not really so, but that the appearance is only caused by the refraction of the light by the water.

Again, the setting and rising of the sun is a daily optical illusion. How many observations, both connected and unconnected with it, had to be compared and mentally elaborated before Copernicus could arrive at the discovery of the real facts which underlie this optical delusion. But for all that, the human eye had perceived a reality, and you trust its evidence as much as ever. You are not shaken in your belief by your knowledge that disease of the optic nerve may simulate flashes of light; you take means to distinguish between the subjective effects of disease, and the revelation of external realities. Thus you do not lose faith in your own senses, and whatever you see, hear, or touch, is, you are convinced, real, without demanding further proof. You are, we all are, in this respect, believers in the five senses.

But is this the only method of cognition, is this applicable to all realities, so that we may affirm that there is no reality but such as we can apprehend through one of the five senses? Not so. In the spoken words which you hear, which are a sound that strikes upon your ear, there is yet something more than a sound; there is a thought also, and he who speaks, and they who hear and understand him, have something within them, nay, *are* something that lies beyond the jurisdiction of the five senses. You say *I*, I *think*—but you have never seen your thought; you can perceive it neither with the eye nor with any other of your five senses, and yet you do perceive it, as certainly, nay, more certainly than you see—you perceive it by your immediate consciousness. You are thus aware of the invisible within you, of your spirit, of your soul. You are not indeed ignorant that there is a modern science which would teach us that this spirit or soul is nothing but a temporary peculiarity or activity of the brain, entirely dependent upon the convolutions of the cerebral substance; whence it follows that a man does whatever his brain necessitates, and that there is no such thing as free-will or reponsibility. It is not necessary to dwell at greater length upon this doctrine, which is not only wicked but miserably foolish; we shall return by and by to something connected with it; at present it may suffice us that we are made cognisant of the invisible power of thought within us not by the perception of the five senses, but through our immediate consciousness. This is a perception which no one doubts or can doubt without madness. It is on this point that every system must be wrecked which is founded on a determination to doubt whatever cannot be proved. For here every one believes without further proof, and without the perception of the senses.

This truth pervades all human life and human action. We rejoice in whatever is beautiful either to the eye or the ear, but it is not the eye or the ear that decides upon this beauty; many hear or see the same thing, and fail to remark its beauty,—they have not the special sense requisite. Again, we see the external action of another man, but the inner nature, the significance of that action,—whether it was well or ill done, just or not, noble or not,—this we do not see with our bodily eye, this it requires a developed faculty of correct moral judgment to appreciate. To this we must bring spiritual perception and comprehension. One who was only a believer in the five senses, would lack the sense wanted here. But if we possess it, we place confidence in it, although delusions in such matters are manifestly more frequent than in optics; and on the strength of our own perception, we believe a man to be upright, intelligent, loveable, or the reverse.

Now let us take one further step. The world around us, and the body which is our instrument, both alike show us most admirable wisdom and order in all their arrangements, small and great; an exquisite adaptation of each organism for its life purpose; a surprising interdependence between separate existences, so that each creature lives for itself, yet not for itself alone, but for the advantage of other creatures; and the eye of the embryo is most carefully prepared in its ante-natal darkness to receive the light that shall break on it after birth —but why go on citing instances? A lifetime were not long enough for this! This wondrous design then we perceive, so that if we were not taught to do so, we *must* needs ask ourselves whence this proceeds, and *must* conclude, even were it not revealed, that the universe owes its origin to the highest wisdom and intelligence. Of this design we see only a small fragment; we cannot exhaust its resources; but what we do see suffices to convince us that all is intelligently ordered, and enables us to hold fast that conviction even in presence of what might almost seem occasional discrepancy; and if this be the case, it is consequently plain that this wise order can proceed only from a *conscious* power: for, to deduce the rational from the irrational, would be the height of irrationality.

Thus our own perception of an intelligent plan leads us to believe in an intelligent, conscious Author of the universe, which, as Socrates said of old, is an affair of purpose not chance.[1] And we have the same good ground for trusting this perception, as we have for believing on the evidence of our senses in the reality of the external world.

For what we see is not the alone real. Most real is the Originator of this wisely-ordered world, whom we do not see, any more than we see our own souls; but whose eternal power and Godhead we perceive by rational attention to the visible, as the apostle says, Rom. i. 20; this we must perceive, must seek after, and seeking find. For we find that although the five senses may indeed suffice to apprehend the material, they are useless as regards the immaterial, and yet the latter is as real, nay, far more real than the former, and our cognition of it by the inner perception of our reason, affords us as positive, as reliable, nay, a far more positive certainty than any cognition of the senses; for our eyes may deceive us, but our self-consciousness never can,—that which says to us, "I am, and I think,"

[1] Xenophon, *Memor.* i. 4.

that does not deceive. Still higher and still more certain must be our reliance in the *existence* of the invisible Creator of the world and of ourselves; for the unconscious material world is not ordered by itself nor by us, nor do we order our own being, but the world and we ourselves are alike dependent on Him in whom we are compelled to believe as the Lord of the world and our Lord also.

But it is possible, as we see, to resist even this belief; possible to say that the world is thrown together by chance. Yes, this is indeed possible. Only we will never allow that this is the knowledge which is the antithesis to belief. We perceive an intelligent plan, we believe that this cannot be self-originated, we deduce thence an invisible but a real and intelligent God; this is our knowledge of God founded on our rational belief. He who can say of this intelligent plan which appeals to his belief, that it is the result of chance; who will not believe, and does not therefore perceive, cannot have any pretensions to knowledge, but rather to utter ignorance. And yet this ignorant man is not entirely without a certain faith of his own, for he has not *seen* that Chance is the creator of the universe, and yet he asserts it to be so; this then is his *faith*, Chance is the God in whom he believes. We Christians have a more rational belief.

Or is it much better than this belief in Chance, to hold the doctrine of unconscious yet wisdom-fraught Nature-power? Is it in very deed rational to attribute the creation to the spirit before it becomes self-conscious in humanity, and to speak of that "which it wrought as an unconscious Nature-power, ordering the relations of the planetary system, forming the earths and metals, and the organic construction of plants and animals."[1] Is this the teaching of reason? Not we think of a reasonable reason. In practical life, at all events, a man would be considered mad who should attribute a mechanical invention, or thoughtful work of art, to an unconsciously working intelligence. And is this to be the rational deduction from the evidences of intelligence

[1] Strauss on *Christian Doctrine,* i 351.

displayed in the universe? We prefer the Christian faith as the more reasonable of the two.[1] For if any one believes in this unconscions Nature-power, it is a faith still, not a knowledge, and hardly a faith to prefer to our own!

We have now seen what faith is in its most universal sense; faith is the reliance that we place in the evidence of our senses with regard to those things that come within their range. In regard to the Immaterial, more especially with regard to God and things divine, faith is the reliance we place on our perception of immaterial reality; a perception not attained to by the medium of the five senses, but by means of the higher sense of our reason. Not that the truth is inherent in this our reason; its office is to take cognisance of that immaterial reality which lies open to its perception, and we place reliance upon this perception. Thus the Scripture describes faith in the Epistle to the Hebrews xi. 3 (we quote from De Wette's translation): "But faith is confidence in what we hope for; conviction of things we do not see. Through faith we perceive that the world was prepared by God's word, so that not out of the apparent came the visible."

Now in what relation do we stand to this God whom we recognise and believe in? What do we owe him? For the question of questions must be this which relates to the law and purpose of our life, since, as Socrates himself declared, the more glorious the God who wills that we should serve him, the more highly is he to be honoured.[2] We now begin to discern that this question respecting the knowing and honouring God is not merely an affair of the head, but of the conscience; that this is the central point of all that conscience demands of us.

What a wonderful thing this conscience is! No doubt we may talk of it incorrectly. Many represent conscience as the infallible inner lawgiver, nay, even the source ot all knowledge of God and of divine truth. But to this an objection at once occurs: Whence then

[1] Compare Gess on *The Person of Christ*, 1856, s. 145.

[2] Xenophon, *Memor.* i. 4.

the instability and variability of all social ordinances? whence the fact that in one age and amongst one nation acts and customs are reputed moral which in another age and another land are held to be immoral? I may instance the marriage of two sisters, which obtained amongst many of the nations of antiquity; or polygamy, which was not forbidden by the Old Testament. Does it not appear as though, instead of a fixed law of conscience, we had nothing before us but variable opinions—the product of a given age and climate?

What shall we reply? In the first place, we must acknowledge that it is just as possible to doubt of moral truth as of the existence of God. It is by no means more philosophical to doubt of God than to doubt the sanctity and inviolability of the moral law. Nor will it ever be possible to remain unshakeably convinced of the last apart from its root, its central point,—the certainty, namely, of our responsibility to God and our dependence upon him. And if that which is best within us, protests against doing away with the moral law, this be it known is closely connected with the bond that unites us to God. You will not, you say, part with this belief in a moral law? you do well, hold it fast, and you will become convinced that it is only in God that you can be sure of it.

But the observations we have just made upon the variable standard of morals among men, proves to us at least that untenable expressions are often used with regard to conscience. Conscience does not most certainly itself lay down for us the special laws we have to obey. But it declares in a general way, even among the most degraded and most savage nations, that there *is* a difference between good and evil; a difference according to which we decide when we are unprejudiced by any considerations of utility, a difference, therefore, other than the mere difference between the useful and the hurtful; a difference that every one recognises, however debased and corrupted his own character may be, for every one will characterize this action as evil, that action as good, call this man upright, that man dishonest; and every one is conscious of something or other in himself of which he is ashamed; nay, this verdict of our own conscience as to whether or no we have done what we knew and acknowledged to be right, is so incorruptible, so independent of human influences, so ineradicable, that even when it has long been silenced, whether the man will or no, it may break out at the very last with a quite irresistible strength. Whence comes this? whence but because it is implanted in us; or, in other words, because the author of our physical life is also the author of our moral sense; our Creator, is also our lawgiver and our judge. Hence the activity of conscience in all who have not ceased to deserve the very name of man. It is true that only in the element of truth can conscience develop itself, very tenderly and sensitively, very freely and joyously, very deeply and enduringly. But even when the intellect is fettered by many errors, the existence of conscience is evidence to itself of the bond that unites men with God.

If, therefore, we duly reflect upon this, we shall perceive how that denial of a Creator of which we spoke just now, is something worse than merely irrational. In fact, to say that Chance has compounded the world, or that it is the result of a creative energy which is unconscious of its own operations, can only be possible through a contradiction not merely of reason, but of the inward voice of conscience as well.

Let us take another example to illustrate the above. A man who intentionally takes away the life of another without being forced to do this in virtue of his office, we call a murderer; a man who unjustly appropriates his neighbour's goods, must submit to the appellation of thief. Now there may be people whose passions prevent their allowing this. They do not lack plausible arguments by which to place these actions in such a light that the actor can no longer be called a murderer or a thief. These arguments may be lucidly expounded, but they are in no way convincing to the simple sense of truth. At bottom they contradict our reason, and what is more, they contradict conscience; nay, the very man who brings forward the argument cannot do so without opposing and resisting the inner voice within him. And is it not the very same with a denial of God, as the self-conscious and world-conscious Creator? Can a man honestly, *de bonne foi*, express such a negation as this? He may indeed point out difficulties in any definition man can give of the Divine self-consciousness. But can he in good truth assert that the *denial* of the Divine self-consciousness is not fraught with still greater difficulties? No, verily, he can only do this by resisting the testimony to the truth afforded by his own conscience.

We now begin to see why the apostle repeatedly speaks of *obedience* to the faith, which he was called to establish (Rom. i. 5). The point in question indeed is an act of the will, a subjection to an acknowledged truth, as we shall understand more clearly by and by.

Hence it follows that no one may take refuge in the excuse that he was not organized for faith; that for others indeed it may be right, nay, admirable, but that for him it is impossible; does not even the apostle allow that all men have not faith? True, he says so (2 Thess. iii. 2); but it is only of unreasonable and wicked men that he says it, so that at least you had better not appeal to him. And, above all, do not use this expression till you have thoroughly and honestly examined whether you have really conformed to all the claims made on you by your conscience.

When I remarked just now that man was often for a long time able to silence his conscience, I implied the fact that in this region of moral self-consciousness defects of insight were especially common. We know what wickedness is in others, every one can bring forward plenty of examples of worthless people; whereas with regard to our own condition, self-complacency not unfrequently prevails; we have the same delusions about our character as that which inflated the Pharisee of old above the publican. Even the various misfortunes we are called upon to suffer are by no means certain to help us to self-knowledge; on the contrary, they often render hard and defiant, lead us to entrench ourselves in a certain dogged obstinacy. The right discernment of our sinful condition before God is only to be learnt in the way the Scripture describes: the Holy Ghost shall reprove or convince the world of sin (John xvi. 8). It is thus the inner eye must be cleared and sharpened. And this is only thoroughly done by a man's attaining a deeper perception of the Divine will and being.

When, however, this is done, then the human heart learns what real misery is; its cry is now, Who will help me, who will forgive me? I must have forgiveness, peace, and deliverance from evil; where shall I find these, how shall I attain to them? For *this*, conscience does not of itself reveal. It discovers the disease indeed, it convinces the man of sin; but it does not show him the healing of the disease, the removal of the sin. To try and comfort himself with believing "that no one can overstep the barrier of his defects and evil tendencies, but that yet each in his weakness and his limitations plays his own appointed part in the eternal destiny of the human race," affords no true calm, is only a miserable suppression of conscience. Wherever conscience is alive, it will require some better comfort than this. It occasions the most intense need to be felt of forgiveness, but it cannot itself satisfy that need; indeed, any forgiveness which we could ourselves devise, a forgiveness thought out only by ourselves, would amount to *no* forgiveness at all. Forgiveness can only come from God against whom we have sinned.

But the knowledge of the Being of God, which we have deduced from the creation, does not bring with it this message of forgiveness. On the contrary, this natural revelation leaves many a question unanswered, many a dark mystery unsolved. How much disorder meets us in all the domains of creation; in how ghastly a manner Death, with its pains and terrors, reigns therein! It was with reference to this that we spoke a little while ago of apparent discrepancies. True, we are in a measure able to perceive how each disturbance of order but promotes a higher order, how each death subserves a new life. But this consideration does not suffice to still the cry of the wounded heart, oppressed by the sadness of death all around. It is true that even the heathen were more or less aware, that between the ills that we suffer and the evil that we do there is a close and intimate connexion. But the more earnestly we examine into this, the more we find ourselves involved in fresh and insoluble problems, and deliverance from sin is clearly not to be found in this direction.

The case then stands as follows: either there is no deliverance and no forgiveness, and so no solution to this dark problem of human life; or that which we need can only come to us from God, revealing himself to us as the Deliverer. *And he is there and invites:* Come unto me, all ye that labour and are heavy laden, and I will refresh you (Matt. xi. 28); I am come to seek and to save that which was lost (Luke xix. 10). Here we have a new discovery of God; one which the stars never hinted at. No man knoweth the Son but the Father, and no man knoweth the Father but the Son, and he to whom the Son will reveal him (Matt. xi. 27). It is only through the Son that we learn to know God as a *Father*, as our merciful, forgiving Father. But no man can call Jesus Lord but through the Holy Ghost (1 Cor. xii. 3).

Such then is the testimony of the Sacred Scriptures; not only that God is the Creator of all things, but that he is the just and holy One, and at the same time the tenderly merciful, and that he is this not only in himself, but *towards us.* Now this last fact we could never gain from our knowledge of God drawn from the works of Nature. Be the argument for the necessary belief in a Creator ever so well conducted, it leaves the truth as it were still in a measure outside of us; in spite of our agreement we are not thoroughly at one with it; we see, indeed, that we are bound to believe in the reality of God, but none of the proofs of it fill us with that full, tranquil certainty of reality, on which we build. It may be true; but it is not, so to speak, positively true *for us.* This God in whom we are compelled to believe, is dumb towards us; he does not speak plainly to us of grace or reconciliation, so long as we do not know or wish to know the testimony of the witnesses of God. The question then is: Have we the purified and opened inward sense for the reception of this testimony? Do we employ it to apprehend this testimony? De we trust it, or do we not trust it? Do we believe or do we not believe? This cannot possibly be an immaterial thing. Man can deny this testimony. But also lofty spirits can heartily assent to it, and I adduce as an example the epitaph which Copernicus chose for his tomb, giving a faithful translation of the meaning of the Latin verse—

> Not such grace as Paul's do I require,
> Not Peter's pardon do I ask; but that
> Which on the cross thou gavest to the thief
> I earnestly pray for.

Thus we see the great astronomer did not seek for the salvation and blessedness of his soul in the stars, but in the grace of Jesus Christ; he was not only a believer in the five senses, but a believer also in that inward sense awaked by God in the consciousness of man.

Such a faith as this, however, we clearly perceive is no more only an affair of the intellect; it becomes evident that the *will*, nay the *whole man*, must share in it. It is a mutilation of faith to suppose it a mere lifeless opinion of the mind, an indifferent holding of the mere *fact* that there is a God. Such faith as this the devils have and tremble, says Scripture (James ii. 19). By a saving faith, the Bible invariably understands an active, practical principle founded on the knowledge of God. This the very word itself shows. The Hebrew word for "believing," in the Old Testament, signifies *to lean* firmly upon something; the Greek word means to *trust in*. Nothing can be further removed from mere opinion. The Bible conception of believing is compounded of Trust and Faith.

I will give another word of Latin derivation, which conveys the same meaning—the word *credit*. Yes, credit is the faith, credit is the trust that a merchant enjoys; and you know well that he can get on in business as little, nay, less without credit than without money. And if no mercantile enterprise can prosper without faith, so too no friendship can; no marriage, no blessed relation between parents and children, no upright, honourable, peaceful intercourse of any kind, can exist without reciprocal confidence. All human relations require trust and faith. Shall our God then, our Creator and Redeemer, have a less claim upon us? No great undertaking, no important discovery ever came to pass without a mighty faith which filled the soul, and taught it to hope for what seemed beyond hope. Columbus could never have reached America but for this confidence of a mighty faith. And is less than this required in order to reach the eternal aim of human life? We are now in a position more fully to understand why it is said both in the Old and New Testaments, The just shall live by *faith*.

The prophet Habakkuk is bewailing the manifold iniquities, and the spoiling and violence that prevail among the people of Israel. God answers him by declaring that he will raise up the Chaldeans, that hasty and bitter nation, to execute judgment upon Israel. This only dismays the prophet the more. Are these heathens, who are worse than ourselves, to have power over us? O let us not die! And this is the answer he receives: The vision or prophecy will not tarry (the prophecy, that is, of the terrible events which are ordained only as temporary judgments, those who are really and heartily humbled finding favour at the last); though it tarry, wait for it; it shall surely come, it shall not tarry. Behold, his (the powerful adversary's) soul is lifted up within him (therefore, though he is employed as the instrument of God's judgment, his own fearful judgment will eventually overtake him); *but the just shall live by faith* (Hab. ii. 4).

It is the same in the New Testament. Faith, trust, is that upon which all depends. Christ ever demands faith, confidence in his person. When about to heal the sick, he asks, "Believest thou that I am able to do this?" (Matt. ix. 28.) But it is not only to the sick in body, to the pardoned sinner as well he says, "Go thy way; thy faith has saved thee" (Luke vii. 50). And St. Paul especially preaches faith, because through the works of the law can no man be justified; for by the law is the knowledge of sin; therefore God has manifested his righteousness;—the righteousness which is of him, as being through faith in Jesus Christ, unto all and upon all them that believe" (Rom. iii. 20-22). "*The just shall live by faith*" (Rom. i. 17).

This faith is confidence, reliance in God's mercy through Christ. But such confidence is not easy, natural, self-evident to the human heart. In this higher province there is also needed *an obedience of faith*, an overcoming of distrust, a submission to acknowledged truth, a profound earnestness, a willingness to live by this faith.

God is willing to give us his grace; we must be willing to receive it. *Not* to believe, signifies not to accept his saving, forgiving, helping, healing grace. Now, if we do not believe the testimony to God's grace, if we remain obdurate in our non-believing and non-accepting, we ourselves make God's work of salvation of none effect, so far as we are concerned. Can this result in anything else but our ruin?

It is thus the Bible speaks of faith; it is thus that our fathers understood the Bible, and preached faith, in our Reformed Church. Let me cite one only, but one very important passage in evidence of this, the 21st question in the excellent Heidelberg Catechism. This is how it runs: "What is Faith?" *Answer*, "Faith is not only a certain perception through which I receive as true whatever God has revealed in his Word, it is also a hearty trust which the Holy Spirit works in me through the gospel, that not alone to the sins of others, but to my sins forgiveness will be granted, and eternal righteousness and blessedness bestowed on me by God, out of free grace, and for the atoning merits of Christ."

You see plainly that the faith here spoken of does not mean a mere opinion, or semi-knowledge, but a firm and lofty confidence in the grace of Christ as the reality of realities. But there is probably something besides in this clause of the Catechism which is repugnant to some among you: I allude to what is said therein about a certain perception through which we receive as true whatever God has revealed in his Word. Is this not, it may be asked, that Bibliolatry, that belief in the letter, which would constrain us to receive as literally true even the speaking of Balaam's ass, and the standing still of the sun at Joshua's command, with other incredible and unbearable things of the kind, and would make blessedness or perdition hinge upon our doing so? And here I should need to speak more at length about the Bible, in order to determine that it is this Bible that witnesses to us of God's saving work. But you will understand, that of such an extensive and comprehensive theme I can only give the merest outline. In the first place, it must be laid down that the *ground* of our faith is not a literal belief, such as might result from external evidence, without reference to the nature of the revelation, as thus: these Scriptures have come from God; *therefore* you must receive as true whatever is contained in them. Not so; the root of our faith is *personal* trust in Christ. Then, indeed, we learn to understand that we cannot believe *on* him without believing *him*. We cannot rightly trust in *God*, without trusting the *truth* of God.

Now if God *is*, which our observation of the outer world and our own consciousness compel us to believe, how could he be without making himself known? How could he be love, whence should we know confidently that he was love, if he had not revealed himself more fully than in the outer world, or in our own consciousness? This may indeed tell us that we need love; but that God really *is* love, as we require it, forgiving, redeeming, saving love, how should we know this but for the testimony of the prophets and apostles, to whom he revealed it through his Spirit, and, above all, the testimony of Christ, who is to us the incarnation of this love? What nation is there, that, not having had the Bible, *knows* that God is love? Where do we find the eternal fundamental truths on which our salvation rests, the truth of God's justice and judgment, the truth of God's grace and mercy, as we find them in this Book?

And remark once more, that these Divine truths are not mere ideas, but God's thoughts are at the same time *acts* of judgment and mercy, discipline and deliverance, developing themselves in an ascending scale from the beginning of the human race till the coming of Christ. Consequently, the history of God's *acts* cannot be an immaterial matter safely to be thrown aside. Everything contained in the Bible is not alike nearly and vitally connected with the main point, namely, salvation. There is much in which we can hardly trace this connexion at all, much which is, at first sight, repugnant to us, but a careful examination shows us how closely even this is interwoven with other parts which are not only historically essential, but of highest moral importance. What is wanted is a careful, patient, laborious, but self-rewarding and thoroughly conscientious searching of the Scriptures. But how many reject the Bible without ever having *searched* it, merely on account of a few stumbling-blocks which they are continually bringing forward. If, however, it be not a matter of indifference whether we believe or believe not in God's truth, can such conduct be right? Is it right in those who have the Bible within reach to neglect it? For of course I am not speaking of those who have never received the Bible revelation, we may safely leave them to God's mercy, for he is no unrighteous Judge to require what he has not given. We, however, are not in that position, and our responsibility is, therefore, of quite a different character.

Let me sum up what has been already said. We have seen that if it be really true that everything depends upon faith, then it is nothing but the love of God that utters the warning cry, "He that believeth not shall be damned." You will now, perhaps, be less surprised than you would have been at first at my saying, It is also nothing but the love of God that has ordained that all should depend upon faith. It is, indeed, love which leads him to put such honour upon us, as only to have us his *free* servants and children; for the God of love will have *free* love. In the beginning he said to man: Thou art at liberty to obey or not. And with regard to his work of redemption also, he says to us, You have liberty granted you to receive my salvation or not. To such, however, as obstinately resist all his judgments and all his mercies,—all the warnings and leadings of his Spirit, all his paternal and gracious knocking at the door of their hearts, and who consciously resist their own conscience as well,—to them he *must* say at the last, Thou hast not *believed*, thou hast not *willed* to believe. Nothing is left but this: "He that believeth not shall be damned." For God will not constrain us, just because he is the God of free love. The dignity conferred by God on man consists in this his power to stand upright or fall; to lay hold of deliverance, or destroy himself completely.

But if this awfully severe sentence that must be passed on the resisting does not impugn the love of God, neither does it in any way pledge us to hatred against unbelievers. On the contrary, the God of love educates us for love also. Truth compels me to confess that, from olden times till now, many sins against the loving character of God have been committed in the name of Orthodoxy. It is possible to know the truth of Christ, and to use that knowledge without the love of Christ. And yet he himself has cast eternal disgrace upon unloving orthodoxy by the example of the Good Samaritan. But all unbelievers, however, are not good Samaritans. Still less are we to be misled by the statement, hear it often as we may, that the same pious feelings and dispositions may co-exist with the most opposite forms of theoretical belief; or even that a high and pure morality is compatible with a denial of God, and of a future life.

It is true, we must admit, that there are men who are upright and irreproachable in all their relations to their fellow-men; nay, who, by their nobleness of mind, put many of the nominally pious to shame, and yet are resolutely opposed to the Christian faith. We must not underrate this fact. But who knows how much these men are unconsciously indebted to gospel influences, and to early religious education? For, after all, we must once more earnestly ask, If God be God, do we owe nothing to him? Should we place so high a value upon unbelieving rectitude of conduct, upon a morality which is even compatible with a denial of God?

Are there many who exhibit a high morality in combination with this denial? Would such morality hold good under the secretest, hardest, extremest trials? Can it produce any other salvation, any other forgiveness of sins, any other eternal deliverance, than that which God has offered us in Christ?

Or will any one assert, assert in good earnest, that we do not need such? Can there be true virtue if we have not God; and what will be the fate of him who owns himself *not* virtuous, but sinful? Or if you concede that a faith is essential to man, but not exactly the Christian faith, then tell us what other faith? but tell it us plainly, so that we may be able to perceive whether it will do to build on in life and in death. Show us the well-founded subjects of faith that surpass the fundamental truths of Holy Scripture. We meanwhile assert, that all morality that unites itself with a denial of God, wants its vital centre. This does not imply that there is no such thing. After the setting of the sun there is still light, the Alpine peaks still glow; but by and by it grows dark and cold. And so is it with the moral man without the firm foundations of God's truth, without humility before God, without prayer to God, without gratitude towards God, without the fear and love of the living God.

We cannot read the heart, and are not called upon to judge our fellow-servants. We should learn more and more of Christ's infinite mercy. How patiently and meekly he knows to wait for faith! How inexpressibly merciful the answer he returns to his enemies after they have blasphemed him by the malignity of the imputation: He casteth out devils through the prince of the devils. All manner of sin and blasphemy, says he, shall be forgiven unto men, and he that speaketh against the Son of man shall be forgiven; but blasphemy against the Holy Ghost hath never forgiveness (Matt. xii. 31, 32). Thus freely does he admit that it is possible to mistake him, the Son of man, through what is, after all, pardonable ignorance. But at the last, when all the Divine means of mercy are exhausted; when all the light that shows a sinner his own sins and God's salvation has shone in vain; when all the chastenings and all the drawings of the Spirit have been alike despised, and pure unbelief has come to opposing itself to the Spirit, and saying I *will* not, what else can ensue but ruin? what remains to the God of truth and holiness but to execute upon the resolutely defiant soul the sentence, "He who believeth not shall be damned."

From this, however, we are far from deducing the duty of hatred to unbelievers, but rather the duty of love. It is this which Christ's patience should teach us, a love which, however, from its very nature, must be united with truth. Yes, it is for love's sake that we bear witness to a truth which, to the discerning mind, should be as self-evident as the assertion: He who eats not must die of hunger; the truth: "He that believeth not shall be damned."

For, once more, faith is no insignificant thing; faith is no mere opinion or partial knowledge; faith is no assumption of unimportant matters on insufficient grounds; faith is the conviction of invisible realities not capable of mathematical proof, not to be verified by the senses, but real nevertheless, with a higher reality than any sensible object can ever claim; faith, in its highest sense, is the conviction of God's grace in Christ Jesus, as being within our reach, the acceptance of what God has offered us in him, the reliance thereon as on God's truth; the obedience thereto of a perfectly free heart. How can this be a matter of indifference? How can it be all one whether we have any heart towards God or not, whether we seek him or seek him not, inquire after him or not, depend upon him or not, pray to him or not, love him or love him not,—in a word, *believe* or *believe not?* Verily love must needs warn and testify. "He that believeth not shall be damned." But why hearken to these words alone? Why not to the promise that precedes them? "*He that believeth shall be saved.*"

II.

NATURE OR GOD.

NATURE or God? Is the universe self-existent, or does it derive its origin from a being distinct from itself? And supposing this latter hypothesis the true one, and that the universe by its very existence refers us to God as the cause of that existence, what opinions are we to hold respecting Him? Is He a self-conscious being? Does He concern himself about us? Is He present with us? Does He speak to us, and can we pray to Him so as to be heard of Him? Or is the being from whom the world is derived, too high and distant to interfere in the insignificant concerns of earth? Or, still further, is it altogether a mistake to attribute to the being from whom the universe springs, self-consciousness, liberty, or personality? In what manner, in short, are we to think this origin of all things? I enumerate these questions, not with the view of entering at length into them all, but to give you a general idea of the nature of the inquiry we are about to enter upon.

There are two different methods of inquiring into the nature of God. The one is based upon those acts of God, whereby he revealed himself in the midst of the people of Israel, and accomplished the salvation of the human race. From God's *acts* it is possible to draw a deduction of God's *nature*, more especially since the appearing of Christ, whose coming into the world, life in the world, and departure from the world, afford the climax of God's revelation of himself in action. This is the royal road to the knowledge of God's existence, and the one that leads us most deeply into the knowledge of the Divine nature. Indeed, what the apostle Paul calls the deep things of God, are only attainable by this method; nor is it by any means true that none but the credulous make choice of it. Theology can adduce strictly scientific reasons for believing what the Scriptures relate of God's revelation of himself in action. But for all that, we will not on this occasion adopt the theological method, but the philosophical; we will seek to discover the being of God from the consideration of the universe. For it is a want, a necessity of human nature, to search after the highest truth by the independent method of reason; and by the evidences of God in our world-contemplating reason, to prove the revelation of God contained in Scripture; philosophy belongs to the noblest portion of human nature; only it must not be a mere wanton opposition, nor a slavish repetition of the current maxims of the ever-changing spirit of the day; but a genuine philosophy, that is, a genuine love for wisdom, and hence, an earnest, sober, profound examination of ultimate principles. There is an old and frequently quoted saying, to the effect that philosophy when it sets to work superficially, leads away from God, but when it examines more deeply, leads back to him; and I trust that we shall find this saying true.

We will set out then from the easily intelligible admission in which we shall all concur, that the external world is pervaded by *profound intelligence.* At the first sight of any working-machine, say, for example, a locomotive engine, all decide that it must needs be a work of the intellect, because we find that everything in it is a means to an end. But nature is not less pervaded with purpose. Not that this is to be understood in a sense to which it has often been perverted, as implying that everything which we find in nature is adapted for the use of man; this is a low point of view, and must lead to many absurd conclusions. Both in the plant and in the animal, we find that every detail subserves the development of that plant or that animal's peculiar existence. In our own bodies, more especially, we admire the ada tation of every part to the development of our physical life, and not only so, but to the requirements of our intellectual life also. But further, this earth on which we live is more and more recognised by science as a great organic whole, whose parts all tend to one great aim, namely, the progressive intellectual development of humanity. But this law of interdependence extends even beyond the earth; the earth is only what it is through its relation to the sun, round which it moves. And when we consider that our solar system is also related to the other solar systems, so that they all interdepend, what a display of Omnipotent intelligence opens out before us!

But here we must not fail to notice one essential difference between the adaptation of any humanly constructed machine to the particular end it is destined to serve, and the adaptation of the forms of nature to their final purpose. You will all readily apprehend the distance between the most elaborate mechanism, and a plant, or the human body. This difference does not consist alone in the machine remaining what it was originally made, without growth or life, while the plant shows its life by growing; but the plant is far more intimately and universally pervaded with unity of purpose than any machine can possibly be. If we take the different parts of machinery to pieces, no doubt the purpose of that machinery can no longer be fulfilled, but the parts remain what they were, they are in themselves unaffected by the purpose they subserved. Whereas if we take a plant to pieces, this is death to every part of that plant; thus the life of all their parts consists in their unity; and if they are deprived of their pervading unity of purpose they die. Still further, in order to construct machinery the materials are taken from different sources, those materials have first of all an existence, then they are wrought and combined in the manner requisite for the purpose in hand. But the tissues of the plant are not there before the plant itself; the plant evolves itself, and what it derives from without it assimilates most completely in its own special manner: no purpose is skilfully infused into the plant from without, but the primal germ is, equally with the developed tree, pervaded by its own particular law of being; the apple-pip is already thoroughly impregnated with the nature of the apple-tree, and if placed favourably for its development, can develop into nothing but an apple-tree, just as, from the first moment of conception, the human embryo is adapted to be the instrument of a personal and intellectual life. We give the name *organism* to that which thus evolves itself; developing its germ into a number of limbs or parts, which are all suitably related, and which all tend to the accomplishment of one common life-purpose. In plants, animals, and in the human body, we perceive organic life in an ascending scale of organization. Again, in the intellectual life of man, whether of individuals or nations, up to the whole of humanity, we see an ever new, ever higher organization, which increased organic perfection both consists in the increasing complexity of the parts, and in their more intimate and vital unity. So essential is this conception of an organism to the right understanding of the world, that we may pronounce the highest discovery of natural science to be this of systematic gradation in organic nature. And even the study of human history can hardly propose itself a higher task than to establish how the original constitution of man, and the progress of mankind during the centuries past, tends to make of different nations and countless multitudes of individuals one great organism, in which each nation and each individual has its special bearing upon the whole.

Thus the universe is all pervaded by one purpose, displayed alike in the relations between its giant members—the suns and planets—and in the least vein of its least living creature; nay, we may call the whole universe itself a great organism. Thus the whole is pervaded by one intelligence. We learn the same truth, too, from the beauty of the world. We call a picture beautiful if it represent some significant thought, some tender emotion, or some strong inward struggle, in such a manner, that the sight of it at once convinces us of the feeling by which the mind of the artist was moved.

And so we call a man beautiful if form and countenance are the harmonious expression of a noble soul, an energetic intellect. A soulless man may be well made, may even be handsome, but cannot be beautiful. Now if beauty in works of art, or in human beings, presuppose intelligence, this cannot be less true of the beauty of nature. Impressions of tenderness, of sublimity, of peace, are made upon our minds by nature, and it is because of these that we call a landscape lovely, sublime, beautiful. Now love, sublimity, peace, and repose belong to Mind; if therefore there was no reason, no intelligence in Nature, we could not speak of its beauty.

Now let us take one other step. How is this fulness of design, this beauty in the world, to be explained? The purpose or design of a machine is given to it by its inventor; the meaning which the picture expresses has been transferred from the mind of the painter to the canvas; but whence the reason, the meaning of the external world? We Christians indeed answer this question in the words the Psalmist sang three thousand years ago, and in those of our Lord himself: The heavens declare the glory of *God*, and it is our heavenly *Father* who clothes the lilies of the field. God's Spirit has from the beginning brooded over, developed, and shaped the life-germs scattered by God's hand, and at the present time this self-same spirit of the living God pervades, animates, and develops the immeasurable realm of Being, so that everything in its appointed place and appointed number, moves in its pre-ordained orbit, and all living things grow and mature according to their appointed laws.

For God, the Self-Existent, is the only source of all existence, all movement, all vitality, all order and harmony, all beauty and joy. This is the scriptural view of the world, and by the side of it there is another view, and a very ancient one too, at least in India, and among a portion of the Greeks; and this view seventeen centuries ago ranged itself under the name of the Greco-Roman paganism, in opposition to the Christian faith, was then conquered in the war of mind, and slept silent in the West for about a thousand years, till about two centuries ago it once more began to lift up its voice. I allude to so-called Pantheism. The Greek word expresses its own meaning, according to this view, the *All* is *God*. Thus Pantheism also speaks of a God, but it uses the word in a quite different sense to the Christian. It says, you must not look for God outside of the universe; on the contrary, the universe, the *All* is itself God. Of course, this does not mean to imply that everything in the world, every tree, every animal is God; in that case we should have the utter absurdity of a world consisting of countless deities. The language of Pantheism is this: You must distinguish between the world of Phenomena, and the inner Formative Energy, from which the phenomena spring. A tree bears fruit yearly. That fruit falls as soon as it is matured, but the vital force of the tree remains, and in spring it will break forth anew. Our earth has already undergone many revolutions, but the formative energy which has worked for ages is still at work, though in a different way, and may work on indefinitely. If then the multitude of spheres be one whole, one constantly active life must pervade it all, a life of which the formative energies of individual spheres are only separate rays. This one Essence, or Substance, which lives in all living things, and itself invisible, reveals itself in a sense that is visible: this is what Pantheism calls God. Goethe makes this One describe himself as follows:—

In the waves of life,
In the storm of action,
I roll up and down,
I weave here and there,
Birth and death,
An eternal ocean,
A changing web,
A glowing life,
Thus I work at the roaring loom of time,
And weave the living garment of the Deity.

This is an excellent imitation of the Pantheistic Idea, but only an imitation, a poetical rendering, not the exact expression of the idea that the language of philosophy aims at conveying. There are two inaccuracies therein, first that which rolls in the waves of life to weave the living garment of the Deity, appears to be something distinct from the Deity, whereas Pantheism affirms that it is by Deity itself that the phenomenal world is woven; and, secondly, this working, weaving, rolling agency speaks in this poetical representation of itself, names itself *I*, comes forward as a personality, while Pantheism explicitly denies personality to the Deity, maintains that he is not an Ego, but calls the unconscious world itself its God. Pantheistic philosophers have characterized in different ways this One and yet *All*-animating, this unconscious yet all-organizing agency; but the most striking, and at the same time intelligible name has been given to it by Spinoza, the gifted Jew, who two hundred years ago revived Pantheism in Europe. Spinoza distinguished between *natura naturans* and *natura naturata:* the latter he understands as the constantly changing world of phenomena; the former as the cause out of which and into which every effect is constantly emerging and sinking. This *natura naturans* is, according to Spinoza's view, God.

And here let us remark, that this confusion of God with Nature does not seem to be quite confined to the schools. Many men in our day have, without being in any way philosophers, acquired a habit of constantly referring to Nature only; it is from Nature that they expect recovery from sickness, fruitful harvests; it is the powers of Nature that they admire when they contemplate the shining world of stars; it is on these powers they seem to depend, as though Nature were indeed the highest that we know of. I am aware that all who use this phraseology do not mean to assert thereby that Nature is God, and to deny the existence of a supernatural God; but the latter, it appears to them, is so remote from the world that he created long ago, that virtually man has now only got to do with Nature. They, however, who are acquainted with the history of philosophy, at all events of German philosophy, from Kant to Schelling and Hegel, need not to be informed that amongst scientific men, one never now hears of this remote god of the English deists; if any voice be raised to revive that doctrine, it is at once assumed that the speaker is unacquainted with the progressive development of modern philosophy. At the present day the choice can only lie between the God of the Bible or the god of Pantheism, whether he be named *natura naturans*, or, according to Hegel's kindred expression, "absolute idea." And any one, even if unaccustomed to these speculations, may convince himself by serious reflection that a God remote, or not universally present, not actively beneficial, can be no longer considered God,—neither the Living, the Loving, nor yet the Absolute.

Well then, the question before us is this, Is it from this all-*engendering*, but also all-*devouring* Nature, from this God of Pantheism, that we derive our existence, or from that God in whom our fathers hoped, to whom the Lord Jesus Christ prayed as to his Father, and on whom he has taught us also to call in a filial spirit? The advocates of Pantheism often assure us that there is no important difference between the two views; but in point of fact, we can hardly imagine a greater contrast. No rational man can pray to Nature, whereas the Christian looks upon his communion with God by prayer as the highest blessing of his life. If *Nature* be the source of all life, and so of man's spiritual life, why, then, whatever happens, *sin* included, is the result of an iron necessity, growth in holiness is an impossibility, and our faith in a holy Saviour a mere dream; whereas the most earnest desire of the Christian is to become holy, and his rejoicing in the holy Son of man is his strength. Finally, if this all-engendering and destroying Nature is the ultimate cause, life after death is out of the question altogether; whereas heaven is the Christian's goal, and this earthly life is but the way to that goal.

Before I proceed to a further examination of Pantheism, I would point out that the very assumption of Nature being its own cause, being self-existent, involves a contradiction, the idea of self-causation implying self-consciousness. I might further show, that if God be only the underlying substance, or the formative energy of the phenomenal world, the origin of the world-material, the existence of this vast organic whole remains quite inexplicable; and we shall be obliged, if we try to shape our conceptions in words, to presuppose, as the Pantheists of Grecian antiquity expressly declared they did, the eternity of matter. But in order to confine myself strictly to the admission from which we set out, I will only ask whether Pantheism is able to explain to us the wisdom and beauty we see in the *material* world before us; for example, the harmonious order in which the several thousand stars rotate so regularly that astronomers are able to predict the very hour at which they will become visible and invisible to us, their conjunction and opposition.

Pantheism tells us, that it is Nature itself which is pervaded by this ordering wisdom; but Nature knows nothing of itself, has no self-consciousness, is no Ego, no self-existing personality. And Pantheism attributes perfect wisdom in action, works of beauty, and wonders of design, to an agency that knows nothing of itself! To unconscious wisdom, in short! But is not this as self-contradictory a conception as a triangular circle?

We will not, however, be precipitate in our answer. If the possibility of unconscious wisdom is to be maintained at all, it must be so on the ground of a twofold experience, one relating to the animal kingdom, the other to human life. I allude to the range of animal instincts, and to the origin of human language. For instance, does not the way in which the spider spins its web, and the bee makes its cell, exhibit the most perfect adaptation of means to an end? And yet no one will assert that these creatures ply their relative arts with self-conscious reflection; neither do they acquire them from teaching, but they practise them from the force of an indwelling instinct. And again, how does a nation get its language? It is the national spirit which produces the national mode of speech. But this is not effected according to any premeditated *plan*, not by definite and *conscious contrivance*. Man cannot think except in words; a people must already have a language before they can attain to thought-life. Nevertheless, languages are an intellectual product, an artificially woven web; at least the languages of the most cultivated nations,—of the Greeks, the Germans, are this. Nay, more, the languages of those races that have never as yet learned to express their ideas in writing, are at all events fraught with certain rules and principles. There are tribes in different parts of Africa, to whom most certainly it has never occurred to reflect upon the construction of their language; yet when the ambassadors of Christ visit them, they are able to lay down grammatical rules regarding even the poorest of those African dialects, able to discover the laws by which these people have unconsciously been guided in the formation of their language. It is, therefore, indisputable, that there is such a thing as a half-conscious exercise of the human mind; nay, more, that there is a dreamy working of the animal intelligence which is capable of producing effects full of beauty, adaptation, and law. Moreover, it is just in this scarce conscious working, that we hardly ever discover a mistake or failure of any kind, while, on the contrary, the thoroughly-conscious labours of the mechanic, the philosopher, and the statesman, abound in errors.

May not Pantheists, therefore, be justified by this analogy in ascribing the design and beauty of the organization of the universe to the agency of unconscious wisdom? If the human intellect, if even the animal intellect can produce such results without self-consciousness, are we not authorized in attributing to the universe a self-unconscious, a merely dreaming soul; and deducing from this universal soul, although it be not self-conscious, the wisdom-fraught organization of the whole world? We reply, that to one who merely bestows a superficial consideration upon the subject in hand, this view may indeed seem plausible, but on closer examination the plausibility vanishes. We could only be justified in inferring the unconsciously wise agency of a world-soul from the unconscious wisdom of the animal mind, in the event of such wisdom being really inherent in the animal mind itself; in other words, to give any force to our argument, the purpose-fraught working of animal instinct would need to be actually self-originated. But this is not the case. The instinct which impels every creature to certain works of art, and the unvarying perfection of the art it displays, like the impulse and the power to sing possessed by the singing-bird, is inherent in its bodily organization, which organization it has not produced, but has from some source or other received. In the same way, man's impulse to speak, and faculty of speaking, are inherent in the duality of his nature; and the peculiarity of different languages springs from the peculiarity of natural constitution in different people. If then the wisdom which displays itself in animal labour, and the higher wisdom displayed in the construction of languages, does not primarily belong to the animal nor to the national intelligence, but rather to that power from which men and animals alike have derived their organization, it follows that the want of self-consciousness, which we find in the wisdom of their several instincts, does not authorize us in drawing the conclusion that the first originating cause of human, and animal, and all life whatsoever, works unconsciously.

Again, neither animal nor human life is a thing apart and complete in itself. The life-activity of men, and still more of animals, is intermingled with the universal stream of natural life, is excited and guided thereby, so that we must describe the wisdom displayed in animal life as belonging not to it, but to the universal life with which animal life is inextricably intertwined. Now, unconsciously working intelligence, as implanted by a higher power, is, as we have seen, a matter of experience, but unconscious wisdom, as the final cause by which the universe has organized itself, is an idea which fades away before steady thought, is a mere phantasm. What a strange anomaly it would be, that the intensely conscious mind of the natural historian should, with delighted admiration, continue throughout life to search into the wisdom of a blindly working power, should be ever learning from it, ever bowing down before it! No; as in mathematics there are certain axioms, certain ultimate principles, which afford proof for the whole structure of mathematical science, without themselves requiring proof, or even being capable of it; so in order to attain to a truly philosophical view of the world, we must proceed from the self-evident proposition that the original intelligence, from which all other existing intelligence is derived, is not and cannot be itself blind and unconscious, must be self-conscious, in the most exalted sense of the term. In other words, so surely as the world is a wisdom-fraught and beauteous organism, so surely does it refer us to a creative Spirit, who *knows* himself as he *manifests* himself,—to a personal God, in short, such as the Bible reveals, unconscious creative wisdom being as palpable a contradiction as a triangular circle.

But now let us turn to that portion of the universe with which we are best acquainted, to our own earth and its inhabitants, and we shall find that it abundantly confirms the view of God's nature to which we have arrived. We would lay especial stress upon the evidence afforded by a science which many have looked upon as a formidable enemy to the Christian faith—upon the history of the progressive development of our earth. Now, if there be anything firmly laid down by geological science it is this, that the vegetable and animal world, still more the human race, are far more recent than the earth itself, the first conditions of this globe of ours having been quite incompatible with vegetable, animal, or human life. Since, then, these arose at successive epochs, we naturally inquire how it was that they did arise. Natural philosophers, on their side, confess that they do not see how organic life (whether vegetable or animal) could have developed itself out of inorganic, and in its earlier stages our earth consisted simply of inorganic matter. Now this fact places Pantheism in an awkward predicament. With its assertion that Nature is the final cause of all, there is united this other assertion, that Nature never produces an immediate and isolated effect, but that it is in the collective unity of all individual things that the World-Soul dwells, and that this collective unity of whatever is related in time and space, forms an indissoluble sequence of cause and effect, so that nothing which was not included in the original plan ever comes to pass, while nothing so included is ever omitted. In other words, Pantheism does not allow the possibility of a miracle, and it looks upon this exclusion of the miraculous as its peculiar boast. Well then, if there be no miracles, how did vegetable and animal life arise? above all, how arose the spiritual life of the human race, self-conscious and free? Are men the descendants of apes, or have they sprung directly out of mud?

The well-known David Strauss, seventy years ago, hazarded the desperate conclusion, that since the tape-worm, which has been known to exceed seventy feet (so that in point of length it far out-does man), was produced by spontaneous generation, out of the alien substance of human intestines, it was not impossible that man should have been originally developed from some earthly material, however unlike in composition that material might have been! Especially, he adds, since in those remote periods the formative energies of the earth were undoubtedly greater than at the present time![1] I will not now dwell upon the fact that the science of our day entirely denies to the tape-worm the spontaneous generation above assumed; I will only observe, that Alexander von Humboldt, who was certainly not predisposed in favour of Christian truth, writes as follows: "What displeases me in Strauss is the scientific levity which leads him to see no difficulty in the organic springing from the inorganic, nay, man himself from Chaldean mud."[2] I have only to add that it would be a strange thing if men who parallel tape-worms with the human race were to prove the leaders of exalted humanity. Nevertheless Strauss, in this passage, reasons logically enough from the standpoint of Pantheism. If Nature be the final cause of all life, then there can be no miracle. If there is no miracle, man must have arisen in some such fashion as he presumes.

But, on the other hand, if man be *not* a descendant of apes, nor a child of mud, then man is a miracle; and if there are miracles, then there lives a personal God; for miracles, as is universally acknowledged, presuppose a

[1] Strauss *On Christian Doctrine,* vol. i. p. 602.
[2] Humboldt's *Letters to Varnhagen,* First Edition, p. 117.

personal God. We now see that men who reject the Bible because it narrates miracles regarding nature, or at least human nature, cannot have reflected very deeply, otherwise they would have discovered that the book of nature also tells of miracles. These remarks, however, have led us to a new train of thought, upon which I pray you to follow me for a few moments.

The point from which we set out was the fact that the whole of natural life, from the gigantic spheres that harmoniously circle in space, down to the least of the grasses that sprout on the earth, are pervaded by a law infinitely varied, and yet identically one, on the exercise of which all vital development, all adaptation of interworking means and ends, all beauty and harmony, depend. But besides this law of nature, the investigation of which is the never-ending task and delight of the man of science, there is another law, the *moral*, and this is certainly deserving of equal attention and admiration. The mere comparing and contrasting of these two laws has the greatest possible charm for the inquiring mind. The stars in heaven and the grasses on earth obey the law of nature with undeviating punctuality, century after century; and even the comets, those vagabonds of the sky, which appeared to be an exception, are found to be no ways exempted from an obedience of their own to the same law. True, this natural law, so faithfully followed, is unknown to these its subjects; they fulfil it unconsciously, or rather it fulfils itself. It is otherwise with the moral law, which dwells in the consciences of men. This cannot get itself accomplished before it has been realized in consciousness. Now, in some way or other, it is realized in the consciousness of every human being; but in some it shines like a bright star, from childhood upwards; in thousands it only exists as a faint reflection; thousands, again, are aware that at times it has died down within them to a weak glimmer, while at other times it has burst out into a vivid flame. If we inquire into the *cause* of this increased light, experience will return a twofold answer. Sometimes the brighter radiance succeeds a steadfast and determined fixing of the eye upon the light; sometimes the fire will kindle into flame without, or even against a man's will.

But this brightening of the moral law in the human consciousness by no means insures the accomplishment of this law. And what constitutes the second point of difference between the law of nature and the moral law is, that the former *must* be fulfilled, while the latter, though doubtless its aim is to get itself fulfilled, yet depends for its fulfilment or its non-fulfilment upon the free choice of man. And every man has the consciousness of not having so fulfilled the law of his conscience as he ought. Now, if at the first glance it should appear as though this moral law were not equally fraught with power as the natural law, since the latter is irresistibly accomplished in the vast system of the universe, while the former is left dependent upon the human will, a little fuller consideration will serve to transmute this apparent weakness into strength. We men are subject to both of these laws; our physical life is governed by natural law, while the moral law addresses itself to our will, and between these two laws a conflict may arise. For example, the natural law enjoins the satisfaction of our hunger; the moral law commands, Thou shalt not steal, shalt not kill. An animal so unconditionally obeys the natural law, that, in so far as his strength allows it, he will always procure himself food by violence, and thousands of human beings will, if pressed by want, act in like manner as the animal; but there are other men who would prefer dying of starvation to infringing the moral law, which forbids theft and murder. Neither is it by constraint but by gentle persuasion that this moral law succeeds in counteracting the natural impulse to satisfy hunger and preserve life. But it may be asked, how does this moral law assert its majesty with regard to the myriads who, without concerning themselves therewith, follow only their natural impulses? For a long time, indeed, it may keep silence, but sooner or later it will begin to hold a tribunal within the soul, and then the man will be bowed beneath the burden of his guilt, his conscience having pronounced sentence of death upon him.

Now let us turn again to our first question respecting the being of God, and inquire what fresh light has been thrown upon that subject by our glance at the nature of this second law, the law of conscience. First, we have it thereby established that it is not from unconscious nature, but from a personal God that all life is derived: for we now see most clearly that man cannot have arisen as the highest product of natural life, but miraculously, through a creative act of a personal God. Man is capable of hearing the silent speech of the moral law; he is conscious of being bound to obey his conscience in despite of his natural impulses, and if he fails to obey it, he is painfully aware that his disobedience has degraded him. Now, every intellectual system based upon a belief in Nature as the highest power, is absolutely incapable of explaining the origin of this law, which ventures to contradict man's natural impulses, and often, with gentle supremacy, triumphs over the pressure of the law of nature. We may most confidently assert, that no Pantheist will be found able to bring forward any views on this point scientifically correct or satisfactory. Thus, as every one acquainted with the course of philosophical development during the last decade knows well, without my reminding him, the new impulse given to Pantheism has been followed by the revival of Materialism, the most irrational of all cosmical theories whatsoever; for if the *Natura Naturans* be the source of all life, material life alone can proceed from that source, therefore liberty and spirit must be mere figures of speech; phosphorus is the noblest agent in existence, and self-love is the only lawgiver, the only source of all that men esteem holy.

But if, on the other hand, a personal God be the Creator of man, and if a soul be, as the Scripture teaches, spirit of the Divine Spirit, it is self-evident that our soul must be free and amenable to a different code of laws than that which regulates our natural life. And here new views of the Divine Being open out to us. If the Eternal Original Spirit, whose omnipotent wisdom has given laws to natural life, and to whose inherent harmony and exalted blessedness all the beauty of the universe testifies, has given to man liberty, that is, the power to determine by the choice of his will whether he will follow the impulses of nature or the law of conscience, why, then, this God, who is the creator of liberty, must be a God of liberty, and not bound by an iron necessity, as must inevitably be the case with the *Natura Naturans*.

And how fraught with inferences this proposition is! Since God is a God of liberty, we can readily understand that power of prayer which so many utterly repudiate. And further, since the law of conscience addresses itself to us with such majesty, that the conscientious man recognises his obligation to give up his life rather than refuse it obedience; and since the consciousness of disobedience thereto inflicts within us the suffering of self-contempt, while the consciousness of having been faithful in obeying it fills our souls with the highest rapture,—must we not conclude that the God from whom all these laws are derived must be in perfect harmony with these laws; must he not, in other words, be absolutely good, his will absolutely holy?

Finally, we inquire what could have been the motive that moved such a God as this to create? That he should have, by the exercise of his will, called into existence all the infinite wealth of life which we compress into the word "universe," gives us some idea of that ocean of life inherent in his own being. And He himself is the fountain of that ocean; his life is a self-derived and self-containing circle; consequently he, the source of all life, must have been self-satisfying, self-delighting. Why, then, since he was self-satisfying, should he have created? The answer can only be: He who had life in himself created, because he would have external to himself, and through himself, beings who also rejoice in their lives; in other words, God creates because God is Love. If then he be love, how can he possibly fail to call the soul-endowed human race to fellowship with himself? For it is only in fellowship with the Eternal Creative Spirit that the created spirit can meet with the satisfaction of its desires; and, therefore, what a degradation of humanity it is to seek, as is done in our day, under the pretext of exalting the dignity of man, to dissever him from that Original Spirit who is our Creator!

And now, having been led step by step to form these views of God, it is difficult to break off here without proceeding both to draw further inferences as to his nature, and to fill up the outline we have traced, with more living colours. We might, for instance, having cast a glance at the world of nature and the intellect of man, go on to consider the argument afforded us by the history of the human race. Its progressive development depends on the countless arbitrary resolves of countless minds, and nevertheless the philosophical historian discovers therein a fixed plan. How often in the course of history, it has seemed as, through the waywardness and passion, the apathy and unreason of the human race, all further progress were rendered impossible, when suddenly unexpected occurrences, new powers, great men, have changed the whole aspect of affairs, solved the problem, and opened out the way. It were easy to show that this intelligential progress of history, accomplished through all the confusion and clashing of wills of millions of free agents, is only to be explained by the superintendence and providence of an omnipotent Divine Personality; the unconscious wisdom of nature pitted against the liberty of man, being incapable of insuring this historical progress. However, as time to carry out this argument fails me, I will only ask leave to make one further observation.

We have seen that to make a god of Nature offers no intelligible theory of the world as it is, and is therefore quite unsatisfactory to an earnest thinker; that the world as it is, is only explicable as being created by the power of the will of an eternal and self-conscious spirit; that such a God must be a God of miraculous power, for facts prove to us the introduction into the already created of new creations such as cannot be considered mere developments of the previously existent; that such a God must also be a God of liberty, since he has created mankind free; must be a holy God, since the law that he has written in our hearts reveals itself to us as a holy law; that, finally, this God must be love, for it is only a benevolent will to impart his own life that could move a self-blessed God to create at all. Many amongst you will perhaps be disposed to say: "What necessity can there be to prove all this? It is self-evident; it needs no skill to convince the simple mind that it is not Nature, but an eternally self-complete and self-conscious God who is the original cause of the universe." I reply: Yea, verily, so it is, and one of the triumphant proofs of the truth of our faith is, that the glance of a simple eye can overtake its flight; but still there are those to whom it is indispensable to follow truth by the measured steps of severe reasoning, and it is to those that I would prove that earnest, exact, and thorough examination of the subject will find itself shut up to one conclusion alone, the conclusion announced by the first article of our venerable creed—"I believe in God the Almighty Creator of heaven and earth."

And, further, I would urge: If this eternal Creative Spirit indeed lives, and calls us to fellowship with him, he being holy and each one of us unholy, where then is the way by which the unholy are to be led to the holy? For of a truth, the more deep and earnest the researches of human thought, the more momentous must this question become, and the more anxiously will the inquiring spirit direct its inquiry to Him who has spoken those incommensurable words of himself: "I am the way; No man cometh to the Father but by me." And therefore it is that even this primary belief leaves us with a presentiment that besides that truth of an almighty Creator of the world upon which we have been dwelling, there must be another truth which shall bring us tidings of a Mediator between God and man, a presentiment that the gifted Roman Tertullian was right, when having, in his ripe manhood, turned from heathenism to Christianity, he summed up the result of his researches and his experiences in these words,—"The soul of man is naturally Christian," which means that it is drawn by its very constitution to find the way, the truth, and the life, in the Lord Jesus Christ.

III.

SIN, ITS NATURE AND CONSEQUENCES.

"IT is no especial depth of reflection," says a well-known theologian, in his work on our present subject,[1] "it is merely an average degree of moral earnestness that we need, to keep us steadfastly gazing on one aspect of human life, and constantly renewing our researches into its nature. I speak of human life's *evil* aspect; of the presence of an element of disturbance and discord just where we most intensely feel the need for unity and harmony. This element meets us whereever and whenever our minds review the history of the human race, and its progressive development *as a whole.* It reveals itself no less clearly in countless ways when we fix our attention upon the *particular* relations of human society, nor can we conceal from ourselves its existence, when we look within the recesses of our own breasts. It is a dark shadow which casts its gloom over every circle of human life, and constantly swallows up its gayest and brightest forms."

We may confidently venture to assert, that if there be any one point in our nature and our condition respecting which all men whatsoever are agreed in their estimate, it is upon this great fact of the existence of Evil, in us and around us; of the radical incompleteness of human nature, and consequently of all that proceeds from or is connected with it. First of all, each one of us experiences this personally. While feeling in the very core of his being a consciousness of a Divine origin, of being created for peace and joy, and full enjoyment, he sees himself in point of fact en-

[1] Julius Müller.

tangled in and given up to a diametrically opposite destiny.

Men in their social existence are set one against the other, and mutually hem in and hinder free activity. The judgment of the reason opposes the wish of the heart, the aspirations and efforts of the mind are kept down and frustrated by the flesh; our best thoughts and motives, the accomplishment of which would, we feel, satisfy our inmost needs, these we are not in a position to accomplish. From some cause, in some way or other, our constant and abiding experience is that of the Apostle: "What I would that I do not, but what I would not that do I." And as this discord in our innermost nature never allows any one of us to attain to full enjoyment, or perfect and abiding peace, so this universal experience gets itself outspoken as by one voice wherever human lips open to bear their testimony to the joy and the sorrow, the destiny and experience of our race. "The best is never to be born," cried the greatest of the Greek poets at a time when his native city was in the fullest bloom of prosperity and splendour; and "Whom the gods love, die young." The singers of Israel proclaim human life to be "labour and sorrow, full of trouble and unrest; at its best estate altogether vanity." Solomon, in close agreement with the Greek poet, praises "the dead which are already dead more than the living which are yet alive; yea, better is he than both they, which hath not been." And there is no need to tell you how these declarations have been repeated, unchanged in spirit, though in varying words, during the course of centuries, and how it is in no way necessary to adopt the Christian view of man's fall and man's depravity, to feel most acutely that our nature is disturbed and shattered to its very centre, and, to burst out into the heart-rending acknowledgment of Schiller:—

> "The world is perfect everywhere,
> Where man comes not with his grief and care."

Nay, even say that there were among us some one or other who did not unqualifiedly feel this; say that he had so far relinquished and ignored his claim to inward contentment and satisfaction as to disregard his own heart's unrest, and to satisfy himself with mere external pleasures, possessions, and enjoyments; and say that these were always attainable, and he always in a condition to appreciate them,—would not such a one still find in the world without, in the society of other men, the same sorrowful experience from which he was attempting to escape, the bitterness he would fain put away? Would not a perversity and a confusion confront him there, frustrating and disappointing his wishes, poisoning his enjoyment, forcing upon him the evil and the repulsive instead of the good after which he was reaching? Selfishness, envy, hatred, falsehood, duplicity, anger, injustice, uncharitableness, and all other sins that shake and taint human intercourse, would meet him on all sides, turn which way he would, and cause him most sensibly to feel the nature of the moral condition of our race. And it is a significant fact, yea, verily, significant as to his own true state, that the very man we are supposing would by no means treat the offences of his neighbours, the wrong done *to* him, in the same light-hearted manner that he treats his own short-comings and offences; on the contrary, he would be perfectly ready to concede with respect to others, that we meet with little that is good among men, but with much unkindness, injury, and untruthfulness. He would ascribe all manner of evil to those who in any way opposed him, nowise extending to them his favourable opinion of human nature, but rather agreeing with prophets and apostles so far as they were concerned, that there is "none that doeth good, no, not one!" And yet such a man might all the time forget that others on their side would be justified in holding the same opinion respecting him; that his conduct to his neighbours is pretty much the same as that of those neighbours towards him; and that their errors, for which he has so keen an eye, may in a word be taken as the reflection of his own, which he is so determined to ignore.

Thus, then, so much is certain and indisputable, and established in one way or other by the testimony of all, a perversion, a corruption, is existent in the race of men; nor is there any part of their condition, nor any relation in which they stand exempt therefrom. And as the very words "perversion and corruption" imply, this melancholy state of things cannot have belonged to the original nature of man, but must have sprung up in despite of and in contradiction to that original nature, else we should never be sensible of it as a discordant, alien, and anomalous element in our moral being. If we were from the first framed for selfishness, what should we know of love, and love's claims, and how should we be painfully affected by their violation? If we had never had experience of a harmonious personality, of inward joy, of perfect heart-satisfaction, never been called and fitted to seek after and finally to attain them, whence that spirit-yearning, spirit hunger and thirst after these blessings, by which we are all in our measure impelled and consumed? Whence would arise that incurable discomfort produced by the discord between our judgment and our will? Whence that most painful unrest of every individual among us, and of the whole race? Whence these sad and heavy hours which come unsparingly to us all, so soon as we are removed out of the world's distracting uproar, and face to face with ourselves? Whence that inward dissatisfiedness and incapability of satisfaction, which we may indeed appease for a while by fresh possessions, but can never really overcome; which breaks out ever anew, and extorts from each one of us at intervals, throughout life, the cry and confession of St. Paul, "O wretched man that I am!"

How indeed could we possibly account for all this, if our present condition were the original one for which our nature was adapted, and the only one it could ever attain to? How could we miss that which we never possessed, of which we were ignorant, which our natural disposition and capacities did not require? If, therefore, we never do feel satisfied in our present state, if we suffer therein and long for something better, it is self-evident that we must once have been in a different condition, must have lost that which once we possessed; evident that our actual state fails to respond to this peculiar constitution of our being and our inner wants.

"Sin itself," says St. Augustine, in one of his deeply significant passages, "bears witness to the originally different and higher destiny and existence of man, since even in sin he seeks out for himself not evil, but rather good, pleasure, happiness, joy." We must somewhere and somehow have sustained a fall; we must have forfeited our best possessions; we must be deposed kings, who wander about in exile, and eat their bread in the dust. "Yea, verily, thou art not here below in thy rightful place or order," exclaims the great French thinker St. Martin; "a single good heart-impulse which tends to raise thee, a single hour of inward unrest, proves this to thee more clearly than all the arguments of philosophers can ever prove the converse." And another writer observes: "Neither the state of mere nature in which the savage lives, nor our own corrupt civilisation, can be right; our inward being points us to a simple life, led in God, consisting in fellowship with him. Our present condition speaks incontrovertibly of a fall of man, which is the only key to the whole of his history. And therefore it is that the world (that is, the unchristianized, unredeemed) ever retrogrades in a moral sense, while the intellect is ever striving to progress; consequently, in our present state, man's highest wisdom is only a looking back, a recalling the past, and virtue itself only a return to God. This great truth appears more or less distinctly in all religions. There is, indeed, no science occupied with spiritual matters which is not based upon it."

Any one possessing even a superficial knowledge of the various religions and philosophical systems of the world (not including Christianity), will be perfectly aware of the truth of this last assertion. Amongst every people possessing traditions and a literature of any kind, we meet with legends of a "golden age," as the Greek and Roman authors call it, when the earth brought forth spontaneously whatever its inhabitants required; when the gods walked among men, were beloved by them, and held converse with them; when hearts were still pure and innocent, not desecrated by vice or passion; when peace and joy everywhere prevailed, and the wolf pastured beside the lamb, and did him no injury. This golden age, they go on to say, was followed by one of silver, the silver age by one of brass, the brass by the age of iron, the hard, unjust, perturbed age in which we find ourselves now. But as to the *how* and *wherefore* of this; as to the reason of the degeneration of our race, no satisfactory answer was ever returned by Greek or Roman. They stood before the fact of the existence of evil as before a mighty and gloomy problem, and finally they carried sin and guilt and conflict up even into their heaven and its deities, in order to give some sort of explanation of the dark mystery under which the whole universe confessedly lies.

There is only *one* tradition that goes to the root of the matter, and presents us with a solution of the problem in perfect accordance with the history and the consciousness of man. I speak of the tradition of the people of Israel, the tradition of the Bible, which, however, is no mere human tradition, but a revelation from God to our race, of its heavenly inheritance and the way that leads thereto. And the tenor of this tradition is briefly this: The reason and cause of the thoroughly shattered and ruined state in which man finds himself is *sin*, and sin in its essential nature is the creature's attempt to sever itself, and its actual severance from the Creator; the creature, willing to be something through and for itself, and yet to reach the end for which it longs, the being content and glorious and blessed, while, in point of fact, out of God this end is unattainable, the creature being able to find in God alone the peace and full enjoyment to which its nature is adapted.

Let us then proceed to examine this universal experience somewhat more closely, and from a Biblical point of view, combining therewith, as far as our limits allow, what we know respecting the origin of this same sin, and the cause of its universal prevalence amongst men. You may easily convince yourselves how thoroughly reasonable and conformable to the wants of our nature the Scriptural answer to the momentous question is, if only you take counsel with your conscience and your experience, the two great authorities upon this subject.

God, who is love—as was so forcibly and logically proved in the last lecture—called the human race into existence, in order that it might enter into loving fellowship with him, let itself be loved by him, and love him in return, finding in this mutual love the same eternal blessedness with which he is blessed. For, as we all know, to love and to be beloved is blessedness. Even earthly love, the reciprocal love of created beings, is rightly acknowledged to be the source of the highest rapture of which the heart is capable; how much more then must this be true of the pure, all-embracing love of God, to which there can be no hindrance, into which no imperfection of any kind can enter, and which includes every other love, so that through it we stand in one great bond of love with all that has the power of loving, and is worthy of being beloved in earth and heaven. Hence it is that the law of the Old Testament, and later the Redeemer, were wont to repeat: "All that is enjoined thee, O man, all that is needful to the fulfilling of thy destiny, is comprehended in one word, Have love, love to God, and love to thy fellow-man; Thou shalt love the Lord thy God with all thy heart, and with all thy mind, and thy neighbour as thyself. This is the first and great commandment; herein are contained the law and the prophets."

Now it will be at once evident to every one of you, that real, genuine love can only be the product of liberty,—must be essentially free. Wherever there is constraint or necessity, whether external or internal, there love, in the proper sense of the word, cannot exist. It is only owing to the poverty of language that we say of the domestic animal that caresses and obeys his master, because it is in his nature so to do, that he loves that master, for his attachment is merely instinctive; merely dependent upon the relation in which he stands; he could transfer it from one master to another; and he gives it as fully to the lowest and most degraded of men as to the best. Such love as this does not constitute blessedness, cannot enter into fellowship with God or embrace him. If we would have loving relations with God, we must adopt these with definite consciousness and from free choice, because we discern him to be the best and most love-deserving portion. And that man should be capable of such relations arises from man having being created a free agent, with free will to fulfil or to frustrate this his highest destiny; free will to love or to love not. In man's heavenly calling, in his very capacity for fellowship with God, there is, accordingly, inherent, a possibility of falling away, of rejecting the calling, of missing the highest end of his being. And it is just this which is more immediately expressed by the word *sin*. The Hebrew and Greek correlatives for sin used in the Bible almost exclusively imply a departure from the right and prescribed way; a walking along crooked and mistaken paths which do not lead to the goal aimed at, and therefore a missing of the end, such as happens to the wanderer who has lost his way, or to the careless and unskilful marksman.

Hence we at once see in what sin most especially consists. If the rightful aim of the human being be love, and if sin be the straying from or missing of that aim, why, sin must necessarily be the want of love, lovelessness, or, to use its most significant and exhaustive epithet, *selfishness*. Man becomes a sinner, and forfeits his high destiny, because, instead of having his being in loving fellowship with God, and seeking in him all he needs: life, joy, blessedness; he determines to have his being in himself, and to reach all he requires by his own efforts. He will not surrender himself; will not be dependent; he misuses his freedom so as to have a will of his own, contrary to the will of God, and he directs his steps according to that blind self-will. This is the special root, the germ, and, so to speak, the vital principle of all and every sin. But how many ramifications proceed from this one root; in how many shapes this principle, this spirit, incarnates itself! For even in the sinful and selfish heart the desire for happiness and perfect satisfaction continues to exist, and, accordingly, it must unavoidably seek to gratify itself with all possessions external to God which lie within its scope, and require no submissive love on its part, but rather seem passively to offer themselves to its use and service. The heart turns, then, from the Creator to the creature, from God to the world; from the invisible to the visible, in order to attain here below what it imperatively needs, and to still the painful hunger and thirst it feels.

Every individual, each according to his temperament and his circumstances, seeks to satisfy himself: one by the lusts of the flesh; another by the greatest amount possible of worldly possessions; a third by a high and commanding position among his fellow-men, and so on. A few less sensually minded, who find no delight in any of these aims, leave externals altogether; leave, so to speak, the material nature of such things alone, and seek to enjoy them merely in a spiritual fashion. Intellectually, they embrace and contemplate the fulness of creation and the riches of the world, and endeavour to win their inmost heart's desire by what earthly arts and sciences call the perception of the beautiful.

And now there arises a quite peculiar, unexpected, unforeseen fact, which is yet at bottom thoroughly natural, inherent indeed in the very constitution of our being. For since this our being is originally adapted to fellowship with God, that is, to loving self-surrender and dependence, we may at once perceive that by severing ourselves from God we do not and cannot attain to the independence we hoped for, but can only exchange the object of our submission and dependence. We thought to use and enjoy the world as free agents, as rulers over that world; but lo, and behold! so soon as we begin to deal with it, man, who by his departure from God has limited himself to his own strength only, and thrown himself from off his proper inward centre of gravity, finds himself far too weak to obtain or keep mastery over this world. That portion of our nature most intimately connected with it, that flesh and blood, as the Scripture calls it, which the soul if united with God could easily have subjected to itself, glorifying and spiritualizing it by that very subjection—now tears itself away from the control of its enfeebled ruler, as that ruler has torn himself away from God; makes common cause with worldly objects, which our perversion has caused to assume a perverted relation to us, and so drags us away with irresistible might. We thought to win the world, we lose ourselves in the world; we hoped from the height of our own free unbiassed will to choose out for ourselves what most pleased us, and we are inwardly conscious that whenever we come for this purpose into contact with the world, it invariably gets the better of us. Even though we are forced to own that we do not find what we seek, that the world cannot offer us the satisfaction and blessedness which we crave, yet we are no longer able to escape from it, and we become more and more powerless with regard to it, the more—through its intercourse therewith—the sensual element within us strengthens, and finally sensualizes and secularizes the spiritual. Pleasures and selfish efforts of every kind, to which we first willingly surrendered ourselves, become pain to us, become passions which never indeed afford us what we expected from them, and yet will not let us go. As a mighty stream overpowers the swimmer who, in presumptuous reliance on his own strength, dared to plunge into its rush of waters, so we are swept ever farther and farther away from our original goal, ever separated more widely from God, our eternal destiny ever more hidden out of our sight, till finally we sink into a vortex where we completely forget all that is above us. Therefore it is that the Scripture proclaims, "He that doeth sin is the servant of sin." He who will not be God's is not on that account his own; rather he makes a God of, and belongs to, that which is not God, and therefore cannot possibly satisfy man's own essential nature, can only oppress and destroy it.

And here is it necessary that I should seek to prove how, from such a state as this, a disturbance of all God-instituted relations must ensue, not only in the human heart, but the world around? Since selfishness is the only impulse that governs individual thought and action, it follows that selfishness everywhere clashes with selfishness, and the possessions and enjoyments of the world not being illimitable, but having to be parcelled out among mankind, and the selfishness of the one being hindered and limited by the selfishness of the other, offences, quarrels, and conflicts of necessity arise. And thus selfishness develops into enmity against all who oppose it. It turns to hatred, envy, bitterness, in all their forms. "We not only do not love our neighbour, but we are by nature disposed to hate him," says the Catechism of our Church. And if we consider the matter a little more closely, we shall be obliged to admit that this is no exaggerated statement. For even in those cases where we *do* love our neighbour, as we say, this is often no real love, but rather a form of selfishness. We love our fellow-creatures either because they are members of our own family, and we are drawn to them by a certain natural impulse, or because we receive pleasure and satisfaction of some kind from them, and hope by their society to fill up the aching void within us.

Hitherto all that we have advanced has only touched one side of our subject. We come now to observe that sin is not only a wandering out of the way, a missing of the mark, an absence of happiness, but is also *debt* and *transgression;* a *debt* which, if there be a righteous government of the universe, must necessarily be brought home to us. For we do not wander as those might do who knew not the right way; nor do we reject God's will and our own high calling as being ignorant of these; but in some degree or other, each one of us is conscious of his wanderings and his failures; conscious that he has turned aside out of the way marked out for him, and persisted in thus diverging; conscious that both in conduct and condition he finds himself in constant opposition to that which is in the highest sense *Right* and *Law*, and therefore that he has done *wrong*, and been guilty of a breach of *duty*. Even where men are without any external revelation of the Divine will, it is, we all know, *conscience* that writes that will in their heart, and keeps alive within them the sense of having offended against the highest and best. This conscience, this most wonderful and supernatural power in human nature, differs from all other of our faculties in this, that while the rest serve us and are liable to be controlled at our pleasure, conscience, on the contrary, is independent of our will, and puts forward a claim of its own, which we can never entirely suppress, to direct that will and guide it to its own aims. And these aims of conscience are, we well know, the very opposite to those of our perverted wills and our fleshly inclinations.

True, conscience itself shares the deterioration of our nature, and is often clouded; but still it never ceases, in the midst of confusion and sinfulness, to point us to the opposite of these, to the good, and so to the *one* highest good from whence all goodness flows, namely, to God. And while it lives and witnesses within us, no man can remain entirely unconscious of being, through his selfish and carnal feelings and actions, in opposition to some higher and holier order of things, of offending against some eternal law, of incurring some responsibility towards a superior power, which is righteous and wills righteousness. And if, nevertheless, man persists in the feelings and the actions which awaken this consciousness, does not our moral sense at once tell us that his perverted condition cannot in such a case be only an evil, a misfortune, such as sickness is (which is a view of sin man is prone to take); but a *conscious* transgression, a *conscious* contempt of a power which he ought to obey; an abnegation of his calling, and a denial of him from whence it proceeds, against his *better knowledge and conscience.* It is *this* which constitutes guilt in the most special and emphatic sense of the word, as is unmistakably affirmed by the same conscience that at the first warned us of the fact of our deviation. It is no empty figure we use, when we speak of a bad, a guilt-laden conscience,—a conscience self-terrified, that like Adam after his fall would fain hide itself in darkness.

Again, it is scarcely necessary that I should remind you, for this also is a self-evident truth, that the more clearly and definitely we are instructed as to what we should do and be, the greater and the darker our guilt, if we nevertheless persist in disobedience and resistance. It is in this sense that the apostle speaks of sin, "by the commandment, becoming exceeding sinful;" and this must apply most of all to the perfect revelation of the divine love in Christ. Henceforward, there is a possibility of the open and thoroughly conscious opposition to the leadings from above, which our Lord characterizes as that sin against the Holy Ghost which has never forgiveness. Well therefore may the apostle say, that if the gospel be not a "savour of life unto life, it is a savour of death unto death;" and we have but to reflect how we view and judge the disobedience of our own children when they not only do what is wrong in itself, but utterly disregard our most explicit prohibitions, thus rebelling against the parental will, and shaking off the parental authority: we need only, I say, think of this to make us most keenly conscious of the aspect our sins must wear to him who has enjoined us to lead a loving and holy life, and who continually reminds us from within and from without, that this is indeed his will and commandment respecting us.

Thus, then, the sinner stands in the position of one who is both erring and guilty, subject both to evil and to punishment; for that there is and must be Divine punishments, will be evident to the simplest mind, unless we are content to throw contempt on the nature of God. What should we—to use once more a familiar illustration—what should we think of a father who daily delivered some command or prohibition to his children without ever giving them a hint of his displeasure in the event of their direct disobedience to either? To every onlooker, as to the children themselves, such a man would appear lamentably weak; one whose person and whose words would only provoke ridicule and scorn. And shall we dare to transfer this weakness, this absurdity, to our God? Shall we not rather acknowledge that the sense of justice inherent in ourselves, which claims expiation and punishment for every offence, must dwell in far higher and holier measure in him after whose image we are created, and therefore in a certain sense may, and indeed must, deduce his nature from our own?

But further, as nothing arbitrary can be attributed to God, but all that he does is grounded in the very nature of things themselves, and necessarily comes to pass, so also the punishment that he has connected with sin is no arbitrary, externally-imposed punishment, but one whose perfect justice is self-evident, because it proceeds out of the very nature of sin, and is indeed nothing else but its fruit and completion, as the Scripture comprehensively expresses it, "Whatsoever a man soweth, that shall he also reap." Now if sin sows selfishness, *i.e.*, the tearing one's-self away from God, and making one's-self dependent on the created, what else can be reaped but separation, an ever-increasing and finally complete separation from him, and a submersion in the perishable creature whose destiny we must henceforth share, having voluntarily made common cause with it? But God is indisputably the one and only source of all life and all good; to be separated from him, therefore, implies a separation from all goodness and all life: in one word, implies death. "The wages of sin is death," exclaims the apostle Paul; and St. James declares, that "when lust hath conceived it bringeth forth sin, and sin when it is finished bringeth forth death." Nor can anything exceed the logical correctness of the statement; for if sin be the effort to sever one's-self from God, and to depart from him more and more, the result sin at last reaches can be nothing else than such severance and departure realized; and this involves at the same time a severance from everything that truly deserves the name of life. Our temporal and natural death is an evident image of the eternal; the *other* death, as Scripture calls it, that which is the ultimate and extremest consequence of what sin, without knowing or wishing it, has striven after and attained to. We cannot, however, enlarge upon this subject, particularly as we shall have hereafter the opportunity of doing so in our Lecture on the Future Life. For the present it may suffice to observe, that this eternal death is what the Scripture, viewing it as proceeding from the punitive justice of God, calls damnation; that fearful sentence, "Depart from me into darkness," to be spoken by the Lord. God punishes man *by* his sin, by allowing sin to have its way, and attain to its end. The sinner both condemns and punishes himself, and is punished and condemned; both separates himself, and is separated from life; nor can any one say that he is overtaken by a doom unconnected with the nature of his transgression, each one experiencing that alone which he willed.

Which he willed, and yet, however, *did not will;* for it is a further characteristic of sin (and one so intimately involved in its very nature that we cannot even think it otherwise) that it is also falsehood. How, indeed, could sin ever mislead men's wills, if it appeared to them in its true form, presented them with its actual consequences, and allowed them to discern that it ruined their capacities for happiness, and subjected them to the despotism of evil? No one wills to choose such a lot as this, but rather one diametrically opposite; it is after good and after enjoyment that each one is striving. It is only by picturing to us and promising us what we wish, that it allures us to its ways. Sin never comes before us but in the form of some gain, some fuller life and fuller liberty, and this it invariably proffers at a small price; some isolated act, say of wilful disobedience, which is to remain unlinked with consequences or with further acts of the kind. Sin invariably feigns to abnegate its comprehensive character, and conceals its might to capture and to tyrannize from its victim. It does not at first allow us to discover that the individual evil action to which it invites, contains in itself the principle of universal evil; on the contrary, it affects still to acknowledge the law of goodness, and to honour and obey it on all points save this one. And thus it is that it deceives us, veils from us its true nature, and leads us to expect from it the satisfaction of our needs and wishes, while, on the contrary, we are reaching out our sadly deluded hand to receive the frustration and blighting of all these. By promising us pleasure for the flesh, and satisfaction for our sensuous requirements, it lures us into its toils; and once there, it actually robs us of legitimate and God-ordained bodily gratifications, shatters health, deadens the senses, takes the external means of enjoyment away. By the prospect of a position that will satisfy all personal rights and claims, it impels us to ambitious efforts, and what we actually attain to is the fate of Tantalus, the position fraught with this imagined satisfaction, ever receding as we advance, till at length we are landed, not on the promised heights, but in the abyss. And if at length we, the long deceived, do open our eyes; if we become inwardly convinced how in every instance the exact opposite of what was promised is what really falls to our share; when the bitter dregs have succeeded to the sweetness of the first draught, and evil has dropped the mask it wore at the beginning, and stands before us in its own thoroughly hateful aspect of enmity against God and our own souls, even this discovery may come too late. Sin has reached its aim. The toils into which it lured us by its deceit, may still hold us so fast we cannot escape from them, though we know them now to be the toils of misery as well. "The devil is a liar and a murderer from the beginning," exclaims our Lord. "When he speaketh a lie, he speaketh of his own, for he is a liar, and the father of it." He promises life, the fulness of life, the joy of life; promises us each delight in larger measure than before, and meanwhile he is actually destroying life, the life to come as well as the life that now is, till finally we attain to eternal death.

I am well aware that in quoting these words of our Lord, I have spoken a name which will probably provoke in many among you a laugh of compassion. No doctrine of Scripture has in these latter days excited more contemptuous opposition, or been more utterly repudiated, than this doctrine of the existence of the devil, and in numberless circles he who should in any sense adhere to it, would hardly escape the imputation of benighted superstition. Time does not permit me to enter upon any lengthened refutation of current objections, but you will allow me to make one passing observation: Most certainly the Scripture nowhere admits the existence of such a devil as the popular imagination has constructed, and popular legends describe, a "teeth-gnashing, tailed and horned subordinate deity." In Scripture, Satan intrinsically appears as the head of the preter-human domain of evil, the tempter and misleader of creatures originally adapted to abide in God. And what is there in the belief in such a preter-human evil one, and in his influence over us, which is contrary to reason or to experience? Or who is there who has ever so remotely succeeded in proving the impossibility of the existence of such? Nay, further, if we dwell seriously upon what we have just been proving, that sin is, in its essential nature, *falsehood*, and can only get a hold over us by plausible and deceiving lies, why, then, we must necessarily assume a personal liar and misleader, who in this way gains admittance to our spirit. But for this, would not human sinfulness be itself devilish, that is, a rebellion against God out of original self-will and self-consciousness, and so one from which there could be no deliverance; while, on the contrary, we have the comfort of knowing that we, who were deceived at the first, and who continue to be deceived again and again by lies and semblances, are yet capable of being restored to liberty by that Truth which maketh free.

And now having considered the nature of sin under both its aspects, it remains to us to dwell awhile upon so-called original sin, and the various opinions that differ from our own concerning it. But before we enter upon this topic, you will allow me some brief parenthetical remarks, nay, you will even require them of me; for, as one question, that, namely, of the origin of evil and its first beginnings amongst us, becomes the more pressing the more fully the horrors of evil are disclosed, the remarkable chapter at the beginning of the Bible, which professes to give an account of this origin of evil, must occur to the minds of us all, nor must we fail to examine how it tallies with what we have already said. And nothing is more wondrous than the fact, that in this very chapter, simple as it is, and intelligible to any child, all and everything is to be found concerning the nature of sin, which we may have gathered from the later developments of Biblical thought, or from our own experience. The narrative seems a nursery-story, yet the researches of the greatest thinkers have been directed to it, and failed to exhaust it, so that we are forced to inquire where we shall find, even considered from the stand-point merely of reason, a more lucid explanation of the problem in question? What old tradition, what last result of human wisdom, will help us further? Of all passages of Scripture, this chapter most emphatically illustrates the truth, "that the Bible is a stream through which a lamb may wade, but which an elephant cannot fathom."

First, let us observe, that what is told us of the blessedness of the first pair in their communion with God, and the first commandment enjoined them by Him, manifestly agrees with our assertion at the beginning of our discourse, that man was formed for loving fellowship with God; and further, that he must choose and enter upon this loving fellowship of his own free will, beginning with that believing and obedient conformity to the Divine precepts, by which that will increases in energy, and becomes more and more one with the holy will of the Creator. Now, this free will of man had to be subjected to a test by a command of God's. Man was to decide whether he would seek his standing and his happiness in truthful, filial submission to God, or in some self-elected way which should even dare a departure from the Divine will. "Thou shalt not eat of the tree of knowledge of good and evil," was the command; in other words, "Thou shalt not gain the knowledge of evil by evil-doing; gain it experimentally, know it, so as to become a sharer in it; but by my prohibition, placing the possibility of obedience or disobedience before thy mind, thy good shall become a self-conscious good, and shall stand out to thee in clear and recognised opposition to the evil from which thou turnest away." The will of man, in short, was not only to remain good and holy, but to be exalted to a consciously holy will; and this was the first step that he had to take towards his eternal destiny.

But since man, following the dictates of his originally pure nature, would have conformed to this, the evil temptation had to come from without, from the divinely permitted instrument of the divinely appointed probation; and the mode of its procedure was the very one we might have anticipated, having a thousand times experienced it. First, there was the coarse falsehood, which would throw doubt upon God's commandments: "Yea, hath God said;" and when the woman replies to this by simply narrating the facts of the case, and treating obedience as a thing of course, then follows the more subtle insinuation, meant to shake her confidence in the benevolent meaning of that commandment given, "God has commanded thus that you may not be equal to him; that you may not become too highly exalted; only make the experiment; only eat, and you shall be as gods, knowing good and evil." Just as in the present day, God's saving ordinance, Christianity and its claims, is represented as a scheme to stultify the human race, to keep it down, to prevent it from reaching to its full happiness and greatest height.

And see further, how in every clause, black and white, truth and falsehood, are mixed up in this typical serpent-speech! It freely acknowledges the divinely ordained aim of man's existence, and apparently seconds it; for verily, to know good and evil, and to be like God, is the very end for which man is adapted. "We know that when he shall appear, we shall be like him," exclaims the apostle. But it is about the way to that end that the temptation lies. "Seek it not through God, not through abiding in his word but rather seek and win it by your own independent will and power. This is the only possible and worthy way of development. Disobedience to God will be a transitional stage to perfection and completeness; without it you will never reach them, but must ever remain in a state of childhood, and ignorance, and degradation." The whole system of Pantheism, the most subtle of all falsehoods, is contained herein: "Yes, there is a highest good," so runs the pleading now as then; "yes, you are fitted for that highest good, and will ultimately attain it, but not through obedient faith and submissive love; on the contrary, you must rise out of this lowly condition to a higher one of independence and self-exertion." And this deceived the woman. The pleasure of pitting her own will and power against the will of God fascinated her: "When the woman saw that the tree was good for food, and pleasant to the eyes, and a tree to be desired to make one wise, she took of the fruit thereof and did eat, and gave also unto her husband, and he did eat."

And no sooner was this done than the consequences which we have represented as inevitably linked with such departure from God began to ensue: First came the emancipation of the flesh from the spirit, with which it had been up to this moment unconstrainedly and perfectly one. Now the body began to put forth its own separate claim; now there was forced on the beings who wanted to exist independently, such a view of their own physically limited, mortal, animally organized individuality, as, contrasting with their newly-awakened pride, created in them a sense of shame. Yes, their eyes were indeed opened, as the serpent promised, only not opened to look around them as gods; rather to look around in most ungodlike degradation and subserviency to the creature; "they knew that they were naked," and they sought to cover their nakedness. Moreover, the impulse to untruthfulness, the delusive falsehood of sin, has eaten into their nature. They now deceive themselves as sinners ever do, they seek to deceive God, and yet they are not able to shake off the terror of an evil conscience, and the sense of guilt and profound alienation from him. They flee from God; they endeavour to hide from him, to excuse themselves before him by specious pretences. And finally, they undergo that which had been foretold them as the unavoidable result of self-separation from the original source of life: "In the day that thou eatest thereof thou shalt surely die." The tree of life in the garden of Eden, typifies the constant flow of living energy imparted by God to man, so long as man abides in fellowship with God. The driving of the fallen pair out of Paradise, and away from this tree of life, denotes that in their present state of separation from God, their earthly bodies must undergo the condition attached to all earthly created things of perishableness and decay, and their organism having degenerated from its original unity and normal development, must be now fretted and destroyed by the conflict of its own divided elements, unless it can be in some way restored to union with God, and thereby to harmony with itself.

Such is what Scripture, with incomparable clearness and truth, teaches us respecting the entrance of sin amongst us. It does not, however, proceed to afford us an explanation of the origin of evil, and we would just observe that any explanation which should really enlighten our understanding, is neither possible nor indeed conceivable. For evil, as the opposite of true reason, the reason namely of God, is essentially the reason-*less*, the *un*-reasonable, that which blindly and arbitrarily averts itself from the law of Reason. How then could its origin be explained on reasonable grounds, its possibility and actuality demonstrated by any intellectual process? We can indeed contemplate evil as an existing *fact*, we can observe its appearance and its influence among and over ourselves, but we cannot say, *why* it appeared, nor why the first free will that turned away from God chose that fatal direction.

There is, however, another far plainer and more intelligible subject, that now challenges our attention, and to which the Church has affixed the technical appellation of *Original Sin*. We all know what is meant by the phrase. It expresses the conviction that *All* who belong to our race, without any exception whatsoever, appear as aliens and sinners before God, and prove themselves so from the very beginning of their life; and it explains this truth of which we are convinced by a reference to that law of connexion between parent and offspring, owing to which the perverted will and disposition which manifested itself as *sin* in the former, is handed down to the latter. This, too, is one of the doctrines peculiarly repugnant to many in our day. This assumption of original sinfulness is often declared to be a glaring degradation of human nature, a narrowing, if not a denial of human liberty, a blasphemy against Divine justice, and much more of the kind. But can these and such like declamations against the *theory* do anything to alter the *fact* upon which the theory is based? Can our opponents anywhere show us a man who is thoroughly perfect even as our Father in heaven is perfect, who loves God with all his heart and all his power, and his neighbour as himself, as the ideal of human perfection requires? And if they cannot do this, what other explanation have they to offer of this universal sinfulness of the race? Will they suggest the singular idea that each man undergoes his own special fall, and sins as Adam did? Or will they adopt that most superficial notion that it is defective education and bad example alone, which pervert originally pure and well-inclined creatures into practical sinners? But do we not daily see in the case of our own children, even before they can sin *consciously*, before education or example can have had any effect upon them, that their very first feelings and impulses are those of anger, selfishness, resistance, disobedience, even though it is true, that as contrasted with adults, they are relatively innocent? Yea, in their very earliest days, before they are cognizant of anything, still less of good and evil, do they, while uttering their angry, uncontrolled cries, make upon us the impression of pure, holy, and complete beings? or do they not much rather most vividly recall to the shame of us their parents, those words of the Psalmist, "Behold, I was shapen in iniquity, and in sin did my mother conceive me?" And if this be so, can there be anything irrational, anything contrary to experience, in deducing this defective and perverted condition from their relation to defective and perverted parents? Does not the most universal and incontrovertible experience suggest such an explanation? Do we not see children bear the impress of their parents in every other point? Is not the form transmitted,—the features, the talents, temperament, disposition? And is the *sinful* element in all these to be omitted? Is the *will* to be inherited, but not the discordant and perverted *direction* of the will? Is the natural character to be handed down, but not its disturbances and defects? Nay rather, are not the very bodily ailments so constantly transmitted from father to son, through several generations, sufficient to oppose such a theory as this? You see yourselves into what contradictions and improbabilities we wander when we try to contradict the teaching of Scripture, which harmonizes so perfectly with observation and experience.

There is only *one* objection to this doctrine of the universal and hereditary corruption of human nature through the fall of our first parents, to which I can concede any sort of plausibility. It is an objection of the following kind: "If this be true, every one of us is innocent of his own sinfulness, and it is a crying injustice on God's part that we should be born in a condition that leads us to miss our eternal goal, and subjects us to eternal misery. Why," continue the objectors, "is not each man created afresh, immediately by the hand of God, with the same liberty of choice our first parents possessed? *Then* only would it be true of each that he reaped what he had sown, whereas we have to reap and to eat a bitter harvest we never planted?" But even this objection will be found easy enough to reply to. For if we possess any insight whatsoever into the nature of religion, we shall soon see that the whole of it is adapted to and presupposes a social and interdependent state. Humanity is to be and form a whole, an intimately connected organism; and in order to this it is essential it should have a common origin, should not consist of innumerable and independent humanities. It is not as *single individuals*, but as members *of a body corporate, as humanity as a whole*, that we are elected to fellowship with God. Scripture speaks of a fulness, a completeness appertaining to the heirs of salvation; the heavenly inhabitants are to make up *one body*, of which all the members are to be intimately connected, and Christ the Son of man the head. And therefore the fundamental condition of fitness for the kingdom of heaven is not only, "Thou shalt love the Lord thy God;" but this as well, "Thou shalt love thy neighbour as thyself."

But, again, this doctrine of original sin in no way impugns the justice of God, since for this sin, and all that it entails, he has instituted a deliverance and a remedy, and he alone can fail of his high eternal destiny who self-consciously and resolutely wills to refuse this remedy and its conditions. Redemption has connected with hereditary sin a hereditary blessing, which we impart to our children in baptism; and the strength of the latter, if it be appropriated and used, exceeds that of the former. Together with the first Adam, we have now a second Adam, from whom a new, God-pleasing, and eternal life proceeds, as from the first Adam a sinful and death-tending life. Nothing, therefore, has any longer power to ruin or condemn us, but a persistent turning away from the Redeemer, for which each man is alone responsible. "I judge no man," says Christ. He that believeth not on me is self-condemned.

From this doctrine of original sin, however, it necessarily follows that we are incapable of delivering ourselves from our sinfulness, incapable of attaining to the moral condition essential to heavenly happiness; for if sin consists in a perverted direction of the will, and this perverted direction is from the first inherent and dominant in us, how can we find within our own nature a capacity for withstanding and rectifying it? Can the corrupted, and, at the same time, enfeebled will, help itself? This were as absurd and impossible an idea as that of a man extricating himself from a quicksand by his own strength; and since all our other faculties are subservient to the will, and receive from it their direction, and consequently all obey its selfish impulse, where, in the whole scope of our being, are we to find that still pure, intact, and healthy energy, by which it were possible to bend this will to the right direction? No; sin requires a conqueror and deliverer whose position is outside of its domain, and who, standing on firm ground, can reach out to us a helping hand, and so raise us from the quicksands in which we sink.

And now let me very briefly proceed to contrast with this scriptural doctrine of sin,—logically conclusive, concurrent with reason, conscience, and experience, as you have yourselves seen it to be,—some of the principal counter-teachings current amongst us. We will not dwell at any length upon the views of those who pronounce it degrading to human dignity and worth to speak of a Fall, a moral deterioration sustained by man, and who, to restore his injured honour, simply deny his sinfulness altogether, and insist upon his still being actually good and well-inclined. To such reasoners we would only reply, "Ye know not what ye say." It is not the Scriptures, it is you yourselves, who, by such assertions as these, most deeply dishonour man's capabilities and destiny, and steal from him his royal crown; for, in saying as you do, "Man is good enough as he is; even in his incompleteness we discover in him moral energies which perfectly satisfy us that he will attain to a high destiny without foreign assistance;" in saying this, what poor and miserable conceptions must you entertain of man's destiny and worth and being, as well as of the nature of moral excellence, and the degree of it to which he is called. Very different is the language of the Bible concerning him. The Bible affirms his nature to be so elected and adapted to the highest, that even the least failure, the least taint, is in him unbearable, and in contradiction to his destiny. So long as he is not holy as God is holy, like him in the purity and the glory of perfect love, so long is he not what he should be, what he can be, what he will be! Yes, it is just because God's revelation sets us upon this loftiest, this almost inconceivable pinnacle, that it considers us in our present state to be so deeply sunk in poverty, misery, and darkness. The human race never is, never can be more highly honoured than when it is said, "Ye are not yet in any sense what ye shall be!"—so infinitely does the royalty destined for you transcend your present broken-down and slavish state.

But there is another conception of sin, which more or less, indeed, acknowledges this, only proceeds to opine, that the present condition of man is an inevitable, nay, an essential transitional stage towards this highest height; that what the Scripture calls sin, is in fact neither guilt nor wandering, but merely a want of development and maturity, just as childhood is a lower stage in the progress to manhood; that just as the child fails at present to possess those manly faculties to which one day it will attain, without being held culpable or even responsible for that failure, so is it with the human race and its so-called depravity. Men only need to develop their being on all sides, and to progress in all directions, and they will gradually work themselves free from carnality and selfishness, and will attain to that condition of perfect knowledge, love, and happiness, which the Bible describes as the Kingdom of Heaven.

But, after all, it is to our conscience that we must appeal respecting this question, and does not this view most definitely contradict its voice? For, according to this theory, sin is nothing but a lower stage of development ordered and willed by God himself, and therefore not wrong, not transgression at all! Wherefore is it, then, that we invariably feel it to be such, so that the commission of it entails upon us an uneasy conscience, and destroys our rest and peace? And wherefore is it that we mutually condemn each other, and condemn our own selves on account of it, if it be after all nothing but deficiency and partial development? No one reproaches the child with its childish measure of intelligence, no one requires from a less advanced stage the fruits of the more advanced; but we do, and are inwardly constrained to make a reproach of sin, and right conduct is demanded of us in every stage of life alike, both by our own consciousness and that of others. And further, does it in any way accord with our conceptions of a holy God, that he should himself ordain and decree sin (*i.e.*, contradiction to himself and disturbance to his laws), even as a transitory and transitional state? It is self-evident that such a theory as this is only consistent with a view of God that differs essentially from that Christian, that holy conception of Him, the necessity of which the preceding Lecture established.

This is one reason that lays a veto upon the acceptance of this theory. But there is another—our *experience*. Let us inquire. Is it then really true, that in proportion as man develops physically and intellectually, he becomes more and more free from sin? From certain low and animal forms of it he indeed may free himself by increasing intelligence and higher cultivation; but *selfishness*, its peculiar germ, selfishness as displayed against God and man, does he overcome and lay aside this by his intellectual growth? Does it not rather increase as he increases, so that the child comes confessedly more near to loving God with his whole heart, and his neighbour as himself, than the full-grown man? And if this be true of the individual, how should it fail to be true of the race at large? We hear much said of progress even in a moral sense; but men forget, that in that picture of humanity which lies immediately before them, there has been the intervention of Christianity, which in a thousand ways breaks and represses the power of sin even in those who are not themselves believers. If, however, we look at other portions of our race, we nowhere find the moral progress spoken of, but rather universal moral retrogression, the longer the more complete. We have all-sufficient evidence how incomparably better off the aborigines of America, the South Sea Islands, China, and India, formerly were, in a moral point of view, to enable us to speak positively on this subject. Now, how could we possibly account for such a phenomenon as this if the above theory were true, if, without the Divine power in redemption, the mere natural course of things tended to bring about an increased freedom from sin, and a progress to ever higher and higher degrees of moral excellence?

No, we must just come back to the truth first laid down, "Sin is enmity against God," and in this respect there is no difference, we are all alike sinful, we are therefore by nature all children of wrath. Our own will, our own powers, are impotent to alter the past: *but we are not on this account lost beyond power of rescue.* When the first man sinned, and sentence was pronounced upon him, there was heard simultaneously the mysterious promise of a future triumph over sin, a future redemption from it: "I will put enmity between thee and the woman, and between thy seed and her seed; it shall bruise thy head, and thou shalt bruise his heel." That is, thenceforward there shall be strife and opposition between the power of evil, between sin, and the special, essential, God-adapted nature of the human race. The task, the need, the great life-effort of humanity, so long as its history endures, shall be to wrestle with the ruin which sin has introduced into our midst, and to trample over it. But in this agonizing conflict victory shall not finally remain with the Evil One, with Sin, but with the Seed of the woman. Out of the human race one who belongs to it shall arise, one born of woman like the rest, who shall tread down the powerful foe, and rob it of its conquering strength, though not without wounds and blood. And as the first part of this prophecy has been accomplished, and is still going on before our eyes,—the ceaseless strife, namely, between humanity and evil; so also we know that the second part of it has not remained unfulfilled, that the Conqueror has already appeared, and that we through him stand opposed to a baffled and vulnerable foe, tread a redeemed world, and behold the way once more opened that leads up to our God and our heavenly home.

IV.

THE OLD TESTAMENT DISPENSATION AND THE HEATHEN WORLD.

IF we trace back the history of our race to its dim and distant commencement, we shall find that it was even then divided into different peoples, each having their own special languages and religions, and that these peoples were not only mutually unintelligible, but in a state of enmity and warfare. Now, this is no normal condition, but one arguing disorder and disruption. Its worst feature, however, was not the inimical separation of these peoples from each other, but their being separated from the living God, steeped in polygamy and idolatry; so that, according to the language of Scripture, the very word Gentiles signified heathens. For God is the source of all life and all true life-enjoyment; without him the nations, be their external existence ever so ornate and brilliant, are but as sheep without a shepherd, lost children without a home; and God is not only the source of all creatures, but also their bond of union. It is because humanity severed itself from God that it lost this true point of union, and became itself internally divided. Thus we discover that there must have been some great original cause, some world-embracing catastrophe, in which humanity as such rebelled against God, and was therefore parcelled out into different languages, nations, and religions; so that enmity, opposition, and exclusiveness replaced that beautiful many-sided unity in which the different races were to constitute one great family of God. The people of Israel, who, possessing the true knowledge of God, possessed also the true knowledge of mankind, and retained a correct memory of their primeval state, in their sacred records refer this great historical fact to the building of the tower of Babel. For after the deluge we again find mankind in a state of universal apostasy; and their disruption into heathen and inimical nations, is the great historical manifestation of the sinful condition described to us in the previous lecture.

But amidst all these nations one people stands out before us essentially different from the rest, the people, namely, of Israel. While all others worshipped several, and hence necessarily false gods, we find here the knowledge and the worship of the one true God. How are we to explain this singular fact? Can the Israelites have been by their natural constitution adapted to develop correct religious ideas, as the Greeks were to attain the highest place in art? But the parallel will scarcely hold, for all other nations had some artistic faculties or other, the Greeks only brought them to the greatest perfection; whereas the religion of the Jews differed essentially from heathen religion, in that it was true while they were false; and just as religion is a different thing altogether from art, so the difference in kind between truth and falsehood is quite other than the difference of degree between the imperfect and the perfect in art; and moreover, we know that all error, religious error more particularly, is a consequence of sin, and that the Israelites were as little exempt from sin as the other nations of the earth. Therefore the people of Israel could no more have evolved the true religion by their own natural powers, than we can gather grapes from thorns, or figs from thistles.

And this the self-consciousness of the people themselves, as expressed in their sacred records, perfectly confirms. The Jews never claim the honour of having originated their own religion; on the contrary, the Old Testament Scriptures represent them as naturally rebellious to God, and prone to idolatry; in short, as heathenish in their tendencies as any other nation. Their knowledge of God, and their religion, both at the first and throughout all stages of its development, is invariably ascribed to Divine Revelation. The assertions in the Old Testament respecting the nature and the origin of the Divine Idea they held, are inextricably connected, and if we acknowledge the truth of the first, we cannot without inconsistency reject the latter.

Another point in which the Jews differed from every other nation, was their expectation of a Messiah. As God was the origin of the Old Testament life, Israel having from the first recognised itself to be the people and the kingdom of Jehovah, so the Messiah was its end. While heathen nations and empires decayed and fell without hope of deliverance, in Israel, on the contrary, political decline was attended by an increasingly clear expectation of a high and God-sent Deliverer, who should restore the Divine kingdom to a new and far greater holiness and glory than it had ever known before. This idea, too, was always referred by its enunciators, the prophets, to divine revelation, and we have every reason to receive their testimony. For not only is it mere folly to suppose that the announcers of the highest truths of humanity could be themselves mistaken as to whence these truths came, but it is contrary to the very nature of things that such golden fruit as this should grow on the barren thorn of the sinful human heart. Could this have been, surely the great and noble spirits of other nations, Socrates, Plato, Zoroaster, Confucius, would also have confidently expected salvation, whereas we only hear from their lips a few dim and obscure yearnings of the kind. It was only as a powerless ideal, that, in times of decadence, heathen philosophers and other earnest men, as for instance, Tacitus, held out a higher condition to the enervated race around them; it was only as a vanished epoch, a poetical dream or a political panegyric, that heathen poets ever sang of the golden age. The heathen were without hope, because they were without God in the world (Eph. ii. 12). Amongst the Israelites, on the contrary, this Messianic idea did not appear as a mere yearning or poetical ideal; but from the first as a definite, and as centuries rolled on, ever more and more definite prophecy. Now such a prophecy transcends human power. The predictions of even so pious a man as Savonarola were not prophecies, for they remained unfulfilled; whereas we have a fulfilment of this prophecy, which is without a historical parallel; we have, centuries later, Jesus of Nazareth declaring himself to be this promised Messiah, and announcing the dawn of that kingdom of heaven which the prophets foretold.

This leads us to a third peculiarity which distinguishes the Jews from the heathen, I mean the relation of their religion to the Christian, which is represented in both divisions of the Scriptures as connected with the old Covenant (Jer. xxx. 31; Luke xxii. 20; 2 Cor. iii. 6-14). Christianity recognises in the old dispensation its divinely-ordained preparatory stage; while in heathenism it sees the power and bondage of an alien principle (Acts xxvi. 18; 1 Cor. x. 20). This peculiar connexion between the two Testaments, their different stages of revelation being fraught with one and the same spirit, and constituting a marvellous whole, is a witness to the Divine origin of the Jewish (as well as the Christian) religion. And when with conscientious thoroughness of research we examine into the books of the two Testaments, we find, both in their history and their doctrine, a connexion extending through centuries, a gradual progress which points to one comprehensive plan, which could by no possibility have had its origin in the mind of short-lived man, but can only be reasonably explained by that Divine causation to which the Bible itself refers all things; and if we proceed further to test this conclusion, by comparing it with our knowledge of other kinds, we shall find, that not only do the Divine revelations intimately agree together, but with the condition and needs of our human nature, with the fundamental relations of the universe, and with the being of God. Incomparable wisdom, holiness, and love breathe on us from the Scripture pages, and perfectly satisfy the demands of conscience and the search of the intellect after the highest truth. "Nothing has so convinced me," says a very exact and intelligent theological thinker, who has thoroughly studied the whole of Biblical History, I allude to the respected Hess of Zurich;—"nothing has so sincerely convinced me of the truth of

Christianity, its revelation, history, and doctrine, as the having found in the sacred records, on one hand, what perfectly satisfies the needs of humanity both for time and eternity, and, on the other hand, in the Divine provision towards this end, such a connected progress from small to great, from the particular to the universal, as would have been impossible to human invention."

Accordingly, we now find ourselves not only authorized but bound to contrast with the heathen the people of Israel as the people of God, in the undiluted, the Biblical sense of the word. The history of the Israelites is the history of Divine revelation; that of the heathen the history of humanity left to itself. The former shows us the positive, the latter the negative preparation for Christianity; in other words, it affords us a practical illustration of what humanity without God becomes. To use the pregnant expression of the latest historical commentator on the Old Testament, J. H. Kurz, "In the former, we have salvation prepared for humanity; in the latter, humanity prepared for salvation." And the more closely we examine into both these processes, the more we shall discover in the universal history of the Old World a preparation, and so an argument for Christianity. Let us, then, in the first place, direct our attention to the development of the Divine revelation to Israel, as we find it recorded in the Bible annals.

Over the whole world sits enthroned the eternal God, who is love. Because of his love he has from eternity determined to reveal and impart himself ever more and more completely to his intelligent creatures, that they, being filled with his own life and glory, may attain to the perfecting of their existence in him, and thus God be all in all. Nor did God relinquish this loving plan upon the entrance of sin into the world; on the contrary, he revealed his love all the more gloriously, as that grace which saves the lost, and brings about the perfecting of the world by the process of redemption; and because of his free and inconceivable mercy, he held fast his thoughts of peace respecting humanity against all heathenish apostasy, and determine to accomplish first the redemption, and finally the perfection, the glorification of the world by means of continuous revelations of himself.

But now what position is this Divine revelation to occupy with regard to the false paths into which the nations have wandered? There is to be no fresh deluge to exterminate the ungodly race, this, God—having given, once for all, at the commencement of human history, that fearful example of his judgments—has expressly declared (Gen. viii. 21; ix. 15). Neither was the whole of humanity to be miraculously brought back to the living God, for that would have been a violent and enforced deliverance, while God, on the contrary, most carefully respects the liberty of man. Thus, He could neither annihilate nor convert the human race as a whole; it only remained, therefore, that at certain points of greatest susceptibility to Divine manifestations, he should begin to work for the deliverance of all. God had to adopt individual expedients to accomplish general salvation; therefore, he set apart,—as formerly, Noah,—the Semitic Abraham, to be the especial recipient of his revelation. Abraham, during the early nomadic period, when national life was in process of formation, was chosen the ancestor of one particular family who were eventually to become a particular nation. While God suffered the heathen to walk in their own ways (Acts xiv. 16), he chose Israel for his own inheritance, and by the historical destiny of that one people, prepared the way for the final purpose of all revelation,—the redemption of the human race. This was done by three great successive stages.

In order to bring about redemption, it was first of all necessary that sin should be recognised in its essential nature of a contradiction to the holy will of God, and consequently to the ideal and the destiny of humanity as well. Now, this could never come to pass unless man felt himself inwardly bound to God, and knew it to be his duty to walk before him and to be perfect (Gen. xvii. 1). It was, therefore, necessary to take out and set apart from the heathen godlessness and worldliness around, a holy section of humanity, in which God might once more re-unite the severed bond between himself and his creatures, and thus lead them back to faith. This was done in the patriarchal dispensation under which Abraham, Isaac, and Jacob lived. Upon the basis of this dispensation, it now became possible, the family having developed into the people, that, secondly, God's holy will should be revealed in the law, by which came the knowledge of sin (Rom. iii. 20). To this stage succeeded, thirdly, the foretelling of redemption by the prophets, who led from the law to the gospel, from Moses to Christ. The patriarchal dispensation, the law, and the prophets, are thus the three stages of revelation in the Old Testament, which now claim our more close consideration. But before we enter upon them, there are a few obstacles in our way which it were well to remove.

In the Old Testament, as in the Bible generally, we find numerous miracles, and to these the thinking of the present day is peculiarly averse. Now, the question of the possibility of miracles reduces itself to that other question of the existence of a God who created the world, and in whose power it must therefore be to introduce into it new creations. That we all have abundant reason, nay, are even constrained by the laws of correct thinking, to believe in such a God, has been proved to us in the first two of this series of Lectures; and therefore, the possibility and the existence of miracles may be looked upon as already briefly and inferentially proved. In fact, that simple declaration by which Gabriel proved to the Virgin Mary the possibility of the miraculous conception of the Saviour, "With God nothing shall be impossible" (Luke i. 37), is the best argument for the miraculous that severe and profound thought on God's relation to the world can discover. It is in this sense that the noted free-thinker, J. J. Rousseau, declares in his forcible way, that it is blasphemous to deny the possibility of miracles, and that he who does so deserves to be imprisoned. And one of the most acute of our modern thinkers, Richard Rothe, remarks, in his *Studien und Kritiken*, "I will candidly confess, that up to this present time I have never been able to understand why the idea of miracles should be repugnant to my reason. This may proceed from my being originally of so thoroughly theistic a nature, which has never detected in itself the slightest tendency of a Pantheistic or Atheistic kind." Miracles, indeed, belong to the very nature of divine revelation, and are its necessary phenomena; for revelation consists in God himself acting and speaking directly in humanity, so as to create in it something new which humanity could never have produced out of its own resources, and thereby to bring back the world to its original ideal of perfection in God. Neither should it any way surprise us, that the miracles recorded in the Old Testament are different in character and more marvellous than those in the New; for, from the sensuous, externally-directed spirit of that olden time, and of the still childish people (see Gal. iv. 1), it was necessary that startling and colossal miracles should be brought to bear, having the more exclusively external character of violent and abnormal physical occurrences.

There are, however, other difficulties in the Old Testament which appear more formidable, because they not only threaten to offend our laws of thought, but our moral consciousness; as, for instance, the polygamy of the patriarchs, the command to exterminate the Canaanites, and so forth. Now, in dealing with questions of this kind, it behoves us to be candid and thoughtful enough to judge the part from the spirit of the whole. It is as unfair as it is unscientific to detach particular passages from their context, and to use them as weapons against the Old Testament. Before we venture to accuse it of defective morality, we should remember that those Ten Commandments lie at its very foundation, which have been transplanted into every Christian catechism, learnt by heart by all Christian people, and still form the basis of the morality of the whole civilized world. But though this proves how much of undying divine truth is contained in the Old Covenant, we are still to remember, on the other hand, that it is but the Old Covenant, not the New, only the preparation for, not the perfect revelation itself. Therefore, an unprejudiced and genuinely historical criticism measures the facts of the Old Testament by its own standard, not by that of the New Testament, nor of modern times. It takes up the idea expressed by Lessing, an idea founded on Scripture, that, namely, of a divine education of the human race. Now, it is perfectly reconcilable with the divine educational wisdom, that certain conditions which, after the work of redemption had been accomplished, fell under moral condemnation, as, for instance, polygamy and slavery, should be still tolerated under the earlier dispensation, just as a judicious teacher or parent will only attempt to wean the children under his care gradually from their faulty ways, proceeding from requirements easily fulfilled to those which require greater efforts of self-control. As to the extermination of the Canaanites, it only exemplifies the universal historical sentence that new and vigorous nations have invariably been called to execute upon the worn-out and degenerate; which, for example, the Babylonians and the Romans executed at a later period upon the Jews themselves, the Persians on the Babylonians, the Germans on the Romans. Only in Israel we read that "the Lord laid bare his arm;" in other words, this righteous judgment, which he usually accomplishes by his unseen guidance of the course of historical events, was expressly committed to his chosen people, who found themselves in presence of a peculiarly degraded, ripe for destruction, and yet ensnaring heathenism. Naturally I cannot in the space allotted to me clear up specifically all objections and difficulties that may be found in the Old Testament; it will be enough, in contradistinction to a widely-spread and superficial Rationalism, to lay down the truly scientific method of examination, and to indicate to all earnest seekers after truth, that here, too, faith and knowledge are easily reconcilable, nay, are much more than reconcilable merely.

To return. Abraham then is separated by God's command from all connexion with his previous circumstances and surroundings, and their heathenish tendency; he is to leave his own family, his own country, and to go into a strange land, that of Canaan, which is henceforth to be the chief scene of the divine manifestations. And that it might be made evident that this emigration of Abraham's was not an isolated or accidental occurrence, but rather the ground and beginning of a series of further manifestations, God attaches a promise to the calling of the father of the faithful (Gen. xii. 1-3, 7); which, at a later period, to enforce its significance, he frequently repeated both to Isaac and Jacob. The nature of this promise is threefold: 1*st*, The childless Abraham is to become the ancestor of a mighty nation; 2*dly*, The land of Canaan is to belong to that nation; 3*dly*, Through Abraham and his seed all generations of the earth are to be blessed. Thus the promise from the very first embraces the whole of the Old and New Testament future, and while the appointed *way* is seen to begin with the choice of one individual man and one race, the universality of the *aim* —blessing and salvation for all humanity,—is already revealed, and to Abraham personally, rich recompense was made in this promise for all that he had to sacrifice for God's sake. He was to leave his family indeed, but in return he was in his advanced age to have a family of his own, nay, to become the father of a great nation; he was to forsake his home, but to him and to his posterity a wide and beautiful land was to be given as inheritance. It is thus our God rewards. But this reward was not to be as yet actually possessed by Abraham, he had only the promise of it. Both external circumstances, and the calculations of reason and experience seemed to tend in a quite opposite direction. Abraham's wife is barren, both are old; how then can he expect posterity as the sands of the sea for number? And in Canaan he has to wander as a stranger all his life long, and can call no portion of the land his own, but as much as serves for a grave! Thus Abraham was referred only to possessions to come, which had no present existence for him save in the words of the promise. He was not merely called upon to break through natural ties of kinship for God's sake, he had to do something harder still, to trust unconditionally in God and his word, for a compensation contrary to nature and apparently to reason. It was necessary, in order that Abraham should open a new historical period, that of redemption, that he should be entirely removed out of the soil of nature, and thoroughly rooted in God, in his might and his grace. In other words, he must learn to believe. This requisite belief Abraham possessed; and throughout life, even under the severest tests, he ever rendered a believing obedience. This is that faith of our father Abraham, which the apostles of the New Testament, St. Paul above all, contemplate with the deepest reverence,—that faith which God counted to him for righteousness. The whole narrative is so sublime and yet so full of holy simplicity, that it bears the unmistakable stamp of truth and historical actuality. No later Jew could possibly have invented the history of Abraham, for no other ever reached to his eminence of faith, and even the greatest saints of the Old Testament have only walked in the footsteps of the father of the faithful.

Thus then a living relationship was once more established between the true God and man; resting on God's side upon Promise, on man's upon Faith. God entered into a covenant with Abraham, that is, he solemnly instituted an especial fellowship with him above all other men and people, promising to be his God and the God of his seed in a special sense, even as they were on their side in a special sense to serve him. This covenant of grace is on God's side expressed in the words, "Fear not, Abraham, I am thy shield and thy exceeding great reward:" on the side of Abraham, by the command, "I am the almighty God; walk thou before me, and be perfect;" these sentences being the introduction to the two solemn ratifications of the covenant recorded in Gen. xv. 11; xvii. 1. And as sign of this covenant, God enjoined upon Abraham and his descendants circumcision, which was the first initiation into legal ritualism. Since faith could not be inherited by natural generation, with the latter there was to be at least connected an external sign that should indicate that Abraham's seed was not to be merely his natural posterity, his children after the flesh; thus pointing typically to the true and spiritually-begotten seed of Abraham, that is, to Christ. This is the higher and more sacred significance which the rite of circumcision, —used, no doubt, by other nations,—possessed among the people of God. The Old Testament had many forms and customs in common with the heathen, because it spoke to the people in a symbolic language, peculiarly suitable to that olden time, just as we teach children by pictures; but all these forms will be found to be imbued in the Old Testament with a different and holier spirit and character than belongs to them in the natural religions of the heathen. Promise and faith, covenant and circumcision, are then, we see, the basis of the patriarchal dispensation of the Old Testament.

It was in Egypt that the patriarchal family grew into a people; and it was under Moses, one of the greatest and most gifted men the earth ever bore, that this people as such entered into the light of Revelation. God wooed Israel to be his own inheritance by wonders in Egypt, and in the Red Sea, and in the wilderness. But in so great a multitude it was evidently impossible to reckon upon the faith and obedience of each individual. Yet all the people were to bear a divine impress; this then could only be done incompletely and externally by that legal method already introduced in circumcision, which would but bring more clearly to light inward deficiencies and offences. Now the life of a people shapes itself necessarily into a constitution and laws of some kind. Therefore by a new creative act of love, God condescends to conform to this groundwork of national existence, reveals himself as the King of Israel, and gives them a church and state constitution, a law whereby natural, social, political, moral, and religious life is so governed as in the very smallest detail to bear the impress of the divine election, and collectively to express the holy divine will. Upon the basis of this law, whose core, namely, the ten commandments, the Divine Being personally delivered in awful majesty, and to the obedience of which the people voluntarily pledged themselves, a covenant was entered into at Sinai between Jehovah and Israel, which we are accustomed in a restricted sense to call the Old Testament. Its motto is, " Ye shall be holy, even as I am holy." But no inward sanctification, no holy and living renewal of the whole man, was conferred thereby. The law, although as being the will of God, it must needs be holy, nay, spiritual, is yet itself no life-giving spirit; it stands as a mere letter in opposition to the flesh, chastening and restraining it without bestowing on it a new birth, or having power to produce the true righteousness that avails before God. Thus the law does not itself bring salvation; it is only a schoolmaster to bring us to Christ the Saviour.

More narrowly considered the import of the law was, we shall find, threefold: 1*st*, It was a barrier whereby the people of God were separated from the unholy heathen nations around them, and kept under strict discipline in service to God. Thus a consecrated national soil was set apart from the rest of humanity, like a garden enclosed from out the curse-laden ground, for salvation to grow up in. Hence that Old Testament joy of pious men in the law of the Lord, as the distinguishing and gracious gift of God to his people, the most costly possession of Israel, the way of life to the upright, which we find expressed in the Psalms, as, for instance, Ps. xix. and cxix. And since Israel was thereby distinguished from all other nations as a holy people, a theocracy and special inheritance to the Lord (Ex. xix. 5, 6), the law served, in the *second* place, to convince the people themselves of their own unholiness in contrast to the divine will. The law entered, as St. Paul says (Gal. iii. 19, compared with Rom. v. 20), between the patriarchal promises and their fulfilment in Christ, that the offence might abound, *i.e.*, partly that it should be more fully manifested (as we, for instance, sometimes *throw out* a disease in order to cure it), partly that a full consciousness, an undisguised and humiliating confession of it should be brought about in the minds of men. Nor is this second purpose of the law inconsistent with the first, as it might at the first blush appear to be. To the great and carnal mass of the people the yoke of the law was often grievous, the barrier tempted to infringement, and the repeated falls into idolatry which marked the history of Israel for centuries, show in it an excess of sinfulness above that of the heathen; for the higher the revelation, the greater the apostasy. And therefore the sins of Israel met with denunciation and rebuke, such as we find nowhere else; the calls to repentance, and the threats of judgment by the prophets stand alone in ancient, nay, in universal literature; never was the truth spoken with such impressive and sacred earnestness to any people and its rulers. Thus the law bore fruit in the conscience of the prophets, and rendered them susceptible of the divine revelation for which they were appointed.

Nor was the barrier of the law in vain for the people at large. It impressed upon them a peculiar religious character. We find Israel, after its apostasies and its judgments, again and again returning to its God; and after the Babylonish Captivity, the law was observed with such scrupulous conscientiousness, that the Messiah could grow up and develop in the observance of all Old Testament ordinances. But still more did the life of certain pious Israelites, who were the very essence, so to speak, of the people, prove that the institution of an external holiness, and the revelation of internal unholiness, by one and the same law, were perfectly reconcilable. The more pure these kept themselves from the abominations of the heathen, the more earnestly they endeavoured to keep the commandments of God, the more they discovered that their sanctification was but an external one, which might indeed satisfy the eyes of men, but was incapable of fulfilling the law in the inward parts that God beholds; nay, that the law rather wrought in them all manner of concupiscence (Rom. iv. 2; ii. 28, 29; vii. 7, 8). Accordingly in the Psalms, which reveal to us the influence of the law upon the spirits of pious Jews, we find a depth and clearness of the sense of sin, which we meet with in no other ancient record. The penitential Psalms are the fruit of the law in the conscience of Old Testament believers, who were thus prepared for the singing of "new songs" in the spirit. And those righteous men and women with whom we meet on the threshold of the New Testament, walking in all the commandments and ordinances of the law blameless, Zacharias and Elisabeth, Simeon and Anna, were no self-righteous Pharisees, but the very people who waited for the consolation of Israel, and for redemption at Jerusalem (Luke i. 6, 11, 25, 38); so that it was just in those who most conscientiously observed the law that it produced the deepest knowledge of sin, and the yearning for atonement and redemption. In this sense the law served as the necessary preparation and foundation for the further development of the promises in the prophecies.

But not only so, the law itself offered, if not actual redemption and atonement, at least an external atoning and purifying; and this was its *third* object, which is made more especially apparent in the priestly and sacrificial rites. These showed, in the external and symbolic manner peculiar to the Old Testament, that only by the expiation of sin by death, only by a free-will and unspotted sacrifice, can fellowship be restored between a holy God and sinful men. Under this aspect of the law, the emblematic presents itself as the prefiguring, the symbolic as the typical, the Old Testament, by its sensuous and visible representations, was the preparation for the spiritual and essential blessings of the New.

And now let us briefly review this threefold purport of the law. It served to separate the people of Israel from the rest of the nations of the earth, to lead them to a knowledge of sin, and to afford them a type of redemption. The first of these purposes is connected more particularly with the law's political aspect, the second with its moral, the third with its ritualistic. In the first respect the Old Testament dispensation was the circumstantial way to that of the New; in the second its necessary condition; in the third its type and shadow. And it is in this intimate connexion between the Old and the New Covenants, between the law and the gospel, that we discover a sublime plan which constrains every severe and rational thinker to refer it to the love and wisdom of a personal God. The fault of our sceptics is not too much, but too little thought.

We now pass to the third stage of revelation,—the prophetic. It needed a long course of time to establish the people in the condition aimed at by the law. This was only thoroughly done under David and Solomon, whose reigns mark the glorious culminating point of Jewish history, which was itself typical and prophetic, as the Messianic Psalms show, of a still more glorious future. But to that period succeeded one of declension. Even under Solomon degeneration began, and it increased in the divided kingdom. The northern portion strengthened itself against the south by apostatizing from the pure worship at Jerusalem, and giving in its adherence to half or wholly idolatrous rites. The kingdom of Judah still indeed possessed the Holy City and the Temple, as well as the consecrated royal house of David, from which several pious monarchs sprung. The evil began therefore here, in the mere externality of religious observances and hypocritical lip service, with which, gradually, idolatrous tendencies associated themselves. These defections were met by the remonstrances of the prophets, who, since the days of Samuel (compare Acts iii. 24), had stood beside the kings as messengers of the Divine King, and exponents of his will. These prophets were men taken out of various classes, whom God had called by special revelations, who were from time to time mightily inspired by his Spirit, and commanded by him to appear before king and people as bold and incorruptible witnesses of divine truth.

It will be plain from the above, that these prophets had first to enter upon their public career in the apostate kingdom of Israel. It was here, at the time that, under Ahab and Jezebel, the worship of Baal most grossly prevailed, that Elijah and Elisha sought to bring about a reformation in favour of the true God and his law. The immense strength of the apostasy, which threatened to spread from the court through the whole people, required an extraordinary display of Jehovah in his omnipotence and majesty, and hence both these prophets were armed with the same miraculous power exercised by Moses in the presence of the Egyptians. On the other hand, while working thus by *deeds*, their *words* were not of such importance as to lead them to write down the revelations they had received. The written prophecies date from a later period, when Amos and Hosea arose in the north, and Joel, Isaiah, and Micah in the south, and from that time the prophets appear to have lost the power of miracles, while their prophetic insight, the results of which were to be preserved for races yet to come, was increased. But even these later prophets had for their immediate office the personally and verbally testifying before king and people, and calling backsliders to return to God. In Judah, where with much sinful practice a show of holiness was still observed, the prophetic office was more especially to insist upon true conversion and its genuine fruits. "To what purpose is the multitude of your offerings unto me?" cries the Lord, in the first chapter of Isaiah. "Bring no more vain oblations; incense is an abomination to me, the new moons and sabbaths, the calling of assemblies, I cannot away with: it is iniquity, even the solemn meeting. Wash you, make you clean; put away the evil of your doings before mine eyes; cease to do evil, learn to do well; seek judgment; relieve the oppressed; judge the fatherless; plead for the widow." Thus it was that the prophets contended with the people for a better and more spiritual righteousness, as, later, Jesus did with the Pharisees (Matt. v. 20). While they recalled men to God's rule of order and duty, they became more and more penetrated not only with the external character, but the inward nature and spirit of the law.

Thus, while prophecy rests upon the basis of the law, it is itself a new, progressive, more and more heart and soul affecting stage of revelation. It forms the transitional epoch between the law and the gospel, the bridge from the Old Testament to the New; and, as we plainly see, the prophets were enabled to get an insight into the new and better covenant and its spiritual character.

This leads us to that most prominent, but by no means only and exclusive aspect of prophetic activity—the prophecies properly so called. These, again, have a twofold aspect of their own; they denounce judgment, and announce salvation. The calls to repentance had, to the great majority of the people, been sounded in vain; the awful words had even been spoken to Isaiah at the time of his calling: "Make the heart of this people fat, and make their ears heavy" (Isa. vi. 10). There was consequently no thorough and enduring improvement of character and condition to be hoped for, and so the unrepented sin became liable to punishment. God, who has united the world's history with the history of redemption, had already prepared the rod of his anger for the rebellious people. The rise of the great Asiatic kingdoms of Assyria and Babylon, and their extension to the west, significantly synchronize with the apostasy of Israel. The more, therefore, the people of God strengthened itself in its idolatrous and ungodly position, the more definitely had the prophets to announce that it would become a prey to the heathen, to which it had assimilated itself, and would be carried away out of the holy land of its ancestors. We know how these threats of judgment were fulfilled in the Assyrian and Babylonian captivity.

But nevertheless the covenant of God with Israel still stood fast; the old promises made at the first to Abraham and renewed to David were not yet fulfilled, and could not possibly fail. God's people and kingdom could not be annihilated, and given over for ever as a prey to those heathen who so presumptuously abused the power lent to them. When, therefore, Israel had been chastened by the heathen, these last were to go themselves into judgment, and then when all flesh should have learned to humble itself before the Lord of lords, he would establish his kingdom in new, loftier, and eternal glory. Like to the dawn of a brilliant day, the image of the perfected divine kingdom, the Messianic age, rose before the prophetic gaze from out the stormy night of judgment. That which, beginning even in paradise, had been the light of the whole pre-Christian revelation,—although, so long as the Old Testament dispensation was itself advancing, it could only be the accompanying element of its progressive stages,—the Messianic prophecy namely, now became more and more the principal feature. The old dispensation had now no other office than to point to the new, the no longer typical but actual kingdom of God. The prophets foretold that the Messiah, that is, the anointed King of Israel, was, by an all-sufficient sacrifice, to make satisfaction for the sins of the people. Jehovah was to appear in his own person, and to be the Shepherd and King of humanity. The reign of peace, righteousness, and glory was to spread out of Sion over the whole inhabited world, and even the material creation was to have its share in the revival and redemption, the fulness of power and blessedness of this truly divine kingdom.

With promises such as these, the Old Testament concludes, and must needs conclude; beyond this it had nothing more to give, for here we have the very ideal of the New verbally present. Our place is appointed us in that dispensation of fulfilment which has itself historical stages, as the preparatory dispensation had. But that which has been up to this present time fulfilled in and by Jesus Christ, so eloquently witnesses to the divinity both of the prophecy and the accomplishment, of the Old and the New Testaments, that, respecting the prophetic dispensation, as before respecting the legal, we can confidently challenge each man only to open wide the eyes of his understanding, and bring to bear his utmost thinking powers, in order to convince himself that the cause of revelation is a good cause. He who thinks rationally must inevitably cease to think rationalistically.

On the part of God then, as we have seen, everything had been done to prepare for the new dispensation by the old. We might, indeed, have expected that a people in possession of so many and glorious divine testimonies would have adorned itself as a bride for Messiah, the coming Bridegroom. But such an expectation would contradict the tenor of all history.

"Many are called, few are chosen:" this is the almost universal axiom. Number and rank go for nothing in the kingdom of God. Just as in the days of Elijah there were but seven thousand in Israel who had not bowed the knee to Baal, and as in our own time we are wont to distinguish between the visible and the invisible Church of true Christians, so was it amongst the Jews during the period of expectation that intervenes between the close of prophecy and the beginning of the fulfilment. The externally restored nationality that succeeded to the exile, was the husk in which grew the kernel, that little flock of the elect who were being educated by the law and the prophets for a secret life in the fear of God, and the confident waiting for the consolation of Israel. This little flock was the living fruit of the Old Testament dispensation. It is here that, foremost of all, we meet with Mary, the representative, as it were, of believing Israel, who, by her humility and simplicity of faith, was fitted to become the mother of the Messiah. It is here we find Zacharias and Elisabeth, who were chosen to be the parents of the forerunner of Christ; here, too, were a number of fishermen and other Israelites without guile, whom the Lord afterwards chose to be the witnesses and apostles of his gospel. Such is ever the Divine method; with the least possible show an inward wealth, of which, it is especially true, that to him who hath shall be given; while, on the side of heathenism, we have the inverted human method, uniting with a high degree of external power and civilisation, inward emptiness and nothingness.

We must now contemplate those Gentile nations, which God left to their own devices. These innumerable multitudes may be divided into three classes, the unhistorical, semi-historical, and historical peoples. The unhistorical are those who in a more or less degree are degraded almost below the level of humanity, and have hardly attained to the faintest beginnings of culture. Such in our day are the millions of Southern and Central Africa, the American Indians, the aborigines of Australia and of the South Sea Islands, and the countless hordes of the north and the interior of Asia. Although not without religious ideas and customs, these people are yet so thoroughly sensual, that, generally speaking, they appear like the animals, to care only for the immediate wants of the present. They have no clear and connected consciousness of their own past, they know nothing of their own history; whereas it is just this unity of consciousness and memory through which life is apprehended as a connected whole, that constitutes the nature of a reasonable being or a historical people. Hordes and tribes who possess no history of their own, can, of course, take no part in the history of the world. One can only say that they vegetate on, propagating themselves from century to century, till some mighty divine impulse shall restore in them the human dignity they have nearly lost. But it is a heavy mystery weighing upon our race, an awful thought, which is very seldom pondered deeply enough, that so large a portion of the human race should be given over for ages to such an existence as this.

Among the semi-historical nations should be classed the Hindus, Chinese, and Japanese, as well as the Mexicans and other ancient American civilized peoples. Here there is no want of culture or history. These people reached a rapid and important elevation in the early period of their existence; they possessed the art of writing, a literature, and many other elements of civilisation; they are acquainted with their own past, and more or less clearly conscious of its history. But the remarkable fact here is, that after reaching that first elevation they seem to have come to a perpetual standstill. These nations still carefully shut themselves from contact with others, as though retaining something of the old dread that actuated the builders of Babel; "lest we be scattered abroad over the face of the earth." National egotism is, in its highest degree, stamped upon them all; there is an utter deficiency of that universal human sympathy which draws one nation towards another, and brings about historical events by friendly or inimical contact. Thus we have the wonderful spectacle of a history, begun indeed, but stationary, as it were arrested in its course; and this, too, is a mystery to which, taken up as we are with the great historical nations, we have not as yet given due importance, although these semi-historical nations constitute the largest section of the human race.

But these unhistorical and semi-historical nations dwell far away from us in different quarters of the globe; we find the historical grouped round that specially historical people of Israel: in Northern Africa, Greece, and Italy. If we compare the unhistorical races to a mass of stones and fragments; the half-historical races, to some specimen of ancient elaborate architecture, that endures for centuries in stony repose; the historical people may remind us of a city full of life and movement. What the unhistorical nations could never attain to at all, and the semi-historical only imperfectly, is brought to its highest perfection. We have in these last the three principal departments of the natural life of man, Arts, Science, and Politics, developed on a grand scale. In the first two, Greece; in the last, Rome; completed the civilizing process that had begun in the East. The remains of Grecian architecture and sculpture that we still possess, are ideals for all time. What Homer, Pindar, and Sophocles accomplished in poetry, Herodotus and Thucydides in history, is so classical in form that later centuries have ever returned to these sources, and ever will return. The Romans are pre-eminently the juridico-political nation. Within, they fixed their code with so much tact, circumspection, and equity, that even at the present day Roman law is of great importance to all civilized nations. Without, they conquered the whole east and west; it seems as if they had appropriated all the secrets of universal dominion from Assyria and Babylon, Cyrus and Alexander, in order to excel by far their teachers. In imperial Rome under Augustus, it may be said that we behold the heritage of the efforts and attainments of all historical nations. All that the culture of east and west had during many centuries produced, centred and culminated in the capital of the world. Augustan Rome may be looked upon as the historical result of the collective development of heathen antiquity.

If, however, we contemplate the inward side of this brilliant world of power and civilisation, we shall find therein a profound void and discontent. There is a want of the very heart of human life, a want of faith. The great developing elements of Rome's history, of politics and civilisation, necessarily exercised a destructive influence in this direction. The convulsions of disruption most deeply shook the nations during the last centuries before Christ, and uprooted on many sides national consciousness, that foundation of antique life, together with the religious element, intimately connected with it. Still more influential was the progress of scientific thought, which set gradually extending philosophical and historical convictions in opposition to faith in the popular mythology. The rich world of culture in the period immediately preceding Christ was a godless world.

Nevertheless man cannot long live without any religion, and accordingly even then the religious wants of his nature showed themselves in most varied and often in the strangest manners. Instead of the old lost faith, men sought to construct a new one of one kind or other. The secret teaching of the East was explored; the old mysteries of the Greeks revived; an attempt was made to gather truth out of all possible religions and philosophies; recourse was had to conjuration, astrology, fortune-telling, and secret arts of all kinds. The most opposite streams, whether pure or impure, were to flow into one great river, from which the thirsting soul was to drink light and life. The world-empire seemed engaged in giving birth to a world-religion. But no new garment was to be woven out of these old heathen rags; and the internal bankruptcy of Paganism, its incapacity to satisfy the deepest needs of humanity, was more and more revealed. We know from the Acts of the Apostles, as well as from the Roman satirists, that there were in the Roman empire many, distinguished women more particularly, who earnestly sought after

God, and joined themselves to the Jews, with whom they found a pure worship and a true Scripture. And when Christianity appeared, spite of all persecution, it found in the Roman empire a proportionately favourable reception and rapid extension. Now then the religion long yearned after had appeared !

Thus the ages of heathen development show us whereto humanity, left to itself, without God in the world, was able to attain. A great proportion sunk down to a nearly animal condition; another section made a promising start towards the unfolding of its natural energies, but in the midst of its career it stopped short, its strength was paralysed; the semi-historical people became prematurely old and weary,—a notable result this of living without God in the world;—and even that third portion of Pagan humanity, which, by the strenuous exercise of all its powers, strove after and attained the highest development, when it had reached its goal felt itself unhappy. It was without that inner life-spring of human wellbeing, *peace;* and it acknowledged that it could not procure itself that peace,—that salvation was of the Jews. Bethlehem, which signifies Bread-house, that least of all the cities of Judah, was the place where proud, yet in the midst of her abundance hungry Rome, must consent to receive the bread of life.

We are tempted to draw a parallel between the three stages of Jewish development, which we may designate as Patriarchism, Nationalism, and Universalism, and the three stages which we observe in the national life of Heathenism. The unhistorical peoples stand essentially on the patriarchal level. But while the family life of Abraham, Isaac, and Jacob, unfolding in covenant with God, and supported by his promise, joyously expanded and bore within itself the germ of a mighty national life, the corresponding stage of heathen existence either remained within the limitations of family and tribe, or having lost all ideal standard whatever, sank to the miserable condition of nomadic hordes. The semi-historical peoples, again, remind us of the Mosaic stage in Israelitish life, when the people of God began to have an independent and national culture of their own, which developed itself in strict separation from the rest of the nations. This union of internal civilisation, and jealousy of external influence, is just what we have seen to be characteristic of the Chinese, etc. But these latter remain in this condition, decay in it; they lack the impulse to universalism, which pervaded the people of Israel from the first, because they were the people of that God to whom the whole earth belonged (Exod. xix. 5); and knew themselves from their earliest origin appointed to be a blessing to the whole human race (Gen. xii. 3). This impulse towards universalism is the peculiarity of the heathen nations of the third class, namely, the historical. They realized it in the form of a great world-empire, or universal monarchy. But while the nations were in this manner brought out of isolation, they only in point of fact attained to a reciprocal destruction and deprival of national existence. Thus, every great monarchy in its turn destroyed many smaller states, while, on the other hand, Cyrus overthrew the Babylonians, Alexander the Persians, Rome the Greeks. In the same way, Israel too lost its national independence when drawn into the great current of the empire of the world. But to a crushing political universalism it could oppose the new life-giving religious universalism of its prophecies. All the great historical peoples have sunk without a promise, and are buried in the ruins of their former glory, but from Israel, according to the promise, a new divine universal kingdom has arisen out of the ruins of its material political existence; a kingdom that, originally founded in the Spirit, shall hereafter be manifested in external glory. While the people of God lay, like the rest of the nations as to outward condition, beneath the domination of the world-empire, its existence was not only preserved and spared for a better future, as was the case with no other, but in relation to the inmost and highest life of humanity, the law went forth to the rest of the world out of Zion, and Japhet still dwells in the tents of Shem.

At that period, when a meek and lowly maiden was dwelling at Nazareth, and at Rome a world-swaying Cæsar, beneath whose sceptre heathen humanity had reached its fulness of power and civilisation, and at the same time revealed most completely its inward emptiness and poverty, then, on the side of the people of God, and on that of the people of the world, the period of preparation had alike run its course. It is thus we understand the Christmas message,—"In the fulness of time God sent forth his Son."

V.

THE PERSON OF JESUS CHRIST.

IT is of the person of Jesus Christ that I would now speak to you. You feel with me that we enter here into the sanctuary. If God be holy, and we unholy, we are constrained to inquire, Who will lead us to him, so that we may not only know of him, but enter once more into his living and blessedness-conferring fellowship? For we are not to look upon our sinful condition as a *status quo*, in which we have only to do the best we can. Unless we determine to ignore the solemn problem of life altogether, we must needs seek after deliverance and redemption. Accordingly, from the very first this has been promised to us. In the people of the Old Testament, who were elected to that end, we behold the law and the prophets preparing the way for this redemption. The New Testament announces the fulfilment of the original promise in the person of Jesus Christ, the one Mediator between God and men; and also declares this to be no matter of human invention, having its origin in the heart of man, but the work of God for us; not a product of our reason, but a God-given fact for reason to receive. The eye must indeed be related to the solar light, or it could not perceive it; but it is not itself that light, nor can it produce light. Thus no speculations of the human understanding, but only the message of the gospel, can announce to us Christ, what for our sakes he became, and still is.

It is a solemn thing to speak of this. How shall we be so bold as to appear as the Lord's advocate, when needing rather that he should be ours? All we shall venture to do, is briefly to adduce the most prominent reasons we have for refusing to give up our belief in the Christ of our Gospels.

It is well for me that my proposed sketch does not embrace the whole of this great subject. I am not at present called upon to go into the atoning work of Christ, nor into his resurrection, ascension, and celestial reign. This will be the task of succeeding Lectures. I have now to limit myself to the person of Jesus Christ; to the great features of his character as revealed to us in his exalted career.

Regarding this subject, as indeed regarding necessarily all that is historical, we can have no other evidence but the narrative of contemporaries. The great question that at once arises, therefore, is, Whether this evidence be sufficient to substantiate so much that is marvellous and abnormal? A spirit of distrust on this head has become widely spread amongst us at the present day, and this distrust recommends itself as liberty and independence of thought; but thoughtful, serious, and candid examination is a far higher thing than mere doubt or distrust, and indeed it is our positive and appointed duty. Our consciences should recognise it as imperative to beware of relying for salvation upon anything unauthentic and unreliable. To such an examination, the alone genuine examination, beginning with, "If any man will do his will," the Lord himself invites us, as do also his apostles (John vii. 17; 1 Thess. v. 21.) We are not required in matters of faith to throw contempt upon reason and science, and to stifle rational thinking; on the contrary, we need to have thought set free from the prevailing prejudices of the time. We are not to forfeit any of the honour put upon us by God of being his free, his personally-convinced servants. And what does this conviction mean? It means the being overpowered by the strength of his testimony.

The very opposite of conviction is a state of mind which we sometimes hear confessed much as follows:—"How can we be required to place implicit faith in Jesus, when there are no means of positively ascertaining what he was, what he did, or what he said?" But is this indeed so? Christendom has for eighteen centuries held, that on all these points sufficient certainty was attainable, although beneath them all there lay a divine mystery, which we could never thoroughly exhaust, any more than we can the mystery of many comparatively unimportant natural facts around us. It was faith that led Christendom to knowledge; the want of faith, on the contrary, leads merely, as we see, to want of knowledge. Is this, then, to constitute the triumph of advancing intelligence?

Allow me here a few introductory observations. Professor Schmidt of Strasburg, a profound historian, wrote a few years back a beautiful work, on which the French Academy bestowed the crown. Its subject was, "Civil and Social Life in the old Roman world, and its transformation by Christianity." The author began by painting Pagan society in ancient Greece and Rome. Of course he exulted in the beautiful ideas, the noble characters, the brilliant deeds, which are so abundantly found therein, for which reason he felt himself all the more free to disclose the dark side of the picture; and, accordingly, out of the laws and written documents of the ancients themselves, he gives us incontrovertible proof of the grievous evils of their whole condition,—their political constitution, marriage, the relations between parents and children, the treatment of the poor, of slaves, of strangers,—life being, in fact, in all its circumstances, essentially based upon selfishness, and therefore liable to inevitable disorder.

With this melancholy picture he proceeds to contrast the Christian Church, which, recruiting itself chiefly from the poor and despised, always threatened, and often heavily oppressed by persecution, nevertheless held its ground, and offered to the world a new and hitherto unseen spectacle, the spectacle of a society based on perfectly new principles, based in all its relations, not on selfishness, as was heathenism, but, on the contrary, on love and mercy. And more than this, not only was the Christian community founded on unselfish love, but its influence became even over those who hated, persecuted, and sought by most cruel violence to blot it from the face of the earth, so great and irresistible; it so progressed, by slow degrees indeed, silent and unremarked, but irresistible, that even before the time of Constantine many elements appear both in laws and customs, which we can only explain by Christian influence, till at length that great emperor himself considered it the wisest and most politic measure, openly to declare himself on the side of this bloodily persecuted but indestructible sect.

But whence, we would ask, comes this incomparable power that triumphs by suffering and death?—the power which has worked such marvels, which, without outward might, has conquered the world's mighty ones; nay, which has effected what the wisdom of the wise, the strength of the strong, could never accomplish—what neither emperors nor philosophers attained to or even strove after—effected the transformation of the world, and introduced into a social fabric, raised and resting upon selfishness, the new and active principle of unselfish love. From whence does this wondrous power proceed? To what origin are we to refer it? What affects the everyday collective life of humanity must indeed spring simultaneously and independently in many hearts and minds; but the greater any cause, the more certainly do we find that there are few, nay, perhaps only *one*, who first grasps the thought, first speaks the word, or does the deed which afterwards others appropriate, because they find therein realized what *all* vaguely sought, and none could of themselves attain.

Now, this has been in the highest degree exemplified in Christianity. If we inquire what it was that so fundamentally transformed society, whether we direct our inquiries to Christendom itself, which was the instrument of this great achievement, or to the distinguished Christians who were foremost in the struggle, all agree in not ascribing their religion to themselves, all profess to have derived it from the *one* Jesus. He is become as even they who do not believe in him allow, "the great turning-point of the world's history."[1] And is it regarding Him that advancing science has to con-

[1] Hörler *On Faith and Knowledge in Religion*, p. 46.

fess that it is without certainty as to what He was, did, or said? Is it before Him that it must "silently stand as before an eternal problem?"[1] Not as before the manifested mystery of God, in which we believe, but before a problem about which we do not know what to think! Surely, even in a scientific point of view, this were a lamentable result of so much examination and so much learning. Let us see whether something better be not really attainable.

We will set out with what is least open to controversy, with what, indeed, is almost universally allowed. Who, then, was Jesus considered simply in his human character, and for the time entirely apart from the miraculous element?[2] He grew up, we find, in humble circumstances, in the small and despised city of Nazareth, whose inhabitants, whenever they are mentioned, impress us as a rough and limited race. He was so poor that even during his public career he seems to have been in great measure dependent upon the gifts of his friends. The people spoke of him as the carpenter's son (Matt. xiii. 55), nay, even as himself a carpenter (Mark vi. 3); therefore we conclude that he helped his father in his daily work. He had not passed through any school of the Rabbis: "Whence hath this man this wisdom?" was the astonished query raised as soon as he began to teach (Matt. xiii. 54; John vii. 15). We can neither presuppose nor trace in him the many-sided culture springing from intercourse with distinguished men, or the study of choice books. We only observe that he is thoroughly acquainted with the Scriptures of the Old Testament.

Now these are circumstances that would hardly have been invented by those whose wish it was to do him especial honour. These are facts, at all events, that an Israelite would never have dreamed of associating with his Messiah. No doubt they were circumstances in which a man might become, humanly speaking, a worthy character, conscientious, upright, capable. and be advantageously separated from evil surroundings. But, on

[1] Hörler *On Faith and Knowledge in Religion*, p. 47.
[2] See *The Christ of History*, by John Young.

the other hand, we should hardly have expected to see a man who could thoroughly transform a world emerge from such a position. How could he, in a condition of such obscurity, have acquired the culture and the knowledge of human nature, without which influence seems impossible? How could he have gained sufficient self-reliance to appear amongst men, and with keen, free glance to penetrate into their character and their actions?

Nevertheless, Jesus did so appear, this poor, unlearned, unknown, and inexperienced carpenter; and his appearance was made when he was only thirty years of age. He had not attained to the experience of age. Neither do we find in him the violence or precipitation of fervent youth. He appeared without any powerful friends, without support of any kind from the power of those in authority; nay more, he at once excited against himself the prejudice and the jealousy of the powerful. He appeared, and he worked for only a few years, then he died the disgraceful death of a criminal. And in this short time what was it he did? We leave out of the question his miracles, which many doubt or reject altogether. With their exception, he accomplished few positive deeds, in the common acceptation of the word; he conquered no lands, ruled no people, founded no specific social organization, arrived at no results of learned inquiry, produced no heart-stirring poems. All that we know of him beside his disputed miracles, are a few simple sayings, without art or system, spoken incidentally, now in the chamber, then in the highway, here to one or to a few, there to great multitudes,—most simple words; and these have transformed the world, and are still, after the lapse of eighteen centuries, dearer to thousands than their very life. Truly this is a marvellous thing!

But further, he appeared in the midst of a generation that not only the evangelists, whom we might suspect of partiality, represent as corrupt and degraded, but the Jewish historian, Josephus, paints in by no means favourable colours. And this young, unknown, and uncultured journeyman appears as a reprover of these countrymen of his, holds up their sins to view insists upon a fundamental change of character and disposition, and not merely rebukes the evil and adulterous generation, but more especially and severely its highest and most learned class, the Pharisees, with their apparently holy punctiliousness, the men who gave the tone to the rest; and this he does without having the prestige of years, or the vantage-ground of a secure external position, and he is, nevertheless, tolerated for three whole years; and he does this with an inward security in which we never trace the faintest influence of a lowly origin, or the evidence of his having grown up in narrow circumstances and homely surroundings. Calmly and majestically he goes upon his way. No touch of servile fear impedes him. He confronts men alike without timidity and boastfulness. What induced him to come forth from his obscure home in Nazareth? No one knew him, no one called him, not the people, not his disciples, for as yet he had none; nor was it any accidental occurrence which brought him forward, and was the commencement of an activity that afterwards transcended its original aims. Nothing of all this; there was within him a pure, inward impulse, which, in spite of his want of the learning of the schools, or any customary preparation, necessitated his coming forward. It was *his* thought, *his* will, *his* deed, which alone insured him such attention and recognition as he received.

But what kind of recognition was this? Even unmoved, indifferent Jewish people, agreed at least so far with his disciples as to call him a prophet (Matt. xxi. 16); and in our own day, even those who will not be his disciples, acknowledge him to have been "a man of impressive prophetic power." Now, what is a prophet? Many associate the word with one who foretells things to come, it matters not of what nature. But such a one would be rather a fortune-teller than a prophet. It does, indeed, belong to the character of a true prophet to foretell certain facts that afterwards come to pass, but this is not his principal office, not the basis of his character and his calling.

A prophet is rather one who directly expresses the hidden counsel and will of God; who reveals what had been before a mystery hid in God, who announces his Being, his work, and his government, and does this alike on the side of righteousness as on that of grace, of judgment as of mercy. It is true that the preacher of the gospel has the same truths to declare. But the authority for his preaching is the written word. In him there is no original divine revelation such as the prophet knows himself to have received; one of the most remarkable features in the self-consciousness of the genuine prophet, being the positiveness with which he distinguishes between himself and the false prophets, to whom the Lord has not spoken (Jer. xiv. 14; xxiii. and xxviii.), while he, on the other hand, testifies of judgment as of grace in the name of the Lord.

On the side of judgment, the prophet declares to the people the character and the claims of God; he enforces the law, and the law in its internal bearing; he rebukes transgression and points to punishment. Thus his word is the voice of God quickening the conscience of the people. "Your offerings are an abomination to me," says God by the mouth of Isaiah, (i. 11-15), iniquity and solemn meetings together I cannot away with; I will not have the people draw near me with their mouth only (xxix. 13). It was not for this I spake unto their fathers (Jer. vii. 22). In harmony with these prohibitions were the fundamental principles inculcated; dependence upon the living God and not upon idols, practising simple truth and love to their neighbours, learning to do well, judging righteously, relieving the oppressed, judging the fatherless, pleading for the widow (Isa. i. 17). Upon these conditions forgiveness and favour were promised to the penitent.

But, on the other side, the prophets never fail to place in sight of the people new life and salvation in the grace of their covenant God. "I am the Lord, I change not, therefore ye children of Jacob are not consumed" (Mal. iii. 6). "My thoughts towards you are thoughts of peace not of evil" (Jer. xxix. 11). It is true, that the decision lies between conversion and destruction, life or death, and the Searcher of hearts knows how many *will* not listen to the deciding word, and on that account will grow ever more and more dull and hardened (Isa. vii. 9, 10). They have moved me to jealousy with that which is not God, and I will move them to jealousy with those who are not a people, which I shall bring upon them (Deut. xxxii. 21). The heathen whose idolatries they have shared, shall be to them a heavy rod of chastisement. But after they have exercised and abused the power committed to them for a time, the heathen shall themselves be cast away. In Israel, on the other hand, a remnant shall be left. The whole people is not to have a share in the promised salvation by its natural strength, "though they be as the sand of the sea," that will avail them nothing; it is only a remnant that is to "return and to be saved" (Isa. x. 22). This remnant signified those who under the heavy judgments that fell on them thoroughly repented, humbled, and purified themselves; "an afflicted and poor people that trust in the name of the Lord" (Zeph. iii. 12). These shall be holpen, so as to have a share in the promised kingdom of peace (Isa. ii. 2-5); whose King is to be that wonderful Child who is to come forth out of the stem of Jesse (Isa. ix. 6; xi. 1).

At times the representation of his triumphs sounds as though he were to be a mighty warlike hero; but yet the description given of the suffering servant of God, who was to give his soul an offering for sin (Isa. liii.), reminds us that deliverance is to come, "not by might nor by power, but by the Spirit of the Lord of hosts" (Zech. iv. 6). And thus this warrior of the stem of David is to smite not with the iron sword of his adversaries, but with the rod of his mouth, and the breath of his lips (Isa. xi. 4). He is to be the deliverer who will judge the ungodly, establish the kingdom in Israel, and allow to an anointed remnant of the Gentiles a participation in its glories. These also shall be called by the name of the living God whom they serve (Amos ix. 12); and then the whole earth shall be filled with the knowledge of the Lord as the waters cover the seas, for the branch out of the root of Jesse shall be for an ensign of the people (Isa. xi. 9, 10).

Such are briefly the fundamental ideas developed in prophecy. It is on these that the various prophetic utterances are based, however modified they may be by varying circumstances. In all of them, threats and promises alike are placed within the choice of man's free will. "At what instant I shall speak concerning a nation and concerning a kingdom to pluck up, and to pull down, and to destroy it; if that nation against whom I have pronounced turn from their evil, I will repent of the evil that I thought to do unto them. And at what instant I shall speak concerning a nation and concerning a kingdom to build and to plant it; if it do evil in my sight I will repent of the good wherewith I said I would benefit them" (Jer. xviii. 7-10). Thus it may sometimes happen that a prophet promises a certain definite deliverance out of a definite peril, conditionally upon faith, and if the recipient of the promise have faith the deliverance is accomplished. Thus Hezekiah was saved precisely in the wonderful manner predicted by Isaiah, the King of Assyria did not come into the city of Jerusalem, nor shoot an arrow against it (Isa. xxxvii. 33). If, on the contrary, certain predictions were nullified by the unbelief of those to whom they were conditionally made, the ultimate principles of God's counsel and of prophecy were never departed from.

Such then is a prophet. And it was exactly in this prophetic character that Jesus appeared. He, like his Forerunner the Baptist, began with the cry, "Repent ye! Change your ways, for the kingdom of God is at hand." And what the true character of children of this kingdom is to be, he proceeds to lay to the heart and conscience of his hearers in the simple noble words of the Sermon on the Mount,—words which have not only made on his contemporaries, but upon men of all times, an irresistible impression of having been spoken by one possessing omnipotence. How, in his character of genuine prophet, he enlightens the conscience: "Except your righteousness shall exceed the righteousness of the Scribes and Pharisees, ye shall in no case enter the kingdom of heaven" (Matt. v. 20). How he expounds the law as relating not only to the outward action, but to the very thoughts and intents of the heart: "He that looketh upon a woman to lust after her, hath committed adultery with her in his heart" (Matt. v. 28). Nothing short of the highest may suffice: "Be ye perfect, even as your Father which is in heaven is perfect" (Matt. v. 48); and this perfection is to be especially manifested in love to enemies (ver. 44-47). It is thus the law was to be fulfilled (Matt. v. 17), by a twofold love, a loving God with all the heart, and our neighbours as ourselves (Matt. xxii. 37); but this love is to be in very deed, not in appearance, not in hypocritical alms-givings, prayers, and fastings to be seen of men (Matt. iv.); not in lip service (Matt. xv. 7); nor in keeping the Sabbath-day by mere inaction (Mark iii. 4).

The announcement of this promised kingdom of heaven, kingdom of God, is intended to move the hearts of the people to render a free and sincere obedience to the Divine law. But Jesus has the same knowledge as well as the same experience as the prophets of old. He knows and he experiences that many are only rendered harder and duller by his glad tidings of the kingdom of heaven; and it is in accordance with the justice of God, that on those who *will* not hearken, this should be the effect produced. They *must* be hardened and dulled by preaching. "He wills that his word should have on them the effect of rain upon the already saturated ground." If it be the purpose of their stiff-neckedness *not* to return, why, it is God's purpose also; it *must* be be so. What they will not receive to their salvation must subserve their ruin (Matt. xiii. 13). Therefore it is that Christ concludes his preaching with denouncing woe against the Pharisees (Matt. xxiii.); and prophesying against Jerusalem and the Temple, that not one stone of it shall be left upon another (Matt. xxiv.)

If, however, this last prophecy was most strikingly fulfilled, and fulfilled indubitably against the will and actual command of the Roman general Titus, I must not, on the other hand, disguise that the same prophecy contains difficulties which are painfully perplexing to some, to others a glad pretext for rejecting the whole. I allude to the verses, "There are some standing here who shall not taste of death till they shall see the Son of man coming in his kingdom" (Matt. xvi. 28). "This generation shall not pass away till all be fulfilled" (Matt. xxiv. 34). When Jesus so spake, does it not appear as if he gave his disciples cause to expect not only that this doom would fall upon Jerusalem in their lifetime, but Christ himself return to judgment?

There is confessedly a difficulty here such as often meets us in the case of the old prophets; but the main point which we must keep in view in order to clear it up, is, that these divine matters are not to be measured by the narrow scale of short-lived man, and also that a particular prophecy may often have a many-sided fulfilment, differing from the apparent tenor of the words, its accomplishment being committed to the action of human free-will, and contingent upon faith or unbelief. The old prophets, as we have seen, expressly declare this fact. Thus it may happen that the first stage of judgment may begin at a period very far removed from the execution of that judgment as a whole, and the establishment of the promised kingdom of peace. "Henceforth," he says to his enemies, "ye shall see the Son of man sitting on the right hand of power, and coming to judgment" (Matt. xxvi. 64). These words indicate a gradual coming by stages of indefinite length. But this does not in the smallest degree affect the eternal and unchangeable fundamental laws of judgment and mercy, as they were laid down by the old prophets, and for ever confirmed and enlarged in the prophecies of Jesus.

For finally, Christ, too, promises the kingdom only to the little flock (Luke xii. 32); as Isaiah did to the remnant that should return. "The gate is strait, and narrow is the way that leadeth unto life, and few there be that find it." Such is the declaration of the prophet of the New Covenant (Matt. vii. 14). But all who endure to the end shall be saved (Matt. xxiv. 13); and if many of the children of the kingdom, the Israelites who had the first claims to it, are cast out through their own fault (Matt. viii. 12); on the other hand, the gospel of the kingdom is to be preached to the whole world, and out of all nations some shall be saved (Matt. xxiv. 14).

Such, then, is the preaching of the Prophet of Nazareth! Thus he speaks, not hypothetically, dubiously, inquiringly, argumentatively, like the philosophers of old, but with gentle certainty, uttering simple, profound, powerful words, striking home alike to the reason and the conscience, living words, not phrases, not formulas. Even those who see in them much to object to—often probably because they do not understand them, and fail to understand by reason of unbelief—still affirm that "our moral life finds its highest ideal presented there in visible forms," and that "even the religious knowledge and thought of the present time sees its deepest truths expressed in many of these maxims."

And this will be our experience, too—if only we bestow earnest reflection upon them,—with regard even to those words which might at first somewhat surprise us by their appearance of harshness; as, for instance, the prohibition to bury his father, imposed under peculiar circumstances upon a disciple (Luke ix. 60); or the severe check which the help-imploring father receives, "Unless ye see signs and wonders, ye will not believe" (John iv. 48); or the apparently Jewish exclusiveness with which Jesus treats the Canaanitish mother (Matt. xv. 21). Everywhere, when we carefully examine the whole context, we find light where there seemed to be darkness; we discover how strikingly his words apply to the character of the case in point, and express, besides their more immediate and particular application, a universal truth that proves itself suggestive of a hundred other applications, and thus our confidence grows in that which still remains uncomprehended.

In the same manner, in his Sermon on the Mount, he lays down the principles of his kingdom by particular illustrations intelligible to any child, and yet such that the mature man finds in them inexhaustible profundities,—feels, for instance, inwardly convinced that there are cases in which he would fail to conform to the spirit of the words, if he were scrupulously to adhere to their letter. This applies evidently to the plucking out the right eye and cutting off the right hand, and it equally applies to giving alms to some begging impostor,—to do which would be no true almsgiving, that is, no work of mercy;—and to many other cases of the kind. The words of Christ, in fact, are spirit and life. They have a foretaste of eternity, whether, for instance, we take the benedictions with which he opened the sermon on the mount, or that address to his disciples on the evening before he suffered, which St. John has preserved for us (xiv.-xvii).

But is it not indeed marvellous, that a young, inexperienced, and obscure man, in the course of three years' teaching at most, should succeed in doing what the fairest efforts, the most admirable views, the most distinguished writings of the sages of Greece, of a Plato and an Aristotle, failed to do? That he, and he alone, should bring the deepest truths concerning God and man, and man's divine destiny,—concerning the love of God to us, and our love to God and to our neighbour,—within the reach of the Jewish people at large, nay, of all the nations upon earth? Whence hath the man these doctrines? Who is he that doeth such things? We must needs begin to think greatly, and ever more greatly of this prophet.

But the greatest thing of all is, that he himself possesses in full measure the meekness and love that he enjoins. His word is confirmed by his character. This, in some degree or other, was also the rule with other prophets. They too announced God not only by their words, but by their personal conduct. Balaam stands out as an evil exception, when, spite of his insincerity, he is constrained to serve God, and prophetically to announce his councils. For the rest, they whom the Lord employed as his instruments, were men of faith, of holy zeal, of obedience to the truth, at a cost of heavy suffering. "Behold," says Isaiah, "here am I, and the children the Lord has given me, for signs and for wonders in Israel" (viii. 18). How much Jeremiah had to bear in the discharge of his office, and how nobly he bore it! How hard Hosea must have felt it to be commanded, just as he entered upon his prophetic career, to go and marry a woman who was an adulteress,—a most striking injunction, by the way, which has given occasion to much impure ridicule, and which, nevertheless, when we rightly understand the whole context, is one of the passages where the holy majesty and grace of God shine forth most gloriously.

But it is in no way inconsistent with the holy character of these servants of God, nay, rather it belongs to it, that they should occasionally most thoroughly confess the taint of sin that cleaves to their hearts by nature. "Woe is me!" exclaims Isaiah, "for I am a man of unclean lips, and I dwell among a people of unclean lips" (vi. 5). Now this was not the case with Jesus. His disciples are unanimous in testifying that he impressed them as fulfilling the prophetic description (Isa. liii. 9). "He did no sin, neither was guile found in his mouth" (1 Pet. ii. 22). "He," that is in his personal experience, "knew no sin" (2 Cor. v. 21).

Indeed his whole character makes upon us the impression of pure and spotless holiness. It is true that we every now and then meet with passages that at the first glance surprise us; as, for instance, a speech to his mother, which sounds like a lack of filial reverence, "Woman, what have I to do with thee?" (John ii. 4); or again, his impetuous anger against the money-changers in the Temple (John ii. 15, 16); or his attack upon the Pharisee, whose guest he was (Luke xi. 39); or that injury done to the property of the Gadarenes (Mark v. 43); the cursing of the barren fig-tree, and such like. These are incidents that we do not at first comprehend; but gradually, with regard to one or the other, new light breaks in upon us, so that what at first shocked us, not only shocks us no more, but shines out as a new instance of his pure and holy nature. For instance, those words spoken to his mother are, we discover, not hard or irreverent, though distant, and intended to convey to her, at the beginning of his public career, that henceforth she is no more to use a mother's authority, but to let him rest upon his own judgment, when the hour that he knows to be his shall have come. "When Jesus, with apparent severity, admonished his mother to be patient, and not to interfere with his calling, he bestowed on her the lesson she needed, in order to have faith in him. It is evident that, for Mary above all others, it must have been difficult to submit to him as to her Redeemer, on whom she must believe like the rest. Therefore, his very love to her, which must needs be truthful, could not display itself otherwise than by proving to her that when he spoke or acted in his great vocation he no more belonged to her than to others. And by thus placing her in what she herself soon felt her proper place, he made faith in him as easy to her as possible, and gave a counterpoise to the effect of their habitual domestic life. He honoured her as his mother, indeed, but not at the cost of his heavenly Father, his calling, and the love he bore to her soul."[1] And so in other cases, careful consideration easily rectifies our first impressions, while each new light strengthens our confidence even with regard to what still perplexes us. It is not within my power to go further into details in this lecture, but I may be permitted to refer you to what I have elsewhere done in this direction.[2]

There is one point, however, to which I would now call your attention. Even those who demur and criticise such imperfectly understood passages as these, do not, with the exception of a few openly profane among them, venture to assert, that in any instance Jesus sinned,—they only suggest that, if such and such an incident were historically true, it would be a flaw in his perfections, a weakness, or a limitation. Such is the power exercised, over even their spirits, by the "exceedingly grand and exalted image of Christ."

But, nevertheless, it does not suffice to concede to him this indefinite though exceeding exaltation,—the gospel positively declares that he was without sin.

[1] Dorner *On the Sinless Perfection of Jesus*, p. 11. Gotha, 1862.
[2] In my Lectures upon the Life of the Lord Jesus. Basle, 1858.

Sceptics can doubtless continue to reply, that no one can know this for a certainty; can remind us how little information after all we have about him; a few fragments merely of his public life, and one single incident out of the thirty years of his obscure youth. Even though his enemies, spite of all their endeavours, could find no well-grounded accusation to bring against him, but only calumnies, perversions, false witness; even though Pilate could find no fault in him; even though the despair of Judas arose from his having betrayed innocent blood, what, they ask, could all these have known of the depths of his heart? For even his disciples, who received a permanent impression of blameless purity from the spectacle of his daily walk, did not know the whole of his life, and could not read his inmost thoughts.

True, but certainly we ought not to under-estimate the fact that of all which these eye-witnesses did observe or record, there is not the least incident liable to censure except through misapprehension or ill-will. Now we know how liable even those who exercise the greatest self-control are to failure in small things, but here there is no record of such. At the same time, his whole character is far removed from anything of calculation, —anything put on, constrained, artificial. Word and deed are alike simple and majestic. He is most acute and precise in his appeals to conscience; he discovers the very ground of the heart, for he thoroughly knows sinners in their sins, and rebukes them for their good. And yet for all his keen insight, he is no despiser of men, but very pitiful towards them. What tender love he has for the degraded woman of Samaria; for her who anointed his feet, being a sinner; for the fallen disciple that denied him; for Jerusalem that rejected him! He is moved with compassion for the sheep that have no shepherd. "Father, forgive them;" this is the breath of his whole life. Meekness and humility, grace and truth, make up his being; this was the impression received by susceptible hearts, and there was not a passage in his life to disturb that impression.

And this experience of theirs they have handed down

to us in a representation that testifies to its own faithfulness. Whence could they have derived it, if they had not seen and known it? In such a case they must have drawn the idea from themselves, their inward views, their own actual character. But do men afford such an example of spotless purity as this? Our conscience, indeed, may demand it, but who that looks within finds there the fulfilment of conscience's demands? What poet or historian, ever before or after, sketched so perfect a form. True, Xenophon says, speaking of his noble master Socrates, "No one ever saw Socrates do, or heard him say anything that was irreligious or unholy." But how external and low was the standard of holiness among the Greeks compared to that of the evangelists.

We repeat it, a description such as that of the holy character and conduct of Jesus is without a parallel; so spotlessly pure, and—let us observe this well—at the same time so life-like, so true to nature, so individually personified, that no human imagination could ever have created it. What should we men do if we sought, from our own resources, to draw the image of a sinless man? Why, we should harp upon his sinlessness, we should insist upon his freedom from this sin and from that sin, and we should heap superlatives of virtues and excellencies one on the other. But to produce a living, personal, individual character such as that of our Lord in the Gospels allowedly is, and moreover to invent a history in which this personality should be retained throughout most widely varying circumstances, and to do all this simply, naturally, plainly, grandly, this were beyond the reach of the greatest poet. This, however, the evangelists have done; they have done it artlessly, without being highly gifted poets; they have done it so that misapprehension may stumble at much, till further light breaking in upon the mind, each stumbling-block is seen to be a fresh trait of moral grandeur; they have done it so as not to conceal from us how much there was in his character which contradicted their own preconceptions of legal piety, and of what became the Messiah; they have done it, have been able to do it in short, because they speak of that which they have *seen* and *heard* and *experienced.*

And it is in strict conformity with this character of the real and the experienced that they represent this spotless holiness of Christ, not as an unassailed incapability of all temptation, but as a purity which, though inherent, had to struggle and resist to the very end. The most painful part of this struggle consisted in Jesus not finding himself in the condition of original humanity, not growing up in undisturbed peace, but being, from the earliest period of his life, surrounded by temptation, seeing forms of sinful pleasure, bearing the burden of the sorrows of others, scared by sufferings of all kinds which in their totality are called death, and which the Scripture teaches us to consider as the wages of sin. The more pure his nature, the more repugnant and contrary to it must all these have been. This was not sin, this belonged to his very holiness. "I have a baptism to be baptized with," he says, "and how am I straitened till it be accomplished!" (Luke xii. 50.) "Thou art an offence to me" (Matt. xvi. 23); it is thus he rebukes Peter, because he felt how the temptation to avoid suffering might enter into his heart. Thus he bore continually a burden laid upon him by his intercourse with sinners (Matt. viii. 17).

This agony rose at length to trembling and dismay, and to a sense of being forsaken by God. So little is Christ a mere ideal hero. So deeply and naturally human is he in his feelings. But in everything he overcomes. Never is there any assertion of himself, save as a child pouring out his heart before his Father. This pure, this holy impulse of his nature to resist suffering and death, how truly, how entirely he surrenders it: "Not my will, but thine be done." He who does not acknowledge this victory greater than any won on battle-plain, knows nothing of what is great before God. He who can confound this, being made perfect through suffering, as the epistle to the Hebrews has it, with the apprehension and timidity of a sinner, has as yet no discriminating faculty whatsoever.

Such is that perfectly holy Being whom the evangelists paint from the life of which they were eye-witnesses. Do you, however, still insist that our knowledge of him is too incomplete, fragmentary, uncertain, wanting fuller proof, since even the most intimate of the disciples could not vouch for the inward life? I reply, we have a witness that sets a seal to all that has been hitherto said; we have Christ's own account of himself: "Which of you accuseth me of sin?" (John viii. 46) was the challenge he once made to his enemies, who could only answer him by groundless insults. Not one of them could bring a specific charge against him. Yet, what they said, or even what they had not got to say, is comparatively little. What decides the point was his daring *to put such a question.* What man is there, even the noblest amongst us, who could venture to ask such a thing of the rudest of his contemporaries? If we say we have no sin, we deceive ourselves; nay, we make the holy God himself a liar (1 John i. 8, 10). Thus, then, nothing could have been more impious than a question like this, if, in the inmost recesses of the heart of Jesus, there had been the slightest consciousness of sin.

There may, perhaps, be some among you in whom the critical researches of the present day have infused some doubt as to the authenticity of the Gospel of St. John, and consequently of the passage in question. But even this will hardly enable you to escape the teaching of the three earlier evangelists, and they attribute parallel expressions to Jesus. In his sermon on the mount, he says to his hearers, "If ye, then, being evil" (Matt. vii. 11), but he does not range himself among these evil ones, rather places himself in contradistinction to them as one who is not so. His enemies exalt him by the very reproach they bring against him: "This man receiveth sinners" (Luke xv. 2); but no one pretends that he is himself one. "He is come to seek and to save those who were lost" (Luke xix. 10); no need that any should seek and save him. He teaches all his disciples without exception to pray: "Forgive us our trespasses." But however clear and correct his insight into the sinfulness of the human heart, we never hear from him an admission of personal consciousness of sin. In none of his prayers does he ever humble himself and implore mercy; whereas it is in the most distinguished saints that we usually meet with the deepest convictions of natural corruption, the strongest statements of guilt, the most striking expressions of self-accusation. But in all his expressions concerning himself, Jesus invariably appears holy, undefiled, and separate from sinners.

It is thus he represents himself. If then he had not been this in truth, what inconceivable self-delusion, nay, what blasphemous impiety, would he have been chargeable with. It is this that constitutes the strength of his own testimony to himself; testimony to which in other cases we should object, for which of us is impartial in his own cause. But it was necessary that Jesus should bear that witness to his own nature which none other could bear, since none other could penetrate into that holiest place. And we needs must believe the evidence of his own words, since self-delusion, or rather an insane and impious falsehood, united with the sublimity of his being, the exalted holiness of all that comes within the sphere of our powers of judgment, would be simply inconceivable.

But there remains one objection which I may not suppress; it would be the strongest of all, if only it were cogent; that is, if it succeeded in proving a consciousness of sin in Jesus, from any practical admission of his own. Why, we are asked, did Jesus submit to baptism at the hands of that Baptist who preached and conferred the baptism of repentance, and to whom the people came confessing their sins. To this I would reply, that it is most inconsistent to insist upon this fact of baptism without, at the same time, insisting upon the circumstances that preceded and attended it. If we consider these, we shall find that the words exchanged between Jesus and the Baptist, most definitely prove that Jesus in receiving baptism made no confession of any sins of his own; that he submitted to the ordinance not as a sinner but only as a mediator; in the sense, namely, of thus entering upon his office, entering, that is, into sympathy with the wants of the sinner, and by the way of suffering for the sins of the world, fulfilling all righteousness (Matt. iii. 13-17).

But if this objection be relinquished, there is still another and more important one to be made; his own words in answer to the rich young man who asked him (Matt. xix. 17), "Good Master, what shall I do to have eternal life. Jesus said to him, Why callest thou me good; there is none good but one, God." What do we need further, say many; Have we not heard it out of his own mouth? There is none good but one, God! What can be the true and simple inference from this, but, Thou art mistaken if thou callest me good; keep the epithet for God, to whom alone it belongs.

But is this indeed the true inference? It would certainly be so if one like ourselves had spoken these words. But we may not so understand them in the mouth of Jesus, so long as a whole series of quite opposite expressions retain their force. Nay, this very passage, if it be considered together with the context, forbids such a conclusion. For, immediately afterwards follows that declaration about the rich, how hardly they enter the kingdom of heaven, and when the disciples start at it, that other declaration of more universal range, the things that are impossible with men are possible with God.

But according to the tenor of the whole gospel, Jesus is never to be reckoned amongst those who can only enter in not of themselves, but by God's saving might, since the kingdom of heaven is in him, and when he comes, then the kingdom of heaven is at hand, and it is he himself who gives rest to the weary and heavy laden (Matt. xi. 28, 29). Thus he cannot upon this occasion have meant to say, Why callest thou me good? I *am not good*, but only, Why callest thou me good? *Thou* shouldst not *call* me so. Being good is not a thing that can be attained by words, as if thou shouldst need only to name me good master, and I had only to tell thee in a few easy sentences what good things to do, in order to be thyself as good as the good master. Not so; for none is good but the one, God. That he, Jesus, was himself good because he was always in God, and God in him, this very passage proves to the understanding mind. But it veiled for a while both his goodness and his Godhead together from the rich young man. A superficial acknowledgment of the first, without a recognition of the second, will never avail.

If then, Jesus, according to his own testimony, which we are constrained to receive, be perfectly holy, perfectly free from sin, what inferences are to be drawn? We must needs confess him to be *a moral miracle.* And who can venture to assert this an impossibility, because sin is inherent in humanity? In its present condition this is indeed the case, as a former lecture has taught us; but he who would assert that this inherent sinfulness belonged originally to humanity, must have very inadequate ideas of the evil of sin, and must, moreover, impiously accuse the Creator, to whom, according to such a theory, sin would have to be originally referred.

Now the Christian doctrine, on the contrary, commends itself to the conscience by invariably charging the guilt of sin upon man himself, and also commends itself to the understanding by its logical deductions, consistently maintaining, as it does, the fundamental principle that that which is born of the flesh is flesh, and for that very cause insisting that the sinless must have entered upon life in some other way; in other words, proclaiming according to the oldest of our creeds, and in perfect agreement with the gospels, *that he was conceived of the Holy Ghost, born of the Virgin Mary.* This is undoubtedly a miracle. But he who really believes in the miracle of the spotless holiness of Jesus, would be very illogical if he refused to assent to his miraculous conception. He would only have as an alternative to invent a divine interference with the ordinary course of nature, so far as to preclude the transmission of sin; to hold, in short, with regard to Jesus, the same doctrine of immaculate conception which the Pope decreed with regard to the Virgin Mary in 1854; that is to say, to adopt a miracle of his own discovery, instead of the miracle Scripture records, and moreover a far more exceptional miracle. For that sinful parents should beget sinful children, and that a sinless being should not be begotten by sinful parents, are perfectly harmonious facts; whereas that sinful parents should on one occasion fail to beget in their own nature, would be a far less intelligible interruption of a universal law.

However, the mode of thought which more especially claims the name of modern culture, most positively sets itself in opposition to all miracles whatsoever. This breaking through of eternal world-laws, as though God could only attain his ends by supplementary acts, improvements introduced into his originally inadequate creation, is a doctrine they deprecate in the strongest language. It is this element of the miraculous which is so repugnant to them in the Biblical Jesus, and certainly it meets them on every side in the Gospels.

For the present, however, we leave all consideration of the wondrous works of Christ to dwell on what must already have become apparent. There was a time, and its influence is not yet quite over, when many whose belief in the miracles of Christ was shaken, were wont to congratulate themselves all the more that they possessed at least intact his holy teaching, and, more, his pure and sublime ideal. But is it really possible to maintain such a position as this? I pass over the fact that such a mere ideal could have no power to save us, but rather as, being unattained, only to condemn. We must look more closely at his teaching. It will not be found practicable simply to rejoice in its pure morality. The *person* of Jesus is the great leading fact, the central point of all his teaching. Although lowly of heart, in all that he is acknowledging his Father, he nevertheless openly and freely puts forth the highest claims. He does not only preach the kingdom of heaven, the kingdom of God, but he declares himself to be the King of that realm. The kingdom of heaven is *his*, he is *Christ*, which is the the Greek rendering of the Hebrew word Messiah, the anointed King. In this he is consistent from the very first, and he only holds back because the earthly spirit of the people has in so many ways forgotten the prophetic word, "Not by might, nor by power, but by my Spirit, saith the Lord of hosts" (Zech. iv. 6). For this reason they were only too much inclined to use the carnal weapons of insurrection to make him a temporal king, and even his own disciples would scarcely have been proof against such a temptation. This it was which imposed upon him the most sacred reserve. But in himself there is no wavering upon this point. He is the Son of man, as he calls himself, by preference. This is a mysterious title, of simple sound, but high significance. Lowliness and majesty are marvellously blended therein. It is an appellation which carries us back to the prophecies of Daniel (chap. vii.) Daniel beheld the kingdoms of the world under the form of a terrible and devouring beast. In the great heathen secular powers, it is the animal nature of man that displays its might and also its cruelty. Then there enters into the presence of the Ancient of days, one like the Son of man, and to him is given a dominion that is the alone everlasting dominion. This Son of man is in appearance of small power, compared to the beast, but he it is who alone can subdue the sway of the animal in man, and establish a truly human reign. It is this Son of man that Jesus names himself, at once veiling and revealing his glory. "The Son of man hath not where to lay his head" (Matt. viii. 20). "The Son of man shall be betrayed into the hands of men; and they shall kill him" (Matt. xvii. 22). Nay, such his lowliness and humiliation, that it shall be possible for men to mistake his character, and oppose him, without committing the unpardonable sin (Matt. xii. 32). But yet this very Son of man, lowly as he now is, shall return as a king to judge the whole world (Matt. xxv. 31). "He will come in his glory, and in the glory of his Father," that is of God (Matt. xvi. 27). Thus, then, the Son of man is at the same time the Son of God.

Son of God! you may say. This is only the epithet bestowed in the Old Testament to the people of Israel as a whole (Ex. iv. 22), as well as upon Israelites in particular (Deut. xiv. 1; Isa. i. 2), and more especially upon their rulers (2 Sam. vii. 14). It is never understood to express the original natural relationship of a son to a father, but always a new beginning of spiritual and God-derived life, and with regard to the sovereign, this distinguished name signified his being anointed with God's Spirit, in order to execute the judgments of God.

But the evangelists, and the New Testament writers generally, apply this term to Christ in a yet higher sense; they name him thus as drawing in a peculiar and unparalleled manner his life from the life, his nature from the nature, of his Father. The evangelist St. John does so most decidedly of all, when he calls him the only begotten Son of the Father, full of grace and truth; the Word of God, who in the beginning was with God, and was God, but who in the fulness of time took flesh and dwelt among us.

There may, however, be some amongst you who have been persuaded that the doctrine of Christ being in this highest sense the Son of God, was not the doctrine originally taught, but was superadded at a later period by the apostle Paul, and the author of the so-called Gospel of St. John, whoever he might be. It is the fashion with many now-a-days—and really it is a mere fashion—to regard the Gospel of St. John with peculiar prejudice, as being a late invention. But even were this the case, of what avail to their cause? If we examine the three first Gospels carefully, we shall find that they claim for Jesus the very same dignity as that of John. We will now confine ourselves to citing the testimony of these three earlier Gospels.

We have already heard of the Son of man, who is to to come in the glory of his Father (Matt. xvi. 27). This Son of man calls himself repeatedly in discourses, which are least of all open to dispute, the Bridegroom (Matt. ix. 15; xxv. 1). Now this, from olden times, was the appellation of that heavenly Lord and God who was to betroth his people to himself in righteousness and in judgment, and in loving-kindness and in mercies (Hos. ii. 19). Again, this Son of man was expressly declared, by a voice from heaven, both at his baptism and transfiguration, to be God's beloved Son (Matt. iii., xvii). Or even if we set aside this evidence, because the doubters we have in view doubt most of all of such miracles as these, let us at least hear how he describes himself in uncontested passages. After the Lord of the vineyard has in vain sent his servants to the wicked workers in his vineyard, to them he sends at last his well-beloved Son (Mark xii. 6), who is thus expressly distinguished from those servants. Again, he is the King of the heavenly kingdom, and the angels are his servants, whom he will send to execute his judgments, by separating the tares from the wheat, the wicked from the just (Matt. xiii. 41-49). Nay, he exalts himself above the angels, even in that other passage, where he says: "Of that day and hour knoweth no one, no, not the angels, nor yet the Son, but the Father only" (Mark xiii. 32); for it is plain that while as concerning his humanity the Son here places himself below the Father, he asserts, at the same time, his superiority to the angels. And even as early as in the course of his sermon on the mount, he speaks of himself as the Judge of the world. It is he in whose name those false disciples are to preach and to do wonders, and to call him in vain Lord, Lord, whom he shall bid to depart from him (Matt. vii. 21-23). It is he who is to come and gather all nations before his throne (Matt. xxv. 31). And it is a far more important question than any concerning a mere date, whether he could without actual impiety put forth such lofty pretensions as these. If we decide that he could, then the question as to the exact time of the occurrence loses all its weight.

But he does not merely promise, at the future judgment, to manifest his glory; even during his earthly career he speaks with omnipotent majesty. Ye have heard it said by men of olden time, but *I* say unto you (Matt. v). Who is he who dares thus to institute a new law of God in addition to the former? Who is this that dares to say of himself that the Son of man is Lord also of the Sabbath; greater than the Temple, greater than Solomon or Jonah (Matt. xii. 8, 6, 41, 42). Who is this that presumes to place himself in the same position that God occupies in the Old Testament? For just as there the vital question hinges upon faithfulness to the living God, or apostasy from him, so in the New Testament

Jesus asserts, "He who is not with me is against me" (Matt. xii. 30); "He who loveth father or mother, son or daughter, more than me, is not worthy of me" (Matt. x. 37). What man, I ask, being only man, could dare so to speak, dare to annex heavenly rewards to the suffering of his disciples for righteousness' sake, which was tantamount to being persecuted for his sake (Matt. v. 10, 11). Verily this is the language of one omnipotent. So, again, when he speaks of the Baptist as being his Elias (Matt. xi. 14, 15), and exclaims: "He that hath ears to hear, let him hear!" Who was he of whom Elias was to be the fore-runner, but the Lord of hosts himself (Mal. iv. 5; iii. 1), and whose fore-runner was John? Neither is it less an utterance of omnipotence when Jesus granted forgiveness of sins to the leper (Matt. ix. 2-6), or when he gave that gracious general invitation to the weary and heavy-laden: Come unto me, I will refresh you (Matt. xi. 28).

This last passage has for context one that sounds like an extract from St. John (v. 27; Luke x. 22): "All things are delivered to me of my Father: and no man knoweth the Son, save the Father; and no man knoweth the Father, save the Son, and he to whom the Son will reveal him." If he did *once* actually so speak, must he not necessarily have done so much oftener than the earlier evangelists report? Do they not themselves seem here to require that the fourth should come and complete them?

For in all these passages, which we have only collected from the three first Gospels, what is it that Jesus assumes but divine dignity and divine power? Now these necessarily presuppose a divine nature, such as St. John most clearly and definitely announces. But indeed the other evangelists announce it too. When our Lord says to his disciples, "Where two or three are gathered together in my name, there am I in the midst of them" (Matt. xviii. 20); when he tells them, "Behold I send the promise of my Father (namely, the Holy Ghost) upon you" (Luke xxiv. 49); we at once exclaim, what mere mortal could dare so to speak? Take, more especially, those lofty words at the close of St. Matthew's Gospel (xxviii. 18-20): "All power is given me in heaven and in earth. Go ye therefore, and teach all nations, baptizing them in the name of the Father, and of the Son, and of the Holy Ghost; teaching them to observe all things whatsoever I have commanded you: and, lo, I am with you alway, even unto the end of the world." Why, what loftier language than this does John use? Since the days of the apostles we have baptized all members of the Church of Christ; that is a continuous fact. The apostles baptized according to the command of Christ, the Risen One; for he did not institute the ordinance before his death. When he did institute it, he placed his name between the Father and the Spirit, as one in divine nature with them. He commands that men be baptized in his name, as well as in that of the Father and the Spirit; he pledges men to himself equally as to the Father and the Spirit. The most sublime expressions that we find in St. John cannot transcend in dignity this one command. "I am the bread of life" (John vi. 35); "I am the light of the world" (John viii. 12); "I am the way, the truth, and the life; no one cometh to the Father but through me" (xiv. 6); "I am the resurrection and the life; he that believeth in me, though he were dead, yet shall he live" (xi. 25); nay, "He that hath seen me hath seen the Father" (xiv. 9); "For I and the Father are one" (x. 30),—what do all these sayings convey, but what we equally hear in the parting injunction, "Baptize them in the name of the Father, and of the Son, and of the Holy Ghost." What greatest man, loftiest prophet, holiest apostle, durst approach these words ever so remotely without extremest impiety?

This, then, is how the general question stands. We see that it is in vain to do away with, in vain to cut short, in vain to exclude this or that passage, for the doctrine runs alike through every phase of the Gospels. The same Jesus, then, who makes upon us such an impression of perfect candour and gentleness, meekness and humility, wisdom and holiness; the same Jesus who "created a moral ideal in the conscience of humanity, and embodied it in his life, so that whoever would acknowledge, contemplate, or practise what is good, must ever keep returning afresh to the word and the image of Jesus;"—this same Jesus has claimed divine majesty, divine power, nay, divine nature; and were then all these claims indeed false? Was he either a crazy enthusiast or a blasphemous liar? Could such impious deceit as this proceed from the lips of him who did no sin?

This is the problem before which unbelievers needs must stand; nor would they escape it even if, by the critical subtleties of a learning which is only a misuse of mind, they could succeed in throwing suspicion upon the testimony of all the evangelists alike. For the apostle Paul,—that powerful intellect in those epistles of his, the genuineness of which no rational man can controvert,—is a sufficient and a most trustworthy witness, not only to that crowning miracle, the resurrection of Christ, but also to the divinity of Christ. "A man in whom the yearning of the soul after moral sanctification connects itself with the person of Jesus; a man who, for decades, labours as a missionary in all patience and self-denial, in countless perils by land and water; a man who, by the depth of his own convictions, affects the consciences of other men, and to whom his hearers put the most searching questions, —such a man as this used, we may be sure, every opportunity afforded him of proving the grounds of his belief." In point of fact, no reasonable person, who is capable of appreciating Paul's character, can believe that this man, who kept himself so independent of the earlier apostles, would ever have based his own salvation, and his whole career of activity and influence, upon the divinity of Christ, without the most indisputable certainty that the historical Christ did indeed in very truth speak of himself as divine.

And then, again, there are in these very Gospels, together with all those miracles that the children of our time despise, such deeply impressive, such unexampled touches of sublimity,—touches that bear so incontrovertibly the impress of historical truth,—which it is so utterly impossible to dissever from the marvellous and the repugnant, that every opponent of the faith must needs stand in fresh and growing perplexity before the riddle they present.

Thus we see Caiaphas stood. When nothing definite was to be proved by all the false witnesses procurable, he conjured Jesus to confess whether he was the Christ, the Son of the living God, or no; and Jesus answered, "Thou hast said: hereafter (or henceforth) shall ye see the Son of man sitting on the right hand of power, and coming in the clouds of heaven" (Matt. xxvi. 64). It is thus the bound prisoner bears witness in presence of the angry judge, knowing well that his words will bring him to death! Henceforth he openly declares himself to share the royal power of God, and to be the Judge of the whole world; and this he asserts to one who was in a position, before the day was over, to contradict, and in appearance put his words to shame. Were they really put to shame? Who was right, the High Priest or Christ? This is in point of fact the great, the momentous alternative. If we take up the position of the High Priest, and proceed upon the axiom, he is *not* the Son of the living God, equal with the Father, and Judge of the world; he is not, and he *cannot* be this, and yet he declares it of himself, and elevates himself to this loftiest altitude without really reaching it,—why, then, we cannot stigmatize his conduct as less than blasphemy against God; nay, it was the most daring appropriation of God's majesty that insane presumption ever attempted; and this crime was committed by the very man who makes upon us such an unparalleled impression of perfect holiness! This is a problem, indeed, that no unbeliever can solve.

Thus highly, thus divinely, then, does this lowly, youthful, uncultivated, unesteemed carpenter of Nazareth characterize himself! This prophet, we see according to his own declaration, is more than a prophet. He is not only the keystone of the whole series of prophets, he is in his own person the subject and the end of all prophetic enunciations. He it is who, by word and deed, has made known to us the paternal name and paternal character of God (John xvii. 6). In him, in his teaching, and in his work, God's will to renew the creature is practically announced. If we receive his own account of himself, we have acknowledged him as the miracle that personally he *is;* and if so, it is nothing else than the natural consequence of the miracle that he *is*, that he should also *do* miraculous works.

This then is the main point of our controversy with you who stand on the opposite side; you cannot fairly treat it as though it related merely to a few isolated facts, the swine of the Gergesenes, or the breaking of bread to the multitudes, and the seven basketfuls over. Our controversy relates to the Saviour himself. It relates to the God of the Christians, who is not yours, and to nothing less. Why is it that you stand so helplessly there, before the eternal problem of this personality? Because you proceed upon the assumption that Jesus can only be a man like ourselves, and yet the original documents that bear record of him, invariably represent a man who is higher than a mere man; represent the Son of man as the Son of God in a sense in which we cannot be so, and moreover as being this for us, in order to raise, to redeem, and to perfect us. But you will not acknowledge such a miracle as this, and yet, God be praised for you! you have not the impious daring to say with Caiaphas, he hath spoken blasphemy; he is guilty of death. Therefore it is that you stand before the problem as before a closed door, the only key to which you have thrown away, but which is far too strong for you ever to break down.

We would, however, remind you of what has been said before in the second of these lectures; and then would ask you whence came *man* himself? He is here incontrovertibly, but he has not always been; his appearance was an interruption to the till then existing law. He is composed of elements that are unlike him, and which can never explain his existence. He arose *miraculously*, the work of that God who does miracles. How will you prove that the Son of man may not also have appeared in humanity as a higher miracle still? Whence do you derive that comfortless conviction, necessary to assert that this is not possible, that nothing can transcend man, nothing can be superadded to his present position, nothing can interfere with the present order of things? For this is what you say, and must say. Even Jesus you will not allow to have been perfectly holy. If he was not, he could not have been a Redeemer; nay, he must himself have needed one. Or, rather, according to your teaching, there is no Redeemer, and need not to be any; you need no Saviour to "die in peace," no Saviour to forgive you your sins and awaken you out of death. It is enough that the history of the world is a "triumphant march of moral and intellectual culture" (though it may well be questioned if it could have been so, had not Christ the Saviour appeared in it); and that no world history outside of Christ tends to a reign of perfection, but without him, sin and death maintain an unbroken dominion, beneath which we must spend the few years we have as well as we can, till we pass away, and become mere dust and corruption. This is the human dignity promised you by your God, that universal and original Spirit, which as true Being pervades the universe and ourselves, unconscious of himself, knowledge being too low and limited. We only know him, only in us does he know himself, because we are one with him!

But we Christians have a different God, and in him a different human dignity. It may indeed be humbling to need a Saviour. It implies the consciousness of being sick unto death, unable to deliver ourselves from the extremest danger. But even this disgrace is an honour. The Bible tells us our state is not good, is not right; that we are fallen from our original nobility, that we are called to something better; the highest and most glorious point to which you without a Saviour can hope to attain, is far beneath that to which God has appointed us,—to holy, blessed, and eternal life. It is thus that the God of the Christian honours sinful men; the Holy God, with whom we are not by nature one, as the delusive faith of Pantheism would teach, but with whom we are to become and do become one in Christ.

And further, we honour humanity in submitting to

this holy and gracious will of God concerning us. If we really are sinners, how can we degrade ourselves more deeply than by refusing to hear of repentance, determining to call wrong right, denying sin altogether, or making light of and painting it fair. What, on the other hand, can be more sublime, what can better reveal the dawn of human grandeur, than the publican striking on his breast, and crying, God be merciful to me a sinner! and the monarch bending beneath the prophet's rebuke, and confessing before God, Against thee only have I sinned!

This moral grandeur Jesus Christ will bring to perfection. He heals and he glorifies humanity; yea, the world itself. He is what Christendom, in accordance with the gospel, expresses, when saying in her creed: *I believe in Jesus Christ, God's only begotten Son, our Lord.* This is the manifestation of divine mystery before which we bow. The endeavour to see how much we can by our own efforts succeed in gaining of the knowledge of the person of Christ, of his divine and human nature, is indeed self-rewarding; but not while we set aside his own expressions about himself, rather while we make these the basis of all our knowledge; neither is it any disturbance to us, nor any reproach that this knowledge should remain fragmentary till we come to know even as we are known. Meanwhile we *live* in his fellowship, and know without visible proof, or extraordinary experience, that this is a holy and blessed reality. For, as the Scripture says (John iii. 33), and as those referred to experimentally know, "He that hath received his testimony, hath set to his seal that God is true."

VI.

CHRIST'S ATONEMENT FOR SIN.

THE atonement of Christ for the sins of men, the blessed mystery to the contemplation of which we devote one solemn week in every year, this is to be the subject of this Lecture.

God has given Free-will to man; it is with him a matter of choice whether he shall act in this way or in that, more especially whether he shall follow the voice of his conscience or not. But how if man perverts this his liberty to a consciously sinful course of action? And, in truth, fearful is the stream of unrighteousness which has for ages run through the history of humanity. What an amount of cruelty of man to man, not only on the battle-field of the invader, or in the markets of the slaveholder, but in the stately houses and the lowly cottages of our own land! And what an amount of wrong inflicted by the licentiousness of man! But how immeasurably greater would this dark tide of sin appear could we pierce below the surface of action into the thoughts and motives of the heart! Plato on one occasion divided human beings into three classes. He placed the unjust and the dissolute in the lowest class, as deserving to be transformed, after their death, into wolves and apes. The second class was made up of moral and well-behaved people, who were temperate and upright indeed, but lacked the spiritual sense, and held no communion with the Eternal; these he, in his half-jesting, half-earnest strain, pronounced well-qualified for transmigration into wasps and ants. We see, therefore, that the Greek philsopher had no very profound respect for mere outward propriety of conduct. It was only those belonging to the third class, those who occupied their lives with the contemplation of the Eternal, and departed this world free from stain of any sort, who were after their death to be admitted among the gods. Thus this wonderfully gifted man anticipated in a measure the great Christian verity, that not mere morality of conduct, but inward and spiritual righteousness leads to blessedness. We seldom find this recognised amongst ourselves. We are far too ready to judge character from without. This tendency to rest in the external is a very prevalent evil now-a-days in theory and practice.

"Thou shalt love the Lord thy God with all thy heart, with all thy soul, and with all thy strength;" this is the eternally stringent law for beings made in the image of God. Now, if this be the law, how heavy the condemnation that attends upon our actual condition! The law of God is *holy*. Consequently, from the opposition of our lives to this law, a fearful alienation, a profound unhappiness, must needs ensue. And so indeed it is, and we each know by experience how heavy a burden of woe rests upon our race.

This burden of woe is ordained by God for a twofold purpose; for the purpose of discipline, and the purpose of retribution.

The purpose of discipline:—The wretchedness which proceeds from sin is intended to lead us to see the folly of ungodliness; they who will not take it upon trust shall feel experimentally that out of God there is no life: and it is thus that the Holy One, who delighteth not in the death of the sinner, would recall us to himself, the only fount of life and joy. The inspired writers are unwearied in their forcible declarations of this purpose of divine love to improve us by suffering. But God's chastening has also another aim. The sin of man is a violation of the divine law, a dishonouring of the divine name. This is especially evident in the case of perjury, but it is true also of all sin; God has made himself known to man, he has revealed his name in our midst; sin is an ignoring of God, a desecration of the Divine Spirit who dwells or desires to dwell in the human soul, just as impurity is a desecration of the Temple of the Holy Spirit, whose temple the human body should be. Now, as surely as God is a living God, so surely must he support his holy law and name; the consequence of such desecration must fall on him who has attacked the sanctuary; the sinner must, in the language of Scripture, "bear his sins;" God must recompense sin by punishment.

This purpose of retribution is not less emphatically dwelt on by the prophets, apostles, and our Lord Jesus Christ himself, than that other purpose of discipline. Take, for instance, the passage, "With what measure ye mete it shall be measured to you again;" and where is the man whose conscience does not at once recognise the incontrovertible truth and justice of these words? The necessity of retribution is most deeply imprinted upon the human mind. When misfortune comes, how frequently is it accompanied by a flash of conviction that it is the righteous reward of some evil action or other. This law of retribution is the fundamental idea of many of our noblest poetical works; not only do we trace it in the lives of individual men, but in the life of nations also. Whoever sets himself in good earnest to gain a comprehensive view of the history of humanity, will infallibly find, on the one hand, such clear traces of a fixed and wise plan, as in spite of co-existing confusion force upon him the conviction that the course of human events is ordered by the wisdom of a personal God; on the other hand, such disturbances and hindrances as can only be viewed as punitive acts of this same God. I would instance the fearful sway permitted for many centuries to the fanaticism of the followers of Mahomet. How many lands that might else have yielded a rich harvest of spiritual life they have trodden down into barrenness! But, above all, the law of retribution has been displayed in the history of the Jewish people, the people of revelation as we may emphatically call them. A long series of prophets down to Jeremiah had foretold (this every critic concedes) their carrying away by the Assyrians first, and then by the Babylonians, as

God's judgment upon their disloyalty; and this really did come to pass 600 and 700 years before Christ. Again, Christ himself prophesied their overthrow as the retribution for their rejection of the Messiah, and in the following generation Jerusalem was destroyed, and for 1800 years Israel has been scattered abroad among the nations; still retaining so marked an individuality, that wherever they may meet Jew recognises Jew; a people without land or home, indestructible limbs of a torn and scattered body, a body from which the spirit has fled, because they sinned against the Spirit of life. Schiller has missed the truth in saying that the history of the world is the judgment of the world; the true statement is rather this: The world's history is a judgment *upon* the world,—" The wrath of God is declared from heaven upon all ungodliness of men who hold the truth in unrighteousness." In these words St. Paul deliberately states the nature of that relation of things and events which history records for us.

What follows, then? If each one of us individually, and the race as a whole, lies under the retributive justice of God, how are we to escape its sentence? Many have their answer ready prepared: " God is Love, consequently God will forgive us." But this is too hasty a conclusion. Doubtless God is love; he, the God of life, has called us into existence that we might enjoy it, and he is willing to call the dead in sin out of that death into life again. But, on the other hand, humanity lies under the retributive government of God. The sorrow that weighs upon the sinner practically teaches him, that joy, well-being, life itself is inconsistent with alienation from God, since he alone is the source of these blessings. Thus must the majesty of God be glorified in those who have desecrated it. Every one who has reflected upon the Divine Being will acknowledge that God's actions are not as ours, *arbitrary*, but that which *he* does is *necessary*. And it is equally clear from the very nature of God, that he cannot enter upon any course of action and then relinquish it, as is often the case with us changeable mortals. God's purpose cannot fail of its accomplishment. Hence it follows inevitably, that since men lie under the divine law of retribution, that law must take its full course, and attain its ultimate purpose, which is no other than the triumph of the Divine Majesty over the sins of men. God is indeed love; he delights not in killing, but in making alive; but his quickening and saving of those who have dishonoured his great Name *can* only be brought about by a full display of that Name's inalienable glory. Imagine a man called to the death-bed of a friend; imagine that dying friend confiding to him that his conscience is heavily laden by guilt, and entreating some consolation; what would he say to him? We are often told, that according to the fundamental principles of Protestantism, all Christians should be priests, and doubtless this ought to be the case; what priestly word then would you have to utter on an occasion like this? Imagine yourself ignorant of all connected with Christ's atonement, and retaining at the same time a firm hold of the truth that God by his very nature can neither be arbitrary nor changeable, and you will find that this alone remains for you to say: "My friend, God's justice must indeed mete to you that measure with which you yourself have measured; you must needs bear whatever retribution you have incurred. But submit yourself humbly to God's sentence, acknowledge its justice, let your heart be melted in the fire of the divine judgments, and turn under their influence to the Lord, so will he who is still Love—after his majesty has been manifested in you, as well as practically acknowledged by your humble submission—manifest also his quickening and saving power in your behalf." This is the only answer that you could possibly—of course I am now excluding Christ's atonement—make to your sorrowful and dying friend.

But is this a comforting answer? He who looks deeper into the human heart will find no comfort here. "Bear ye the weight of the divine judgments!" Surely these are fearful and melancholy words. "Be converted by the divine judgments!" Good; but Christ has said, "He that doeth sin is the servant of sin;" and even the heathens of antiquity were well aware that nothing is so difficult as to gain the empire over one's own heart. "Let your hearts be softened by the chastening fires." That were well, did not experience teach us that a self-seeking heart—and this is what a sinful heart is sure to be—does *not* become softened by the furnace of tribulation, but rather embittered, rather kindled with hatred and even blasphemy against its judge. "The law worketh wrath" (Rom. iv. 15), says St. Paul. "The people when hungry and hardly bestead shall fret themselves and curse their king and their God," wrote Isaiah nearly three thousand years ago; and as it was in his day, so is it experience teaches us in our own. And as it is on this side death, so will it be on the other, for death can in no way change the heart of man.

How then do we stand? On one side, so certainly as the voice of conscience which proclaims the fact of a divine law of retribution to be no self-delusion, and so certainly as the hallowing of the divine name is the highest law of all, that is, so certainly as God is a living God, even with equal certainty must the sinner remain separated from God, that is, from the source of life, till he bears the divine judgments in a fitting spirit,—in other words, till he is sanctified by them; and on the other side, if we must needs bear the judgment our dishonouring of God's name has incurred, to the end, we shall infallibly wax worse and worse, and add new debts and new guilt to our old. And taking these two truths in connexion, we must needs come to the conclusion, that no one can show us a way of escape from the penalty we lie under.

But now let us look to Christ. He tells us that he is come to seek and to save the lost. In what way then does Christ propose to save these? Even his first step towards such an end is of the utmost importance. He submits, we find, to that very baptism in Jordan which the Baptist instituted as a typical confession of sin for the sinful people to whom Messiah came. While the baptism of the people in the Jordan typically declared that only in the way of deep repentance could they meet their Messiah, the Messiah's own participation in the rite testified, that only by the way of *Death* could he bring help to the people. Messiah must die to save the lost; with this conviction Jesus went on his saving way. But how does this death of the Messiah bring salvation within the reach of the lost? I will content myself with citing some of the Lord's most striking statements upon this subject. On his last journey to Jerusalem, two of his disciples entreat, as a mark of favour, to be placed the one on his right hand, and the other on his left, when he shall come in his kingdom. He, however, replies that they must leave domination to the princes of this world, that their greatness must consist in serving, " even as the Son of man came, not to be ministered unto, but to minister, and to give his life a ransom for many." This expression clearly denotes the significance of his death. Are any disposed to inquire how it was that a just God could deliver over Jesus to death? He himself gives the answer: " the Son of man came to give away his life for you." And for what purpose did the Son of man give his life away? Hear his own words: " To be a ransom for many." Now, where a ransom is needed there must needs be prisoners. And where the ransom is a life, clearly the life of those prisoners must be involved. And if this ransom has to be paid for many, it is plain that they are unable to pay it themselves, though they owe it; and therefore He steps into their place.

A few days later the Lord was keeping the holy festival of the Passover, the memorial of the gracious sparing of Israel in Egypt at the time of the slaying of the first-born in every Egyptian family, as well as of their deliverance from Egyptian bondage. This supper was the last, the parting meal of Jesus and his disciples, for his death was to take place on the morrow. The Lord therefore took bread and said, " Take, eat, for this is my body; and after that the cup, and said, Drink ye all thereof, for this is my blood, the blood of the new covenant which was shed for many for the remission of sins: this do in remembrance of me." He substituted the feast of the new testament for that of the old, and this feast was to commemorate his death. But why should the remembrance of Christ be most especially a remembrance of his *death?* He answers, "My blood is the blood of the new testament." But how can Christ's blood ratify the new testament? He says, "It is shed for many, for the remission of sins." Thus it is the forgiveness of sins that leads to a new covenant, this forgiveness being brought about through the shedding of Christ's blood. It was on the selfsame evening that Christ offered up that prayer (John xvii.), which we are accustomed to call the sacerdotal prayer. I may here mention that even De Wette speaks of this as the most exalted portion of the gospel, the purest expression of the divine consciousness and divine peace of Jesus, having previously observed of several others of our Lord's discourses, recorded by the same evangelist, that they ray forth a greater than earthly brightness, so that it is inconceivable that John should have himself invented them. In this prayer, then, the Lord says, in reference to his death, "For their sakes I sanctify myself, that they also might be sanctified through the truth." And this significant expression, interpreted by the sacrificial language of the Old Testament, is to be understood thus: I devote myself as a *sacrifice* for them; this being the only way by which even the disciples of Jesus became holy men.

The last allusion made by Christ to his death, which I shall here quote, belongs to the same occasion. When he was about, as he was wont, to set out with his disciples to the Mount of Olives, he said: "This that is written must yet be accomplished in me: 'and he was numbered among the transgressors,' for the things concerning me have an end." Christ here alludes to a most remarkable prophecy in the 53d of Isaiah, concerning that servant of the Lord who was to come forth as a root out of dry ground, without form or comeliness, despised and rejected, a man of sorrows and acquainted with grief, taken out of the land of the living, but bearing the people's grief and carrying their sorrows, the Lord having laid their iniquity upon him, who, like a sheep before the shearers, was dumb, opening not his mouth, but making his soul an offering for sin, interceding for the transgressors, being the righteous servant by whom many should be justified because of his having borne their iniquities. It is not possible to set forth in plainer words than these that sinners are saved through the vicarious suffering of one who has borne their penalty in their stead; and Christ, we have seen, declares that these words are accomplished by his death.

You know that a few years after Christ's death, Stephen died a martyr for his faith. After a few years followed James, Peter, Paul. And who can count the numbers down to the time of Wycliffe and Huss, who sealed their witness with their blood? Well, the enemies of Christian truth at the present day would make the death of Jesus nothing more than a martyrdom. The Pharisees, they say, who hated him because of his reproval of their hypocrisy, accused him to Pilate; Jesus remained unshaken in his testimony to the truth, and this cost him his life. Now, it is doubtless a glorious thing to lay down one's life for the truth, and there are not many in this age of ours whose souls are lofty enough for such a sacrifice. But Jesus is so exalted, that a deed which confers the highest renown on mere men, would be in him poor, and small, and inadequate. If Jesus be the great witness for the truth, and if the most important revolution in the world's history be brought about by him, those who have any proper historical discernment should first of all ask of Jesus himself the meaning of his own death. His answer we find far transcends language applicable to mere martyrdom. "My life, he declares, is a *ransom;* my blood is the blood of the new covenant,—it is shed for the forgiveness of sins. Thus the Saviour reveals the *atoning* character of his death; for, whatever act of suffering is a quality to expiate offences is called *atonement* for those offences, and it is through *atoning* for human guilt that Jesus brings about the reconciliation of man with God,—his restoration to the character and privileges of a son.

But how does his death atone for our sins? In order to understand this, we must be careful clearly to *distinguish* between the two fundamental ideas found in our

Lord's own words. When he says that at his death he sanctifies himself for his disciples, he characterizes his dying as a free-will and holy offering of his life to God. And when he declares that the Son of man came to give his life a ransom for many, this giving his life is represented as a perfectly free act, and the life given as a costly gift, for a ransom must needs be costly. This is the first fundamental idea in all our Lord's statements concerning his death,—in free love he gave up his holy life to the glory of God. But, on the other hand, Christ describes his death as the fulfilment of that prophecy which declares, that the righteous servant dies because God has laid on him the iniquity of the unrighteous,—their sentence being executed upon him,—their transgressions the burden under which he sinks. This is the second point of view in which the Lord teaches us to consider his dying. If, then, we would know the real truth and the whole truth, we must grasp both points of view in their vital *unity*. And if this be done, one class of objections, often adduced, will die away of themselves. For, with regard to all profounder truths, the great desideratum, but at the same time the most serious difficulty, is to apprehend by a living glance the essential oneness in which two different truths converge, and from whence they radiate;—the beating heart, so to speak, from which, and to which, the streams of truth flow; superficial minds discerning often nothing but contradictions in the profound subjects which reward a deeper insight with the highest intellectual enjoyment, because it is just in those profoundest depths that it recognises harmony.

I must now revert to our supposed answer to the dying man, convinced by his awakened conscience that for a guilty sinner it is a fearful thing to fall into the hands of the living God. We have imagined ourselves telling him that he must needs submit to the consequences of his actions, be they what they may; but that if he, in another world, bows humbly to the just judgment of his God, and turns in penitence to him, his Creator will, after the expiation of his sentence due, cause his face to shine upon him once more. But, in point of fact, the retributive justice of God does not begin in another world: the life that now is, is often fearfully shattered by sin, and the weight on the conscience most oppressive here: nay, we trace the effects of this law of retribution in national as well as individual life, and through the whole progressive history of the race. Now, there are two points which must be taken into consideration, before we can rightly understand the nature of this retributive justice. The holy men who spake by inspiration of God, both in the Old and New Testament, most distinctly state that physical death is the wages of sin. Not that we can suppose, that even had we been sinless, these earthly bodies of ours could eternally have clothed our immortal spirits. But the manner in which our earthly life now ends, in complete severance of the spirit from all material organization whatsoever, this, the Scripture teaches, is not the original ordinance of the Creator. According to that original ordinance our spirits would, during our mortal life, have evolved for themselves out of these earthly and material bodies a higher and an undying corporeity. But physical death as it exists now, or, to adopt the language of St. Paul, the "being *unclothed*" instead of the "*being clothed upon*," this it is which is the wages of sin. Now, what is it that constitutes the distinctive character of the judgment which sinners have incurred,—what is the special root out of which death grows? It is the alienation of the sinner from that communion with God which is the only source of life. If we take a tree out of the soil from whence its roots derive their nourishment, it will die; and so it is with our own life, which we have, by reason of our sin taken out of the very element of life—that is to say, out of fellowship with the living God.

Thus we see that the sentence of death treads on the heels of sin by invincible necessity. And now remember, also, that since there is no shadow of repentance or turning, with God, this sentence cannot end before it has accomplished its aim, its purpose, which purpose is the manifestation of the Divine Majesty. Just as the symptoms of bodily disease will not disappear, till the cause of the disease be removed, so the processes by which death saps human life cannot disappear till the separation of man from the Source of life be done away with, and the Spirit of the living God be restored to the human race. Yet how shall the Divine Spirit be ours till we have in humble submission borne God's judgment, borne it in a holy frame of mind, and borne it to the end? This brings us back to the very point we stood at before: there is no human way of escape from the sentence of condemnation under which we lie! But we stand in a different attitude than before, for now we have heard the words of Christ. The judgment which we had to bear has been already borne, for Christ declares himself to be that righteous servant who was, according to prophecy, while bearing the sins of many, to give his life as a sacrifice for their guilt. And thus God's judgment has been holily borne, for he who bore it sanctified himself, as he himself says, "I sanctify myself for them." Christ has not merely *suffered* death in consequence of sin. He has suffered it with the full consciousness that Death was the wages of sin, submitting with holy, loving, and reverent submission to the conditions of Divine justice; and hence is it that his death has power and virtue to atone for our sins.

But I must show, with still greater distinctness, what we are to understand by Christ's holy bearing of the Divine judgment. Jesus the Holy One, who could declare that no one knoweth the Father but the Son—Jesus might have had joy (Heb. xii. 2), uninterrupted; he might have withdrawn himself from the guilty race who did not desire him, and have lived solely in the blessed contemplation of his heavenly Father. For, as he himself says, "This is life eternal, to know thee, the only true God" (John xvii. 3). It was his zeal for God's glory, his love for mankind, that forbade this; he desired to reveal his Father to men. Why, we may ask, did he not limit this revelation to the true Israelites, to a Nathanael, a Peter, a John? His love could tolerate no such limitation; it impelled him to seek the publicans and sinners. But why, at least, did he not remain at a distance from the Pharisees, who had been already declared by the Baptist to have rejected the counsel of God?[1] Because his love could tolerate no limitations of any sort: the Son of Man had come to seek the *lost*, wherever and whatever they might be. Now, any one who is feelingly alive, on the one hand, to the sinless purity of him who condescended to sit and eat with sinners; and, on the other hand, to the fact, that this pure and sinless one was *very man*,—not a mere, but still a true man; in all things susceptible of pain, sorrow, and temptation, even as we are,—will at once discern how great an effort of absolute self-denial is implied in this companionship of Christ with sinners, and will see that his inward agonies, inward crucifixion, must have begun long before his bodily death. If an unholy man feels constrained and distressed in the company of the holy, surely the fellowship of worldly men must have been a deep grief to the divine holiness of the Saviour. But when we further take into consideration the practical bondage of men to sin, and the hatred of men to God's judgment upon sin, we may well say that Christ, in his intercourse with men, bore the punishment which God has affixed to human guilt.

Christ knew well the inward anguish that awaited him, when he appeared as a Prophet in the midst of rebellious men; but, for the glory of God and the welfare of those men, he willingly took upon him all the miseries which Divine Justice has associated with human intercourse ever since the Fall; he, so to speak, accepted the conditions under which alone, according to God's ordinance, it is possible for a holy being to act and work amongst sinners, and in this manner he practically acknowledged the holiness and justice of God, in evolving out of human sinfulness itself the penalty that attends upon all human intercourse. On the other hand, we have seen that Christ gave up his life voluntarily. As he himself said, no one took his life away from him; he gave it up of himself. At the very moment of his capture in the garden, he might have prayed to his Father, and he would have sent him down legions of angels; those even who came to take him fell to the earth at his

[1] See Christ's own words, Luke vii. 30.

words, "I am he." This voluntariness of the sacrifice of Christ appears pre-eminently from the narrative of his Transfiguration; the Holy Jesus might have returned from the Mount to the invisible world, without undergoing death. Wherefore, then, was it that he submitted to die? It was that amidst the myriads of men who *must* of necessity die, being sinners, and who, before Christ's spirit was shed abroad, never rightly *understood* either their sinfulness, or the sentence of death that they lay under,—to say nothing of their powerlessness to undergo that sentence in a right spirit,—it was that amongst all these myriads there should be *one* who suffered death with full *comprehension* both of the nature and penalty of sin; full comprehension that the law of mortality is a holy judgment of God passed upon sin; that one amongst the many should suffer death in holy *submission* of his soul to the *justice* of this divinely-appointed penal law.

Again, in the third place: the root from which death springs is, as we have before seen, the separation of the sinful soul from life-giving communion with the living God. The bitterest drop in the cup of the lost will be that they have lost their God, torn for ever with their own hands the bond between themselves and him. For —for him who hath sinned against the Holy Spirit there remaineth no forgiveness, and his will be a fearful isolation when it is finally decreed that he is and must continue separated from him who created him, and who is the alone source of life. Even now, the men who are without God in the world, know something of this terrible loneliness; but what has only faintly begun here, will be fully developed hereafter; what is now felt in secret will then be made manifest. On the other hand, the highest happiness of the Christian, even now, is that of which St. Paul speaks, the Spirit bearing witness with his spirit that he is the Son of God. And now consider these words of Christ: "My God, my God, why hast thou forsaken me?" Not, indeed, that this forsaking of the Son by the Father could resemble the forsaking of the wicked by the God whom they have rejected. Christ expressly states, the very evening before his death, "I am not alone, because the Father is with me," and his cry on the cross is, "*My* God, *my* God!" But for the dread time during which he was given over into his adversaries' hands, the Father's inner voice, witnessing of his communion with the Son, was hushed, that so the Son might, in this *silence* of the Father, experience the darkest portion, the very essence of God's judgment against sin, and, by believing and humble submission, recognise the linking of even *this* awful consequence with sin, to be a righteous law of the Righteous Judge; thus, by his holy bearing of the sentence accomplishing its purpose, and by fulfilling it to the end, doing it away. For the atoning power of all our Lord's sufferings lies in this *holy* bearing of the judgment which God has indissolubly linked with human sin; not in his physical pains, his wounds, his blood as such, but in the holy travail of his soul, when he voluntarily underwent the penalty affixed by God to sin, received the bitter cup from God's hand into his, the Son of man's, thus, by fulfilling its purpose, accomplishing its aims—*exhausting* the judgment. This is what is included in the atonement of Christ; a profound suffering, not merely *external* suffering and submission, but inner and intense; the most free and most absolute spiritual act of sacrifice that ever was recorded in the history of humanity.

Any one who has followed the above train of thought with deep attention and spiritual recollection, will find in it an answer to the two following questions: Why could not God's forgiveness be obtained except through the death of Christ? and in what manner does Christ's death bring about the forgiveness of sins? But there are two other questions which spring out of the above statements, to which I have yet to reply: and these are, first, How can the holy sufferings of the one man Christ Jesus atone for the sins of hundreds and thousands of millions? and, secondly, In what way can Jesus appear before God as the representative of humanity? And these two questions I the more willingly propose to answer, because of the deeper insight we shall thus gain both into the wisdom of God, and into the mystery of the Saviour's person.

How, then, can one man's holy endurance of the Divine judgment upon sin atone for the sins of millions? The briefest answer I can give to this question is as follows: If you compare humanity to a tree, Christ's relation to this tree with countless leaves, is not that of a leaf like other leaves; and if you compare humanity to a body with many limbs, Christ is not a limb like other limbs. In all organic life, each part is doubtless vitally related to the whole, but the different parts are not alike vitally important to that whole. Look at the facts of Nature; the tree includes root, trunk, several arms, a multitude of smaller branches, a countless abundance of leaves; if of these leaves you take away numbers, your eye will scarcely note their loss, the tree will not suffer; but if you take away the root, what becomes of the tree? So with regard to the body —we deprecate the loss of a limb, yet how many a soldier returns, seriously maimed indeed, but in good health and spirits, to his home: whereas if the bullet reach the heart, all is over with him. And so it is in the organism of human society. The members of the family are father, mother, children, but we call the father the *head:* the duty of the children is to obey, even when they do not understand him; while his part is to understand the wants of wife and children better even than they themselves can; and not only to understand, but to supply. The State, too, is divided into members, into citizens and governing authorities, and every citizen is of use to the State, but in the most free Republic it has never been imagined that each citizen could be a statesman. We call statesmen those who have insight to discern, and power to execute, that which is best for the many-sided life of the people at large. So, too, in ecclesiastical organization; each member is of use to the whole body, but there are some who have more especially *the cure of souls;* whose vocation it is to assist and support in all questions relating to spiritual life, men of various ages, positions, callings, gifts, and temperaments; and this can only be rightly and really done by one who can connect his own experience with the experience of men of every shade of character, and take by sympathy the varied life of others into his own: only such a one can speak the appropriate word of help to each separate case that comes before him. But how remarkable the extension of the horizon both of thought and action in those highly-gifted spirits that God sends among us from time to time. Some live in the narrowest sphere, and hardly understand themselves; others have not only a deep insight into their own life, as well as into the lives of a wide circle of their fellow-men, but are able to enrich all alike with special and appropriate gifts. This may, in some degree, prepare us to understand the relation of Christ to the whole of humanity. Christ was an Israelite according to the flesh, and he remained dutifully subject to the law which made the Jews what they were. But the name by which he was wont to name himself was, "*the Son of man*;" the field in which he sowed the seed was *the world*; all nations were to be his disciples, and of *all his disciples* alike he required that they should love him with their whole power of loving.

And, in point of fact, how wondrous the might with which for these eighteen hundred years one Jew has actually subjected to his mild yoke thousands and thousands of souls out of every nation! Syrians, Egyptians, Greeks, Romans, Saxons, Celts, Sclaves, have said to him, as said his Jewish disciples of old: "Lord, to whom shall we go? Thou hast the words of eternal life!" Yea, not only hast thou the *words* of life, but *thou thyself art* the life. "He who hath the Son of God hath life." For wherever the religious life of Christians really exists, there will be found a fellowship with Christ's person, there the language held will be: "Thou art the Vine, we will be the branches." All such souls have acknowledged that it was this Jesus, this personal Saviour, who awakened and quickened their inner man; that it is this fellowship with him which enables their better nature so to triumph over their lower, that they can partly reach the goal towards which their conscience strives. This intimate and indissoluble bond which unites all such spirits to Christ, to his *person*—and the closer the bond, the completer the liberty—this is the most remarkable fact in the history of the human race, the highest problem with which psychology can possibly occupy itself. Now, the only possible explanation of this fact lies in this, that he who calls himself the *Son of man* was not a mere man, but the eternal and incarnate Lord, for whom and by whom all human spirits were created.

But, however, I will not dwell further here on the person of Christ; I will only show in what way this one man can be the priestly representative of the whole race. He who appears before God as the priest of sinful men must be able to take an adequate view of the guilt of the people whom he represents; he must not look upon it as less than it is in the eyes of a holy God; he must apprehend its depth, its full extent, its wide-spreading ramifications. I say its *ramifications*, because, as humanity in God's sight is not a mere aggregate of separate men, but an organic whole, having a common moral sense implanted in it by its Creator, sin has necessarily a *common* and *corporate* existence, the *world* lies in wickedness, the *spirit of the world* is become a spirit of evil. Now no man, except Christ, has ever yet been able rightly to discern the nature and extent of sin, because only one who is sinless can see how black its stain; only one who himself stands in the light can truly know what darkness is. And this *Son of man* is also the only one whose penetrating gaze can apprehend the whole of the glory and worth of which God created humanity capable, the whole tenor of its downward way, and the high end it may yet attain; none but Jesus has ever sounded the whole extent of the aberrations, degradations, and disorder of our race. He, however, *has* sounded all these depths, his heart has been pierced with adequate sorrow for all that dishonouring of God's holy name of which the beings whose brother he became were guilty; and consequently he has fully apprehended the righteous severity of divine justice in connecting sin with death, death in its various forms. And because he has manifested the righteousness and justice of the divine sentence—not in words only, but practically by his silent and holy endurance of its penalty—he has accomplished the *purpose* of divine punishment, and has terminated it—on behalf of whom? On behalf of all those who by faith appropriate this his holy endurance of the divine judgment as their own.

This last sentence contains also an answer to the second question—In what sense is it that Christ stands in the place of other men, or how is he to be my representative, and how am I to avail myself of his work? It is in and by faith, living faith, that I appropriate that work, and make it mine. Of course it is essential to the satisfactoriness of this answer that we should thoroughly understand what is meant by faith. No doubt, to any who hold, as the opponents of Christian truth in our day generally do, the fundamental error that faith is a mere *belief* or opinion, the whole of Christianity, but most especially the doctrine of the atonement, must remain hopelessly unintelligible. But are these enemies of faith, who would willingly give themselves out to be theologians, quite unacquainted with the writings of the Reformers, or if they know them—if, for instance, they only know Luther's famous Introduction to the Epistle to the Romans, or his work upon Christian Liberty—how is it possible that they can now attribute to us that poor and inadequate conception of the nature of faith with which the Church of Rome sought to oppose the Reformation? Are not these theologians aware that one of the fundamental differences between the Church of Rome and the Reformed Church lies in this, that the former confounds faith with mere belief, *i.e.*, the assent of the understanding to a fact or facts; whereas the Reformers understand thereby an affair of the heart, the will, the very core, so to speak, of personal consciousness. When our Lord said to the woman who was a sinner, "Thy sins are forgiven thee, thy faith has saved thee;" are we to understand by this, "Thy opinion, thy mere *belief*, has saved thee?" When St. Paul writes to the Galatians, "It is no more I that live, but Christ that liveth in me; and the life that I now live in the flesh

I live by the faith of the Son of God, who loved me, and gave himself for me;" are we to cut down these beautiful words to "I live by mere theoretical belief in the Son of God?" And again, are we to affix this lamentably inadequate interpretation to those other words of St. Paul to the Philippians: "I count all things loss, that I may win Christ, and be found in him, not having my own righteousness which is by the law, but that which is by the faith of Christ, the righteousness of God by faith; that I may know him and the power of his resurrection, and the fellowship of his sufferings." Truly we need not be theologians, we need only have a sound intelligence, to discover at once from expressions such as these, that to have faith in Christ means to trust him, to draw near to him, to be found in him, to live in him. To have faith in Christ implies such an experimental knowledge of our own unrighteousness, as leads us to distrust our own wisdom with regard to the things of God; such deep and dominant conviction of Christ's wisdom, Christ's holiness, Christ's spiritual majesty, and such inward experience of his quickening power, as makes us trust only in his word, and experience in ourselves a real communion with him who was dead, but who now liveth for evermore. It is self-evident that those who believe in Christ assent to the truth of his mission; but they do this, not from hearsay, not on outward evidence, but from personal spiritual experience, just as he who walks in the sunshine is convinced by his sensations that the sun is up there in the sky, even if—his sight having been weak from childhood—he has never gazed full at the radiant orb.

Now, it is this personal experience which is the very soul of faith, and without which the mere assent of the understanding is a lifeless thing, which the enemies of evangelical truth ignore in their description of faith, although it is surely illogical and unfair to omit the main point of a definition. But, on the other hand, they who know what is really implied in believing in Christ, living by faith of the Son of God, being found in Christ, have no difficulty in understanding how the believer has a property in all Christ is and has, more especially in his holy bearing of the divine punishment of sin. We take an illustration: Christ has given us the Lord's Prayer, a prayer so short, so simple, and yet so perfectly complete, that surely no man will presume to say he himself could ever have invented such a one. Thousands repeat these words thoughtlessly every day, and call this repetition prayer; and at last fifty repetitions of it at a time are called a rosary, and held to be meritorious, though every intelligent mind knows well what a wide difference there is between parrot-like repetition and prayer. Such saying over the Lord's Prayer as this, of course, is alike without virtue or result. But how is it when a man whose soul thirsts for the living God hears this filial prayer of the Lord Jesus, and feels at the same time the Holy Spirit of Adoption dwelling within him? It may be that for a long time he fails to apprehend all the depths and heights there are in this prayer, but he breathes its spirit; the Spirit that maketh intercession therein is blended with his own, and when he approaches his Father which is in Heaven in those words which did not, indeed, spring from his mind, but from that of Christ,—think you that, in the eyes of that Father, it is not all one as though from that praying human soul the prayer had originated? Yea, verily, by the very equity of the divine holiness it must needs be so. Here we see that Christ's act of prayer is the property of mankind; just so is it with the work of suffering by which he acknowledged and satisfied the justice of God's sentence upon sin. As the Lord's Prayer was originally not ours but his, so are his holy sufferings his not ours. And as his prayer may be repeated mechanically, and to such repetition the name of prayer be given, so may a lifeless assent be paid to the fact of his atoning work, and that assent may be confounded with faith. And as such repetition of the Lord's Prayer is a useless and barren thing, so this assent of the understanding to the fact of the atonement may leave the soul of the man year by year unatoned for.

But, on the other hand, just as the holy spirit of the

Lord's Prayer may take such hold of a human soul that the man's whole delight is in it, that he inhales its spirit as the sick man inhales the pure mountain air, so also may the holy spirit in which Christ submitted to God's just anger against sin, become the spirit of the sinful man who is bowed beneath the sense of personal guilt and divine displeasure. And now, how does such a one stand in relation to Christ's act of expiatory suffering? Christ's death fills him with the keenest *sorrow*, for he truly says: It is owing to the sins of the world, and to my sins also, that this sentence of death, which the holy Saviour bore, came upon the world; but, at the same time, the sacredness of Christ's death inspires him with a joy equally keen; he praises and blesses the Son of man who bore *righteously* and *holily* the punishment of sin, and thereby acknowledged and submitted to God's justice, and thus did what the whole world never could have done, *endured* and *exhausted* the penalty, and magnified God's moral government, so that the sentence having accomplished its purpose, was done away with. Such a man will say: "I ought to have done what Christ did, but I was not able. I thank the Saviour that he did it." Such a man will confess that his whole being is nothingness and unworthiness. It is the holy sufferings of Christ with which he identifies himself, in which he delights, and which he takes for his only portion. So that henceforth he lives not to himself, but to Him by whom the saving work was done. Of a truth, a very different relation to Christ's death is herein implied than that mere *belief in the fact*, which the unenlightened confound with faith, could possibly afford; *this* faith is nothing short of a dying with Christ in order to live with him, and he who thus identifies himself with the atoning work of Christ, must needs be held by the divine justice to have a property in it; for *not* to forgive a man who thus, in the sufferings of Christ discerns, confesses, and magnifies God's holy judgments *upon his own sins*, would be to continue the sentence after it has been undergone, the penalty after its purpose had been fulfilled.

It was thus that the apostles believed in the death of Christ, and history tells us what great things they gladly did in the strength of such a faith. Let, then, the Church of our day so believe therein, and it will once more be strong and joyful as the Apostolic Church was. For the foolishness of the Cross is wiser than men; and as the great poet said of the works of God's creation—of the rushing of the rivers, the flash of the lightning, the waves of the sea, the rotation of the earth, the triumphal march of the sun—"these incomprehensibly great works are glorious as on the first day," so is it true of all Christ's works; it is true of his atoning work (to-day, yesterday, and for ever), that "its love is incomprehensibly great and glorious now, as on its first day."

VII.

THE RESURRECTION AND ASCENSION OF JESUS CHRIST.

THERE is hardly any fact in the history of the world so well attested and corroborated as the Resurrection of Jesus.

This assertion may, to some readers, sound a bold one. My task must be to justify it. The New Testament records afford us a fourfold proof of this great fact,—two different apostles, John and Paul, and two bodies of men, the first Christian community, and the apostolic band who made it the fundamental theme of the preaching on which the whole Church rests, presenting themselves as witnesses of the resurrection of Jesus.

Out of the evidence afforded by the Evangelists, we shall only cite that of John, because the latter so convincingly conveys the impression of *eye-witness* to an unprejudiced mind. It is very true, that of late this Gospel of St. John has been rejected as not genuine, though only by a small number of writers who occupy the extreme left,—by Baur and his school. They are, moreover, opposed by incomparably the majority of biblical students. Even De Wette himself does not venture to deny the genuineness of the fourth Gospel; and men like Ewald, who are most free in their criticism of the Scriptures, have of late maintained this genuineness in opposition to Baur. Now, there are two ways of carrying on the controversy with the opponents of the resurrection. We may either say to them, You reject the Gospels, we receive them; but we will for once go over to your stand-point, and seek our evidence only from the records you yourselves consider authentic, namely, from the universally acknowledged Pauline epistles, which will afford us three out of the four proofs that we have already alluded to; or we may adopt another mode, and prove that we have a good and scientific right to use the Gospels as sources of historical truth, and, in these Lectures, the intent of which is to give *reasons* for the *faith* we hold, this is the course we choose. Time, however, compels me, to limit myself to the Gospel of John, to which, as we have already said, the present tone of critical inquiry is decidedly favourable, and which is not only rich in external testimony afforded to it by the Fathers, but possesses internal peculiarities which must invariably impress the unprejudiced seeker for truth with its apostolic origin.

We will not dwell upon the fact that this especially pneumatic or spiritual Gospel, as old Clement of Alexandria calls it,—this tender, genuine chief Gospel, in the language of Luther,—discloses to us the inner mystery of the nature of Christ in a manner only intelligible from one whom Jesus loved, and who had lain on his breast; but we would especially recall to you the self-witness of this disciple standing below the Cross: "And he that saw it bare record, and his record is true; and he knoweth that he saith true, that ye might believe" (John xix. 35). There is indeed an amazing degree of subtlety and evasion of the plain, straightforward meaning of words required to pass over so lightly, as certain critics do, such a declaration from the mouth of the author of such a work as this. We see that we should have to suppose a narrative, pressing on our conscience with all the sanctifying force of truth, to be itself chargeable with falsehood; and the writer, while expressly asserting the truth of the testimony he bore, to have been consciously lying all the while.

But with the force of the moral evidence, we have combined that of the æsthetic to verify the statement: "He that *saw* it bare record, and his record is true." From the first chapter onwards this Gospel bears the most unmistakable traces of ocular testimony, so that even such a rationalistic critic as Credner observes, "If we were without any historical data whatever as to the authorship of the fourth Gospel, we should on internal grounds,—from the freshness and vividness of the narrative, the preciseness and minuteness of the details, the peculiar mention made of the Baptist and of the son of Zebedee, the inspiration of love and devotedness which the writer evinces towards Jesus, the irresistible charm that pervades the whole evangelical history,—have been led to the conclusion that the writer could only have been a native of Palestine, an immediate eye-witness, an apostle, a favourite of Jesus, could only in a word have been John." Lachmann, that acute, not seldom over-acute critic, says, he for his part has left off reading works against the genuineness and historical character of the Gospel of John, for he knows beforehand that they are worthless.

It is in the account given by St. John of the Easter morning that this impress of personal experience is more especially noticeable. Mary Magdalene had been at the sepulchre in the early dawn, and had found it empty. In her agitation she hurries back to Peter and John, the thought of the resurrection not having occurred to her. She exclaims, "They have taken away the Lord out of the sepulchre, and we (I and the other women, by whom, according to the other evangelists, she was accompanied) know not where they have laid him." Filled with kindred perplexities, Peter and John forthwith hasten to the grave. On this occasion the impulse in the heart of the loving disciple is even stronger than that of the usually more impetuous Peter, and he is first to reach the spot. But when there, he stands, in his contemplative way, by the sepulchre, and only looks in, and, looking, discovers the linen-cloth in which the body had been wrapped. Peter follows him, and at once, as might have been expected from his fiery nature, goes in, and sees not only the linen-cloth, but also the napkin which had been bound round the head of Jesus, and which was carefully wrapped together in a place by itself. This little circumstance, of which John convinced himself by going in also, was enough to dispel the idea of the removal of the Lord's body. If that had been the case, the clothes would have been taken too, or at all events they would not have been thus deliberately arranged. This incident at once led John to a truer train of thought; faith in the resurrection dawned upon his soul. But he blames himself for having required to see in order to be convinced, and owns that they had not known, that is, understood the Scriptures, according to which the resurrection of the Messiah had long before been a foretold and a divine necessity.

If the slight rebuke, here implied to both apostles, comes best from the mouth of John, much more does the extraordinary vividness with which apparently trivial matters, such as the slower or swifter running to the grave, the standing without or going in, and the actual position of the napkin, prove distinctly that the narrator was one of the two actors in the scene. To no one else would such details have seemed of any importance, to say nothing of the improbability of any one having invented them; whereas to John they were of the highest value, as having served to awaken his faith in the resurrection. It was equally as decisive a time in his life, as that in which he first met Jesus, and describes with such inimitable life and truth in the first chapter of his gospel.

Whoever is capable of appreciating the natural truthfulness of a narrative, will find himself more and more irresistibly compelled to acknowledge that such passages are self-evidencing as the light of day, and that their peculiar colour and significance can only be explained as the result of the personal experience of the narrator.

Thus, then, in the apostle John, we have an indisputable witness of the resurrection of Jesus. The value of his testimony consists especially in his giving us the circumstances in their original freshness and liveliness, in his transporting us back to the very Easter morning and the empty sepulchre. It is true that John only certifies us in this passage of the sepulchre being empty; he had not yet at that time himself seen the

Risen One. But not only are these preliminary facts important as having served to develop faith in the resurrection in the apostle's heart, but it is in immediate connexion with them that he tells us of that first appearance of the risen Saviour, at the same place and in the same hour, to Mary Magdalene, and then of three other appearances at which he was himself present. If, then, the first narrative, and the Gospel, as a whole, be deserving of faith, these further reports must equally be so. But we will not at present pursue this subject. We leave John in order to hear St. Paul, the second witness we have cited of the resurrection of Jesus. His testimony will be the more weighty, because it transports us to a quite different place and period, and throws light upon the question from a quite different point of view.

Paul, in his Epistle to the Galatians, had to defend his apostolic claims against those who maintained that he had not been himself directly a disciple of Jesus, but had received the gospel at second-hand, as it were, and through human instrumentality. In refutation of this charge, he begins his epistle by calling himself an apostle, not of men, neither by man, but by Jesus Christ, and God the Father, who raised him from the dead; that is, he derives his apostleship, not indeed from Jesus during his earthly career, but from the risen Lord. This he goes on still more distinctly to declare in the 12th verse; he had not received the gospel he preached, of man, neither was taught it but by the revelation of Jesus Christ. That in speaking of this revelation, he referred most especially to the occurrence before Damascus is plain from the 17th verse, in which he expressly names that city. Thus, then, Paul deduces his apostolic character and doctrine from a supernatural revelation of the Risen One on his way to Damascus. Only he does not on this occasion distinctly state whether this revelation was subjective merely, or objectively visible. The first theory would seem to be supported by the fact of Paul elsewhere speaking of visions and revelations of the Lord which he had experienced, as well as by his saying in the context of this passage in Galatians (16th verse), "It pleased God to reveal his Son *in me.*" Yet, on the other hand, we cannot hence fairly conclude the mere subjectivity of the event, for the apostle evidently intends, in these words, to express the result, which was to reveal the Son of God in his inmost heart and conscience. Without this internal conviction, a mere external appearance would have remained inoperative. Indeed, we should be disposed *a priori* to conclude that such a persecutor and destroyer of the Church of God as Paul represents himself to have been, must have needed some objective and powerfully-impressive circumstance to bring about the radical and remarkable transformation that he underwent. And that such was really vouchsafed, he himself expressly states in two places in the First Epistle to the Corinthians, ix. 1, xv. 8.

In the last passage, after mentioning some of the different appearances of the risen Lord, he says: "And last of all, he was seen by me also, as of one born out of due time. For I am the least of the apostles, who am not meet to be called an apostle, because I persecuted the Church of God." Here again he is speaking of his marvellous conversion from a persecutor to an apostle, and he ascribes it to an appearance of the risen Jesus, whom he describes as visible in the ordinary sense of the word. And in chap. ix. ver. 1., he exclaims in the same tone: "Am I not an apostle? Have I not *seen* Jesus Christ our Lord."

Thus Paul testifies that the transformation of his whole life and character was effected by the visible appearing of the risen Jesus, whereby he revealed himself outwardly and inwardly to Paul as the Son of God. Nay, he insists upon this fact of his having received his calling and commission as an apostle directly from the risen and ascended Lord, as that which constituted the strength of the apostolic position and claim which he had to defend. For, he argues, he whom the Lord has called to bear witness of him, and instructed in the way of salvation, is an apostle indeed.

But how then if Jesus were not risen after all? If Paul had deluded himself both as to having seen the eternally living Son of God before Damascus, and as to his subsequent wonderful inward communion with him? Is it at all probable, we reply, that so powerful an intellect should be transformed, by a mere self-delusion, from a persecutor of Jesus into his most zealous advocate? Is it probable that so sagacious a man in other matters, so acute and clear a thinker as from his writings we know Paul to have been, should, for the sake of a mere imagination, have braved countless pains and perils, and finally have suffered death? Is it possible that a man who (setting apart Christ himself) has had more influence in the history of the world than any other man whatever,—the whole standing of our Christian world being based on the exertions of the apostle of the Gentiles,—is it possible, I ask, that such a man should be under a mistake as to that which he himself affirmed to be the especial foundation of his life and his efforts? I appeal confidently to all who are well acquainted with the writings of Paul, Does the man who wrote the Epistle to the Romans make upon you the impression of a dreamer? Is it conceivable to you that, as to the very main point of all, he should have leaned upon a mere chimera? Have not his sayings been to each one of us a light shining on our life-path? Do not the hours that we have spent sitting at his feet reading or listening to his words rank amongst our best hours? If he has already raised millions of men above earthly cares, above the anguish of remorse and the fear of death, how can this have been done but by the energy of that spiritual life which he derived from the risen Lord?

Thus the influence daily exerted by the epistles of Paul, and indeed by the whole Bible, practically prove the truth of the witnesses to the resurrection. Shall all this go for nothing? Are we still to keep doggedly repeating, Resurrection from the dead is contrary to our experience, is inconceivable to us; consequently Paul, distinguished man as he confessedly was in other respects, must have been self-deluded in what was to him confessedly the most important point of all, in a manner that is undoubtedly very remarkable.

We, on the contrary, maintain that Paul, as well as John, is a most credible witness of the matter in hand. And now mark the advance in this second witness over the first. John only comes forward as an eye-witness to the external fact; Paul is a *life*-witness to the inward significance of this fact. The Living One has revealed himself to him as the life-giving, so that henceforth the man Paul is a practical proof of the resurrection life of Jesus; and is able to express the nature of his inmost being by the words: "I live, yet not I, but Christ liveth in me" (Gal. ii. 20). If Christ be not risen, the whole historical aspect of St. Paul is a riddle and a contradiction.

A similar relation to that between the witness of John and Paul will also be found to exist between the two collective testimonies, which we now proceed to consider.

There were in Corinth those who denied the resurrection of the dead altogether. To this false doctrine which was then prevalent, as it is to-day, Paul, in the 15th chapter of his First Epistle to the Corinthians, opposes the resurrection of Christ. That this was a positive fact he calls upon several eye-witnesses who had seen the risen Lord to vouch for. He was seen, we read in vers. 5-8, "of Cephas, then of the twelve. After that he was seen of above five hundred brethren at once, of whom the greater part remain unto the present, but some have fallen asleep. After that he was seen of James, then of all the apostles, and last of all he was seen of me also."

These five hundred brethren or more must have constituted the whole of those who had been brought to believe by the ministry of Jesus himself. In other places, the only numbers given in addition to the twelve, are those of the seventy disciples whom the Lord sent out, and the one hundred and twenty who were gathered together at Jerusalem between the Ascension and the day of Pentecost (Luke x. i; Acts i. 15). Hence it seems probable that the aggregate number of believers, whom Jesus left behind, including the Galileans, could not have exceeded a few hundreds, and that Paul accordingly cites as witnesses of the resurrection nearly the whole of the original Church, with the apostles at its head.

But some among you may be inclined to declare that this bringing forward only disciples and brethren, and not indifferent and impartial witnesses, to prove the fact, is the very circumstance that excites suspicion. Why, you ask, if Jesus had indeed risen, did he not manifest himself in glory to all the world? Then the whole question would have been decided once for all, and there would have been no need to be constantly reviving and strengthening the arguments for faith in him, and in his resurrection. We reply, that the Risen One will yet show himself in his glory to the whole world, to the dismay of his foes, and the eternal joy of his brethren and disciples. But this was not, and ought not to have been the condition of his first appearing; he did not then design to convince the world of his divine majesty, by an external display of omnipotence. It was just such a method as this that the tempter suggested when he challenged him to throw himself from the pinnacle of the temple, and by this marvellous spectacle convince the people of his Messiahship. But Christ was no magician; he was the Redeemer; he would not outwardly overpower humanity, and bind it to him by mere wonder, he would rather inwardly convince and renew it. This is the sublime, free, only truly moral method which Jesus has carried out by the spiritual instrumentality of his word and holy life. He did not, indeed, lack the power of working miracles to authenticate his divine mission; there was a sufficient display of these to remove all pretext for unbelief in his contemporaries; but these were never independent and isolated occurrences, but had always a close connexion with the holy person and doctrine of Jesus taken as a whole. And hence the Risen One could not appear to the world, but only to those who had believed his simple word, and discerned the divine glory through the disguise of the form of a servant; to these he now showed himself in his risen majesty as a reward of their faith.

But these men, who had the true sense for the divine, and afterwards became not only eye-witnesses, but life and death witnesses to the fact, afford us irresistible evidence of the resurrection of Jesus. These repeated appearances, not merely to individuals, but to dozens, to hundreds, have a peculiarly convincing power. Granted that an individual might easily deceive himself, or fall into some abnormal and visionary state in which he could fancy that he saw a dead man still living, here we have more than five hundred reliable men, who, being in their sound senses, saw the crucified alive before them; or, even granted that on some one occasion several men might be deluded, here is a whole series of different cases happening at different times, where now one, now twelve, now hundreds, see the risen Saviour. There must, indeed, exist a strong prejudice, to say the very least, where such evidence as this can be explained away as hallucination, *i. e.*, mere imagination of diseased minds.

Again, there is another notable fact to be taken into consideration. We know that in the first Christians, and especially in the twelve, a decided change was effected by the appearance of the risen Christ, not indeed so marvellous a change as that experienced by Paul, but still a deep and influential one. The death of Jesus had, as was inevitable, deeply depressed them, and shaken their faith; but soon after we see them appear full of confidence and joy, as witnesses to this same Jesus, ready to undergo, on account of their faith in him, shame, imprisonment, and death. If then the Lord did not rise from the dead, how are we to explain this mighty transformation? How are we to understand the early Christians making this very fact of his resurrection the groundwork of their doctrine, nay, their professing their vocation essentially to lie in witnessing to it?

This leads us to our fourth and last proof. We find the two apostles, John and Paul, not only testifying to the fact of the resurrection, but to its significance and its consequences; and this indeed is the case with the primitive Church in general. Paul reminds the Corinthians (xv. 1) of the gospel which he preached unto them, which also they had received, wherein they stood, by which also they were saved. The import, then, of these good tidings, upon which the whole life and blessedness of Christians rest, is that Christ died for our sins, and that he was buried, and that he rose again the third day. To which Paul adds: "Therefore, whether it were I or they (the other twelve apostles), so we preach, and so ye believed."

Here then we have it plainly declared that all the apostles, and together with them the whole primitive Church, held the death and resurrection of Christ as the central fact of the gospel, as the essential foundation of Christian faith. Christianity is indeed nothing else but the fact and the doctrine, that through the death of Christ the sins of the world were judged and expiated; and through his resurrection spiritual life and glory restored to humanity. He who denies the resurrection of Christ, does not deny this or that main feature of Christianity; he denies Christianity as a whole. For, as says St. Paul (vers. 14, 15), "If Christ be not risen, then is our preaching vain, and your faith is also vain; ye are yet in your sins, and we are found false witnesses of God: because we have testified of God that he raised up Christ; whom he raised not up."

It is therefore an untrue and misleading idea that some of our unbelievers put forth, when they profess to retain the essentials of Christianity, its moral element, namely, and merely to eliminate from it a few external and minor details connected with wonders and dogmas that no longer suit our enlightened times. In the same spirit we sometimes hear it said: "We will firmly retain the sayings of Jesus, on account of their indisputable moral truth and excellence; we will only dispense with faith in his miraculous works." But, as has been more fully put forth in the previous Lecture, the sayings of our Lord abound in testimony to the great all-inclusive miracle of his person, the source of all individual miracles whatsoever, and to his superhuman and divine nature. And so too is it here. It is impossible to dissever the morality taught by Christianity from the faith it teaches.

Christian morality depends on faith, and faith depends on the fact—the miraculous, divinely-wrought historical fact—of the resurrection of Jesus; nay, Christian morality itself is nothing else than the new life which the risen Lord imparts to us by his Holy Spirit.

If then Christ be not risen, not only the apostles and early Christians, but the Christianity of all time is in error respecting precisely the chief article of its faith. What Paul says of himself applies to the whole Church; it becomes a perfect riddle and self-contradiction, since, in spite of the world-renewing vital energy which facts prove it to possess, it is all the time based upon a merely imaginary life. Surely, if it had been a house thus built upon the sand, it would, like so many other fanatical sects, have gone to pieces long ago beneath the countless storms that have beat upon it during more than eighteen centuries; instead of which the Church of Christ still stands, the gates of hell not having prevailed against it, and numbers amongst its members not only all the civilized nations of the earth, but also a countless number of those who are life-witnesses of the resurrection of the Lord, being able to say with Paul: "We who were dead in sins, hath he quickened together with Christ, and hath raised us up together, and made us sit together in heavenly places in Christ Jesus."

On the ground, then, of the fourfold testimony borne by John and Paul; by the first Christians who had seen the risen Jesus; and by the apostolic doctrine on which the Church is founded; we may now more confidently than before assert the resurrection of Christ to be a fact. If anything whatever in the world be susceptible of historical proof by contemporary evidence, we are obliged to confess this marvellous occurrence to have really happened. Even a member of the Baur school, Dr. Volkmar of Zurich, in his in other respects unqualifiedly negative work on the Religion of Jesus (p. 76), finds himself constrained to admit: "One of the most certain facts in the world's history is, that Jesus, the Crucified, appeared in glory to his disciples, whether we understand or not, understand thoroughly, or imperfectly understand this fact." We, therefore, consider the assertion, with which we began our Lecture, to have been satisfactorily established, and may now turn to the second branch of our subject, the putting forth of the most important of the necessary inferences from this fact of the resurrection. We deduce a double series of these inferences, retrospective and prospective, and each of these series may be divided into three heads. Retrospectively, we find that light is thrown on the being of God, the being of Christ, and on the preparatory dispensation of the Old Testament.

In the first place, if we ask how the resurrection of Jesus is to be explained, what can be thought to have been its efficient cause, there is only one rational answer. We find ourselves referred to the power of an almighty God, who alone can quicken the dead. Both Jesus and Paul attribute the denial of a resurrection to ignorance of God, and of his power (Matt. xxii. 29; 1 Cor. xv. 34). The resurrection of Jesus is a practical contradiction of Pantheism, which denies a super-mundane and miracle-working God. But together with the form of error respecting God prevalent at the present time, it equally opposes the mode of thought of our earlier Rationalism, in which some of the older amongst us were educated; that so-called Deism, which, while accepting a super-mundane personal God and Creator, maintained that, after completing the creation, he either led an existence entirely apart from the world, or ruled it only by natural and uninterrupted laws, so that the dead must remain dead, and all miracles generally be impossible. Both of these errors, though theoretically contrasted, have one and the same result, in their denial of the miraculous, and of the resurrection; therefore the establishment of the latter fact must alike silence them both. Truth, however, does not conquer error by simply sweeping it away; but rather by separating the component parts of truth and falsehood which constitute error, and by freeing from the veil of falsehood the truthful elements latent in that error, enabling them to assert their rights. Generally speaking, error consists in giving prominence simply to one side of truth, and mistaking the part for the whole, while some conflicting error adopts the other side with equal exclusiveness. The truth lies in a third higher conception, which embraces both sides of the truth (one sidedness being error), and joins them in a living unity. This is the case with the true Christian Theistic idea of God, in contradistinction to the Pantheistic and Deistic. It embraces both the supermundane nature of God, which is held by Deism, and his intermundane nature held by Pantheism. God is the absolutely independent, personally-living supermundane Spirit, who yet, at the same time, as the Spirit of the world, evolves it from within, and fills it with life, so that he both is in the world, and the world lives, moves, and has its being in him. Because he is *in* the world, as its source of life, he can continually work and create therein; and because he is *above* the world, and has in himself a higher life than that of the world, he can create *new* things in it, quicken what is dead, and impart to it his own higher life. This he has done in the resurrection of Christ, through which the perfect spiritual life of God in the Son of man is represented to the world, just as out of the darkness and confusion of chaos the world was framed a harmoniously-ordered *Cosmos;* and, as by the creation, in the image of God, of the free agent, man, the domain of history was superadded to that of nature, so again, by the resurrection of Christ, a new kingdom was based upon the existence of humanity, the kingdom of a glorified and perfected life. Hence we must needs have a living and life-giving God, since he is not only the creator, but also the renewer and perfecter of the world.

Next, what does this resurrection of Christ teach us concerning himself? This fact, by which his whole existence is exalted to a new and higher stage, reveals him as a personal miracle. If Christ be risen, there can be no rational ground to doubt his divine origin, but rather the strongest reason to believe in it, his supernatural birth into the new life by the Spirit, harmonizing closely with his supernatural incarnation in the womb of the Virgin Mary. And it is equally natural that we should find narrated between the initial and the final miracle connected with the person of Christ, a succession of miracles done by him. Thus the resurrection of Christ is the essential proof of the authenticity of the evangelical records of miraculous works. What might indeed well have perplexed us would have been to find that such a one as Jesus, whom God called into natural and supernatural life in a miraculous manner, was not himself furnished with superhuman might. In short, Jesus Christ is, as St. Paul says, by the resurrection from the dead, declared to be the Son of God with power (Rom. i. 4). And, further, since this very Jesus teaches us to understand his divine Sonship in the sense of his having been, before his appearance on earth, nay, before the foundation of the world, with the Father, sharing his glory, and beloved by him (John xvii. 5, 24); since he introduces himself between the Father and the Spirit as one of the three divine sources of salvation to humanity (Matt. xxviii. 19), it is only rational to repose belief in the self-assertions of one whose testimony has been so miraculously authenticated. It is not only in its vitally Theistic, but in its Trinitarian aspect, that the Christian conception of God finds its confirmation in the resurrection of Christ.

Let me now very briefly point out the inferences respecting the Old Testament dispensation to be drawn from this resurrection. All that I remarked to you on a former occasion touching the miracles of the Old Testament, finds further support in this great fact. If Christ be the light from which the Old Testament received its enlightenment and its deeper meaning, so is his resurrection the crowning miracle which affords corroboration to all the miracles related in the Old Testament. I cannot here enlarge upon how the two modes of its preparatory revelation, the condescension of the divine in the heavenly manifestations, and the exaltation of the human in the prophecies, meet in Christ the Risen One. I will only remind you that in him all the prophecies of the Old Covenant begin to have their fulfilment, from that first gospel of the bruising the serpent's head by the seed of the woman, down to Isaiah's declaration of the swallowing up of death in victory, and of that servant of the Lord who after his sacrificial death should prolong his days, and the pleasure of the Lord prosper in his hand (Gen. iii. 15; Isaiah xxv. 8, liii. 10). But so much is logically conclusive; God having by the raising up of his Son shown himself to be a miraculous God, we are bound to recognise his miraculous power in the domain of the introductory revelation. And if the miracles recorded there be different, be more externally amazing than those in the New, this not only was inherent, as has been already shown, in the very nature of the Old Testament, but it surely does not become creatures to draw a line as to how far the miracles of the Creator and Lord of the universe ought to go. Rather should this resurrection of Jesus inspire us with fresh confidence in the earlier dispensation, and lead us utterly to relinquish that miserable logic which will in some measure assent to God's miraculous dealings in the New Testament but not in the Old.

We turn to the second series of inferences to be drawn from this great fact. They supply answers to three questions, namely, What does the resurrection of Jesus teach us as to his present existence? What as to his influence in our own times? and What as regards the future?

Christ is risen; that is, not only has his soul or spirit survived death, but his body has been reunited with that spirit, and this not only in the manner of an earthly, material existence, such as previous to his death Jesus himself was subjected to, and after their revival the widow of Nain's son and Lazarus continued to lead (compare 1 Cor. xv. 42-44). The spiritual body is no longer so oppressed by the burden of matter as to weigh, drag down, and impede the very spirit itself; rather it is the perfectly free and facile instrument of the spirit to which it is unconditionally subordinated. Accordingly we see the Risen One enter through shut doors, change his actual appearance, and vanish at will. And yet in spite of this perfect independence of the limits of matter and space, he is still on the other side capable of being touched and of eating with mortal men; for such the free sway of the spirit over the spiritual body, that it can mould and adapt it to every kind of circumstance and purpose.

This is certainly something strange and new to our customary range of ideas. But so indeed it ought to be. It relates to a new, a more exalted life for humanity, degraded as it at present is beneath the ban of the world and the flesh. If we reflect somewhat more deeply, these scripturally attested miracles will reveal themselves to us as most truly consistent with reason, in that they raise human nature to the full perfection of its ideal and its destiny. The perversion of our sinful condition consists in the higher elements of our being, the spiritual, having fallen under the dominion of the lower elements, which are sensual. This condition the Bible pointedly expresses by the word *flesh*, which has death for inevitable consequence, while it is in the *spirit* alone (wherein lies our relation with God), that we can have life. If then the great fact of the resurrection certifies us that the higher, better portion of our nature shall be made free from the ban of the lower, the animal portion,—nay, shall attain to perfect unlimited sway over it,—how should we fail to receive such a message with a joyful welcome? Doubtless, we of ourselves were powerless to bring about such a result, the resources of our reason could never have devised it; but since God, by means of his creative power and love, has done this, surely the thankful agreement of our reason should not be wanting. For it is not something obscure, arbitrary, unreasonable, that he presents to us in this risen Christ, but, on the contrary, he is the Light of the world, who alone dispels all gloom and darkness, and solves all the problems and perplexities of our existence. In him the gloomy spell that held humanity enthralled is done away; in him humanity is rendered free, restored to its true nature, because restored to full and unclouded life-communion with God. He is the glory of our race, the pledge of an eternal perfection. Surely we should rejoice and be glad, since the Prince of life comes forth to meet us in the radiance of the Easter morning, instead of scanning and criticising his appearance by the narrow and inadequate measure of an earthly horizon.

There are many among us who rightfully revolt from the idea that death ends all, and that man has no personal duration beyond it, but who yet take exception at the doctrine of the resurrection of the body, and profess themselves satisfied with the immortality of the soul. This again was the opinion of the earlier Rationalists, and it is still held by many who imbibed it in youth. Doubtless this view is a far higher one than the later Pantheistic-materialist delusion, that man dies out like the beasts. But still it is an error, a one-sidedness, which only duly honours one part of human nature—the soul—and depreciates the worth of the body. This spiritualistic view, which contemplates man exclusively as immaterial, appears as the antithesis to materialism, which asserts the claims of the body in so exaggerated a strain as to reduce the soul to a mere product of the highest forces of that body, so that obviously the dissolution of these involves that of the spirit also. It is easy to see that these two theories, spiritualism and materialism, are antithetical errors with regard to the nature of man, analogous to Deism and Pantheism with relation to God. Pantheism merges God in the world; Materialism merges the soul in the body; whereas Deism, on the other hand, contemplates God apart from the world, and spiritualism the soul apart from the body in lifeless separation. The true, the scriptural view, combines the elements of truth in both extremes, while rejecting their errors. It deprives neither soul nor body of its due worth, but in spirit it recognises an independent, higher, God-derived being, which finally so fills the body with its might and glory that the body itself as a glorified spiritual body gains an eternal and incorruptible life (1 Cor. xv. 42-47). Thus in the resurrection not one alone but all sides of human nature attain to perfection. And this is what we see typically represented in the risen body of Christ, and secured to all those who in faith and spirit are one with him.

This glorified spiritual life, upon which the risen Saviour has entered, is essentially heavenly life, in contradistinction to earthly and material. Accordingly, the earth can no longer hold him, and the ascension of Jesus is the natural consequence of his resurrection. Here, however, we are met by an objection derived from modern astronomy. "We know now," say our opponents, "that the heaven, which an obsolete view of the universe was wont to place in opposition to the earth, consists of numberless star-worlds, solar systems, amongst whose planets our earth is one of the least. Thus that contradistinction between earth and heaven that obtained in earlier conceptions of the universe is now at an end, and we can no longer speak of an ascension into heaven." But we only need a little closer examination to find out and dispel the fallacy of this plausible but erroneous assertion. The heaven into which Christ is gone is the invisible spiritual heaven, while the starry heaven belongs to the visible and material universe. There is, therefore, between the two the essential difference of the visible and the invisible. Let the starry universe extend far as it may, that does not prevent there being an essentially different and higher sphere of existence, in which God specially manifests the fulness of his glory, a reign of perfect spiritual life, a Father's house with many mansions, which belong to the angels, and to the spirits of just men made perfect (John xiv. 2; Heb. xii. 22-24). Thither Jesus went when, in the words of St. Paul, he ascended up far above all heavens (Eph. iv. 10). Just as the law of gravitation cannot hinder the bird's flight, the fact of the Copernican system or Herschel's later discoveries in no way interferes with the ascension of Christ. Where higher forces and laws come in, the lower must necessarily give way.

Above all heavens then hath Christ ascended, and there he hath sat down at the right hand of the Majesty on high. No inferior place becomes the Son of God. He hath entered into the perfect glory and absolute dominion of the divine throne. The Father hath said to him, All that is mine is thine (John xvii. 10; xvi.

15). Thus, then, we think with certainty of him above, not only as living an eternal life, but dwelling in all the fulness of the Godhead bodily (Rom. vi. 9; Col. ii. 9). No man hath raised him to the throne of God, but God himself hath highly exalted him, and given him a name which is above every name (Phil. ii. 9). Therefore, no man can ever depose him from that throne; no power of any kind can be brought to bear against him: he is invulnerable by spiritual as by carnal weapons. It is on this that we base our confidence in Christianity. For what, indeed, is Christianity but this very Christ himself, living at the right hand of God? To assault him is to seek to overthrow a rock by paper pellets. To all such attempts the language of that psalm of old applies, "He that sitteth in heaven shall laugh; the Lord shall have them in derision," and again, "Sit thou at my right hand, till I shall make thy foes thy footstool (Ps. ii. 4; cx. 1).

Our second question relates to the present office of the ascended Saviour. He is in his heavenly glory the Mediator still between God and man. He appears on behalf of humanity as a Priest before God, and on God's behalf before men, as a King, who has to subject the whole world to himself, that he may fill it with divine life. In his whole personality as God and man, he represents before God the perfect propitiation for the world, yea, he is himself the atonement for our sins, so that his people have in him a priestly intercessor, who can save to the uttermost those who come to God by him (1 John ii. 1, 2; Rom. viii. 34; Heb. vii. 25). But while his priestly influence is hidden in the profundities of heaven, and only recognisable by faith, his kingly sway, on the other hand, is openly made manifest on the earth.

But is this indeed the case? some may ask. Nearly two thousand years have rolled away since Christ sat down at the right hand of God, and we see not yet that all things are put under him (comp. Heb. ii. 8). On the contrary, we still see prevail, and that in an eminent degree, much that is evil, ungodly, and unchristian. How does this accord with the sovereignty of him whose sway should be divinely omnipotent? We reply: In this world of ours, the whole is subject to the law of development, of gradual growth from within. Thus Jesus himself underwent a process of development out of the manger and the cross up to the glory of the resurrection and the sitting down at the right hand of God.

His kingdom is now undergoing the same law; it is gradually advancing from its lowliness, its crucified aspect, to the highest perfection and splendour, because Jesus is, by great periodical stages of development, subjecting the world ever more and more to himself.

And already we may trace many bright signs of his kingly power in the history of mankind. A king has two ways of displaying the might and wisdom of his government: by its beneficent effects upon the internal life of his people, and its triumphant conquest of all external foes. Thus too does Christ, in the history of the world, assert his sovereignty, both by blessing and judging.

We reckon years and centuries from the birth of our Lord. Universal history is placed beneath his influence, divided into the periods *before* and *after* Christ. The whole of the civilized world celebrates his birth, his death, his resurrection, and ascension, and the year is divided according to these festivals. Each week begins with the Sunday, the memorial-day of his resurrection. Thus, to begin with, our whole life is outwardly pervaded and governed by his name. Such honour and homage as this was never paid to any other, either in ancient or in modern times. An attempt was openly made about seventy years ago by the French people to discard the Christian mode of reckoning time; but after a few years this new system died away of itself. Again, is there not a regal sway of Christ over the nations? And which are the nations which own it? They are not a few, insignificant, uncivilized peoples, hid away here or there in corners of the earth; no, the nations that confess the name of Christ combine the greatest power and the highest culture in the world; they alone represent humanity in its loftier aspect. We need only dwell by contrast on the condition of the Turks and the Chinese, who in their way are also great and cultivated empires, but based upon Mahometanism and heathenism. The Turks only continue to exist by the sufferance of the Christian Powers; and in the so-called Celestial Empire we have recently seen a handful of Christian soldiers succeed in driving the Emperor from his throne, plundering his palace, and taking possession of his capital. We need, indeed, only to spend a few years in a land that is not Christian, even if it be the much-lauded Greece of old, to estimate the privilege of a Christian atmosphere. But we need not occupy more time in proving the moralizing and civilizing influence of Christianity; its opponents are themselves the most convincing witnesses of this, laying as they do such stress upon the retaining of the moral truths of the gospel. Their error only consists in believing it possible to cut down the tree, and yet to gather its fruits in coming years.

Thus we see the heavenly King exercises his power to bless even over those who are but outwardly subject to his sceptre. And he equally proves himself to be a judge by overcoming all his enemies, one after the other, whether they oppose him by political or merely intellectual weapons. First of all, Judaism rose against Christianity. It was at Jerusalem that the earliest martyrs died; but that city was destroyed, and to the present day the Jewish people remain scattered over all the earth. Then heathenism entered the lists, armed with the whole might of the Roman Empire, and the persecution of the Christians continued from the first to the fourth century; but the result was, that the whole Roman empire, as well as the Germanic nations that replaced it, finally embraced Christianity. In the seventh century, Islamism arose, and soon became a considerable power, that for fully a thousand years oppressed the Christian Church in different places, and tore great sections away from her; but in the present day, we see the Mahometan power in ruins, and the world belongs to Christians.

Thus, too, has it been with the intellectual assailants

of Christianity. In the first century of our era, it was attacked by heathen philosophers, such as Celsus and Porphyry, with all the resources of their ingenuity, but they were unable to check the world-subduing progress of the kingdom of Christ. In later times, the attempts to undermine have been made from within the nominal Church, and have gone the round of all the most civilized peoples. In the sixteenth century, the field was taken against Christianity by Humanitarianism in Italy; in the seventeenth, by Deism in England; in the eighteenth, by Materialism in France; in the nineteenth, by Rationalism in Germany. But all these modes of thought have passed by, the gospel is still living and powerful, and in our day spreading itself to the very ends of the earth. The sharpest weapons of criticism and philosophy have been blunted, the most promising systems succeed each other on the arena, but they only reciprocally destroy and dispel each other; they are, in short, gone by. They have merely led to Christian truth being more thoroughly inquired into, more deeply based, more freely developed, more convincingly proved. And thus, too, when Antichristianity shall at some future time gather together all its resources, and unveil its last mystery, the Lord himself will appear in his majesty as judge, and the breath of his mouth shall destroy his enemies.

Thus, then, the whole of Christian history is a fulfilment of that word spoken by Jesus in the day of his deepest humiliation: "Hereafter shall ye see the Son of man sitting at the right hand of power (as king), and coming in the clouds of heaven" (as judge). Nevertheless it is true that this subjection of the world to the sceptre of Christ, which we have been dwelling upon, is not yet what it shall be; that even the Christian world is still *the world* in which much that is ungodly and unchristian in character, both in small things and great, continues in vogue.

But the happy influence of Christianity upon the manners and customs of nations is, after all, only an influence of a secondary order. That which the heavenly King primarily designs and effects is something much higher: the regeneration of mankind by the Holy Spirit. Now that Christ is exalted at God's right hand, and has received the promise of the Holy Spirit from the Father, he has shed forth this that ye see and hear. So spake Peter at the feast of Pentecost (Acts ii. 33), and in these words he expressed the inmost and essential nature of the royal rule of Christ. Because the glorified Son of man is now spirit, even as God is spirit (2 Cor. iii. 17; John iv. 24); because he has taken his human nature into the divine spiritual glory, he is become the personal source of spiritual life for humanity. It is through him that the everlasting energies of God flow into humanity; it is because he is gone to the Father that the Comforter can come to us (John xvi. 7).

Since that first Whitsuntide, when Peter spoke those sublime words, the Holy Spirit has been in humanity so far as it has believed in Christ, and this is more especially the great and new dispensation which we are to look upon as the result of his resurrection and ascension. He in whom this Holy Spirit dwells is, in the full sense of the word, a subject of the heavenly King, a member of him who is the head. This Holy Spirit, shedding abroad divine light and life into the hearts of humanity, is the continuous proof that Jesus was not holden of death, but lives in eternal glory. For this Spirit is a reality, yea, the reality of realities in this world. Whosoever will, may know this by experience. It is through this Spirit that the gates of hell never could, nor can prevail against the Church; it is his might that transforms all heresies and perversions into reformatory agencies and witnesses to the truth. We in Basle, who have had so many proofs of this Spirit's power, should indeed be readily convinced of his reality. I, as one not belonging to the place, may at least state, not to the praise of man, but of God, what has been my experience, and what students from other countries have remarked to me: that there is here in our churches, our Christian societies, institutions, and individual men, in the labours of love which follow after the lost in all corners of the globe, a manifest breathing of the Holy Spirit. No doubt a man may, in broad day, resolutely close his eyes, and assert that it is night. Blindness is much the same as darkness, only the sun still shines in the sky. So is it with the influence of the Holy Spirit.

But although the risen Lord does, as we have shown, both inwardly and outwardly, manifest himself as King, yet, nevertheless, this is by no means the full revelation of his kingly power. There are still great antagonisms to be done away with; the antagonism between the Church and the world,—as well as that within the Church itself, between inward spiritual glory and outward weakness and imperfection,—and in every individual Christian there is the antagonism between the flesh and the Spirit. Nevertheless, the risen Lord is our personal security for the removal of all these contradictions and obstacles, and for the shedding abroad in all the world of the perfect life which he himself is living. It is not my task to dwell more particularly upon the different stages of resurrection and world-perfection, which St. Paul gives as the result of the great event of the latter day: Christ the first-fruits; *afterward* they that are Christ's at his coming, *then* the end (1 Cor. xv. 23, 24). But suffer me, in a few words, to call your attention to this *end*, this final stage of the world's gradual development.

The resurrection of Jesus Christ is the living cause and commencement of a glorified world; a new heaven and new earth, wherein dwelleth righteousness; a condition of internal and external completeness of life, where tears shall be wiped away from all faces, sin and death, and all the antagonistic influences of the world being done away; and God, with his inexpressible glory, being all in all (1 Cor. xv. 28; 2 Pet. iii. 13; Rev. xxi. 1). This view is the only one that sheds true light both on our own individual lives, and on the historical, moral, and religious aspect of the world at large. It is this alone that points to any satisfactory conclusion to the history of the world, or calms the perplexities of our thoughts respecting its problems and intricacies. Our moral consciousness demands that evil should be actually overcome some time or other, and that good should absolutely prevail in the world. It demands an identity of virtue and happiness; a perfect harmony between the inner and the outer, the spiritual and the material. These demands ought to be fulfilled; every ideal engraved in our conscience ought to be realized. But had Christ not risen, we could have had no positive security for all this. In the Christian's hope of a glorified world lies the true Theodicea; that is, the justification of God regarding the many sins and imperfections in the world. The glory of God requires that he should allow free scope to the liberty of the creature, should allow evil to attain its extremest growth, and first discover to us the inconceivable fulness of his perfections, by making all instances of opposition to himself but new opportunities of grander and grander revelations of his life and love, and by attaining the original purpose of his creation in spite of all apparent obstacles.

For our own parts, this glance of hope into the new world should teach us properly to value the present, and thus alike afford us the true rule of life, and the true consolation for death. This world, with its possessions, enjoyments, occupations, and cares, is not our abiding city; it is soon over; the fashion of it passeth away (1 Cor. vii. 31). To reach our inheritance in the new, the eternal world, is our earthly task, is the genuine wisdom of this present life. Further, we are consoled for the necessity we are under to leave it, to see our loved ones leave it before us. They who sleep in the Lord depart not to death, but to life, life everlasting. The risen Lord will fulfil his own word concerning us: "Because I live, ye shall live also" (John xiv. 19).

VIII.

THE HOLY SPIRIT AND THE CHRISTIAN CHURCH.

THE doctrine of the Holy Spirit is most intimately connected with the doctrine of the Christian Church, the Spirit being the vital principle of the Church. But, first of all then, we must inquire, Is there indeed a Holy Spirit? A superficial mind may throw off the question, and return a confident denial, because, from his very nature, the Spirit is not perceptible to the bodily sense. We ask again, however, Is there a Christian Church? And here ocular demonstration forbids the returning any other answer than one of decided assent. The Christian Church stands before us as a historical fact; nay, as the most influential fact in the history of the world. A new era of national life arose with its first appearance, which forms so decided a turning-point, that even purely secular history reckons time from the birth of its founder. Our whole life, not merely religious, but social and political, is pervaded by its influence, even where we scarcely suspect it. It has consecrated all our family ties; based the relation between husband and wife, parent and child, upon purely moral principles; from it have proceeded popular culture and public instruction; it has originated the recognised obligation to care for the old, the poor, the sick, the widow, and the orphan; and the now universally acknowledged laws of humanity are laws that it first laid down. They are the positive fruits of the faith that this Church holds, and by her preaching of this faith, as well as by its practical application to all social relations, she has displayed an inexhaustible vital energy that endures for century after century.

Since then we find here ideas and principles, since we must confess to an inward world-subduing power of life and faith, which, in changing times and different nations and individuals, remains essentially the same, and bears the same noble fruits, we are irresistibly led to acknowledge that a *Spirit* must have ruled within this Church from its earliest beginning till now, and undoubtedly one only Spirit, powerful and essentially good. We constantly come to a conclusion as to the nature of the indwelling spirit of this or that man among us; we speak of the spirit that prevails in an assembly, a body corporate, a nation; and we also see, in a far higher sense, a spirit pervading and controlling the Christian Church. Just as the universe, by its existence and laws, presupposes a creative eternal Spirit, so the continuance and progress of the Church proves to us the existence of a Spirit by which she is what she is. A Church without a Spirit were an inconceivable and impossible thing. Nor can we reasonably think of this Spirit as a mere idea; the abstract sum and unity of thoughts and deeds found in the Church; an impersonal idea under which was comprehended the many-coloured mosaic of Christian life, that Jews, Greeks, Romans, and Germans evolved. On the contrary, we must confess this Spirit to be a definite and conscious personality, who stamps and develops his own peculiar impress on these various peoples, races, and generations. The countless divisions and offences within the Church must not mislead us; rather should we confess it to be a marvellous fact, that in the course of nearly two thousand years, so much human folly, hypocrisy, and sinfulness should not have quenched this Spirit, and hindered the Church from reaching its aim. A Spirit never led away by the spirit of humanity, but opposing to it, and exercising over it, a definite and ennobling influence, can only be sought and found in God himself. And this is what the consciousness of the Church clearly expresses in that clause of her creed: I believe in the Holy Ghost.

Nevertheless, it was not through her own unaided reflection and reasoning that she came to this conclusion: she received it from above by revelation from God—a truth that both her historical career, and the personal experience of each of her members, unqualifiedly attest. This revelation is most intimately connected with the whole of God's great plan for the redemption of mankind from sin and its consequences, with the revelation of God as the Father, and in the Son.

The Old Testament is the expression of one fundamental idea—the sovereignty of God. To represent this idea, one kingdom was to be established, wherein God himself should be King, and men his subjects; and in conformity to the typical and preparatory character of that period, one peculiar people in one particular land was to be chosen to this end. Hence the Israelitish Theocracy. It might indeed have seemed as though this plan had failed of its primary purpose, since, after the return from the Babylonian Captivity, the people of Israel led a miserable existence, both religiously and politically, and at last fell beneath the Roman sway, their own royal house having sunk into obscurity and poverty. Then however it was, that, according to the promises of God through the prophets, Messiah himself appeared.

Jesus at once took up this seemingly unaccomplished divine plan, not only as one which had not failed, but which had been throughout wisely carried on, and was just about to reach its fulfilment. His first announcement was "the glad tidings of the kingdom of God;" the time is fulfilled, and "the kingdom of God is at hand." But not only was his office to restore and to establish, but to extend and glorify; to carry out into actuality and perfection what had been typical. What, in the preparatory dispensation, had applied to *one* people (as first-fruits) in *one* land, was now to hold good of humanity as a whole throughout all the earth. The doctrine of Jesus was not specially Jewish, but universal, adapted alike to all men and all times; his character is the perfect model, not only of Jewish morality and Jewish customs, but of universal human morality; in his sufferings and death, as also in his resurrection, he appears not only as Israel's Redeemer, but the Saviour of the world. He is not only the Son of David, but the Son of man.

This character of universality is stamped also upon his own sayings respecting that kingdom of God or of heaven which he introduced, sayings that almost invariably assume the garb of parables. We remark two different classes of these parables, recorded by St. Matthew in the 13th, and 24th, and 25th chapters of his Gospel. In the first class, Jesus presents this kingdom under two aspects, of which one is the complement of the other. On one side, it appears as seed scattered by a higher hand, as a treasure, a pearl, briefly, a good that humanity never could itself have produced, and could only receive by revelation from God; on the other side, as something not already complete, not, according to the Jewish idea, coming with observation and outward splendour; not a thing to be at once possessed, like a rich inheritance or a costly garment; but rather a precious germ which must needs find its development and its growth on earth. This double character is especially indicated in the parable of the four kinds of ground on which the good seed fell, and of the tares in the wheat,—the field in the last case not designating the people of Israel but the world;—while the external process of this development, from the smallest beginnings to the most comprehensive results is imaged by the grain of mustard seed, and its inward nature by the leaven which noiselessly but effectually leavens the whole lump, that is, essentially transforms its character. The second class of parables are those spoken at the close of his career by Jesus to his disciples more immediately, it being necessary that they should now have a deeper insight afforded them. Here we observe a significant advance in the ideas conveyed. In the earlier parables, Jesus had not distinguished between his kingdom and his person, but now a marked distinction is drawn between the Lord and the servants, the Bridegroom and the virgins. In close connexion with this, we observe that human efforts and responsibility are now more strongly insisted upon. And consequently the probation, the period of expectation, which was before merely hinted at, is placed in stronger relief, the conclusion of which, however, stands not in the will or power of the servants, but is to be brought about by the Lord through a new revelation of himself.

Thus the sayings of our Lord more and more clearly indicate that the kingdom of heaven as a glorious whole is a *future* thing; that now it is indeed begun, indeed growing, but as a perfect kingdom of God "neither here nor there." Nor is this, as some have insinuated, a fortunate expedient by which Jesus explained the failure of his original idea, but rather we see throughout the course of his sufferings and his life, as well as throughout all his sayings, a uniform and consistent plan. The fact of redemption is the triumph over this world and its prince. Henceforth the partition wall between mankind and God is taken away—men are reconciled and reunited to him. But this can as little be done by external force and might as—in a narrower sphere—Israel could be truly healed and delivered by a Messiah according to its own expectation. The process must ever begin *within*. It would contradict the essential nature of the kingdom of God, to include subjects who only belonged to it by constraint: the primary idea of it implies its consisting only of members who have been made such by inward conviction, who are partakers of it not from necessity but choice. God is the God of love and liberty, and thus it is only through free-will and unconstrained love that mankind can be united to him and made like him. It results, then, that "except a man be born again, he cannot see the kingdom of God." Therefore Jesus not only declined all external dominion over Israel, but did not after his resurrection appear in open triumph to humanity at large; on the contrary, he withdrew his visible presence, and assigned to his kingdom—as not of this world—a purely spiritual career. All that he left behind was a small band of disciples who knew neither the day nor the hour of the end, but had received from him the commission to witness of him to Israel and to all other nations, to spread the glad tidings of redemption over the world, and to make of all people disciples like themselves, by baptizing them and teaching them to observe all things whatsoever he had commanded them.

Thus the disciples being formed into a society, having the Redeemer for their common centre, were (like leaven) to gather man after man, people after people, into their circle. And this community, appointed from that small beginning to grow and spread inwardly and outwardly, and to ripen towards that perfection which the Lord was to usher in at his coming again,—*this is the Christian Church.*

Nor was it any miscalculation that Jesus made when he trusted this task to the hands of weak and sinful men; far otherwise. When such simple witnesses as these appeared with the tidings of Jesus the Saviour, there was indeed neither constraint nor illusion practised upon their hearers; on the contrary, their own convictions, and their free choice, were most scrupulously respected; and nevertheless, no more powerful, no more engaging testimony could be afforded, than from the lives of men who—by nature sinful as themselves—yet showed forth the fruits of peace, and a holy sense of reconciliation to God in word, deed, and character. What Christ needed to found his Church were confessors, who were willing to stake their persons, their lives, on the truth of their confession. It was in this sense that he had said to Simon, the boldest confessor of all the disciples, "Thou art Peter, and upon this rock will I build my Church." Of course the foundation-stone of the kingdom of heaven could be none other than Christ himself; but the society on earth which was to bear witness throughout the world, needed for its foundation and support, a man firm as a rock, as confessor of the truth; and this Peter proved himself in the first instance to the mother Church at Jerusalem, and through her to the Church at large. This of course is not the place to enter upon the Romish misconception of these words of Christ's; I would only point out, in passing, how little apprehension it shows of the meaning and spirit of the Saviour, to ascribe to Peter over his fellow-disciples, or to the Bishop of Rome over his brother disciples, any pre-eminence in rank, and how far removed Peter himself was from such an opinion when he wrote; "neither as lords over God's heritage, but as examples to the flock" (1 Pet. v. 3).

In placing his Church upon this foundation, however, Jesus concealed neither from himself nor from her, that she was to be a suffering and a struggling Church; that hell, opening wide its gates, would send forth its hosts to battle with her; but he at the same time promised her with divine certainty that she should stand firm, like a lighthouse tower, amidst the foaming breakers.

Yes; Jesus has prescribed for his Church the way he himself trod: from a lowly beginning, through opposition, mockery, and apparent defeat, to final triumph and everlasting life. And in this we discern a majestically great idea, that bears the impress of internal truth and divine origin. It is true that the prophecies of the Old Testament had already spoken of a share borne by the Gentiles in Messiah and in his kingdom: but that by such a company of confessors this kingdom should be brought home to these Gentiles (and even to the people of Israel itself); brought home to their understandings, consciences, and affections; carried on in its character of a pre-eminently spiritual, outwardly despised and oppressed kingdom, to glory and triumph; nay, humanity at large shown its highest development and the attainment of its highest aspirations within this very Church;—this is indeed a sublimely original idea, or, let us rather say, one of Divine profundity and wisdom. We know, too, how narrowly those former promises had been restricted to the Jews by even the most pious among them, and that it was only gradually that the loved and trusted disciples themselves attained to a full comprehension of their Master's marvellous plan.

Hitherto we have been dwelling upon the task which the Lord set before his Church; we must now seek to show how, in the Holy Spirit, he bestowed upon them the only and adequate means for fulfilling that task.

If by setting such an aim before the Church, Jesus gave the highest authority to mankind, as well as the highest task of which in accordance with its divine origin they were capable; in the means towards the attainment of that aim, he has evinced the wisest and tenderest consideration for the humiliations and errors to which sin had subjected them. We see on each side the gradual up-springing and converging of that mighty arch whose bold firm span is to bridge over the abyss between the ideal and the real. Great thinkers had in former ages devised fair systems and high ideals, but these ever lacked the living and generating energy to get themselves accomplished. But the creative words of Jesus were not the product of abstract thought, but the fruit of the Holy Spirit, by which he had in the first instance fully realized in his own person the ideal of human perfection. Thus, on one side, he had, from his own inmost experience, the knowledge that his sublime thought would have been, without the living power of God's Spirit, a mere still-born ideal; and on the other, he could lay down the mighty plan on centuries to come, the more confidently and calmly because conscious of his ability to carry it out, this omnipotent Spirit being his own to promise and to bestow.

Hitherto, personal intercourse with Jesus had been to the disciples a constant source of increasing knowledge of God, and also a means to uphold and confirm their moral character. This pulse of divine life was not to be interrupted even when their Master departed; and hence he promises, I will not leave you orphans, I will come to you; but henceforth in God's new dispensation, that of the Holy Spirit.

This Holy Spirit had already been known and named in the old dispensation, but in each of its successive stages, the Spirit had only been imparted to a few especially chosen men; as, for instance, the prophets, and this only at certain seasons of inward enlightenment. Now, on the contrary, he was to come to all the disciples of Jesus, and this as an abiding gift of glorification for their spirit, soul, and finally their body; as had been the case with our great exemplar, the Lord himself.

Now such a purely spiritual fellowship as this with God, one so independent of bodily presence, required evidently an incomparably higher measure of independent spiritual exertion and free will on the part of the disciples. This was just what Christ desired. They were henceforth to be for the first time his thoroughly genuine disciples, united with their God and Saviour by nothing but the closest and tenderest bond of essential union by free love.

Yes, the Lord describes the inner transformation his disciples were to undergo, as of necessity to be carried out in this way alone: It is good for you, he says, that I should go away; for if I go not away, the Comforter will not come to you, and not to you alone, but to mankind generally. This Comforter he promises as the Spirit of truth, the one who will lead the disciples into all truth, and testify to them of the Lord himself, thus transforming them into spiritual and moral completeness, into the divine nature. On the world at large, Jesus, on the contrary, describes the effect of the agency of the Spirit to be its conviction, by the light of his testimony, of sin, righteousness, and judgment. These words ascribe to the Spirit a peculiar influence, which, wherever the influence of Jesus extends, makes an ignoring of him, a mere attitude of indifference towards him, an impossible thing; and inwardly constrains the world to assume in regard to him a positive relation of one kind or other; the want of faith in him amounting to enmity against the human incarnation of truth and love, and being *sin* in fact and principle, so that they must needs be conscious of it; while in the going of Jesus to his Father, in his death and his ascension, the righteousness of the sinner in the sight of the holy God is established by an all-sufficient expiation, and by this too the Prince of the world (and in him evil in its essential nature) is judged as untenable for eternity.

Thus the preached gospel is the immediate agent, the vessel through whose intervention the Holy Spirit, after he has been received by the disciples on the day of Pentecost, is to be extended over mankind. Without him even the gospel would be a dead and death-dealing letter; only when he breathes through it does it become the word of eternal life, and it puts forth its first vital influence in change of mind (repentance), this first-fruit of the combined action of the truth preached and the conviction of the hearers. Accordingly Jesus has associated baptism with this word, as the solemn celebration of that implanting in the new spiritual life of the individual, by which he becomes a disciple—a member of the body of Christ.

What we have said indicates the organs by which the human spirit apprehends and receives the divine, viz., Reason and Conscience. As the bodily eye needs light from without, so these organs of the human spirit have not light inherent in them, they too must receive it from the Holy Spirit. By him the reason appropriates the pure knowledge of God afforded in the Gospels; by him the conscience attains to an acute and correct moral discernment, which we find neither in heathenism, nor yet in Judaism, and which as common property only belongs to Christendom; this, again, leads to the purification of the will, and to its being, by the new living energy of the Holy Spirit, exalted into the love of God. Thus divine truth becomes the personal spiritual possession of a man, nay, becomes his very being, his new nature; what my reason discerns in the light of the Holy Spirit, is most essentially my own knowledge; the decision of my conscience is no strange superimposed decision, but that of my inmost convictions; it is what my will now demands; it is *my* will, *my* love. Again, the moral perception of my sinfulness and my repentant rejection of evil is my own personal mental act, and so is the believing acceptance of reconciliation with God in Christ; the will and the power to take a divine view of life, and to lead a new course of life, are made mine, so that I recognise myself in my own consciousness as a new man born again into the nature of God; and yet all this is not of myself, but owing to the life-power of the Spirit of God shining through my spirit. This is that inward conviction of being God's children by the Spirit, which teaches us to cry, Abba,

Father! And even when man (as his free will leaves open to him to do) resolutely hardens himself against the influence of the Holy Spirit, the testimony of the gospel, owing to the indwelling strength of the Spirit, is yet so mighty because divinely true, that in point of fact no intelligence can entirely evade Jesus and his work of salvation, but sin must needs take the form of unbelief in the Son of God, the Saviour, and register itself as enmity against him, and no conscience have power to call evil good, except as a conscious lie.

Thus we see in the action of the Holy Spirit, the highest power of conquest and transformation united with a perfect recognition of human personality and freedom; whole peoples are changed by Christianity both as to their religious and moral life, and nevertheless the new element leaves the national impress unaltered. An individual becomes a new creature, and yet he retains his own character, peculiarities, temperament, but all these are purified, ennobled, sanctified by God's Spirit. Each nature, each period has its own special Christian life; every individual knows and apprehends the eternal God according to his personal mode of apprehension,—has in him most significantly *his* God and Saviour; and thousands upon thousands of sanctified human spirits reflect back each in his own individuality the one infinite Spirit, who is all in all. Such is God's creation,—inconceivable variety, yet unity in him.

This unity, moreover, is not merely one discerned of God alone, but each individual is naturally—through the Spirit—conscious of it, and it constitutes in all who belong to God in Christ, the closest tie of spiritual blood relationship, so to speak; for the children of the same Father must know and feel themselves to be brethren, and that without relation to the barriers interposed by their earthly life, whether of nature, sex, or position. The Spirit which, as regards man's position towards God, appears as a spirit of renewal and adoption, manifests itself in the reciprocal relation of saints to each other as a Spirit of communion. In this communion of saints we have the realization of the truth, which, without the Holy Spirit, is a mere shadow or caricature, nay, a mere powerless figure of speech,—the truth that all men are brethren. This communion of Christians with their God and each other, finds its fullest expression in the sacrament of the Lord's Supper, and at the same time its support, its means of growth and increased intensity.

It is evident that while this influence of the Holy Spirit can, and at the last must display itself as absolute and complete, it may also be exercised and progress relatively and gradually. Humanity can neither as a whole, nor in its individual members, attain at one bound to the heavenly height of full divine knowledge and unspotted holiness; but on the ground of the revelation it has received, and by the confluence of divine vital energies, it is capable of development even to perfection. It is in the Lord Jesus that the highest type of divinely informed humanity appears, and the Church is sent by him into the world with no less lofty an aim and promise than the final attainment of the measure of Christ. The Holy Spirit, on his part, appoints to the human being his shorter stages of gradual development; fills him, as water fills a vessel, according to his capacity for holding; affords from time to time just as much light and inward power as he has knowledge and holiness to appropriate and use,—and thus it is ever to him that hath, that more is given till he has abundance.

It now remains that we take a short general survey of the development of the Church under the Holy Spirit's dispensation of Life and Light.

The day of Pentecost was the Christian Church's day of birth. Up to that time the company of believers had resembled an unborn child, whose life is as yet dependent on that of its mother; thenceforth it was to enter upon its individual, independent, self-conscious life and growth. At first it was a thing apart. The line of demarcation between it and the outer world very sharply defined,—a drop of oil on the water, so to speak; and even when after its first persecutions it grew in numbers, and new churches were founded here and there, they were all consciously parts of one whole, they were "the" Church, the universal Church potentially, though not as yet actually embracing all nations. The members of this Church were holy in the sense in which St. Paul wrote, "Ye are washed, ye are sanctified, ye are justified in the name of the Lord Jesus, and by the Spirit of our God" (1 Cor. vi. 11). And between these holy members there was a communion of faith and love, which last showed itself practically in reciprocal support, hospitality, and kindred services.

In accordance with the spirit of the period, we now find in this early apostolic Church prominence given—not as it had been by Jesus to the doctrine of the kingdom of God, but—to the doctrine of the Church. Her nature and her relation to Christ are generally represented in the epistles of the New Testament under three figures: She is likened to a building; she is the temple of the Lord; her members are stones of this building. Here she is described as a whole, the parts of which, according to a well-ordered plan, are joined together for a holy purpose; and it is indicated at the same time that she has an externally visible form, in which God in Christ lives and dwells. This whole appears again as a living organism, having different members; under the figure of a body, whose limbs are all vitally connected by their dependence upon Christ the Head. Finally, the Church is called the bride of Christ. It is instructive to see how this image includes the two former ones, and superadds to them another important idea; it represents the consciousness the Church has of an independent existence of her own, as contrasted with that of her Lord, and yet of her perfect union with him in love. And, further, we have therein an allusion to a future and final completeness; for though the bride enjoys perfect security and happiness, yet she is still in an attitude of expectation and longing.

The Church, at her first appearing, possessed in very deed all the characteristics of a holy, universal Christian communion of saints, as she is called in the apostolic creed. But she was not yet that in an absolute sense; the first-fruits only were there, not the full harvest; it was but the blossoming season of the Church. Between the fragrant, promise-fraught blossoms and the sweet fruit, a long and tedious season of ripening had to intervene. This throws a light upon a phenomenon that we must not overlook; the display of peculiar spiritual gifts—the *charism*—which we observe after the day of Pentecost in the earlier decades of the Church, and which gradually retreated (although they have never entirely disappeared). It lies in the nature of the case, that if man were to be transfigured into the image of God, his spirit would have its share of light, holy joy, penetrating and comprehensive (prophetic) insight, healing power for soul and body; the fulness of spiritual gifts, in short, would be his own. Now this was to find its expression in the early Church, agreeably to its character of first-fruits and type of future completeness. The apostles needed these gifts, likewise, to establish and cultivate their inner life, and to afford strong confirmation of their divine mission. But such gifts were not to be an abiding nor a common possession; this they will only become in the kingdom of heaven, when mankind shall have been, by the slow but thorough method of sanctification, made capable of their universal use and enjoyment.

Thus, then, the Church stood before the world as the company of Jesus Christ's witnesses, testifying of him by their preaching and their lives, and sealing their testimony with their blood. The vital force of the Spirit grew both inwardly and outwardly, but that growth, that influence of divine revelation on human reason, that new form given to the inward moral life, could only proceed through great conflicts. The human mind develops itself by resisting and overcoming antagonist influences; and just as of old, when the Spirit of God brooded over the waters, so now, when at this second creation, the same Spirit spread over the nations, and the "Let there be light" of the gospel rung through the chaos of the sinful world, the new day was made up of the evening and the morning, of the night and of the dawn.

Partly the false assertions of her enemies, and partly the errors arising from false conceptions among her own children, obliged the Church to express her faith in distinct dogmas; each period having its own measure of energy and knowledge for the task, and each successive period treading in the footsteps of the last, widening and deepening them, and at the same time opening new veins in the great mine of Christian truth. But as soon as a unity of faith was formularized into a humanly limited dogma, there was danger lest it should stiffen into a mere lifeless form, or be perverted by false deductions and additions; nay, one whole branch of the Christian stream, the Eastern Church collectively, did fall into this stagnation and distortion, and the Western too seemed threatened with the same fate, so that Christianity, like a suddenly-cooled lava stream, would at the present time have shared the fate of Islamism, if the quickening breath of the Holy Spirit, after many preparatory movements of the kind, had not, with triumphant might, burst the hardening, confining crust, and asserted the right as well as the necessity of private reflection and judgment, and of a personal and spiritual laying hold upon salvation.

The Reformation brought once more to light the fundamental evangelical truth of justification by grace, insisted upon the personal and the spiritual regeneration of the individual, and placed the Bible in the hands of the people at large. It is evident how mighty an advance was thus made in the task appointed to the Church, that of becoming a company of free disciples, inwardly and thoroughly persuaded, and consciously living in God. Nevertheless, even now there is to be no progress made without resistance and struggle, and the evangelical Church may not as yet sit under her own fig-tree and vine; rather is she more than ever the Church militant, more than ever reminded of the declaration of her founder: "I am not come to send peace on earth, but rather a sword."

She has to fight for no slighter cause than her spiritual rights and existence, and her triumph insures her eternal duration. Above all, she must guard against the old danger of growing stiff and inert in her settled dogmas, against having a name to live and yet being dead, for the kingdom of God consists not in ecclesiastical traditions and formulas. Nor does it consist any more in philosophical formulas. Philosophy, indeed, lends powerful aid to the Church in her spiritual appropriation of the truth of revelation, but she is not herself revelation, nor can she ever become religion. For the Church is not a product of human thought and intelligence, but a historical reality, brought about by the saving power of the living God; the *need* of redemption is no mere idea, but an awful objective fact, like the pain of the poisoned and the hunger of the famished, and therefore the *fact* of a redemption was essential; and to bear witness to this fact, accomplished by the historical Son of man,—and to set forth its result in the pardon and moral elevation of mankind,—this it is that constitutes the work of the Church, as the great apostle of the Gentiles proclaimed in defiance of all philosophical opposition: "We preach Christ crucified, to the Jews a stumbling-block, and to the Greeks foolishness, but to them that are called, the power of God and the wisdom of God, that your faith may not stand in the wisdom of men, but in the power of God."

It is inevitable that the more decidedly the Church insists upon the free, self-conscious faith and holy life of individuals, the less any outward pressure is employed, and any outward assent is felt to suffice, the more openly and decidedly will indifference and enmity appear; and accordingly we now have the remarkable phenomenon before us of a Church growing in the earnestness and thoroughness of the inner life, and displaying that life in renewed missionary efforts, as becomes her vocation, while, at the same time, there is among her members a great falling away from her faith and practice, partly into open Materialism, partly into scientific disguises of it. That which the Lord of the Church foretold is coming to pass: "Iniquity shall prevail, and the love of many shall wax cold;" the tares are to grow and ripen with the wheat. Here we tread upon the borders of the task appointed to the earthly Church. When she has attained the full maturity of her spiritual life, the Lord has promised his return in glory to judgment; and then and thereby the now existing spiritual reality shall find its corresponding embodiment. For then first shall the company of saints have become capable of that complete communion between the Godhead and humanity; whose highest reach and profoundest intimacy is expressed in the promise: "To him that overcometh, will I grant to sit with me in my throne, even as I also overcame, and am set down with my Father on his throne" (Rev. iii. 21).

Further, as the Church had to penetrate with her message into the dark winding ways of human knowledge and human will, to exalt and to purify them, so too had she to enter into the political and civil life of humanity, to enlighten all its different departments, to draw thence all good elements into her own sphere, and to sanctify them; in other words, she had to become a State Church. But in this capacity it was not her office to rule and constrain; rather, after the example of her Master, to reach her aim and victory by serving and humiliations. Here, too, she has only advanced through the antagonism of human errors, and the wise leading of the Holy Spirit.

It was a brilliant idea that crossed the mind of the Papacy in the Middle Ages, and appeared to have reached its realization under Innocent III., that of making the Church the mistress of the world, and the power of the State only her proxy; but the truth that lay in that idea was distorted to a violent anticipation of the kingdom of God, in positive contradiction to the example of the Lord of the Church, of whom it is written, that however exalted his claims he humbled himself. In close connexion with this false attitude, rose the most unevangelical separation between a spiritually ignorant laity and a privileged clerical body. Such an inward degeneracy of the Church led infallibly to an outward fall. The Reformation brought about the recognition of the spiritual vocation of the Church, and the universal priesthood of all her members; but it was not able to prevent a disruption of the universal Church into many separate national Churches, neither could it bring about a purely Presbyterial institution, but these Churches fell under the protection and rule of the State power.

Thus we now find in the Church much internal apostasy united with external dependence upon the secular power. This is the twofold reproach that she has to bear from many who have on these accounts separated themselves from her into different sects, and who stigmatize her as a worldly Babylon. But this belongs to her crucified condition, and fulfils the prophetic declaration of her Lord. For her part she knows that she is equally removed from a Papal temporal power and from the Hegelian conceptions of a State, and she rejoices that it is so; but she also knows to how many waverers she offers just the helping hand they need; knows that she acts as a dyke and a support to much that is weak; knows that she is the Church of Him who ate with publicans and sinners. And while she does not presume to break the yoke of the State before her Lord himself frees her from it, she reaches nevertheless the right hand of fellowship to all who in other churches and communions love the Lord Jesus Christ in sincerity. She knows, too, that in every circle, and often where the tares are thickest, there are genuine ears of wheat to be found, and that, in the great day of his appearing, the Lord will gather from the four corners of the earth all who bear the impress of his Spirit, and own them as members of his risen and glorified body. Then shall be fulfilled that which is only in progress now; then shall we *see* what now we believe, the one universal Christian Church, the true communion of saints, the kingdom of God.

Therefore, if in our days there be great agitation both in spiritual and temporal spheres, and on all sides the waves rise high, yet let the living members of the Church discern in these grave signs of the times no tokens of fear, but rather welcome in them, while lifting up their heads, the morning breezes of the coming day.

IX.

THE DOCTRINE OF JUSTIFICATION BY FAITH.

THE subject that is now to occupy us, the doctrine of justification by faith, is, in a dogmatic point of view, based upon the foregoing Lectures, more especially those that treated respectively of Sin and of the Atonement. We are now, however, about to consider this subject from the *moral* point of view. For, apart from the dogmatic objections which have been already combated, this doctrine has often been objected to in the supposed interests of morality. Now it is a doctrine which, in the New Testament, appears with especial prominence in the epistles of St. Paul, and which, at the time of the Reformation, constituted the fundamental point of difference between Protestantism and Catholicism. To prove this latter assertion, we have only to review a few passages of Protestant Confessions of faith. First, we will take the Basle Confession of the year 1534: "We acknowledge the remission of sins by faith in Jesus Christ the crucified. And although this faith be continually practised, proved, and confirmed by works of love, yet we attribute justification and satisfaction for our sins not to these works which are the fruits of faith, but only to our true reliance on and faith in the blood-shedding of the Lamb of God. For we freely acknowledge that in Christ, who is our justification, sanctification, redemption, way, truth, wisdom, and life, all things are given to us. Hence the good works of believers do not expiate their sins, but are done solely out of gratitude to God the Lord for his great benefits to usward in Christ." The Heidelberg Confession also gives a most striking and hearty popular expression to this doctrine. Here is the answer to the sixtieth question, as to the mode of justification before God: "Only by true faith in Jesus Christ, whereby, although my conscience accuses me of having grievously transgressed all God's commandments, and never having kept one, as well as of being continually inclined to all that is evil, yet God, without any merit of mine, of pure grace, bestows on me, imputes to me, the perfect satisfaction, justification, and sanctification of Christ, as fully as though I had never committed any sin, and had myself rendered the obedience Christ rendered in my stead, if only I will accept all these benefits with a believing heart." As to the teaching of the Lutheran Church on this point, I only need to recall the fourth article of the Augsburg Confession: "*On justification.*—Further, be it enjoined, that we are unable to attain to forgiveness of sin or righteousness before God through any merits, works, or expiation of our own, but that we obtain forgiveness and are counted righteous before him through grace by faith, and for the sake of Christ, we believing that Christ has suffered for us, and that on that account our sins are forgiven, and righteousness and eternal life bestowed on us. For this faith, God will look upon, and reckon to us, as righteousness, as St. Paul says to the Romans (chap. iii. 4)."

In direct opposition to this Protestant testimony, we will only here adduce on the side of Catholicism, the twelfth canon of the sixth session of the Council of Trent: "If any man shall say that justifying faith is nothing else than trust in the Divine mercy which forgives the sinner for the sake of Christ, or that it is by this trust alone that man is justified—let him be accursed."

This Protestant doctrine it was which, at the time of the Reformation, not only formed a fundamental difference, but, at the manifold negotiations to which it led, was the chief hindrance to a reunion of both Confessions. It was vehemently attacked from a moral point of view, not merely by its Romish opponents, but by many who, in other respects, were inclined to Protestantism; and we may safely assert that numbers who were violent against the night of error and abuse in the Church of Rome, and who highly estimated the merits of Luther, yet in relation to this doctrine, which was in fact the essential point at issue, remained—perhaps without suspecting it—very good Catholics all the time. Now men are perfectly justified in applying the standard of morality to an article of faith, and it ought to be acknowledged a step in the right direction when any doctrine, which cannot legitimize itself both by its own moral character and its influence on mankind, awakens suspicion. Only we must be careful to draw our moral standard not from a superficial survey, but a profound search into the real moral needs of our nature.

The attacks which have been made in the interests of morality upon the doctrine in question, may be reduced to two questions—1. Is it not in itself an immoral idea that God should, on account of a man's faith, pronounce him to be righteous, when in point of fact he is not so? 2. Would not such an imputed righteousness as this necessarily destroy all moral effort?

This charge of immorality naturally suggests to us an easy, practical refutation; for as Christians, we cannot admit that Pauline Christianity, and as Protestants, we cannot admit that the Reformation, rests upon an immoral basis. Neither has the doctrine called in question, whether as exemplified in Paul, or in the champions of the Reformation—a Luther, a Melanchthon, a Calvin, etc.—or in the social history of Protestantism generally, had practically any immoral tendency. However, we will not allow this train of thought to interfere with the examination of the doctrine, but rather encourage us to carry it on very carefully, and to enter more deeply into the question, before we allow ourselves to come to a decision.

It is evident that, within our present limits, we cannot set before you an account of all the controversies to which our doctrine gave rise, or a special defence of all that has been said on *this* side, and a special contradiction of all brought forward on *that*. This would lead us into a web of occasionally most subtle distinctions.

The conflict has been actively renewed within the last thirty years, by the appearance of a very spirited and learned work of the Catholic theologian Möhler; and in defence of the Protestant doctrine, several have taken up the pen who certainly cannot be reproached with a narrow orthodoxy: I may instance Marheineke, and the recently deceased Professor Baur of Tübingen. A closer examination of the controversy shows how in the Protestant camp, in the heat of argument and opposition, several maxims, expressions, and illustrations have been employed, which certainly betray a rather one-sided, strained, and harsh spirit, and must therefore be sometimes qualified; as, for instance, when the Lutheran Nicolaus of Amsdorf undertakes to prove that the proposition, "Good works are injurious to salvation," is a true and a Christian one. On the other side, we observe how those Catholics who feel anxious to grasp the deeper meaning of the doctrines of their church, and to defend them by scientific weapons, have unconsciously drawn nearer in many respects to Protestant views. But all these points we must at present leave untouched, confining ourselves to the thorough examination of the true Protestant doctrine, and seeking to justify it from the charges made against its morality.

I. First, then, "According to the Protestant doctrine," say some, "a righteousness external to man—alien to him, is imputed to him; he is declared righteous by God without actually being so. This is an untrue and immoral principle." Here we must set out by reminding our opponents that it is necessary for them to understand the idea of this reckoning, or imputing, in the sense that we hold it. In this, as in all cases where divine actions are represented by expressions borrowed from human life, it is essential to make allowance for the inadequacy inherent in these expressions. Thus this reckoning or imputing of which we speak, is not an external affair, as in the business of daily life, when a discharge is written out and given and reckoned to B., because A. has undertaken to be a surety for him, whether as to work to be done or payment to be made. This is, indeed, a purely external matter to B., however closely it may affect him, affect him even while he knows nothing of it. Not so, however, is it with Christ's representation of humanity. Here we are not treating of a certain amount of virtue, of good works which have got to be done, it matters not by whom, and Christ has done them; or, again, of a certain amount of punishment which has got to be endured, it matters not by whom, and Christ has endured it. Most assuredly we are to entertain no such lifeless conception of Christ's representative righteousness, and of the active and passive obedience he has rendered. Rather Christ's holy life and holy works on the one side; his holy sufferings and holy death on the other,—constitute that work of redemption and expiation, which brings about a decided reaction against sin and its consequences; atones at once for the sins of mankind, and is to mankind both a new origin of life—whence Christ is called the second Adam,—and a new condition of life—mankind having now through Christ fellowship with God.

But at the same time, every man is not, as a matter of course, without anything further, a sharer in this new life; faith in Christ is the necessary condition to its attainment. By faith, however, as has already in these Lectures been frequently observed, in connexion with different subjects, and from different points of view,—by faith we are by no means to understand a theoretical process, which only affects the human intellect; but rather, a specially practical relative position; the energetic laying hold by man of that grace of God which was by Christ realized in humanity, and is now in Christ offered to humanity; or, more briefly, it is the energetic laying hold of Christ himself; and consequently, it is a process which affects spiritual life in its very core, a process by which the man is implanted or incorporated into Christ, and thus has, by fellowship with him, a share in that reaction brought about by Christ against the sin and guilt of humanity.

Thus are the believer's personal sins and guilt now atoned for by Christ, and he stands in that fellowship with the divine life which Christ has restored in humanity. Luther, in his famous treatise on the liberty of a

Christian, has treated this truth in a most profound manner, mystically if you will, but mystically in the best sense of the word, mystically in so far as he was discussing the tenderest and intimate *mystery* of godliness. These are his words: "Faith unites the soul with Christ as a bride to the bridegroom. From which union it follows, as St. Paul says (Eph. v. 20), that Christ and the soul become one body; and also that they have their possessions, their mischances, and all things in common, that which is Christ's belonging to the believing soul, that which is the soul's belonging to Christ. If Christ has all holiness and blessedness, these belong to the soul. If the soul has all unrighteousness and sin, these belong to Christ. Here then we see a glad exchange and emulation. Because Christ is God and man, who never sinned, and his holiness unconquerable, eternal, and almighty, he, through the bridal ring, which is faith, appropriates the sins of the believing soul as his own, as though they had been committed by him, and thus the sins must needs be swallowed up and drowned in him. For his unconquerable holiness is too strong for any or all sin. Thus the soul is purified from all sin through its dowry; that is, on account of its faith, and not only goes perfectly free, but is endowed with the righteousness of its bridegroom, Christ."

Thus it appears that to the believer the righteousness of Christ is no more an external and foreign thing that can only be arbitrarily imputed to him; but rather it is something appropriated by him, essentially his own, by reason, if I may so speak, of the solidarity which has been brought about between himself and Christ. The believer has no longer a separate existence, but lives henceforth in fellowship with Christ, as a member incorporated in him, and accordingly he is looked upon by God, not as what he is in and by himself, but as what he is in that relation to Christ which faith has occasioned.

And further, it follows that faith cannot possibly be indifferent to morality, as is presumed by that often repeated charge: "Very convenient, indeed! no matter how a man thinks and feels and lives, he believes, and therefore is declared righteous." On the contrary, faith in its energetic laying hold of Christ and his righteousness, is a spiritual action of a positively moral character. "Faith," says Luther, in his preface to the Epistle to the Romans, "is a living, well considered reliance on God's grace, so sure and certain that I could die for it a thousand times."

Again, the Heidelberg Catechism calls faith "a hearty trust, worked in us by the Holy Spirit, through the gospel." Now, if according to Protestant doctrine it is the Holy Ghost who produces faith in men, and without whom they never could attain to it (as Paul himself had already declared, "No man can call Jesus Lord, but by the Holy Spirit" (1 Cor. xii. 3), it is equally true that it is the human spirit in which he works, and whose energies he sets in motion, and it is the human will to which he imparts this decided direction towards Christ, so that faith can in no sense be a purely passive relation, but rather a condition of the highest activity. Only it behoves our Protestant doctrine vigorously to guard against faith itself having a certain kind of merit attributed to it, as though, as the subjective condition and indwelling quality of a man, it made that man so well pleasing in the eyes of God, that *therefore* God counted him to be righteous, in which case man would indeed have a righteousness in himself, that is, in his faith. Whereas the believer has *no* righteousness in himself, but only in Christ, his faith being but the means whereby he appropriates to himself Christ and his righteousness. It is against this mistaken estimation of faith that the Heidelberg Catechism expressly guards when it follows up the 60th question, the answer to which we have already given, by the following words: 'Wherefore sayest thou, that thou art justified by faith only?' and replies to them, "Not because I, on account of the worthiness of my faith, am well pleasing to God; for the satisfaction, justification, and sanctification of Christ are my only righteousness before God, and I do nothing by my faith, but receive these and make them my own."

But the moral character of faith will appear still more distinctly, if we consider how inseparable faith is from the negative moment—*Repentance;* repentance in the biblical sense, which nowhere means expiation of guilt by punishment, but change of mind with regard to sin; a condemning of sin, not merely in a general way, but a condemning of a man's own personal sin, which takes the form of regret; of a sorrowful consciousness both of individual sinful actions, in thought, word, and deed, and of the sinful nature from which these actions have proceeded; of a sorrowful consciousness, too, of personal inability to make up for past evil, or even to shake off all connexion with evil in the future; of a sorrowful consciousness, in short, of how hateful sin is in the eyes of the holy God, and how it separates a man from him. A consciousness this, whose intensity in no way depends upon the relative greatness or uncommon nature of these individual sins, but upon the depth of the moral feeling and the measure of susceptibility to the contrast between a holy God and sinful man. But still less here than with regard to faith, should there be any idea entertained of merit, as though a man's repentance were in some sense his righteousness. Rather, repentance is that painful sense and acknowledgment of utter want of any righteousness whatever of a man's own, which drives him to seek a righteousness external to himself, and is consequently the preparatory condition of that faith which finds it in Christ.

These observations indeed contain the peculiar features of the Protestant doctrine of justification, but still we have not as yet brought them out with sufficient prominence. That men become righteous and are saved by the merits of Christ, and that faith is necessary to the appropriation of these, both Churches concur in affirming. The difference between them first makes itself apparent in their conception of the *process* of appropriation, in their definition of what justification is in itself, and how man attains to it. According to Catholic theology, justification is not a *declaring*, but a *making* of the sinner righteous, *i.e.*, through the merits of the holy sufferings of Christ the Holy Spirit pours the love of God into the heart of man; man becomes inwardly renewed, and can and will now keep the law of God, and do such good works as are conformable thereto. All this together, they hold, constitutes justification. "In justification itself," says the Council of Trent, in the seventh chapter of the sixth session, "man receives through Christ, in whom he is engrafted, together with forgiveness of sins, faith, hope, and love." At first sight this view may not seem to differ very essentially from the Protestant; but if we look at it closely, we shall perceive how much here the moment of pardon, of forgiveness of sins, is pushed into the background, justification being confounded with what we distinguish as sanctification,—never, therefore, coming to an end, but understood as a subjective process which goes on throughout life, for the justified, as the tenth chapter of the same Session expressly declares, are ever more and more justified. The Protestant doctrine, on the contrary, distinguishes justification as an independent moment, from the sanctification which is its immediate consequence; justification itself, according to this doctrine, consisting in God declaring man righteous, *i.e.*, judicially absolved from all guilt, so that from that time forth, man may be fully conscious of being reconciled to God, assured of his pardon, and in the enjoyment of his peace; and, further, if with this experience in his heart he should immediately die, he would be certain of dying saved, and of escaping judgment; and all this, not on the ground of any worthiness whatever of his own, as though his righteousness were in himself; but for the sake of Christ, with whom he is so incorporated by faith, that he no longer lives in himself but in Christ, and thus is no more viewed by God as existing independently, but as connected with Christ, as a member of the spiritual body of which Christ is the head.

It is possible, indeed, that at the first glance this Catholic doctrine may appear the more comprehensible and clear of the two to what one calls man's common sense; but still the closer examination to which our deeper religious and moral wants invite us, will reveal truth on the side of the Protestant. Let us make this evident by reverting to the experience of the two men in whom this doctrine of justification by faith appears to be equally embodied: to that of the apostle Paul, who first defined it in all its distinctness, and of Luther, who not only made it the principle of his own Christian life, but of his whole work of Reformation. When Paul, after the appearance of the Lord to him on his way to Damascus, underwent a three days' mental conflict, his bodily eyes being sealed, but the eyes of his understanding opened to recognise the whole of his former life as mistaken,—spent in unbelief and resistance to that God whom by his bloody persecuting zeal he had thought to serve,—*pardon* was already bestowed upon him, he being baptized in the name of Jesus Christ. He, on his side, brought nothing to insure it, except sorrow for his past life and faith in Christ; he was only conscious, as far as he was himself concerned, of being laden with guilt, and of seeking righteousness in Christ, and yet he could thenceforth feel certified of God's grace, for the sake of that Jesus whom he had persecuted. While his repentance could discover nothing in himself but wrath-deserving unrighteousness, he already knew by experience what it was to be found in Christ, and to have for righteousness *that* which is through the faith of Christ, the righteousness which is of God by faith (Phil. iii. 9); for his being in Christ was owing to faith alone. This was his justification, an independent act of divine mercy, which was antecedent to the new life he was now entering upon, and the origin and the source of all that followed. This consciousness of justifying grace, laid hold of only through faith in Christ, is henceforth the key-note of his whole life, and sounds throughout all his epistles; this his conviction once for all and for ever, that man is justified without the works of the law,—justified by faith.

Let us now glance at the spiritual history of the reformer, Martin Luther. He is living in his cell at Erfurth, a pious monk, in the best sense of the word. He keeps the rules of his Order with conscientious strictness, and he does this not with the hypocritical intent to make up as it were to God, by outward observances and mortifications, for neglect of far more important moral duties; no, he is seeking in earnest to please God and make his peace with him; and, according to the belief of the age, he considers this monastic life, with all its privations, the most certain way of attaining that end; asceticism is to be to him a means of sanctification and subjugation of all evil tendencies. This course, however, in no way leads him to peace with God; on the contrary, he becomes only more strongly convinced of the wide gulf between his sinful nature and the divine, and he sinks into profound anxiety and gloom. Nothing comforts him but a speech of an old brother monk, who reminds him that the Christian creed contains the words, "I believe in the remission of sins." The significance of this remission of sins, as an independent moment, already dawns upon his mind, and his office of doctor of the Holy Scriptures giving him an opportunity of thoroughly studying the epistles of St. Paul, he soon enjoys the full light of truth and consolation. In them he finds laid down as a fact,—experimentally verified and most clearly impressed on the writer's consciousness,—the mode of man's justification and attainment of spiritual peace. His own experience assents to the declaration of the apostle, "Therefore being justified by faith, we have peace with God through our Lord Jesus Christ" (Rom. v. 1). Henceforth this is for him essentially the gospel of salvation. This certainty of being forgiven by God, not on account of any righteousness of his own, not because of the measure of love and holiness to which he had already attained; but looking away altogether from his own moral condition (so little satisfying in his own eyes, so much less so, therefore, in the eyes of a Holy God), and looking to Christ alone, and being bold to say, "Whatever Christ has is mine, because I am his through faith;" this certainty it was which gave him that cheerful heroic strength in which he triumphantly waged war not only against all hindrances to his own personal sanctification, but against the Papal power so dominant in his time. The energy with which he was inspired by the thought, "If God be for us, who can be against us?" rested on this justifying faith. He knew it experimentally, as "the living, deliberate, reliance on God's grace, so certain that I would die for it a thousand times."

These two examples strikingly illustrate the importance of justification considered according to our Protestant doctrine as an independent act of grace. The greater the truth and intensity of the moral sense in any man, the more aware will he be of the difference between the ever-sinful and utterly imperfect creature, and the holy God, and therefore the more compelled to seek for righteousness not in his own imperfections, but in the perfections of Christ. And again, the very possibility of loving God from the heart, and because of this love striving after holiness with that freedom and joy which constitute the very essence of love—in other words, all truly moral efforts at self-improvement,—must be based upon a justification not dependent upon the measure of sanctification already attained, but independently bestowed on us as the very condition of this sanctification. For so long as I am not certain that God has pardoned me, that I have peace with him, that the sins that still so easily beset me form no wall of partition between me and my God, so long I am unable to love him with all my heart. It is the experience of the love of God as having freely forgiven me a sinner, for Christ's sake, that first calls out in me free, pure, active, and influential reciprocal love. Now this happy certainty of being forgiven is the very point at which the Catholic Church takes especial umbrage. The Council of Trent, in the ninth chapter of the sixth Session expressly states:—"Every man by reason of his own weakness and defects, must be in fear and anxiety about his state of grace, nor can any one know with infallible certainty of faith that he has received forgiveness of God."

II. This leads us to our second question; which is this:—Will justification by faith—in other words, the certainty of being forgiven and declared righteous by God through faith in Christ's merits,—will this actually have sanctification for its result? Will it not rather paralyse moral effort, man being satisfied with immunity from God's judgment, and not careful or desirous to strive after progressive sanctification?

This question may be very simply answered, if only we bear in mind that Protestantism invariably insists upon justification being dependent upon faith, and understands faith as placing us in living relation to Christ. He then only is justified who is virtually related to Christ, and when this is the case, it is wholly inconceivable that a man should remain as he is, that he should not become sanctified. For Christ, through his Spirit, lives in all the living members of the Church, which is his spiritual body, and the effect of this life is their sanctification.

That this inseparable connexion between justification and sanctification may be clearly and distinctly represented without identifying or confusing the two, or in any way encroaching upon the Protestant doctrine of justification as an independent moment, Calvin has shown us in the third book of his Institutes. Thus, in the eleventh chapter, and sixth paragraph, he says, "As Christ himself cannot be divided, so these two, justification and sanctification, which we receive together from him, are alike indivisible. For whom God receives into his favour, to them he also gives the Spirit of adoption, by which power they are transformed into his image. But should we, because the heat of the sun is inseparable from its light, speak of the earth being warmed by its light, and lighted by its warmth? This comparison is well adapted to illustrate the subject, the sun both by its heat making the earth fruitful, and lighting it by its rays; here then we see a reciprocal and inseparable connexion, but still reason forbids our attributing the peculiar nature of one of these processes to the other."

How closely connected justification and sanctification are, how the last is the necessary consequence of the first, shines out brightly from the testimony of St. Paul to the facts of his personal experience. "If any man be in Christ"—that is, be by faith placed in that relation to Christ to which we owe justification—"he is a new creature; old things are passed away, behold all things are become new!" (2 Cor. v. 17.) Now this renewal is not to be thought of as taking place at once, but the decisive beginning of it synchronizes with the being engrafted into Christ, and progresses continually in sanctification. The ruling motive in the souls of those who are justified by the death of Christ is the love first shown by the Lord himself, and now felt for him. "The love of Christ constraineth us," writes the apostle; "because we thus judge, that if one died for all, then were all dead: and that he died for all, that they which live should not henceforth live unto themselves, but unto him which died for them, and rose again" (2 Cor. v. 14, 15). This love to God and Christ, which governs the souls of the justified, is the principle of all moral life.

Again, we are not to think of this subject as though the Christian, in his own person, had a repugnance to all that was holy and good, to virtue and good works of every kind, but yet, out of personal love to God and Christ, was enabled to make the effort, and do good. Rather are goodness and holiness God's essential nature. "God is light, and in him is no darkness at all" (1 John i. 5). To love God signifies, therefore, to love the source and sum of all goodness; and to love Christ signifies to love the most perfect revelation of this goodness in the form of human life. By means of this love is that prophecy fulfilled (Jer. xxxi. 31-34) which promises a new covenant between God and his people, consisting of his law put into their inward parts, and written in their minds. And according to the epistle to the Galatians, as soon as we are engrafted through faith into Christ, we receive the Holy Spirit, and he is a powerful, vital impulse within us, his fruit being "Love, joy, peace, long-suffering, gentleness, goodness, faith, meekness, temperance: *against such there is no law.*"

Thus, through the Spirit of God as ruling motive and vital principle, if we surrender ourselves to him, and follow him, and in his strength overcome the impulses of the flesh, we are placed in a position, and enabled to lead a life, which is in conformity with the law: the expression of the Divine will concerning us. Thus far the apostle Paul. And now let us hear how Luther in his Introduction to the Epistle to the Romans, lays down man's moral renewal as the inevitable consequence of true and justifying faith. "Faith," he says, "is not the mere human delusion and dream that some hold it to be. And hence, when they see no improvement of life, nor good works following therefrom, and yet hear a great deal said about faith, they fall into error, and declare that faith is not sufficient, that a man must have works also in order to be holy and saved. Whereas this is only a hearing the gospel and being struck by it, and calling up thoughts by their own strength, and exclaiming, I believe. Now, this being but a human idea and imagination, which never stirs the ground of the heart, it has no influence, and no improvement follows thereupon. But *Faith* is a divine work in us, that changes us, and begets us anew, and kills the old Adam, and makes us different in heart and spirit, mind and strength, and brings the Holy Spirit with it. Oh! it is a living, creative, active, mighty thing this faith, to which it would be impossible not to bring forth good works continually! It does not inquire whether there are any good works to be done; before the question can be put, it has done, and ever is doing them. He who does not do these good works is an unbelieving man, who may indeed keep groping and peering about faith and good works, but knows neither what faith is, nor what good works really are, however much he may chatter about them both." And again, "Therefore (that is, by reason of his faith) the man is without constraint of any kind, ready and delighted to do good to any one, to serve any one, to suffer anything for the love and to the praise of God, who has shown him so great mercy. For it is impossible to separate good works from faith, as impossible as to separate from flame its burning and shining properties. Therefore, beware of thine own false thoughts, and of useless chatterers, who pretend to be very wise in deciding as to faith and good works, and are all the while great fools. Pray to God to work faith within thee, else thou wilt remain eternally without it, think or do what thou wilt or canst."

According to these statements we may reduce the whole of the previous argument to this alternative: Either a man is really justified by true faith, and then sanctification and good works will inevitably ensue; or sanctification and good works do not ensue, therefore there has been no true faith, and so no justification. What, in such a case as this, a man may still call his faith, is something to which Paul positively denies the honour of such an appellation altogether, while James calls it a dead faith, a form which may indeed retain the sharply-cut features impressed on it by doctrine, but which is only a pale, cold, lifeless thing. It is—if such a name be to be given to it in any sense—a faith which, because it is dead, is perfectly powerless, and as it cannot morally renew man, so it cannot procure him justification either, because it can in no way bring him into living relation to Christ.

If enough has already been said to refute the charge of often paralysing and impeding moral effort brought against this our doctrine of justification by faith, it still remains that we call attention to two points which prove how, on the contrary, it is this very principle that guarantees to moral effort its purity and earnestness. One of these points relates to the undeniable amount remaining, even in the regenerate, of fleshly lusts or inclination to sin. The Catholic doctrine, which makes justification dependent not upon faith, and the righteousness of Christ imputed and granted thereto, but on the actual condition of the man himself, is consequently constrained to assert of these lusts (*concupiscentia*) that they are not in themselves sinful, or objects of divine displeasure. According to this doctrine, they are allowed to remain in man that he may struggle against them, and the apostle Paul designates them as sinful only because they are derived from and incite to sin. But they only become positive sin by the concurrence with them of the human will.—*Trid. Sess.* v., *Decr.* 5. But how, we ask, can that which is derived from sin and incites to sin, and which is not external to the man, but internal in him, how can that be otherwise than itself sin, and therefore displeasing to God? Again, how are we to draw such a hair-breadth line of demarcation between lust and will? If a man feels conscious of some intensely ardent desire, even if it be never shaped by a formal act of the will into a bad resolve or purpose, still, must not the will be in a measure influenced and implicated? Where does the domain of mere desire end, and that of the will begin? How easy, how almost unavoidable, the temptation to draw the line of distinction in our own favour, and to set down many lesser sins of the will to the score of mere lust or inclination! Whereas, according to Protestant principles, the regenerate man, although waging the genuine warfare of the Spirit against the flesh, and advancing in sanctification, yet owes his justification, in God's sight, neither to his individual conduct nor character, but to that relation to Christ into which he has been brought by faith, and owing to which Christ's perfect righteousness is imputed to him. The more pure and earnest therefore, the more *ideal* (to use a modern expression) can he now be in the work of sanctification set before him. His aim is not merely to prevent the will from formally coinciding with the evil desire, but to kill that very desire. He sorrows for and regrets not only every actual sin of thought, deed, or word, into which he falls, and which must deeply grieve him as being symptomatic of a relapse into his old disease; but every rising of a sinful desire excites in him sorrow and repentance, as symptomatic of that diseased nature that still cleaves to him, as something that must be in him most especially displeasing to God, and he feels himself so much the more bound to cling with all his energy to Christ, who of God is made to us both righteousness and sanctification.

The second point touches the merit of good works. We need here only to contrast the two doctrines to see on which side the essential nature of morality—unselfish love in all its purity and profundity—is best guarded. According to the Catholic doctrine, no doubt, all good that the regenerate soul is able to do, is in so far the gift of grace that it can only be done in the power of the Holy Ghost, which God has bestowed for Christ's sake. But by means of this gift (so Catholics teach), a man is able to do such good works as satisfy the divine law as regards this life, and, in the true sense of the word, *deserve* increase of grace, eternal life, and increase of heavenly glory. And from this ground there has sprung the doctrine of supererogatory merits, which, although not formally sanctioned by the Catholic Church, has still less been repudiated by her, but, on the contrary, practically acknowledged by the system of indulgences. This doctrine implies (so are Catholics taught) that they who not only do what the divine law requires, but who also follow the so-called evangelical counsels, more particularly as to voluntary poverty, celibacy, penances, etc., performing so many of these good works that the Church canonizes them, that is, enrolls them among the saints, —that these have deserved more grace than they need for themselves, and therefore these works of supererogation, united with the equally supererogatory merits of Christ, form a fund, a treasury of merit, out of which the Church has the power of drawing indulgences, that is, of remitting to her members the penances or fasts, or temporal obligations of any kind, that would otherwise be necessary. This sketch of the Catholic doctrine will at once convince you how dubious it is in general, and also how it degrades the true nature of vital and inward morality, to suppose that there can be any merit in man in the sight of a holy God. If the doctrine of creature merit before a God who is absolutely almighty, and to whose love and mercy we owe all we have, if the idea that *He* can be indebted in any way to us, be wholly untenable, still more hopeless must the case seem when we remember that he is a *holy* God, in whose sight our best works are impure and imperfect.

Nor, again, does our individual character ever reach such conformity with the divine law, *i.e.*, the *holy* law of God, as to empower us to say that we have deserved eternal life and heavenly happiness. To acknowledge this in sincerity and humility, to confess the imperfection and sinfulness of all they do and are, and thus to be morally correct and just in their estimate of themselves, is rendered imperative by conscience upon all who are justified by faith. While building confidently upon Christ and his perfect righteousness, they disclaim all merit of their own in the sight of God. The good works they do are done not to *merit* eternal life, but out of thankful love to God who has *given* them eternal life in Christ. And while they gratefully allow that the Holy Scriptures do indeed promise a reward to good works, they look upon this reward not as a right or a thing deserved, but only as a happy result or consequence. If they persevere in faith and holiness to the end, the consequence will indeed be their blessedness in eternity; but this does not imply that they have deserved eternal blessedness. If in this life they grow in grace, and thus in peace and true happiness, they see in this no merit of their own, they only exclaim with the apostle: "Being made free from sin, and become servants to God, we have our fruit unto holiness, and the end everlasting life." And if they experience the joy of seeing that their labour is not in vain in the Lord, but that what they do the Lord maketh it to prosper, they neither speak nor think of merit of their own, but give praise to God, who has used such imperfect instruments and feeble efforts to accomplish his gracious ends. Thus the Heidelberg Catechism answers the question, "Have then our good works no merit, since God rewards them in this life and that to come?" by the simple truthful words, "This reward is not of merit but of grace." Or to put the same thought into modern language, we may say that, according to the Protestant conception, The reward of good works is the consequence of the grace shown on the one side, conditioned by the consequence of Faith on the other side.

I have thus endeavoured to answer both the questions brought before us by our subject, and now that I have come to an end, I see too plainly how little exhaustive my treatment of it has been. God grant that I may at least have succeeded in some measure in making you feel how this doctrine of justification by faith alone truly and completely satisfies not only the requirements of deep and logical reasoning, but more especially the deeper moral need of reconciliation with God, and renewal in his image. If I have so succeeded, I may confidently close this lecture by the entreaty that, as we all have cause to hold fast the precious privileges of various kinds conferred on us by the Reformation, so from henceforth this doctrine of justification by faith may be cherished by us as having been the very life-blood of that Reformation, and as being, in its practical application, the chief jewel of our evangelical Church.

X.

THE FUTURE.

PART I.—THE IMMORTALITY OF THE SOUL.

IT is on the old question of the immortality of the human being that we have now to dwell. A question this, which I at first believed so little to stand in need of argument amongst us, that assuming its universal recognition, I was prepared to pass at once to the consideration of the nature of the future life. But to my deep sorrow I discover that this is not the case; that even with regard to this subject, the ground of a once general conviction is undermined, broken up, and that, therefore, it will be necessary to relay the foundation of all that deserves the name of divine communion, salvation, peace, life, before we proceed to meditate upon those lofty blessings themselves.

The task that is thus appointed me is by no means an easy one. For not only am I more restricted as to space than I could wish in opening up such a subject as this, but we all know by old experience that it is just those truths which appear the most self-evident and incontrovertible, which are the least amenable to scientific proof. But, on the other hand, one circumstance encourages me, and that is my conviction that on this question, less perhaps than any other, is there any need to excite your interest or solicit your attention.

For so much is indeed indisputable: no knowledge is more important to man, and none can concern him so nearly, as that which relates to his own destiny, nay, to his very existence, in the truest and fullest sense of the word; which gives him decisive information as to whether he, with all his living and striving energies, his inmost being and feeling, are to be swallowed up in death by the silent night of annihilation; or whether there is within him something destined to outlast this great catastrophe, which death only transplants into another form of existence. "To be, or not to be, that is the question," exclaims the poet, when representing a highly gifted and deeply-perplexed human soul, occupied with the problem that was to decide his whole life, and give a definite direction to his collective thinking and acting. And he goes on to wonder if there be indeed "something after death;" if there be an "undiscovered country from whose bourn no traveller returns," what is it that awaits us there? "To die; to sleep! To sleep? perchance to dream,"—

> "Ay, there's the rub;
> For in that sleep of death what dreams may come
> When we have shuffled off this mortal coil,
> Must give us pause."

That in these words this great poet, who knew the human heart better than any other, expressed the universal searching and straining of humanity at large, and not that of any one individual or class in particular, we all know perfectly well. From the ignorant child returning from the grave of his mother to the empty home, and trying to picture to himself where she can now be who hitherto had always loving words and deeds for him, up to the most philosophically-minded man who strives unceasingly to discover, and perhaps to comprehend the cause of all things, *this* question is revolved as the highest and greatest of all,—What becomes of us when this living form, in which we now move, falls into decay, as we know it inevitably must? What is death, this dark and solemn riddle which we all have to solve? What becomes of those relationships and unions of every kind in which we at present stand; which form the richest element of our life, and which yet in the course of years we have to see one by one severed and dissolved?

And just as in this question the most ignorant and most wise concur,—uttering it, as it were, with one lip,—

so also is it with the answer which they immediately give and receive. For it is an indisputable fact, that amongst all nations of the earth, so far back as their history extends and our knowledge can embrace, we meet with the faith in human immortality, in a new life after death. And, further, this is no mere popular superstition, which fades away before the highest attainments of science and efforts of intellect; but just the reverse. Amongst those whom, according to their time and circumstances, we may pronounce greatest; amongst those whom the human race—whatever its epoch or clime—reveres as its leaders and benefactors in the sphere of spiritual and moral life, holding their names sacred still,—amongst all these there is not, we dare affirm, *one* who did not assert this doctrine of man's immortality, or at all events assume it as a fundamental principle of his own knowledge and teaching. In this the Confucius of China is at one with the Zoroaster of Persia, the Buddha of India with the Socrates of Greece, the philosophers of Rome with the apostle Paul, and if only we read the Old Testament intelligently, we shall admit with Moses also, not to speak of Him who stood in a different position from all these, since he could say of himself, "He who is come down from heaven—the Son of man—knows what is in heaven."

And truly one of the most remarkable, the most suggestive of facts, is just this universal knowledge, this universal agreement. For we are speaking at present of men in their natural estate, men to whom no revelation on this point had been vouchsafed. In the world around them they saw no trace of everlasting life; on the contrary, passing away, decay, and annihilation, seemed the general law. Even creatures who were in a special sense living—the animals—were subject to this doom; man himself, the highest and noblest of all animals, was in no way exempt from it. In the same way as the grass of the field and the creeping thing, man entered upon existence, had for a while his being, then felt his strength fail, and at length gave way, and went to the dust from whence he came. No power of mind, no moral worth, no strong bond of affection, availed to avert this destiny. On all sides it met the eye as an inevitable ordinance, alike for the individual and the species, that all being was only a transitory phenomenon, the very least trace of which was doomed to vanish away. And yet despite this invariable experience, despite all this indisputable testimony of the senses in all members of our race whenever and wheresoever they existed, we find the certain, the ineradicable condition, that as far as they were themselves concerned, this decay and dissolution was only apparent, only affected their bodily form; that their inmost being was untouched by it, and that unlike whatever else they saw, or knew, or experienced, that being would endure without ever becoming subject to annihilation.

Now whence comes such a marvellous conviction, and how is it to be explained? A difficult question to reply to this, with the very meagre records that we possess of the spiritual life of primitive man. The first explanation that suggests itself is this—that those great leaders of the race in spiritual matters, of whom we have made mention, were those to whom the mass of the people owed this transcendental doctrine. But this answer can in no way stand the test of history. For some of those men, as for example Moses and Confucius, did not expressly teach the immortality of the soul, nay, they seemed purposely to avoid entering upon the subject; they simply took it for granted; Moses when he spoke of the tree of life in Paradise, of which if the man took he should live for ever, and called God the God of Abraham, Isaac, and Jacob, thus implying their continued existence, since God could not be a God of the dead, but only of the living; and Confucius, while in other respects avoiding all mention of future things, nevertheless enjoining honours to be paid to departed spirits (thus assuming their life after death), as one of the chief duties of a religious man. And although others, as for instance Socrates and the Roman philosophers, appear to occupy a different position in this respect, and to argue and prove the doctrine of the soul's duration as if new; yet still they only did this because their age had grown sceptical on the subject; no one pretends to date from them the earliest, the original entrance of the idea. On the contrary, it is lost in the darkness of prehistoric times. All that we know is merely this, that the very first intellectual utterances amongst the nations that we are now alluding to, seem to have proceeded upon the assumption that the immortality of man was a doctrine self-evident and universally received. I will only recall to you in proof of this, the description of Hades introduced into the Odyssey, and the Pythagorean doctrine of the nature and destiny of the soul.

Another explanation of the universality of this conviction has been attempted. It has been suggested on the biblical side, that it must have had its origin in some brighter era of humanity than the rude, perturbed, historical era; in some period nearer the beginning, and so having a purer and more powerful consciousness of divine things than existed amidst the desolating confusion and disruptions of idolatry. With all the prestige of a holy tradition from a better time, the faith in immortality may, it is suggested, have been handed down to following ages, and may have maintained itself through them in spite of all the distortions and disguises to which it was exposed from the gradually darkening human consciousness. But this, again, is a solution of the question which I, for my part, dare not accept. For, in in the first place, it is entirely without any support or authority from biblical sources. Nowhere in the Bible do we read of a revelation from God on this point to the early race of men, nor even of any clear conceptions obtaining among them concerning it. And, in the second place, it seems to lie in the very nature of such a cognition as this, that instead of at once appearing in full maturity, even in the deeper and purer spirits, it should begin there as a presentiment, as an almost unconscious, a latent knowledge, out of which it was to develop only gradually, only step by step, and by the united spiritual efforts of many, into a definite view and a conscious conviction. And, in so far as I can judge of the history of this doctrine, it seems to me to corroborate this latter theory. For, to confine myself tc the most familiar example we have, it is plain that, to the people of Israel in the early period of their existence and culture, this doctrine of the immortality of the soul was only as a rough unpolished jewel, the value of which the possessor scarcely knows; while during the later days of their development, in the book of Job, the Psalms, and the Prophets, it assumed more and more a definite shape, and entered more actively into their mode of thought, till at last, even long before the appearance of Christ, it had been elaborated into a certain, an indisputable conviction amongst all believing Israelites.

But in what way, and by what spiritual agency, was this development carried on from a mere foreboding to a definite conviction; from an unconscious feeling to a conscious knowledge?

The essential point for us to grasp firm hold of in our inquiries—else the whole phenomenon will be inexplicable—is, that such a foreboding (the germ of future knowledge) is universally met with in humanity, nay, essentially belongs to, and forms part of it. Nor need we long remain in doubt as to why this remarkable possession of the human mind exists, or on what grounds it rests. One word explains it. Man feels and knows himself to be a spiritual being, having self-consciousness, able to think and to will, and therefore he feels himself placed in a different life-sphere altogether from that visible and material one to which all things around him belong. This gives him an inherent right, nay, this compels him to draw a distinction between himself and those things, to claim for himself a different law of being and of action from that which they obey. It is only as regards the physico-animal side of his form of existence, through which he is related to and homogeneous with them, that he can conceive of, and acknowledge sharing their destiny, and being as transitory as they. As regards that other element of his being so thoroughly different in character, and so in every sense transcending them all, he must inevitably feel that its existence has quite different conditions, and is subject to quite different laws. And the more he learns to distinguish between himself and surrounding nature, the more clear and distinct must this consciousness become. In the earliest stage of our race, it is evident that this conscious distinction must have existed in a very slight degree, since intellectual life was only beginning, while natural life was already mature, and could thus assert its predominance; man must needs have then been chiefly conscious of his material being and his relationship to nature. But it became otherwise as the race progressed. Step by step the sum of intellectual life grew, one accretion led to another; thoughts, ideas, perceptions, arose, which had nothing in common with physical nature, and which led man to conclude that he belonged essentially to a different order of existence. And now, while reflecting more closely upon what it was that constituted the difference, it must have burst upon him that he was a *person*, self-conscious, self-deciding, free, in short, to choose and to do. While each individual animal existed only as an exemplar of the species, and was therefore, after having filled its appointed functions, subjected to the annihilation of its individuality, he found on the contrary that the human individual was a separate entity, perfectly distinct from the rest of the species, one who existed for himself, and had his aim in himself. Yes, on deeper reflection, it must soon have become apparent that this peculiarity not only appertained to man in the same manner as the physical portion of his nature did, but that it was essentially the *basis*, the *core* of his being, essentially that which made him what he felt himself to be. He learned to say *I*, in the emphatic sense of the word, designating by this *I*, not merely his natural frame, but rather his inmost personality of self-consciousness and self-agency. "I think, therefore I am," as a comparatively recent philosopher expresses it, must have become the conclusion of the earlier thinker we are imagining, respecting himself; that is to say, "in this capacity for thought, with all that it includes, lies my peculiar being; if I could not think I should not know that I was, and hence I should not be; that is, I should not be an *Ego*, a being that is able to distinguish between himself and others, but only a part of the whole of nature."

And this perception once attained to, that other perception of the immortality of this *I*, this human being, must have grown up spontaneously. It became evident to man, when once consciously differentiated in being from the rest of nature, that his destiny could no longer be confounded with hers. He who had once learned to say, "I think, therefore I am," must necessarily have gone on to say further, "I shall think, therefore I shall be." For just make the experiment of trying to conceive your conscious, thinking spirit as other than perpetually conscious and thinking. See whether this whole inner life—that has thus in its self-consciousness apprehended itself in opposition to nature—see whether it is capable of entertaining the idea of its existence dissolving into a non-existence; of its being, in point of fact, nothing more than a type of the species like any other animal, whose individuality is of no importance, but is simply to be absorbed again into the race at large. Without being able to afford any mathematical demonstration of the fact, which indeed must always be unattainable in the spiritual domain, do we not all feel with one of the speakers in Plato's *Phœdo:* "The soul is something more powerful and enduring than the body, for in everything it far exceeds it." To the inner being, filled as it is with such wealth, life, and individuality, it is intolerable, nay, impossible to believe that all these have no actual life, but are only transitory phenomena, like a bubble on the water, to form for a moment, and then vanish away. So long as we love, know, cultivate spiritual fellowship, feel within us those religious and artistic propensities, which lead us out of ourselves towards some ideal, so long will it become more and more certain to us that all these imply the gift of something that cannot do other than live and work on, and strive towards an end in which it is to find its fulfilment.

It is these feelings, this consciousness, and the reasonings connected with them, that I hold to constitute the primeval source from whence the human race drew the conviction of the immortality of its inward being. And indeed, the method by which recent philosophers have conducted the argument for this great truth entirely supports this conclusion.

But, together with this primeval source, we must also take a second into the account. I allude to that which lies in the *moral* feeling, in the *conscience* of human beings. We have already been shown in one of the earlier lectures (in that on the Being and Nature of God), that every man, even the most deeply degraded, has some power of distinguishing between good and evil. And since he is able to make such a distinction, it follows necessarily that he is able to make a distinction also between the *destiny* of the good and the bad. For every one feels in his conscience that by doing good he incurs good, by doing evil, punishment. And yet it is, at the same time, certain that, in the present life, the course of things by no means invariably follows this law. Nay, even when it does, the reward or the punishment incurred, is far from satisfying the idea of retribution which the mind entertains. In the midst of his happiness, the highest joy of the good man consists in an inward promise of some still higher happiness; while, in the midst of his punishment, the bitterest pang of the bad man is the threat that his conscience holds out of fuller and more terrible punishment. Now these feelings imperatively proclaim another life, in which both these previsions will have their full accomplishment, and so surely as these feelings exist, that other life exists also. "So then it is quite certain," says Socrates, at the conclusion of an argument of the kind, "and we have not been deceived in believing, that there is another life, and that the souls of the dead have still an existence, and this of such a kind that with the good it fares better, and with the wicked worse."

And not only in the arguments of philosophers, but in all popular religions whatsoever, we see that from this train of thought the conviction of another life after death immediately arose, for everywhere we find it conceived of as a life of retribution. It was felt that the beneficent, heroic life of a Heraclius could have no other result than an ascension to the gods, and an admission into their glory and blessedness. The crimes of a Sisyphus, of a Tantalus, of the Danaides, instantly suggested the punishment that awaited them in the under world; and on account of those punishments which the inborn sense of justice unconditionally demanded, it was felt impossible that the end of their existence on earth should be looked upon as the end of their existence altogether.

Thus it was from both these sources that the conviction of our being's immortality arose; first from the perception of its spiritual nature, its self-conscious personality, by which it is so essentially separated from all that constitutes the perishable nature around; and, secondly, from the inevitable feeling that each must reap what he has sowed, that it must needs be that good is reserved for the good, and evil for the evil. And these are the two points, as it appears to me, on which the argument for the truth in question must be based.

Of course, therefore, it is just here that its opponents direct their attacks. With regard to the first point, they positively dispute that the soul has any such indwelling consciousness of its immortality; and "least of all," says the author of Five Discourses on Faith and Knowledge, "can believers in the Bible appeal to this, since according to their creed, the minority only attain heaven, *i.e.*, eternal life, the rest incurring hell, that is, another death, so that they have to renounce all which we can affirm to be desirable to our nature." With regard to the last observation, the frivolous distortion of the case that it implies, will, I am sure, be evident to every one. For believers in the Bible nowhere assert hell, or a condition of desolated and unhappy existence, to be the *original destination* of the majority; on the contrary, they proclaim eternal life to be that for which all are originally destined, and they speak of their lost estate as including the most utter failure and perversion of what lay in their nature, and was required of them. But to draw the inference, that because such failure and perversion are possible, and exemplified in many, there is therefore no general consciousness and need of eternal blessedness, is just as unreasonable as to pretend that it is not in the nature of man to wish for a good government because so many are ill governed; or that it does not belong to his constitution to desire, and that he has no claim to enjoy his lawful daily bread, because there are so many who have no share in it. "We are not appointed to wrath, but to obtain salvation through Christ Jesus," is the language of Scripture. And that the consciousness of this, despite all disguise and obscuration, does still reveal itself in a thousand ways in the heart of each man, reflecting itself in most varied previsions and hopes, is a fact that we, believers in the Bible, are above all others entitled to appeal to.

But further, this consciousness, these hopes and previsions themselves, are denied their real significance. It is asserted that in these faculties of our soul there is nothing that gives it any right to expect endless duration. If we allege that the feeling of mankind revolts against annihilation, that our inmost consciousness, our communion with our loved ones, all assure us of eternal life indwelling in us, these, we are informed, are merely sentimentally agreeable phrases, which cannot stand rigorous examination. The animal, too, even the worm, revolts and defends itself against death, and yet it dies.

We answer that we perfectly concur in this last observation, and avail ourselves of it to carry on our argument. Thus, then, it lies in the nature of life to revolt against death, and to feel it to be something unsuitable, contradictory to its essential being. Even with regard to life in its lowest scale, to the life of a worm, or some less highly organized creature even, we find this the case. Therefore it follows necessarily that the higher the scale of life, the more powerful, intensive, perfect, the more decidedly must it feel this opposition to death, and seek to guard against it. And if we reflect a little further upon the subject, we shall of ourselves come to the conclusion that somewhere and somehow life must reach such a height and strength as to be actually able to offer an availing resistance, and to be no more liable to interruption. For, if indeed this were not so, if there were no such thing as a life that did actually exclude death, how should we be able to explain this universal repugnance felt towards death by all living creatures? In such a case it would be part of the very nature of life itself to include a liability to death, and no being can feel repugnance or strive against that which is actually inherent in its nature.

And now, is it not most evident that this higher degree and energy of life, that so resists and repudiates death, begins just there where life passes over from merely natural life into that quite other, infinitely higher, specifically different form of which we spoke before,—into the form of the self-conscious, free-willing, or, as we are accustomed to express it in one word, *spiritual* personal life? That *this* life cannot be compared with that of the worm, or of any unconscious or soulless creature whatever, we have already seen; but we may further inquire whether it does not contain a living *consciousness*, and repudiate annihilation in a manner which bears no relation to the repugnance our earthly nature feels towards death? "Our outward man perisheth," says the Apostle, "but our inward man is renewed day by day." And our own experience has afforded each one of us numberless corroborations of the truth of his words.

We might now proceed to take up a line of argument used by philosophy both in ancient and modern times —from Socrates down to Fichte—to prove the immortality of the inner being; an argument derived from the assertion that the soul being a unity, is, as such, incapable of decay, it being only in the case of the complex that a falling to pieces, or a dissolution, is conceivable. But the limits assigned to us, as well as the abstruse nature of this method, lead us to renounce a line of argument from which we freely confess we expect little profitable result. For, after all, what absolute proof have we of this unity of the soul? Can we subject it to the microscope or the scalpel, as we can the visible and the tangible? It must content us for the present, simply to indicate that the instinct and consciousness of immortality have nothing to fear from the most searching examination of the reason, but find far more of confirmation and additional proof than of contradiction in the profoundest thinking. And further, that this instinct and consciousness do actually exist, and are traceable through all the stages and ramifications of the human race,—as the brief historical survey with which we began proved,—is confirmed to us by our opponents themselves; as, for instance, when the author before alluded to, laments that so many, who in other respects are free-thinking in religious matters, should not be able to shake off the old ideas on this subject, but go on insisting that the human mind feels an irresistible need to believe in its eternal duration. If such men do this, as the same authority affirms, "in spite of reason and intelligence," what are we to infer thence but that there is in man something which is deeper and stronger than the maxims of a self-invented philosophy, namely, the divinely-created nobility of his nature, the inherent breath of life breathed into him by God, the relation to the Eternal, which secures to him Eternity. And surely to trace and feel these energies within us, and to be convinced and decided by them, is no slavish subjection of which we need to be ashamed, any more than those are to be envied the mournful victory they have won, who have crushed their eternal forebodings under the yoke of their temporal demonstrations, and confess that they do not esteem themselves worthy of eternal life, and know nothing of the imperishable portion of their nature.

And here you will allow me to call your attention to the different tone in which the so-called humanitarianism of the Pantheists, and the religion of the Bible, speak of and estimate man. This modern view of the universe seeks in the lowest orders of animal life for analogies with the human being. It appeals to the tapeworm and to the earth-worm, to illustrate man's origin and his end. And indeed why should it not do so, if man and worm alike are held the products of the same *natura naturans*, which evolves the whole out of the same elements, and for the same destiny? The Scripture, on the other hand, knows of nothing on earth, not even the highest and the most beautiful, that is worthy to be compared to the being of man. Scripture rises to the heavenly, to the fulness of the divine life itself, when seeking an image for it, or throwing light upon its nature and its faculties. "And God created man in his own image, in the image of God created he him," is the testimony that it bears; and again, "we shall be like him, for we shall see him as he is." I think we have every reason to be thankful that such a mighty and undying advocate has undertaken to defend the honour of our race against the presumptuous folly of its own members, who would tear the crown from its brow!

But it behoves us to inquire whether we may not be doing injustice to the opponents of immortality, when we affirm that they know nothing of an imperishable portion of our being? For, with the exception of the materialists, who indeed will not hear of any spiritual element at all in man, but regard all that we include under that category as the mere activities of his physical nature, doomed therefore to decay, and die therewith,—with the exception of these, the opponents of our doctrine are the so-called Pantheists, whose views have been fully described to us in the earlier Lecture upon the Being of God. Now these hold that the World-soul, which in their opinion produces and fills the universe, also fills and rules man; nay, that it is only in him that it reaches its special end, which is self-consciousness, and attains to thought and will. It is true they go on to say, that at the death of the individual this World-soul retreats from him, just as the setting sun seems to draw back its rays into itself; and that what had been for a period individual existence and self-consciousness, now sinks once more into the great, unconscious, undistinguished spirit-ocean of the whole. But still they call this eternal life; they deny that there can be any question here of annihilation, since nothing is lost of the sum-total of spiritual being, but the individual has merely been merged once more into the general, out of which it proceeded.

But is this really the case? Is it true that such a process implies no loss of that which forms the basis of our spiritual nature, and belongs to the being of spirit in general? To me it appears that much, on the contrary, nay, to speak out at once, that *all* is lost which really concerns us, and in which our life consists. For manifestly in such a case we lose our *self-consciousness*, our *personality*, our *ego*, in other words, just that which essentially constitutes *our* being. The substance indeed remains out of which we were formed, but *we ourselves* are no longer there, we ourselves are as completely annihilated as though we had never been. That life that knew itself, felt itself, thought itself, distinguished between itself and others, has vanished into unconscious and indistinguishable universality; in other words, into *annihilation* and *death*. For, if it be true, that if "I think, therefore I am," it must also be true that if "I think no more, therefore I am no more."

Or can it be any compensation to know that our substance at least is imperishable, and will endure? *Our* substance! Why, *we* no longer are, therefore *we* have no longer any substance! Can it be anything more than an empty, delusive play of words to tell us, that "we have nevertheless an eternal life, and are of an eternal nature." If I myself no longer am, how can *my* nature be spoken of? *I* am not, what life then can there be for me?

Again, do not these very men, who would feed us with such unmeaning phrases, judge exactly as we are now doing, and call things by their right names, when they treat of our *bodily* existence? For with our bodies that process actually does go on which they would transfer to the soul. Our bodies are not lost at death, in the sense of their substance being annihilated; on the contrary, they simply return to the mass from whence they were taken, dust to dust, earth to earth, and new forms of life spring from the mouldering bones. But does any one affirm, on this account, that bodily life is imperishable? Is this return into the sum-total of the material world anything else than *death* to the individual? Does it remove from any one the feeling and the fact of his annihilation on that side of his nature? Is any one at all reconciled to it by those words of Schiller's, which the author so often quoted holds forth to us:—

> "Thou fearest death, thou wouldest live eternally.
> Live in the whole; it remains, though thou hast long passed away."

Nay, the same authority seems himself not to be much influenced by them, but, on the contrary, to discern —when the *body* is concerned—a very serious difference indeed between life and death, and to hold the latter to be the cessation of all that our nature values; for he says, "It is not necessary to believe in a future retribution; mere prudence teaches us to set limits to individual sensual enjoyments, in order to enjoy *life* as long and as completely as possible." Thus, then, some value is to be attached and some care taken of the preservation of bodily life, for when the body is once more absorbed in universal nature, all is at an end with it; but this does not hold good, forsooth, with the spiritual life! *This* can be quite comfortably surrendered to precisely the same absorption, and yet it can be pretended that its death is not thereby implied, and its eternal duration can still be spoken of; no philosophy feeling itself strong enough to oppose and openly contradict the inexterminable need in our spirits for eternal life, but rather seeking to mislead and deceive it by all manner of plausible delusions. And in relation to this, it is significant that even the most acute Pantheistic philosophers, when they touch upon the subject of their "eternal life," seem as it were to lose their head, and in almost comic contrast to their general tone, take refuge in sentimental enthusiasm; a poem of some kind, as, for instance, Rückert's Dying Flower, or an extract out of Schefer's Lay Breviary, taking the place of a clear philosophical analysis.

We therefore maintain that we do the Pantheists no injustice when we say that they attribute to our inner being exactly the same annihilation as to our outer; that they know not eternal life, that they do no justice to the consciousness that our souls have of their own immortality.

But having come to this conclusion, there is still another objection brought against us, which must just be touched upon, though you will hardly be disposed to give it much weight. We are reproached with the *immorality*, because the *egotism* of this hope of a continued personality after death,—told that it only arises from a selfish wish, from a "sentimental tenderness for one's own *ego*." The opposite view is presented to us as evidently a far more lofty one; we are called upon to admire its readiness without more ado, to share the universal doom of instability, to surrender individuality to absorption into universal life, after it has accomplished the purposes for which it was appointed.

What shall we reply to such a charge as this? In order to show the strained and artificial character of the whole objection, and of its pretended morality, it will be enough to quote a reply that has already been made. "If it be egotism to desire to live *eternally*, it is just as much egotism to desire to live the next moment, and every one is an egotist who eats or drinks, or does anything whatever with a view to the preservation of his life."

But there is far more to be said in refutation than this; we can prove that the hope of eternal life, in the *Christian* sense, is the very reverse of egotism, and overcomes the radical principle of this perversion of our nature. Allow me first of all, however, to appeal to your own feelings and consciousness. One of the most acute of the French philosophers and critics of the present day, Ernest Renan, himself nothing less than an adherent of Christianity, as is unfortunately but too explicable in an educated French Catholic, has in his late work on the *Future of Religion*, very earnestly protested against a positive religious faith, grounded on God and immortality being looked upon as a low and subordinate stage in the spiritual life of mankind, and in corroboration of this protest, he adds, "It is in his best moments that man is religious; it is when he is good that he feels that virtue corresponds with an eternal order; it is when he contemplates things from a *disinterested* point of view that he finds death revolting and absurd. Let us then boldly declare that man comes nearest to the truth when he is most religious and most sure of an infinite destiny."[1]

And now I would ask you, whether this be not your own experience? Put it to the test: In which mood do all the good and noble elements of your nature most stir within you? When do your duties of every kind come before you in the most earnest light, and your inner being thirst and strive after a higher moral condition than you at present possess, after holiness and love and completeness; when, I ask, is all this the case? When you represent to yourself that death is to be the end of all; of your personality, your activity, your mental and moral acquisitions; or when, on the contrary, you look upon yourself as destined to transplantation into a wider existence, where all that is good, beautiful, loveable, and true, shall reach its end and its perfection: where love will rest in love; where holiness shall be satisfied with holiness; where the fulness of God will open out to embrace all that are made like unto him, and capable of enjoying his fellowship? Yes; I ask you, which of these two theories most tends to your moral earnestness, and kindles within your hearts that holy flame of aspiration after the highest, and love to all that is love-deserving, by which the selfishness of our nature is consumed? We affirm that never are we more selfish, never does that which is low and mean have such free play within us, as when we forget that we are called to an eternal communion of love; when we forget that we are destined to behold the Holy and Perfect One as he is—that thus beholding we may become like unto him—and look upon ourselves as related merely to this world, as earthly beings who may therefore well be earthly-minded.

And this result is most natural and explicable. Here, too, Pantheism has only the word and the semblance,—the deed and the reality belong to Christianity. We allow that self-surrender does stand higher than self-holding, and that it must indeed appear egotistical to insist in preserving one's own life, merely because it is

[1] *Revue des Deux-Mondes,* 15th October 1860.

one's *own*. But such self-surrender as Pantheism propounds can have no moral worth. For it is not a voluntary one, but a constrained, an inevitable natural necessity; and we might just as reasonably call our physical death an act of self-denial as this self-loss of the soul. Christianity, on the contrary, does place before us a veritable and actual self-surrender, not such a one as the *ego* must passively *undergo* (not having the power to surrender itself even if it had the will); but a self-surrender which is self-consciously *accomplished*, which is voluntary, which actually involves self-denial. For how does Christianity represent eternal life? In one word; as an eternal *love*, which, as is implied in the primary idea of love, is perfectly divested of all selfishness, all living in self, and willing for self; and henceforth lives only in and for God and Christ, in and for the fellowship of its glorified fellow-creatures. And where such love begins, eternal life begins also. "I live, but henceforth it is no more I that live," the apostle declares, "but Christ that liveth in me;" and, again, "Christ died for all, that they which live should not henceforth *live unto themselves*, but to him who died for them, and rose again!" "He who will save his life" (or love his life), exclaims the Lord to his disciples, "shall lose it." "If any man will be mine, let him deny himself, and take up his cross."

I refer it to your own decision, whether this language implies any reprehensible "sentimental tenderness" for the *ego;* whether rather *this* self-losing, and at the same time self-gaining in perfect love for free and personal beings, be not the only worthy as well as the only possible self-surrender to which a moral character can be attributed. It is indeed offensive to hear Pantheism, which destroys and reduces all that is ethical into a metaphysical process, affect nevertheless to oppose Christianity as the advocate of a higher morality than hers.

And this affectation comes out even more fully with regard to the next and last point which we have to consider, viz., the strong arguments for our immortality afforded by the claims of our moral consciousness.

Our opponents themselves point out that, in our estimation, this proof throws all others into the shade, and that it is brought forward most prominently in the Scriptures. For, indeed, St. Paul himself declares that "if Christ be not risen" (and so mankind be left without the expectation of a resurrection and eternal life), "we are of all men most miserable; let us eat and drink, for to-morrow we die." But it is just against this very expression, and the whole train of thought from whence it proceeds, that they protest with a certain degree of bitterness, declaring such a stand-point to be very low and degrading, one only tolerable to the weak, who still need external support to their moral life, while "truly moral, and at the same time thinking men" have long got beyond it. Such, they urge, find their motive for morality within them, and need not the prospect of a future reward or future punishment to incite or to deter.

But I think the first feeling that rises within us will be one of surprise to hear the apostle Paul, that man of profoundest discernment, and, at the same time, intensest zeal for all that is great, holy, and divine,—he who, in an unparalleled fervour of love, could exclaim, in words no other has ever repeated, "I could wish myself accursed from Christ for my brethren, my kinsmen's sake,"—we shall, I say, feel some surprise to find him treated as morally weak, and deficient in correct thinking; nor will it be without a touch of irony that we shall observe how some who really have not the very slightest pretensions to qualities of the kind, coolly rank themselves above him in spiritual discernment and moral susceptibility. And this surprise will increase if we further consider that the same language is held not only by the apostle Paul, as we have heard, but by all those to whom mankind has ever looked up as greatest and noblest in this sphere of thought, as the sources of their highest spiritual insight and their moral life. Of Him who, according to the testimony of his most decided opponents, stands out alone and incomparable in this respect, God-inspired and holy as no other man ever was,—of Christ, I have no need to tell you that this holds good; you will all spontaneously recall those words from his lips which most closely link exhortations to holiness with the promise of eternal life, "Keep the commandments, believe on me, *that thou mayest enter into life*."

But to turn to quite another quarter, we have the same testimony borne wherever pagan thought and pagan morality reach their highest perfection. "For we must remember, O men," said Socrates in his last speech, before he drained the poison-cup, "that it depends upon the immortality of the soul whether we have to live to it and to care for it or not. For the danger seems fearfully great of not caring for it. Yea, were death to be the end of all, it would be truly a fortunate thing for the wicked to get rid of their body and at the same time of their wickedness. But now since the soul shows itself to us as immortal, there can be for it no refuge from evil, and no other salvation, than to become as good and intelligent as possible." Now this is, in other words, the very same statement as St. Paul's. If there was to be an end of everything at death, then we might do what we liked; it was only because there is a future life that there arose the duty of caring for our souls, and following after wisdom and goodness.

And surely what two such voices agree in declaring, is not to be nullified by a few easily manufactured phrases about higher and lower stand-points, but may well deserve and claim to have its meaning honestly inquired into, clearly understood, and thoroughly sifted.

For, first of all, it is evident that our opponents inadequately apprehend the meaning of these expressions of our Lord and his apostles, if they imagine them to convey the idea that, without *the promise of a reward*, eating and drinking and unrestrained indulgence would be the only aim of human nature. Every one to whom the words of the Redeemer, and the epistles of his witnesses, are familiar, know well how, on the contrary, their whole spirit is, in the most positive manner, opposed to such a greed for reward, such a mean and slavish spirit, and how they nowhere say, "Let us love

God, that he may love us in return ;" but rather, "Let us love him, because he first loved us." The truth to which they bear witness is rather this: "If man has no future destiny, he can *live* to no future destiny;" in that case he must be made only for this earth, and the simplest logic demands that he should accordingly live for this earth only.

Now what is implied in this idea, living only for this earth? Does it mean to revel in every species of sensual enjoyment? By no means! Can any one imagine, for instance, that the apostle Paul, even if he had had no belief in a future existence, could, with his lofty, essentially spiritual nature, have led such a life as this? Most assuredly not! To live merely for earth means only this: to plan and lead such a life-career as seems to us most enjoyable, advantageous, best, without reference to anything besides the circumstances of our earthly existence.

Each would then follow, of course, quite unreservedly the impulses and desires of his nature. The sensual man would, as the apostle says, eat and drink, and minister in every way to the gratification of the flesh. Characters of a nobler and more intellectual type, who found no pleasure in such things, would seek to satisfy their *intellectual* needs, and move in an atmosphere of spiritual delights. The rude and uncultivated, in whom unbridled passions held riot, would yield themselves up to their impulses, and thereby very possibly disturb the order of external morality. The wiser and more finely organized, who understood the evil consequences such conduct must entail, would strive to gain a certain control over these natural elements of their being, and to go through life under this self-control. The unloving and envious would keep up galling and aggressive relations with their fellow-men; the kind-hearted and love-desiring would show kindness and love to others, and find happiness in making them happy. In short, each would construct and order his own life according to his taste, his disposition, his intelligence, his idiosyncrasy: the one in carnal, violent, immoral fashion; the other morally, in the usual acceptation of the word, respectably—in much that is lovely and of good report. Together with a Sardanapalus and a Tiberius we should have a Titus and a Marcus Aurelius, side by side with a Cæsar Borgia and a Philip of Orleans, a Spinoza and a Schiller. But still all would proceed upon the same fundamental principle, nor could we blame those for their immoral excesses, or praise these for their moral restraint; for neither the one nor the other *could* have any other law or principle of conduct than just *this:* to satisfy as much as possible the requirements of their own temperament,—for the peculiarities of which they are not responsible,—and thereby to secure the greatest possible amount of happiness.

And, indeed, what other motive could come into play? We could no longer speak of a moral *duty* in a case like this. For to a *duty* there must always belong two moments; first, one that imposes it; and secondly, a reasonable aim proportionate to the efforts required to carry out what is imposed. But according to the theory whose consequences we are now expounding, there is neither a God by whom such a duty can be imposed, nor any future destiny for which we need to prepare ourselves by moral efforts and actions. Accordingly, there is no longer any room for the idea of *good* in the absolute sense of the word, and we must hold, with the Epicureans of olden time, "the good to be what *does me* good, and reckon as good and wise whoever, clearly discerning what tends to his well-being, and what on the contrary disturbs his calm enjoyment of life, knows how to pursue the one and avoid the other." For it is self-evident that the claims of morality would have nothing to depend upon but this one saving clause, "Be moral in order to be happy." Nor do the advocates of Pantheism shrink from admitting this. To quote again from the author we have so often alluded to: "Man must practise moderation and virtue, since it is only by so doing that he preserves the capacity for external enjoyments, or is able to taste the highest joys of which his inward nature is capable: enthusiasm for the beautiful, the good, and the true."

Now, it will be observed in the first place, that, by their own admission, those who, in the promise of future blessedness, held out by Christianity, descry an unworthy appeal to man's self-interested desire of reward, have themselves nothing to allege in support of their recommendations to morality, but just this same prospect of reward, and surely of a reward infinitely below that essentially unselfish and holy joy in the life-fellowship of God, which the gospel sets before the Christian. And secondly, we have to ask them, If, to your admonition, "Be moral in order to be happy," some one should reply, "Moral efforts and limitations do *not* make me happy; they may indeed be the law of your nature, but mine, on the contrary, feels happiest in the perfectly free indulgence of all its passions; and even if the evil consequences with which you threaten me on account of this my idiosyncrasy, do come to pass, and health breaks down, and my fellow-men despise me, etc., why, I have still power over my own life, and can end it as soon as it becomes burdensome." If this reply chance to be made, and there are many natures of this stamp, by what arguments, we ask, can Pantheists meet it? As to what is happiness or unhappiness to him individually, the man himself must be the best judge, and as to any other motive to morality besides this appeal to his own advantage, Pantheism knows of none, nor can it know. Nay, truly, Paul is not mistaken, as our opponents assert, but unqualifiedly right and justified in declaring, that if there be no future life, we may at least, and probably shall say, even though we be not compelled to say, "Let us eat and drink, for to-morrow we die."

Let me set this before you from another point of view. You remember that passage in the lecture upon Nature or God, in which the natural and the moral law were represented as antagonistic. "For it is very possible," said the lecturer, "that they should actually come into conflict with each other. The natural law may, for example, demand the satisfaction of hunger, while the moral law enjoins, 'Thou shalt not steal, thou shalt not kill.' And which of the two are we to obey?"

If we believe in no personal immortality after death, there is absolutely no ground for our preferring to obey the moral law, while there is the very strongest ground for following the dictates of the law of nature. For that this last *has* a claim upon us, and corresponds with the needs of our being, is incontestable. We must, to abide by the above illustration, satisfy our hunger in order to preserve not only health but even life itself. But as to the moral law, what claim can that urge? It incites us to act against the interests of our own being, and to sacrifice our very lives, and we may reasonably ask, Why and wherefore? The only answer that can be returned must be: out of consideration for others, for the general good. But what is it which really pledges me to this consideration? In many cases it is nothing but care for my own welfare, seeing that it would be impossible for the world to go on, and so for me to go on in it, without this reference to the good of others, without respect for their opposite personalities and opposite interests. But if the case in point actually involve my very *existence*, if I am in danger of dying of hunger, how can the care of my own welfare still pledge me to greater anxiety for the rights of others than for my own support? Evidently this argument can no longer hold good. Every other consideration must give place to self-preservation; my nature most plainly and imperatively impels me thereto. I do only what, according to its clearest and most rightful dictates, I *must* do, when I procure for myself, by any means whatsoever, what is essential to the maintenance of my life. And if my conscience protests against these means, without giving me any reasonable grounds for such a protest, if still it says, "That is not right, that will not tend to thy welfare," offering me, at the same time, no explanation of *why* it is not right; while I, on the other hand, see that, from obedience to its injunctions, suffering and death must follow; to what other conclusion can I possibly come but to this, that conscience itself is foolish and unsuitable, a morbid element in my nature that must be resisted and eliminated like any other defect which interferes with that nature's free development and well-being? And such, indeed, we find the most determined and consistent advocates of the so-called "modern theory of the world" openly proclaiming it. Conscience and religious feeling are, according to them, sources of disease in man, which continually interfere with his proper and natural use and enjoyment of life; and this position is really incontrovertible if there be nothing beyond death. For conscience, in countless instances, is in positive opposition to the claims of earthly existence, and each individual life has a need, and a right, and a duty, to defend itself against such disturbing influence, unless, indeed, this right contravene some *other* right, derived from higher authority.

You see then that the moral law can only have a positive and insuperable claim on our obedience when it has for basis the belief, both that while we obey it we are *serving* our life in the true sense, preserving and gaining our life even when our obedience apparently leads to our forfeiting it; and also, on the other hand, are really and truly losing it whenever, by disobedience to the moral law, we seek to preserve life by following the dictates of the law of nature.

In other words: the moral law can only claim a superior right over us to that exercised by the natural law, as being the law of a higher, more important and more abiding life than the physical life, as having the power to hold this language towards us: "Compensation for the self-denials that I enjoin, awaits you in a future state, in every sense far transcending the present. It is not in the present order of things that thy special destiny, happiness, life, lies, and therefore the claims that this order urges are not the highest and final; whereas mine are those supremest and ultimate claims that concern the *truth* of thy being, and hence when the two are discordant, it is mine that should be unconditionally obeyed." For even in the daily life of us men, any law that opposes and restrains our natural impulses and desires, is justified only because the aim it has in view is that of our higher advantage. How could we parents bear to deprive our children of much play and enjoyment adapted to their years, in order to send them to the perhaps hated schoolrooms, if this were an aimless infliction; if it were not necessary, nay indispensable to their after life and higher destiny? How could any ideal, were it ever so fair, excite us to make any sacrifices if it were confessedly without a future? No one undertakes a work knowing beforehand that he will not be able to finish it; no one lives and dies for a cause which is undoubtedly to die and decay with himself. If we are never to attain to the goal of moral perfection, if our loving endeavours are never to find reciprocal love, if there is never to be a realization of that idea of the good which seeks to influence us—and all these allowedly stand or fall with the existence of a personal God and a future life—how can we be reasonably expected, still less bound to laborious and self-denying efforts after these,—efforts which we know beforehand to be powerless, hopeless, and in vain? In such a case the moral law in our conscience, which prompts these efforts, must be not only something useless and unaccountable, but a torture and delusion, and we could not do better than to follow the leading of some of our modern philosophers, and seek to get rid of it as rapidly and thoroughly as possible.

Thus we see that, considered from the most different points of view, we come to the same decision which a healthy natural instinct has long ago anticipated; namely, that with the belief in the continuance of our personal being after death, all essential difference between good and evil must stand or fall; if we give up that belief we lose all absolute ground for moral endeavour, the impulses of nature become the highest, nay, the only laws we have to follow, the doing right, the leading of a loving and unselfish life, may be a matter of taste, but not of obligation; everything within the sphere of morality must be referred to subjective preference,—since there is no longer anything objective, neither a God, nor a destiny set before us by him, which is to serve as the rule of our conduct. For the whole of my argument presupposes that to each of you it is self-evident that the existence of a personal God, and the immortality of our personal being, are so inseparably connected, that as a German philosopher has ventured to affirm, It is easier to believe in the immortality of the soul without God, than in God without the immortality of the soul.[1] But who is there that will, that can in any truth draw the deductions that we are now enumerating? Who is able even to picture to himself a state of things like this, to think human existence from this point of view? Who can shake off not only inwardly but outwardly the habit of calling one person good, the other bad; valuing one man highly for his moral worth, and condemning another for his immorality? We boldly affirm that no one can do this, not even those who, according to our previous demonstration, are logically constrained to such a course. When Carl Vogt, confessedly one of the most out-spoken advocates of the "Modern Theories," according to whom the whole spiritual life of man depends so exclusively upon his perishable corporeity, that his thoughts and feelings of every kind are to be looked upon only as involuntary activities of the nerves, just as saliva is a secretion of certain glands, and phlegm of certain others —even this man, I say, when upon a late political occasion, he expressed his enmity to crowned heads, spoke of them, not as unfortunately organized nervous sys-

[1] Should this not appear sufficiently clear, the following points may be taken into consideration: The immortality of our being is demanded, 1st, by the *truthfulness* of God, since he has instilled the instinct of, and the longing for, this immortality in the universal heart of humanity. "God is not a man that he should lie, neither the son of man that he should repent." 2dly, by his *wisdom*. He creates nothing without a purpose, and everywhere we observe an economy of means to an end. But if man ceased with the present life—to say nothing of his *personality* being entirely lost—many faculties of his soul which have not been developed fully, or at all here below, would exist *unused* and decay unused, there being no further development reserved for them; as, for instance, in the case of those dying before maturity. Thus there would be the most senseless waste of the highest endowments. 3dly, by God's *love and goodness*. For how would these be shown, if the loving and love-needing creature were never to be permitted to attain the full enjoyment of love, but to be annihilated as a mere toy? 4thly, by God's *justice*. For what, were there no immortality, would become of retribution and judgment? 5thly, by his *omnipotence*. Each would, in such a case, have the power of withdrawing himself at pleasure by means of suicide, from the Divine control, etc.

tems, incapable of evolving any but tyrannical and unjust ideas, but spoke of them very decidedly as morally responsible and blameable persons who even, in some wholly incomprehensible way, had it in their power to be and act otherwise!

Yes, these wild theorists are better than their theories; these spring from themselves, but their nature has sprung from God's hand and God's loving spirit, and his work is better than theirs! But can they not see that every sentence they utter containing a moral judgment, witnesses against their own teaching; witnesses that in every man whatsoever, even in those who most positively deny it, there lives and speaks a moral law, which is stronger than he? That hence there must necessarily exist an order of things with which this moral law is connected, from whence it proceeds, to which it tends; an order of things with which the innermost depths of our nature correspond? In so far as we all experience this, we all have an ineradicable and undying witness to our own immortality, and destiny to share this higher order of things. He only who feels within him no conscience whatsoever, who knows nothing of good or evil; or to whom the voice of the moral law which he hears in his heart, speaks with no higher authority, no deeper earnestness, no more attractive suasion than the voice of his material nature,—he alone is justified in considering himself a being for whom no other future exists but what earth can offer. But such a one would no longer belong to our race; he would lack that which makes man to be man.

The nature of this future, which we thus feel and know to be our life's end and aim, will form the subject of the next and last of this series of Lectures.

PART II.—ETERNAL LIFE.

Having in our last discourse proved, by arguments drawn from widely opposite sources, the certainty of man's being outlasting this earthly existence, methinks all that Christianity teaches respecting that life to come for which man must inevitably be reserved, follows of necessity to any logical thinking upon the faculties of human nature, and the influence moral relations exercise upon it. I do not indeed mean to assert that human intelligence would ever have been, if left to itself, capable of developing a correct theory of future things; such an assertion would be instantly contradicted by facts. But my observation aims at pointing out how, with regard to this subject as well as others, Revelation imparts to us nothing essentially new, improbable, alien to our nature and habits of thought; nothing which we have to receive with amazement, and only to believe in because of its lofty origin; but rather that it is pre-eminently *a revelation* to us *of our own being*, which clearly reveals that which already lived and stirred *within our ownselves*, that which we had imagined and yearned after. "We know nothing of ourselves," says the apostle, "we know not what we should pray for, but the Spirit teaches us." So, too, we know not of ourselves what it is that lives and moves in the depth of our soul; we know not how to conceive of it clearly, to express it, to account for it, till Revelation comes to our aid, and furnishes us with the proper clue.

While we contemplate the picture that she holds up before us, while we listen to her utterance respecting ourselves, and compare it carefully with our own inner nature, it is as though this inner nature were interpreting itself, as though its hampered thoughts and perceptions were set free, its chained and stammering tongue loosed; it receives the immediate impression of this revelation that comes from without, being essentially its *own*, and this truth *its* truth. It is indeed with the purport of Revelation that we are filled, in her footsteps that we follow, but it appears as though we were following our own thoughts, and being filled from fountains that spring within our own being. This is what Tertullian alluded to when he called the human soul inherently Christian; and it is in this sense that I assert that our own reason ought to lead to all that divine revelation holds out to us concerning the future life; that while following *her* guidance step by step, it is only conscious of following *its own lead* and *its own laws*, that which revelation vouchsafes being but the natural *development* of what reason itself contains in the *germ*.

And, to begin with, this certainly holds good respecting those statements popularly described as the doctrine of Heaven and Hell, blessedness and condemnation; the plain purport of which is that the conditions of another life cannot be the same for all, but rather that they must be most positively connected with the conduct of each one in this present life, so that the good man will enjoy good, the wicked endure evil. Indeed nothing can appear more self-evident than this to our reason and our sense of justice, nothing more conformable to our whole nature and whole experience. That we must reap what we have sowed, is a law that we daily see put in practice in a thousand ways, in things small and great; that each becomes what he makes himself, is an equally familiar fact which must needs hold as good with regard to the future life as it does to the present. For the laying aside of the body can of itself effect no change in the disposition of the soul; if our personality is to survive physical death, it must needs survive as the same in thought, feeling, preferences, tendencies, character. And what is it that forms *character* but *conduct*, which, in the fullest sense, includes not only acts, but thoughts, feelings, and words. It would be a very superficial and thoughtless way of considering the subject, to suppose that conduct had only external effects, and did not re-act upon our inward nature. The truth, on the contrary, is, that not the very slightest action of a moral character can proceed from us without exercising an influence over us, and leaving its impress upon our soul and our spiritual life. And it is from these re-actions and influences that our inward man gradually acquires form and disposition. Even in respect of physical life, we are accustomed to speak of a *second nature*, brought about by some special way of life, some habitual course of action, or habitual relations of whatever kind. And this must be the case in a far higher degree where the processes of *moral* formation and growth are concerned.

Now, with regard to certain gross and pre-eminently carnal tendencies, drunkenness, licentiousness, etc., it is universally acknowledged that they re-act upon the soul of such as yield to them to such a degree that at length it has no longer sensibility or room for any impulses or imaginations unconnected with them; so that by a course of sinful practice the soul itself becomes sensualized, materialized, sinks to a mere organ of the besetting lust. And what is true in this case is also true in an opposite, and applies equally to right as to evil doing. He who strives to follow the law of love, gradually forms a soul that habitually loves, and has its delight in loving; he who obeys the impulses of selfishness and hatred will inevitably become more and more selfish, and the spirit of hate will grow within him, till its dark influence pervades and subjugates the whole of his nature.

Thus, then, it is undoubtedly true that human souls must, when they enter upon another life, differ essentially in character, and as goodness includes peace and well-being, and wickedness, discomfort and suffering, it is perfectly impossible that the same destiny should await them in that life; but it must be well with one and ill with the other, the one must be happy, the other miserable.

I have before observed that these truths, which form the basis of Christian teaching respecting Heaven and Hell, certainly appear self-evident, nay, seem absolutely required by our laws of thought so soon as we believe in a future life. But it is a very striking fact—and testifies convincingly to the urgent need we have of a revelation from above to set thought free, and prepare its way—that, at a time when Revelation had not uttered its illuminating word, in the era before Christ the Light of the world, man's imagination had not got beyond mere hints and previsions of these necessary truths. We do, indeed, find everywhere a belief in the duration of the soul after death, but that this enduring soul was necessarily endowed with the determining conditions of a happy or unhappy life—to this wider generalization men had nowhere attained. Even the most philosophically cultured, like the Greeks, merely recognised opposite destinies in the case of those who had reached the climax of good or of evil, of the wholly excellent or the wholly corrupt. The more prominent of their heroes, and sons of the immortals, went, indeed, to the Elysian fields, where they led the life of the gods; whilst a Tantalus or a Sisyphus were plunged into Tartarus, there, in inexhaustible torment, to receive the reward of their crimes; but with regard to the innumerable majority belonging to neither of these extreme classes,—for average souls, distinguished by no special endowments or remarkable career, there was to be no difference in their future, however great the difference between their moral character.

And this arose from there being indeed no *actual life* reserved for them at all. In the dark, joyless underworld to which they sank in the mass, they were deprived of all that belongs to active existence; no sunbeam irradiated the grey night of that desolate condition, no communion of spirits with spirits, no occupation to bring about change and stir of some kind in the mournful stillness. The shades press upon and crowd each other in a pale, dim, dreamy state, half-conscious indeed, and yet without any definite feeling or thought, somewhat like fever-stricken sufferers who toss from side to side in a painful semi-slumber, which neither calms down into sleep, nor can be roused to wakefulness. Homer makes the soul even of an Achilles exclaim, "Rather would I be the poorest man, tilling the fields all day long, on the earth above, than reign over the whole swarm of the vanished dead." It was only when they drank the blood of sacrifices that they were able for a short time to resume a human semblance, their souls, instead of having life in themselves, borrowing for a space from the realms of life without, the glow and activity of their lost vitality.

Nor was any other nation, previous to Christianity, able to attain beyond these low and melancholy views of the state of the departed. Indeed, generally speaking, we meet with darker views still, as, for instance, among the savages of Asia, America, and Africa, and indeed among our own heathen ancestors. Departed spirits were conceived of by them as continuing to exist on this earth, as dismal spectres haunting graves, forests, desolate swamps, miserable in themselves, and an object of dread and horror to the living, who had to exorcise them by holy words and sacrifices, lest they should sustain injury from the malicious influence of these forlorn ghosts.

Nay, further ;—and at first sight this may well surprise us—even the chosen people, who, with regard to spiritual knowledge, were a light amidst the general darkness and confusion ; even they, who were not left to their own devices, but favoured with an actual revelation of the one true God, even the people of Israel, the people of the Old Testament, did not on this point differ essentially from the rest. For the Sheol into which the souls of the departed descended (being through Adam's fall cut off from the tree of life in Paradise), scarcely differs from the Hades of the Greeks. True, rest and stillness dwell there, as Job comforts himself by remembering, but it is the stillness of insensibility, the rest of a pale shadowy life. None of the inhabitants of that house of midnight gloom can ever experience joy; in order to hold its prisoners fast, it is necessary that it should be barred and bolted with bands that are strong as love. Even the souls of the godly, though patiently submissive to their Creator's will, are no longer able to stir themselves up to praise his glory, or to retain a lively recollection of his grace and mercy shown them during life. We read in Psalm cxv., " The dead praise not the Lord, neither any that go down into silence." And King Hezekiah, when restored from a sickness that seemed mortal, exclaims, in Isaiah xxxviii., " The grave cannot praise thee, death cannot celebrate thee; they that go down into the pit cannot hope for thy truth. The living, the living, he shall praise thee, as I do this day."

But dark as this shadow of death appears, even in the pages of the Old Testament, it is not there entirely without rays of light. For there we find the knowledge and faith of a living God, and to pious souls such knowledge must *necessarily* have prompted the inference clearly expressed by our Lord: a living God cannot be the God of the dead, or half-dead; he must be the God of the living. Although indeed the Israelites had no definite knowledge of a future life, yet they did know, many of them experimentally, that they were capable of communion with the *eternal* God; and this experience must have excited within them a presentiment, nay, a certainty, that nothing could dissolve such a communion, not even death itself,—that this Eternal would hold fast that which had consciously become his own throughout eternity, and never cast away the nature that had once claimed fellowship with his. The singer of the 49th psalm held this faith, and while declaring of the foolish that, "Like sheep they are laid in the grave, where death shall feed upon them;" he goes on to say, "But God will redeem my soul from the power of the grave; *for he shall receive me.*" And while in the prophecies of Isaiah we meet indeed with the mournful cry, wrung from the consciousness and lips of the people at large, "The dead shall not live, the deceased shall not rise;" we meet also the pious and comforting reply, "Thy dead shall live; with my dead body shall they arise! Awake, and sing, ye that dwell in dust! The earth shall no more cover her slain!"

Nor was it only the truly God-fearing and loving souls amongst the people of Israel who thus rose above the dread of death to the certainty of another life; we see the same fact repeated, though of course more imperfectly, amongst the righteous heathen. We have before cited the testimony of Socrates to the immortality of the soul, but the passage that we are about to give from his last conversation with his friends has a still loftier and fuller tone, and proves to us not only that he believed in the enduring nature of man's spiritual being, but in an eternal *life* that awaited those that loved the gods, and of a condemnation impending upon such as had lived regardless of them. What else could possibly be his meaning, when, turning to Cebes and Symmias, he assures them that he who had really spent his life in lofty meditations, might well be comforted at the approach of death, and cherish the joyful hope that he would after his death attain to the highest blessings? "Yea, it is evident," he adds, and as we listen we are involuntarily reminded of the apostolic declaration, "that all tends to death. And why should it not, since something much better awaits the good yonder? They shall meet again with friendly instructors and companions, incredible as this may seem to the great majority."[1] And in another place he states still more definitely the entire doctrine of blessedness and punishment, as it must needs present itself to human thought when restricted merely to its own efforts, but yet forced thereby to a recognition of the *beginning* of truth: "No," he affirms, "not to annihilation tends my soul, which is formed for a noble place, for a good and wise God, and must without delay, according to his will, go to him. For when the soul leaves the body in a state of purity, dragging nothing that pertains to the latter after it, but fleeing from it and gathering itself into itself; after it has always lived in this manner, it goes to that which is akin to itself, to the invisible, the divine, and immortal, and rational, to which it belongs, there to be happy, being freed from error and irrationality, and fear and lust, and it lives the rest of its time with the gods. But it is certainly otherwise when, polluted and impure, it leaves the body, having been always mixed with it, having served and loved it, having been bewitched by its appetites and enjoyments, and held nothing to be true, thought of nothing but only the material, that which could be touched and seen, eaten and drunk, and turned to sensual gratification; while, on the other hand, it feared and hated and shunned what was

[1] *Phædo.*

invisible to the bodily eye, what could only be seized and apprehended through faith and through the love of wisdom. Such a soul manifestly does not leave the body as independent and purely spiritual, but rather as swathed and encumbered with that which is material; and as this is heavy and earthly, so a soul of this stamp is laden and dragged down into the sphere of the visible, in which it wanders about among the tombs and monuments of the dead, and suffers punishment for its former evil way of life, until, through its strong desire for the corporeal element, it can once more unite itself to a body of some kind, which corresponds with its previous habits of life and inward disposition. The luxurious and gluttonous are changed into asses, or beasts of that kind; the unjust and oppressive into wolves, vultures, and the like; the commonplace, good sort of people, who lived in moderation and social virtue, but yet without seeking after anything higher or really spiritual, will again appear among social and political creatures either as bees or ants, or perhaps as men again of a respectable stamp. But to attain to the ranks of the gods is only permitted to those who strive after the highest wisdom, and depart this life perfectly pure; and therefore we eschew bodily desires and the anxious pursuit of wealth, and care for our souls and not our bodies, and aim at the love of wisdom, and of the liberation and purification she gives."[1]

But methinks I hear you inquire for what purpose it is that I have set before you, first the gloomy popular conceptions of the after-life that prevailed before the introduction of Christianity, and secondly, the widely different testimony of a few individuals in whom the religious knowledge of their age had attained to its highest pitch? By this historical retrospect, you may urge, I have done nothing towards proving the truth of the Christian doctrine regarding a future state, but only broken the course of my lecture by a digression which confuses my argument.

I, however, think otherwise. I, for my part, believe that this apparent digression has been a step in

[1] *Phœdo.*

advance towards the end I have in view, and casts a flood of light on the path we must take to understand aright the very spirit and essence of the gospel announcements respecting our present subject. In the first place, this historical retrospect has served to remind us of the literal truth of the apostolic statements: " Out of Christ, we are without hope in the world. We sat in darkness, and in the shadow of death, as those who had no hope, till the true Light that lighteth all men came into the world;" and again, " Through fear of death, ye would have been all your life long subject unto bondage, but that he hath redeemed you, and deprived death of his sting." Now it is especially with regard to the nature of the future life, a subject above all others calculated to excite general attention, and to call forth the most strenuous efforts of thought, that we can best judge how far the much-boasted reason of man could of itself reach. What results then was this reason able to offer in this confessedly most interesting and most stimulating sphere of inquiry? Where has it proved itself able to set our race at large, free from the most limited and contradictory views? When did it avail to light up the gloomiest and mournfullest darkness by a ray of brightness sufficient to inspire the spirit with confident hope and peace? Or did this reason, in the course of centuries, bringing such increase of knowledge and power in the range of material things, at least approximate more nearly to this happy result? No! The words we have quoted from St. Paul apply directly to his own contemporaries. Of those who lived at the close of the pre-Christian dispensation, and had known and enjoyed the last results of its culture, he declared that they " sorrowed as without hope."

And further, what was it but Christ and his gospel that wrought so marvellous a change (and this not gradually, not by the natural progress of development, but *all at once*), that thenceforth, in opposition to the semblance of things, this *earthly life* appeared to be gloomy, sad, joyless, compared to the fulness of light and happiness that shone around the *life to come?* That this future life became the goal of the best hopes, recognised as the *true* life, and true life's *joy?* That while Achilles must needs lament that the sorrows and troubles of this present life were as nothing to the wretchedness of the future, the apostles could, on the contrary, exclaim: "I reckon that the sufferings of this present time are not worthy to be compared with the *glory* that shall be revealed."

Nor was it only a few pre-eminently gifted spirits, a Paul, a John, who held this faith, and whose life was based on its certainty, but *all*, without exception, who received the gospel declarations,—even the meanest and the most ignorant,—at once felt their truth and their intelligibility; was comforted and made free thereby, and taught to look upon the future world as a world of blessedness and repose in the bosom of God. Now, wherever the name of Christ is named, even the little child, who scarcely knows how to think or speak, wears a joyous face when asked, "Where is thy dead mother, thy brother, or thy little sister?" and pointing above replies, "With God Almighty, as a holy angel, and happy there." Verily, to such as contemplate with an intelligent eye the sudden transformation thus wrought, it is as when the sun has risen, and the darkness vanishes before its rays, and men move gladly on their way, and stumble not, because they walk in light.

Neither is it in the least inconsistent with this fact, that even before Christ's appearance, some of the wisest and best should have been able partially to see their way, for ever the dawn precedes the sun-rising, and they inferred this eternal life only because they aspired after and believed in that capacity of man for *fellowship with God*, which in Christ became "*deed and truth.*" It was *combined* with the hope of a future redemption that pious Israelites entertained the hope of not being holden by death, but seeing God in righteousness when they should awake after his likeness; and even in the account of the last conversation of Socrates, preserved for us by Plato, we have something analogous to this when Simmias, the Theban, uses the remarkable words: "Truly, it is difficult to know anything definite as to future things; nothing remains to us but to depend upon the best and most plausible of human words, till man becomes able, with a certain security and safety, to make the passage upon the *safe bark of a divine word.*"

The second point which this historical retrospect decidedly establishes is this, that by a *mere abstract* conviction of the immortality of the soul nothing is gained, but that this immortality must have a definite character in order to have any importance for us. This is a more important conclusion than may at first sight appear. For it not unfrequently happens that a faith in immortality, merely as such, is looked upon as something Christian and religious, and indeed almost felt to be matter of boast; as, for instance, in the case of Rationalists, whose whole creed is contained in three words: God, Liberty, Immortality.

But what is meant by this immortality, by men who hold their opinions? What indeed *can* be meant? One holds this, another that, as experience shows us; each according to his individual character and bias. It is true, that the gloomy pre-Christian conceptions are universally discarded, and all alike adopt some elements of the Christian school of thought into their own views; generally speaking, the after-life is looked upon as an exalted and beatified continuance of this, the chief stress being laid upon meeting again with those one has loved on earth, and upon freedom from the hindrances, sorrows, and struggles which have embittered and marred our walk here below.

But where do we find any ground or right for expectations like these? Most certainly it is not to Scripture that we can appeal in their favour; for Scripture, as you know, lays the chief stress upon quite other things, and does not even mention this much talked of meeting each other again. If then we do not draw from Scripture sources, what others are open to our inquiries? Do we seek them in our own inward feelings and consciousness? That these by no means hold any such clear and definite language, we have proved by the example of the ages before Christ; and when we come to examine a little more deeply, we shall be forced to confess that we find nothing in ourselves that authorizes these rambling conceptions, that they are really mere unsubstantial and unfounded castles in the air; nay, that they even involve hopeless contradictions, which renders them untenable by exact thought. For, to confine ourselves to one point, what is meant by this our present existence being continued in glorified fashion, and set free from all the hindrances and oppositions that beset it now? Do not these hindrances and oppositions pre-eminently lie in *our own being*—in our selfishness, our discontent, our foibles, and our sins?

And if in that other world we are simply to continue to live on without having undergone a redemption, a moral transformation; without a higher life being inspired into us and embracing us in its fulness, how can our after condition differ essentially from our present? It must be a mere sequel to it; a sequel full of the same sorrows and strifes, labours, achievements, and failures throughout all eternity. And inasmuch as no one can realize such a repulsive, aimless, and comfortless theory as this, the author of those five lectures, on the senses to which we have so often alluded, is perfectly right in affirming that the only idea that natural religion can connect with a belief in immortality, is of an eternally empty and wearisome monotony, making upon us the impression of death rather than life; that idea, in short, which we recognise as prevailing in the world before the appearance of Christ.

And this leads us to the *third* point, incontrovertibly established by our historical retrospect, that there can be no other explanation of a future existence as an *actual life*, than Christ and our fellowship with him. It is one of the deepest and most striking peculiarities of Holy Writ, that nowhere does it *assert* the mere continued existence of the soul after death, although it invariably assumes it, until this fact of immortality had first gained its *true significance*, until it could point us to *eternal life* in the full and perfect sense of the words.

For what is the universal conception of life? A steady contemplation of this our earthly life will enable us to gain a clear comprehension of it. We at once feel that the chief characteristic of life consists in receiving, in appropriating forces, nay, even matter, foreign to ourselves, and returning these in an exalted condition, in the shape of activities and tendencies of most various kinds. Life is an incessant *receiving*, an incessant appropriation, and an incessant *exaltation* and *giving back* of the received. Thus no life, it is evident, can exist by and for itself; at all events, no created life, as we know and experience it; but always it requires another life external to itself, with which it stands in relations of constant reciprocity, constant giving and taking; from which it nourishes itself, through which it fills itself, which is the source and object of all its activity.

Now, if we apply this definition to human life, it is apparent that man can only possess and enjoy life on condition that there be afforded him from without, something that he may receive and appropriate, and with which he may hold fellowship. In barren, objectless space none of us could live, none of us could find materials for life. For we resemble vessels, capable indeed of containing in themselves the most manifold and precious substances, but incapable of originating these, and requiring to be filled from without. We have the capacity for thought and cognition, but we could neither think nor know if no external objects were presented to our knowledge and our thought. We have the capacity for love, but we could not actually love if we were without objects to call forth love; if our heart never met the response of another heart. And the same holds good of every faculty of our nature.

You see, therefore, what inevitably follows with regard to our future existence. It is indisputable, that in this future existence as well, we can have no life unless there meet us some other Life external to our own, with which ours can be united, towards which we stand related by that process of reciprocal giving and receiving, which we have before described. Of what nature then must this life be? Immortal, since we are immortal; the fulness of love, wisdom, peace, holiness, since we feel in ourselves the need and the capacity for all these; and as we have already seen, no one can *think* of the future state as an aimless and continued hungering and thirsting, but each must necessarily conceive of it as the fulfilment and perfection of whatever his nature requires.

Now such a life as we all know exists only, and can only exist *in God*, and there can only be an eternal life for men upon condition of there being for them a *fellowship* with God, God inspiring them, sharing himself with them, receiving them unto himself, entering into a reciprocity of giving and taking, of in-pouring and out-pouring—in one word, into a reciprocity of *love*.

Now, experimentally, this reciprocity has been procured for and proffered to us in and by Christ alone. I say experimentally, because before him, and independently of him, confessedly, no one exemplified in himself or even knew of this kindredship of nature with God, of which we speak; while, as soon as he appeared, all who received him could as with one mouth declare: "We live, but it is no more we who live, but Christ (in whom God lives) who lives in us; the Spirit of God is shed abroad in our hearts; our conversation is no more on earth but in heaven, where Christ sitteth at the right hand of God." And, on the other hand, Christ himself most clearly and explicitly testifies to the truth of this relation. "No man," he affirms, "cometh to the Father but by me; I am the way, the truth, and the life. He that believeth in me, to him will the Father come, and abide with him." And when we proceed to examine more closely how this is to be brought about, we find him declaring further,—He who is one with the Father, he in whom dwells the fulness of God,—that he was able and willing to share his own God-pervaded being with those who believed in him, and by their belief identified themselves with him; so that henceforth their humanity should so have all its needs divinely supplied as to be raised out of the condition of mere empty existence into the condition of true and perfect *life*, the necessary requirements of which we have already enumerated. Everything, indeed, in our Lord's word and work refers to this fellowship, this actual personal fellowship, this identification of the human soul with himself. "For this," he saith, "hath the Father sent me, that I should give you my flesh to eat, and my blood to drink;" that is, that the whole of my special nature should as actually and positively enter into, and be assimilated by you, as the food you partake of, enters into and becomes assimilated with your body. He in whom this does not take place, remains necessarily without the true source of life; remains a mere possibility, a mere potentiality, which never becomes realized, never reaches the perfection for which it was adapted. "Verily, verily, I say unto you, If ye eat not the flesh, and drink not the blood of the Son of man, ye have no life in you. There is no bread that can give life to the world but my flesh, which I give for the life of the world. Whosoever eateth this bread shall live for ever. He that abideth not in me, and I in him, brings forth no fruit, dries up and withers, shall be cut off and cast away."

What a light do these words cast upon that fact of the pre-Christian world knowing nothing of eternal *life*, but only of endless *being!* We can now understand how this was: It did not result from any guilty want of reflection or knowledge on the part of that world, but it could not have been otherwise, for the true life had not then appeared, did not exist for it. The noblest spirits hoped for it, indeed searched after it in vague and sorrowful yearning, but they saw it not, they possessed it not. To us it now sounds like a striking prophecy, to hear the lifeless shades of the under-world entreating Odysseus for life-bringing blood from the world of the living, in order that they might for a while be once more pervaded with vital energy. It seems as though they prophetically confirmed the as yet unspoken words of the Lord, "He who drinketh not my blood hath no life in him," as though they had some foreknowledge that there was indeed a blood in the realm of *true* life that actually and abidingly gave life to its recipients.

And now it is scarcely necessary that I should proceed more minutely to describe the nature of this true, this eternal life. From what has been already said, it must be evident that it is not only a *future*, but a *present* life, beginning from the moment of our receiving

Christ, and with him the actual indwelling of God; nor is it less evident that it must consist in *oneness* with God through Christ, even as God himself, Father, Son, and Spirit are one. "I pray for them," exclaims the Lord in his sacerdotal intercession, "that they may be one in us, as thou, Father, art in me, and I in thee;" and again, "I in them, and thou in me, that they may be perfect in us, and that the love wherewith thou hast loved me may be in them, and that they may share my glory which thou hast given me." Would it be possible to any human lips to bring this life nearer, to explain its details more thoroughly? God be thanked that it is appreciable and intelligible to our inmost consciousness, though it far transcends our as yet earthly faculties of ratiocination and language. It is enough that we know and can assure ourselves of this: "We shall live and be blessed eternally, as God is blessed and eternally lives; for we are in him and he is in us: *one* joy, *one* love, *one* possession, *one* activity, *one* knowledge; an inexhaustible receiving and giving back of what we receive, as in the visions of the Apocalypse the bands of the blessed cast down the crowns of righteousness with which their heads are decked before the throne of the Lamb, and in never-ceasing love and praise ascribe again and again to him the salvation that they have received from him."

Such is the heaven of the Christian, the heaven that the Gospel announces, of which assuredly each one must at least confess that it represents to man the highest conceivable by human thought, nay, more than human thought, left to itself, could ever have attained to. That which "eye hath not seen, nor ear heard, neither hath it entered into the heart of man to conceive," the apostle tells us, "God hath prepared for them that love him."

And this view of what eternal life essentially and fundamentally is, at once dispels all those petty inquiries that curiosity and earthly-mindedness so often raise as to the conditions of heavenly happiness, as, for example, whether we shall meet again, know each other, belong to each other again as we have done here below;

what will be our occupation throughout the infinite eternity, and other details of the kind. I say such inquiries vanish away of themselves; for, if we know even as God knows, we must know whatever he knows; and if we love as he loves, we must love whatever he loves, and love in the same inconceivably lofty manner; and if we are to work as he works, and to be blessed with his blessedness, we must be occupied in *his* work and enjoy *his* inexpressible joy, and the infinity of that work and that joy will be inexhaustible in us as in him. Those who would, on the contrary, maintain that this blessed life of Holy Scripture is in point of fact a mere nonentity, life being only a struggle, a conflict, an opposition of finite forces, and, apart from these, an eternal blank, eternal stagnation, with such indeed we can carry on no further controversy; for what is their position but one that maintains the very condition of the eternal God to be a condition of endless stagnation and emptiness !—A conception this, the philosophical and religious value of which I confidently refer to your own appreciation.

But this word Heaven at once presupposes the antithesis Hell; the *reaching* the goal, implies of necessity the possibility of the *failing* to reach it. And as Scripture speaks of both alike, paints to us the character of the one as well as the other, I should feel myself wanting in my duty towards you were I not briefly to dwell upon this awful subject.

I am well aware that it is against this doctrine of hell, or of the misery of a human soul continuing to exist in a state of alienation from God, that the greatest opposition of the Antichristian, or I may say of the modern spirit of thought generally, is directed. Let us hear the author so often quoted declare himself on this point. "Finally, when we are required," says he, "to represent to ourselves, in contrast with heaven and its blessedness, the HELL where, according to the old faith, the great majority of human beings are burning in eternal flames, we must needs take leave altogether of all conceptions of physical and spiritual things. For this reason, at the present time, it is only that thorough-going Orthodox faith that speaks of hell, which feels no scruple in proclaiming the conclusions of human reason to be mere delusions of Satan, whose interest it necessarily is to blind men to the existence of this hellish state."

We will not criticise the tone and bearing of such polemics, we will only remind you of what we advanced at the beginning of our lecture; of the fact, namely, that the doctrine of heaven and hell rests on nothing else than that old axiom, alike of reason and experience, that each must reap what he has sown, and be what he has made himself, and I think we may somewhat more reasonably than the author above quoted, maintain that he who should dispute *this* position must needs take leave of all conceptions whatever, alike of temporal and spiritual things.

But as, in the course of our historical survey, we have found that the practical application of this universal truth was exceedingly imperfect as regards the blessedness of the good, so also was it with the misery of the wicked. With the exception of a few of the most prominent criminals, the great mass of the ungodly were represented as sinking into the insensible existence of the realm of shadows, and it was only those leading religious and intellectual minds before mentioned, some of the Jewish prophets, or a Socrates and Plato, who definitely perceived that (according to the expression of the latter) just as the good must necessarily fare better in a future life, so the bad must fare worse.

It was, however, the gospel revelation alone that first brought this truth home to the *universal* consciousness and reason of our race. For only then, when it has been once seen and understood what *life* is and includes, can there be any adequate conception of the *loss* of that life, and the remaining in death.

The doctrine then presented to us by the New Testament, as indissolubly connected with its announcement of eternal life, and logically deduced from our moral and psychological conception thereof, is, in its essential features, as follows :—

Human nature, as we have seen, has no true and abiding principle of life without communion, fellowship with God through Christ. If man declines to enter into this fellowship, preferring that self-seeking dependence on and dealing with the creature, which we have depicted in our former Lecture upon sin, he not only evidently deprives himself of all that we have described as constituting the fulness of eternal life, but he also incurs the most utter dislocation and distortion of his whole personality (intended and adapted as it was for fellowship with God), by diverting it from its proper purpose and end. Its various faculties, which would have found their union and satisfaction in God, discordant and dissatisfied as they now are, turn against each other, hinder and destroy each other in unceasing opposition. "The flesh," says the apostle, "lusteth against the spirit, and the spirit against the flesh." The *spirit* destroys, in so far as it can, the soul and the body, because, by its divine consciousness, it opposes and condemns their fleshly nature. The *soul* (the carnal mind), in so far as it can, destroys the spirit and the body, by seeking to blunt and silence the former, and to excite the latter to serve its lusts, and be the slave of its sinful will. And finally, the *body* exercises a destructive influence on spirit and soul, not only by declining to be the organ of the spirit, and thereby injuring the unity of the personality, but by degrading the soul whose lusts it fulfils, by its own degradation, and continually diminishing its energy to desire and to enjoy.

Nevertheless, so long as man lives here below, this fearful process of death is not carried on undisguisedly and sensibly. For he still possesses, both within and without, much that is innately good, independent of his own will, and capable of proffering him a certain amount of life and joy.

No man here below can live exclusively in evil, and practise evil entirely unmixed with the good that lies in his God-created nature. But at death, on the contrary, his personality (as he has constituted it during the God-estranged, sinful condition of his earthly life) is deprived of its externality, thrown back on itself, and restricted to itself alone. Thus he undergoes the fearful decree of retaining the evil which was the result of his will, apart from the good which involuntarily pertained to him; of the accidental good that was in him being swallowed up of evil, since that only which his *will* constituted him may now endure. "Take from the unprofitable servant the one talent that he has," exclaims our Lord; "for from him who hath not, even that he hath shall be taken away." In this second death, there is no one endowed with anything but what tends to his own woe, and the woe of others. The knowledge of God that the soul still possesses only impels it to a fierce and yet eternally fruitless warring against that God, of which it is conscious as the original cause of its fearful existence, the Avenger and Judge that fixes its dark lot; gladly would this soul annihilate in itself this indelible thought of God that disturbs its repose; yea, it would free itself from its God-created being, and sink into nothingness, but ever on and on must burn that awful light, that shines into the darkness, and from which it would vainly bury itself in that outer darkness, with weeping and gnashing of teeth, as the Lord expresses it.

And the same holds good with all the divinely-appointed relations of man to man, as members of one body, destined to bear and forbear in reciprocal love. The perversion which all God-ordained social ties, whether of marriage, family, friendship, or country, have undergone through sin on earth, is now fully manifest. As, in point of fact, it was selfishness instead of genuine love that filled all these relations, they now exist (after the removal of all adventitious good in them) only as relations of unmixed selfishness, and this selfishness necessarily leads to a mutual repulsion that grows and grows (as we see typified on earth) into the most glowing hatred. Each soul would cast off these ties, and not one may ever do so!

To this we add, in the third place, that of all the former possessions which the soul enjoyed on earth, only that remains to it which each unrighteous indulgence fostered; namely, the burning lust and desire which can never more be satisfied, and therefore must glow ever more and more fiercely. The rich glutton in the parable can in the other world think only of the enjoyment of his palate: "Give me at the least a drop of water to cool my tongue, for I am tormented in this flame." The lost soul would continually recall, by imagination, the fleshly life, but it is unable to do so; would continue its sins in memory, and cannot any longer enjoy their fruits. Its spiritual nature ever deprives it of the possibility of illusory enjoyment; all that it can and must do, is perpetually to contemplate that which brought it into perdition; but it is perfectly incapable of dreaming back the pleasant corporeal existence of earth and time. This is what the heathen imaged by the significant tortures they assigned to a Tantalus and Ixion; this is the worm in the soul that dieth not; this is the inward fire that is not quenched.

That dies not, that is not quenched! For there is no longer any *time* to such, seeing that there are no sensuous perceptions, no changes of condition by which alone we have the consciousness of time conveyed. Even in this world there are states and circumstances which supersede the normal relation of the soul to time; agony lengthens, as rapture contracts it. Consequently when suffering has reached its greatest possible intensity, and every mitigation of it is withdrawn—past, present, and future, alike absorbed in a consciousness of pain and an inevitable expectation of pain—time, which the soul still strives to *think*, must dilate itself to monstrous proportions, and between a second and a century there can no longer be any difference. How can there still be a ray of hope for a soul in such a state as this? To escape from its misery it must escape from itself, and that it refused to do while it was still possible, and persisted in this refusal till at length—not through compulsion from without, but by its own quality—this has become absolutely impossible. "There is a sin," says Christ, and he calls it "the sin against the Holy Ghost," which has "never forgiveness, neither in this world, nor in that which is to come." For this sin consists in a corruption of the inner man, so that whatever is good and makes for peace no longer finds place within him, but only excites him to hatred and bitterness.

And it is self-evident that to this inward condition the outward condition must conform, both as regards the saved and the lost. No doubt the expressions used in Scripture, "Fire, darkness, chains," and so forth, are figurative expressions describing in human speech, and enabling us in measure to apprehend, what far transcends our human experience. But, nevertheless, they do express an absolute truth and reality. The fire is the burning desire that is never satisfied, the self-consuming hatred that is never stilled. The darkness is that feeling intensified to the utmost, of which we know something even here when we say, "All is gloom within me, nowhere a ray of light." The chains are that indissoluble consciousness of being bound to a personality and to a misery, which are one and the same thing. And all this pervaded by the unceasing conviction, "This is my own doing, I reap that only which I sowed;" a conviction, however, not involving an admission of the justice of God, but in raging defiance denying it still, and for ever kicking against the pricks by which it is for ever torn.

Such is the Christian doctrine respecting hell, respecting the perdition of those who will not seek after God. A fearful doctrine, we allow, but not more fearful than sin, of which it is the necessary goal, the self-chosen result; not more fearful than the daring rejection of the God of our life, and election to walk on without him and in opposition to him; not more fearful than the contemptuous indifference to the Love which so loved us as to give itself to us in Christ, to seek to receive us into itself, and with us to share all things. And if, when all has been said, the old question should still arise, "How is it possible that God's plan of salvation should not include all?" we have but to return the old answer, "Leave that mystery to God; and see that thou for thy part layest hold on the salvation offered thee. Enough that thou knowest that none, none are eternally lost but by their own fault, none who might not have been saved had they but willed to be so." Yea, we may still further affirm that none are lost while they have any capacity for being saved, while still any longing and yearning for salvation stirs within them, while they are still free from that sin against the Holy Ghost to which every sinner must ultimately attain, "except he repent." That repentance, however, becomes more and more difficult the longer we cultivate the sinful nature, and fill our souls with its ends and aims, is a fact patent alike to our own reason and experience.

It is difficult to break off here, although required by our limits so to do, leaving wholly untouched many points that are equally, with those we have dwelt upon, subjects of doubt and inquiry. And though unable to go into them at length, I feel I shall best consult your wishes by cursorily touching upon the most prominent of these.

First, then, there is the question of the resurrection of the *body*. I confess that it seems to me a striking instance of the lamentable superficiality of so-called *Rational* inquiry, that this doctrine, on account of a few difficulties which attend *its representation*, should be summarily dismissed as impossible. "Here is the point," says the writer so often alluded to, "where the Church requires *faith* of the utmost potency; *i.e.*, faith in contradiction to all that reason can think or maintain." But this is a misrepresentation. What the "Church" (to use his own expression) here demands, is, that reason should really exercise itself on this subject, should bring to it the severest logic and the most searching investigation of which the human mind is capable. For why? Does the body then not belong to this human being? Is the body something foreign from the spirit, a mere external clothing to it, so that the latter may not only continue to exist independently of the former, but continue to *live*, to *act*, in the full sense of the words? Does not our earthly existence teach us that our inner being necessarily requires an organism of externality and activity to give it an objective reality;

that man is constituted a personality by being thus compounded of soul and body, and that neither portion of his being could exist apart without undergoing an essential change of nature and capacity? And therefore, if in the other world we are to continue to be, not as different creatures but as men, we must necessarily have the same vital capacities, only in an exalted degree. Even did not Scripture tell us of the renewal of our bodies, our own exact thinking would lead us to, nay, would demand this conclusion, so soon as the duration of our personality after death was once established, and would demand it under the very same conditions affixed by the apostle: "Sown in corruption, raised in incorruption; sown in weakness, raised in power; sown in dishonour, raised in glory." As the body is one portion of one's own self, which must not remain in ruin and imperfection, so must there also be for it a redemption, a completeness, a glorification to its ideal, if we may so speak,—a redemption and glorification effected, as in the case of the inner man, by the dying off of the old and the transplantation into the new; this inner and outer transformation being most intimately connected.

The resurrection of the believer, like that of Christ, seems not so much an external act that he undergoes, as an act of his own, new God-filled life, which assimilates that which belongs to its perfected state, forming the organism that best corresponds with its nature, and by which its nature is best expressed. For there will then be the most perfect harmony between the inward being and the outward semblance. What is already in a measure true of our earthly bodies, that they are the image and mirror of the inner nature, will be unqualifiedly true in the case of the resurrection body. It will exist as the fully adequate expression of the spiritual character; it will be a faithful embodiment of every feature, every peculiarity thereof. All will then be truth, and all truth will be open and manifest; "the wise shall shine as the firmament," as the prophet declares, while "some shall awake to shame and everlasting contempt" in their undisguised hideousness; all their hidden evil, corruption, and distortion being outwardly revealed and made apparent to the whole world.

It will already appear from these brief hints, that by the resurrection of the *body*, we do not understand those materials of our physical frame, which even in this life are in a state of perpetual flux and transformation, but rather the external *basis of being*, the essential identity of the new and the old body; and that, therefore, we necessarily hold it to be this very bodily *individuality* which is to be raised and glorified to its ideal. "It is sown a natural body, it is raised a spiritual body;" for, as in the case of the dying plant, whose perishable portions are scattered in all directions, there yet remains a living germ, which, assimilating new materials under the influence of creative energies from without, forms for itself a new plant-body, which, through that germ is the *same* with the former plant, and yet *another*, so, says the apostle, shall it be with the human corporeal life. While its earthly elements fall asunder and dissolve, and enter into new combinations, there still remains a germ, the subtlest and innermost—to our senses imperceptible as the principle of growth in a seed—and this will unfold, through the power of Christ's indwelling Spirit, into a new bodily form, equally adapted to its new condition as the former body was to its former estate.

You will at least grant me that there is nothing in these views that contradicts our experience gathered from the natural life around us; and should some one say, "You must show me that imperishable germ of which you speak, and describe more minutely that superhuman coporeity, before I can believe in its possibility," to such a one I simply reply, "Can you, then, even in the lower realm of material nature, preconceive from seeing the germ the vegetable organism that is to arise out of it? If experience had not taught you that plants grow out of seeds, would you, at the sight of an acorn, have ever supposed that from that small dead-looking thing a tree of such might and majesty as the oak would spring? Or would you have been in a condition to describe beforehand the aspect of that tree? Well may we say with our Lord, 'If ye understand not earthly things, how shall ye understand and tell of heavenly things?'"

One thing is certain, this liberation and perfection of human life can only coincide with that of the whole material world, the whole of nature; with the new heavens and the new earth, and the universal transformation, of which these form part. Till then the condition of departed souls must necessarily be a transitional one, respecting which we, in this rapid survey, can only affirm two things: *first*, that during it the maturing of the soul is going on, whether it be a maturing to God's image, or to complete reprobation; and, *secondly*, that for those who are once incorporate with Christ, there can exist no separation from him, but that they must already be living with him in an incomparably freer and higher condition than ours. The Lord, speaking of this state to the thief on the cross, calls it expressly "Paradise."

Again, if we are called upon to answer the mocking questions of unbelief as to the *locality* of this transitional state, as well as of that of heaven and hell, we must be very careful to guard against the idea of there being necessarily an external space, a barrier of matter and time between them and us. Rather is their existence removed far out of all sensuous *space-categories* whatsoever. The tendency of the soul, after death, as an intelligent theologian well observes, is not towards external things, but is rather an internal, an introverted tendency; and far more complete than the modern image of the soul soaring to the stars, is that other view that represents it returning to the underlying innermost mystical chambers of existence. If, however, it be absolutely necessary to think of some localization in space in connexion with spirits made perfect or perfecting, will our doubters permit me, on the other hand, to ask them what precise knowledge they themselves possess of the universe external to our own earth; of that universe which their best telescopes fail to give them the slightest indication of? If, as the poet says. "there are even on this earth more things than are dreamt of in their philosophy," how much more must this hold good of that *infinity* of worlds, the mere number of which neither our eyes nor our intellect can avail to grasp; and finally, as to the realm of *fulfilment*, both as regards the saved and the lost, the Scripture plainly lays it in that new heaven and new earth, of which our astronomers give us no intelligence whatsoever.

For this is the ultimate and highest, and, if we may so speak, the most glorious and exalted feature of the Christian view of the universe, that it recognises for the *great whole*, for all existence whatsoever, a liberation and transfiguration, an exaltation and perfectionment to its ideal; for the least, the most seeming unimportant thing has for its basis an ideal, that is, the Divine thought that called it into existence, and, in the first instance, realized it in earthly matter as a type and image, but never ceases to work within it till it passes through its typical condition to its true being. "All temporal things are a similitude," says Goethe, in deeply significant words, a similitude of what finally they shall really be. "The unattainable," he adds, "will become the actual." It will then be manifest that not one single Divine creative thought, not one Divine work was of only temporal purport, and therefore lost and relinquished; that God destroys nothing that he has ever called into being, but acts according to the declaration of the prophet of the New Testament: "Behold, I make all things new." The veil of earthly materiality and perishableness, which now lies over this rich world, with all its substances and forces, will then be lifted away, together with all the desolation of disturbance and corruption attached to it, and the now veiled and disguised universe shall come forth in the imperishable splendour of its pure form and its real being.

And further, this renovation and perfection will not only proceed from without, but also it will be necessarily evolved out of the innermost spirit of the world, and its original destination. What has been already stated respecting the renewal of the individual body, namely, that it is the indwelling and perfected spirit that includes it (as the organ of that spirit) in its own perfection, is true also on a greater scale as regards the great whole; for as the body is related to the individual soul, so is the world to collective humanity. For *it* the world was created, belonging to it as its dwelling-place and its organ, and therefore it must follow and share throughout the destiny of this humanity. "The creature was made subject to vanity," says the apostle, "not willingly, but by reason of him who hath subjected the same in hope. For the earnest expectation of the creature waiteth for the manifestation of the sons of God. The creature also shall be freed from the bondage of corruption into the glorious liberty of the children of God," into an existence where, as St. Peter adds, "there dwelleth only righteousness."

And just as the body is, as it were, burnt away by the process of corruption, while its germinal principle, out of which the new body is to spring, being connected with the spirit, still abides, so will it be with this our world-system. Its elements will be decomposed by fire, dissolved, as the Scripture says, and out of that dissolution it will rise again, according to its indwelling ideal, in glorified form, to true existence. As one of the most profound theological thinkers of our time remarks, "Chemistry, or the transmutation of matter, will then complete what now it only does piecemeal, and solemnize its highest triumph."

But, as we have before indicated, this will only take place when humanity as a whole has attained to its fulfilment and final destiny. For as for each individual, so for humanity collectively, a day of conclusions, of consequences, must come; a day when all shall have reached the term of their development, and must now stand forth as results of its character; when the gospel has once been preached to the whole world, and all those who would, have entered into the peace of redemption; when sin has reached its ultimate consequences, and those who are voluntarily untouched by Christ's healing hand, have banded themselves together no longer in indifference, but *open enmity* against him, as Antichrist (which we see growing more defined century by century); when, on the other side, the believers, thus opposed and driven out of fellowship with the world, are, by this very experience, matured into the true exemplification of their life of faith:—more thorough separation from the world, and more complete surrender and reliance on the Saviour;—when each of these different tendencies in humanity shall have fully revealed its character, and borne all its fruits; then, when no further development is conceivable, the end must come, the end that actually appoints to each of these tendencies that which it has striven after and attained to, and which is therefore *the last judgment* upon them. When wheat and tares have, according to the parable, grown side by side to maturity, then cometh the harvest, when they are separated, and each is taken to the place to which it belongs.

It is evident, however, that this can only be brought about by the immediate action of the Lord himself, by his personal appearing to judge and to complete. And it is equally evident that, in the results of this judging and completing, all that ever lived on earth, and belonged to humanity, must have their share. For the dead have been, meanwhile, in those transitional states before mentioned, maturing to the last results of their being, either to full capacity for the divine fellowship, or to entire estrangement therefrom, and nothing more remains than the appointment of the definite conditions to which those opposite natures belong. On the one side, the kingdom of God, of which we read: "Then cometh the end, when Christ shall have delivered up the kingdom to God, even the Father; when he hath put all enemies under his feet, and the last enemy shall be destroyed, death; and when all things shall be subdued under him, then shall the Son also himself be subject unto him that put all things under him, that God may be all in all." And, on the other side, the realm of death, of which it is declared, that it is "the other death," that "he who is unrighteous shall be unrighteous still," shall have fellowship with Satan and his angels, with evil and evil ones, so that no germ of possible improvement any longer remains.

"And I saw," spake the Seer of the New Testament, as everything else vanished from his gaze before the image of redeemed humanity having reached its goal, and found the fulfilment of its destiny: "I saw a new heaven and a new earth: for the first heaven and the first earth were passed away; and there was no more sea. And I John saw the holy city, new Jerusalem, coming down from God out of heaven, prepared as a bride adorned for her husband. And I heard a great voice out of heaven, saying, Behold, the tabernacle of God is with men, and he will dwell with them, and they shall be his people, and God himself shall be with them, and be their God. And God shall wipe away all tears from their eyes; and there shall be no more death, neither sorrow, nor crying, neither shall there be any more pain: for the former things are passed away. And he that sat upon the throne said, Behold, I make all things new. And he said unto me, Write: for these words are true and faithful" (Rev. xxi. 1-5).

CPSIA information can be obtained
at www.ICGtesting.com
Printed in the USA
LVHW040431110522
718423LV00002B/374

9 783375 002121